Praise for Joh...

'A magician of genre fiction' *Independent*

'Lindqvist is Sweden's answer to Stephen King' *T...*

'A terrifying supernatural story, yet also a moving account of friendship and salvation' *Guardian*

'Lindqvist has reinvented the vampire novel and made it all the more chilling . . . An immensely readable and highly disturbing book in which grim levels of gore and violence are tempered by an unexpected tenderness' *Daily Express*

'Reminiscent of Stephen King at his best, there are some truly scary bits in the book that will haunt your dreams. Best read by sunlight' *Independent on Sunday*

'Some books are just too good. A masterpiece' *SFX*

'A Scandi chiller with elements of fable and even social satire, but told with great energy and flair that confirms Lindqvist's reputation as Sweden's answer to Stephen King' *Daily Mail*

'A very scary tale indeed from a writer who is master of his genre' *Financial Times*

'Combines an atmospheric coming-of-age story set in Stockholm with a shocking (and very gory) thriller. His vampire is an original, both heartbreakingly pathetic and terrifying. This was a bestseller in Sweden and could be equally big here. Don't miss it' *The Times*

'A surprising and sometimes delightful reading experience . . . Lindqvist manages to maintain a light touch in an otherwise bleak landscape' *Sunday Times*

'A compelling horror story, but it's also a finely calibrated tale about the pain of growing up' *Sunday Telegraph*

'So strange, so mad, so weirdly inspirational' *Guardian*

'Both an eerie, enigmatic mystery and a compendium of fascinating vignettes, this is a third consecutive masterpiece for an author who deserves to be as much a household name as Stephen King' *SFX*

JOHN AJVIDE LINDQVIST lives in Sweden and has worked as a magician and stand-up comedian. His first novel, the international bestseller *Let the Right One In*, was published in more than thirty countries and adapted into two feature films: one by Swedish director Tomas Alfredson, and an English-language version directed by Matt Reeves. *I Am the Tiger* is the conclusion of the trilogy that began with *I Am Behind You* and *I Always Find You*.

MARLAINE DELARGY is based in the UK. She has translated novels by Swedish writers including Henning Mankell, Kristina Ohlsson, Viveca Sten and Johan Theorin – with whom she won the CWA International Dagger for *The Darkest Room* in 2010.

Also by John Ajvide Lindqvist

Let the Right One In
Handling the Undead
Harbour
Little Star
Let the Old Dreams Die
I Am Behind You
I Always Find You

I AM
THE TIGER

John Ajvide Lindqvist

Translated from Swedish by
Marlaine Delargy

riverrun

First published in Sweden in 2017 under the title *X—Den sista platsen* by Ordfronts Förlag.
This English translation first published in Australia in 2021 by The Text Publishing Company
First published in Great Britain in 2021 by riverrun
This paperback edition published in 2022 by

riverrun

An imprint of

Quercus Editions Limited
Carmelite House
50 Victoria Embankment
London EC4Y 0DZ

An Hachette UK company

Cover design based on original jacket design by Jeannine Schmelzer, © Bastei Lübbe
AG, Köln 2016
Cover image of caravan by Jill Battaglia / Arcangel
Page design by Text
Typeset by J & M Typesetting

Paperback ISBN 978 1 52940 828 7
Ebook ISBN 978 1 52940 827 0

10 9 8 7 6 5 4 3 2 1

Printed and bound in Great Britain by Clays Ltd, Elcograf S.p.A.

Papers used by riverrun are from well-managed forests and other responsible sources.

For Thomas Oredsson & Eva Harms
For Blackeberg and Rådmansö
For friendship and champagne

The Underworld

In the autumn of 2016 a wave of suicides swept through Stockholm's underworld. People with links to criminal organisations were found hanged, shot or drowned. In addition, a number of individuals disappeared without a trace.

At first the situation was attributed to some kind of purge, the emergence of a new player determined to do away with the competition. Several of those who died had been big shots, names that could be crossed off the Alcatraz list. There was wild speculation in the press and within the police service; what ruthless force was operating in the city?

As the autopsy reports began to trickle in, the phenomenon became even more incomprehensible. In virtually every single case, all the indications were that the deceased had been entirely responsible for their own deaths. Killed themselves. Hung up their boots.

In one particularly striking case, four men were found dead in a storage depot. Three had been executed with a bullet to the back of the neck, the fourth with a shot to the temple. No one else had been present, there were no restraints or signs of violence, and the report concluded laconically that: 'They all appeared to have been in agreement.' They had worked together, and the last man standing had put the barrel of the gun to his own head.

A total of eighteen people died in September; thirteen more in

October. Then the phenomenon faded away. The police had their hands full trying to work out how the deaths had impacted on the underworld's power structure. It soon became clear that a new player had indeed entered the arena, but they had no success in finding out who he might be. As soon as they got close to something resembling an organised leadership, the whole thing dissolved into a miasma of rumour and hearsay. For the time being, this mysterious new player was known as 'X'.

1. Outside

Tommy T

Tommy T peaked in 2004. That was when he received the Golden Shovel for his investigative reporting into the circulation of cocaine through Stockholm's bloodstream, while at the same time his book *Desperadoes* topped the bestseller lists. He parked his backside on many a talk-show sofa and appeared in the papers virtually every day. There were plenty of his own articles, but he was also consulted as an expert on anything to do with crime. Riots in the suburbs, a double murder, new drugs on the streets? See what Tommy T has to say about it.

The decline began in 2006, around the time Hagge moved in with him. Tommy had written several excoriating pieces on a number of high-ranking officers involved with a drugs case. Short version? All police chiefs were incompetent idiots—'woodentops', in his words.

Gradually it became clear that Tommy's accusations were groundless. The leads the police had been following came good, and seven individuals were charged. Since Tommy always had something of a scattergun approach to his journalism, he'd made this kind of mistake before. The difference this time was that the police refused to let it drop, and he was held to account.

A vicious debate broke out in the press, with Tommy on one side and the woodentops on the other. His talent for ducking and weaving was tested to the limit, and his writing skills reached new heights, but the public had begun to harbour the one suspicion that could prove fatal for his career: Tommy T might possibly *be wrong*.

He didn't crash and burn immediately; there were too many people who still regarded him as a guru, but the phone stopped ringing off the hook and the cascade of invitations through his letterbox slowly diminished. Tommy might be at the top of the tree, but he was beginning to slide down, and he was smart enough to know it.

Thinking to reboot his image, he started going out into the field to research his articles—unlike the deskbound woodentops—and that was how his and Hagge's paths came to cross.

*

Through an informant within the police, Tommy had heard about a raid on a meth lab located in the woodwork room of a disused school in Jakobsberg. Tommy got there before the cops and treated himself to a line of coke while he was waiting outside on one of the swings. The blue-lights arrived, and once they'd cleared the way, he followed them in.

It was an unusually messy set-up. As a general rule the producers were pretty efficient and left the degeneration to the end users, but in Jakobsberg Tommy saw a rare counterexample. Along the chaotic carpentry benches production had ground to a halt due to a complete lack of focus. Three guys lay flat out on the sofa while a fourth was trying, in the slow, uncoordinated way of a sleepwalker, to get through a wall with a chisel.

The ensuing arrests and securing of evidence were straightforward, and as long as Tommy kept his distance, they weren't bothered about sending him away. No excitement, no angle except possibly the amusing little detail of the location. Tommy was about to give up and go home when he heard a whimper. He called out to one of the officers in the room: 'Did you hear that?'

The officer looked around and went over to the sofa. He rummaged around among the cigarette-burnt cushions, and when he turned to face Tommy he was holding a pathetic little creature in his hands. A malnourished puppy, its ribs visible beneath the skin. The cop took a closer look and said: 'Jesus!'

One of the dog's front legs was missing. There was nothing but a bloody stump, as if someone had hacked it off. Possibly with a chisel. The cop sighed. 'Off to the vet with you, my friend. A little injection and it'll all be over.'

The dog looked at the cop. Then it looked at Tommy. Tommy said: 'I'll take it.'

As he drove to the vet's with the dog wrapped in a towel on the passenger seat, Tommy knew it was going to make it, and he also knew that its name was Hagge. Something in its eyes had told him both these things.

Tommy waited until Hagge had finished growing before having him fitted with a prosthesis. By this time Tommy's star was definitely falling. His regular contributions to news outlets in the city had become sporadic, and his picture by-line had shrunk to half its former size. When he contacted his publisher offering them first option on a book on trafficking they said it sounded interesting, but probably for a different publisher. The talk-show sofas were occupied by other backsides. Tommy T's glory days were over.

*

Somehow he kept going. In 2009 he and Hagge moved from his three-room apartment on Birger Jarlsgatan to a two-room place in Traneberg. This freed up just over three million kronor, which meant he didn't have to chase around for work quite so hard. He still had his contacts, and there were still readers who appreciated his bantering style, but Tommy was definitely slowing down.

He'd managed to give up coke, and went for long walks with Hagge in the pleasant surroundings of Traneberg. However, he also spent a great deal of time watching TV, drank a lot of beer and lived on microwaved ready meals. He wasn't fat, exactly, but his belly rested on his thighs when he was sitting on the toilet.

He had an extremely fluid relationship with Anita, a somewhat younger woman he'd got to know while he was researching his book on trafficking. She continued to work as a prostitute, but only occasionally. They met up when it suited them both.

And so the years went by. His book was eventually taken up by a smaller publishing house, and even though his research was a little out of date, it sold pretty well. He even found himself back on a couple of those sofas. He'd started to take Hagge with him wherever he went, partly because he enjoyed the company, and partly because Hagge, despite his slightly alarming appearance, had the ability to make people more positively disposed towards Tommy. As if he were a good person, which Tommy didn't believe he was. Plus Hagge had a *talent*.

A series of articles on cannabinoid drugs in general and the zombie drug, spice, in particular in the spring of 2014 led to a minor upturn in his fortunes, but after a few months he was back to the same old routine. Walks with Hagge, hook-ups with Anita, microwaved meals, TV and beer, chasing editors to try to get the odd piece into the papers. He was considering packing the whole thing in and trying to write a crime novel when his phone rang one evening in October 2016.

*

The silence on the other end of the line after Tommy picked up and said his name told him exactly who was calling. There was only one person who behaved that way: Ove Ahlin, chief news editor for *Stockholmsnytt*.

After a few seconds Tommy heard the rasping voice acquired through long years of smoking: 'Have you heard? About the suicides?'

'Hard not to.'

'You know anything? Picked anything up?'

'I haven't looked into it.'

Another silence. These pointless pauses created the sense of an interrogation, as if Ove was in possession of so much incriminating evidence you might as well confess right away. However, Tommy had been there before, so he simply waited.

'Do it, then,' Ove said.

'Why?'

'Because I'm asking you to.'

'Why don't you send the golden boy?'

Ove made a noise that was somewhere between a wheeze and a

sigh. The paper's current rising star was Mehdi Barzani, a twenty-five-year-old of Iranian descent who had the right connections within the criminal fraternity and also—undeniably—wrote well and concisely. His biceps looked pretty good in his by-line photo too. On top of all this he was a nice guy; Tommy couldn't dislike him, and he had certainly tried.

'This isn't a job for Mehdi,' Ove said firmly.

'Why not?'

'Come on, Tommy. You know. This is the old guard.'

Tommy had realised exactly what was going on as soon as he listened to Ove's introductory silence. From what he'd heard and read, the wave of suicides was almost exclusively restricted to the older generation of criminals, people Tommy had met, and in one or two cases even considered friends.

Since Tommy's heyday many of them had either given up their activities or come in off the street to operate behind a more elegant façade, directing operations without getting their hands dirty. And now more or less all of them were dead.

There was no point in keeping Ove hanging on. The story was interesting, Tommy wanted to find out what was going on, and there was no one better than him to start digging. 'How many articles?'

'Two. Maybe three, but in that case they'd better be good.'

Three wasn't to be sneezed at, given Tommy's current situation, but only last month Mehdi had been given the luxury of four articles in a series about the growing problem of heroin use in Finland.

'Four,' Tommy said, then sat and listened to Ove wheezing. He heard a series of careful thumping noises closer at hand, then Hagge emerged from the kitchen and stood looking at Tommy with his head cocked. Tommy gave him a thumbs-up and Hagge blinked as if he knew exactly what was going on. Tommy sometimes thought he really did know.

'In that case they'd better be *good*,' Ove repeated with a change of emphasis.

'When did I last write something bad?'

'You're so funny, Tommy.'

'When do you need the copy?'

'Yesterday.'

After a little negotiation on the fee, they ended the call. Tommy's question about the timing of the project had been rhetorical; this kind of thing was always urgent. Today everyone was interested, the next day nobody cared. However, Tommy felt that the suicide wave was significant enough that it would take a while for the public's curiosity to wane. It was big international news too.

Around thirty career criminals who'd decided to end it all during the space of two months. As far as Tommy was aware, nothing like this had ever happened before, and certainly not in Sweden. A key element of the mystery was that these were individuals at the top of their game, those who'd made plenty of money. For example, Bengt Bengtsson—Double Bengt—had been found floating on a lilo in his two-hundred-square-metre indoor pool with his wrists slashed.

Why?

Admittedly suicide was comparatively common among criminals, but that applied mainly to younger men. The older ones had a tendency to cling on at all costs. They'd made it this far, and they were determined to keep going as long as possible. So what could have led them all to conclude that life was no longer worth living?

At the end of the day we live in a market economy. If some kind of upheaval occurs, it's always worth asking the question: *who stands to gain from it?* Tommy thought that was as good a place as any to start. He scrolled through his address book—more than half the entries were nicknames—and stopped with his finger on Karlsson.

Karlsson's real name was Micke Prüzelius. As an angst-ridden eleven-year-old he'd started sniffing glue out of plastic bags, and had continued to do so even when he was able to afford more effective ways of sedating himself. These days he had moved on from the product known as Karlssons Klister and was now sniffing Casco contact adhesive; however, the name had stuck. He was a reliable errand boy with a wide network of contacts. He could be trusted as a go-between because his ruined brain meant that he rarely made any connections.

*

'Hi, it's Tommy. Tommy T.'

'Tommy? What the hell…I thought you were dead!'

'Not as far as I know. Why do you say that?'

'Geir told me—about a month ago.'

'Geir was wrong.'

'But he was absolutely positive.'

'Okay, but as you can hear, I'm not dead.'

'He was absolutely positive. I was really upset.'

Tommy rubbed his eyes. When Karlsson was high, he had a tendency to go around in circles. As a circuit-breaker, Tommy asked: 'How is Geir these days?'

'Haven't you heard? He's dead.'

'For real? It's not just a rumour?'

'No, no—I was the one who found him. Last week. He'd hanged himself. I was like completely fucked up.'

'I'm sorry to hear that, I really am.'

Geir hadn't been a major player, but he wasn't small-time either. A year ago he'd been responsible for getting three kilos of cocaine out on the streets, and since then had possibly moved even further up the chain. He was probably a part of the phenomenon Tommy was looking into.

'Did you see anything of him before he died?' Tommy asked.

'Yes—that was when he told me you were dead.'

'How did he seem?'

'Low. Really fucking low.'

'Why?'

'I've no idea. He kept talking about the business of existing, that kind of thing. Said it was a mistake?'

'Seriously?'

'Mmm.'

The Geir Tommy knew hadn't been the type to brood over existential questions. On the contrary, he'd given the impression of being quite a positive thinker, reinforced by the traces of Norwegian that lingered in his accent to impart a lilting rhythm that made a sentence like 'I'm going to kill that fucker' sound life-affirming. The idea that Geir would end it all was…unnatural.

'Okay, so who's taken over his patch?'

'Haven't a clue.'

Tommy bit his lip. He had a great capacity for remembering people's names and characteristics, but somehow he'd managed to forget Karlsson's fixation with *bugging*, his belief that the police had satellite dishes in space that enabled them to listen in to any conversation. Important information could be passed on only by whispering in the other person's ear. Tommy lowered his voice. 'What if we were to meet up. And I had a couple of hundred kronor in my pocket. Would you know then?'

'No, definitely not. I don't know anything anymore. I'm not interested. Bye.'

Tommy opened his mouth, but Karlsson was gone. He tried again, but his call was rejected. He scrolled aimlessly through the names. Karlsson almost always knew what was going on and was so forthcoming that it was a wonder he was still in one piece, but now something had happened. Something that had scared him.

If Karlsson didn't dare talk, then it was unlikely that any of Tommy's other informants would do so either, regardless of promises to protect his sources or the offer of a few hundred kronor. Which left only one option, an option he didn't particularly want to use. He scrolled up the list and stopped with his thumb hovering over 'The Hammer'. Then he slipped his phone into his pocket, called to Hagge and put on his jacket.

If he was going to use his friendship with one of the most feared men in Stockholm to tease out information, then it had to be face to face.

The Hammer's reputation had been cemented during the eighties, when he was working as a security guard at a nightclub called Alexandra's. The place was like a magnet for aspiring somebodies, and the clientele included a fair number of criminals. Some knew how to behave themselves, and were welcomed in to show off their designer clothes and accessories, buying champagne for everyone in sight and tipping generously.

But then there were the ones with a bad attitude to go with their money, and some others who just had the attitude. When they managed to get in the evening would usually end in a fight, often with the police involved, which didn't go down well with the other clients, who'd earnt their millions through honest graft. Kind of.

That was where The Hammer came in. It took a hard man to cope with the threats and violence that could ensue when someone who thought he was the King of Cokeland was refused entry. The Hammer was a metre ninety-five tall and weighed over a hundred kilos and he had hands like cast-iron shovels. And yet there were still people who kicked off, trying to save face and compensate for the humiliation of not being allowed in.

The Hammer had been punched in the eye and roundhouse-kicked in the ear and had on two occasions had a knife pulled on him. His response was always the same: a single solid blow to the chest that knocked the air out of his attacker and sometimes broke a couple of ribs. If there was any kind of investigation, everyone in the queue could confirm that there had been no excessive use of violence on the part of The Hammer. One punch, and not even to the face.

Hans-Åke, which was The Hammer's real name, also supplied doormen to other establishments. If a club already had their own guard, The Hammer pointed out that he was able to offer a better service. If they refused it, then the guard would meet with an unfortunate accident. Towards the end of the eighties The Hammer was in control of more or less every establishment in Stockholm's exclusive nightlife. He stopped working as a doorman and turned his attention to poker machines.

Within a few years he had around a hundred machines in his tender embrace, and there was hardly a venue owner who dared turn him down. Terrible things happened to those who did. The Hammer, having grasped at an early stage the concept of building a brand, made sure these terrible things involved the use of a hammer. Knees, elbows, feet...Of course he didn't wield the hammer personally, except under unusual circumstances, but the use of that particular tool meant that everyone knew who was behind an attack.

He served a few short sentences for minor infringements, and by the end of the nineties he had also survived three attempted murders, but he was alive and well when Tommy first met him in May 2002.

It wasn't their respective professions that brought them together, but a simultaneous need to get away. Tommy was Sweden's most widely read crime journalist, a man who never missed a deadline even though he was working on two books at the same time, one of which would be the highly successful *Desperadoes*. He had insomnia, a stomach ulcer and a coke addiction. Hans-Åke was recovering from a fourth murder attempt, in which one of his closest associates had been killed and he himself had suffered a punctured lung from a dozen or so shotgun pellets.

And so it came about that both of them booked a two-week charter holiday to Majorca, and on the fifth day found themselves relaxing on adjoining sun loungers. Needless to say Tommy recognised the big Swede who looked like a butcher, but unlike some other tourists he didn't move away when The Hammer crashed down onto his chair. After a few minutes Tommy heard a surprisingly high-pitched voice say: 'You're Tommy T, aren't you?'

'Yes.' Tommy turned to look at the man, who was lying on his back with a tortured expression on his face.

'Do you know who I am?'

'What do you think?'

The Hammer sighed. 'How the fuck do you relax? Do you ever *switch off*?'

'Sometimes when I'm asleep. How about you?'

'I don't sleep.'

'Right. So what do you do?'

'I'm not sure. Fancy a beer?'

The two men wandered over to the beach bar and sat there until the sun disappeared below the horizon. They talked about everything except the activities that had prompted them to seek refuge in Majorca. Hans-Åke had two dogs, and he worried about them just as much as Tommy worried about Biggles, the dog he had at the time. They both called their dogsitters, whom neither of them really trusted. They were both Hitchcock fans: they spent a good hour comparing their favourite scenes and actors. They agreed that nothing much had happened on the music scene since Bowie's most successful period.

Hans-Åke had put away fourteen beers and Tommy twelve by the time the bar closed, and they made their way back to the hotel through the park. When Hans-Åke stopped to piss in some bushes Tommy stood there swaying—and listening hard. He couldn't hear any footsteps, any kind of movement. Even though he knew he was entering sensitive territory, he couldn't help asking.

'So where are your people?'

'What people?'

'You're not here on your own, are you?'

'What the hell are you talking about?'

'Nothing. Forget it.'

Hans-Åke zipped up his trousers and turned around. 'Are you here on your own?'

'Yes, but...'

'Excellent. In that case we'll go up to my room and bugger each other senseless.'

Fortunately this was a joke, but Tommy never worked out how Hans-Åke could be so foolhardy as to travel without protection, given the number of people who wanted him dead. When they parted a few hours later after having shared a bottle of whisky, Hans-Åke—who finally seemed a little tipsy—said: 'The thing is, Tommy, what happens happens. Once you really get that, you can throw your ulcer meds away. Do you understand me?'

'I think so.'

Hans-Åke clenched his famous fist and held it up a couple of centimetres from Tommy's nose. *'Do you understand me?'*

Tommy fixed his eyes on Hans-Åke's thumb, which was the size of a matchbox, and said: 'You need to cut your nails.'

Hans-Åke lowered his fist and studied his fingers. 'You're right.' He looked up at Tommy. 'I'll have to ask *my people* to help me.'

He made a noise that was somewhere between a laugh and a death rattle before he closed the door. As Tommy walked away he heard Hans-Åke's voice echoing along the corridor: 'Tomorrow! Same time, same place!'

*

The two men spent a fair amount of time together in Majorca, and kept in touch once they returned to Sweden. When The Hammer went away, Tommy looked after his dogs, and as soon as Tommy published a new book or a series of articles, the Hammer would read them and make extensive, often savage, comments.

There was of course one complication with their friendship—a complication so serious that on Tommy's side it was almost tantamount to corruption. Over the years he learned a great deal about Hans-Åke's activities, one way or another, but he never wrote a word about them. Since Hans-Åke's empire was large and comprised many different areas it was impossible not to brush against its outskirts occasionally, but as soon as Tommy sensed Hans-Åke's guiding hand behind an illegal gambling club or the hijacking of a truck, he drew back and referred to an 'unknown individual'.

It wasn't just a question of a dubious sense of loyalty; Hans-Åke was also very helpful to Tommy in professional terms. Once they started talking about their work, it became clear that The Hammer was in possession of a huge amount of information that was hard to come by in any other way—who was doing what with whom and where. Tommy was smart enough to realise that The Hammer was also exploiting him for his own ends, enabling Tommy to expose things that The Hammer's rivals would have preferred to keep hidden.

So yes, Tommy was corrupt, but he had two arguments that helped to salve his conscience. First of all, he worked with crap and filth. Expecting him to be spotlessly clean was like criticising a garbage collector because he didn't smell like a newborn baby.

Secondly, he genuinely liked Hans-Åke and didn't want to do him any harm. This was highly unprofessional, but it was deeply human. He knew quite a lot about the terrible deeds that had been done by The Hammer, or in his name, but it was *Hans-Åke* that Tommy hung out with, just as he could be *Tommy* when he was with Hans-Åke, not that know-all Tommy T.

Hans-Åke had a fondness for silly jokes that contrasted sharply with his physical bulk and general appearance. On one occasion when they were chatting about the possibility of going over to Majorca for a week, for old times' sake, Hans-Åke said: 'Oh well, in that case I'll wear the little black number so it'll be just like *the first time*.'

Tommy enjoyed Hans-Åke's company and possibly regarded him as his best friend, which is why it went against the grain to go to him with a concrete question. He'd only done so once or twice in the past; their unspoken agreement was that Hans-Åke told Tommy as much or as little as he wanted to, then Tommy was free to use the information as he wished.

But now he needed help. Something terrible was going on, and the rats and mice were retreating into their holes. Tommy needed someone higher up the food chain, someone who could talk without the fear of an unexpected trip along an isolated forest track and the certainty of ending up as an unidentifiable corpse in a burnt-out car. And if there was one thing The Hammer had, it was courage.

Tommy slid behind the wheel of his Audi A2, a remnant of his glory days, with Hagge riding shotgun. To begin with Tommy had tried putting him on the back seat, but Hagge always wriggled over into the front. He liked to keep an eye on the road ahead. Tommy hoped the airbag would save him if anything happened.

He turned right onto Tranebergvägen and got stuck in a jam as usual, heading towards the Brommaplan roundabout. Hagge studied the other cars with the air of a connoisseur, and Tommy scratched behind the dog's ears.

'We're going to visit Hans-Åke,' he explained, and Hagge glanced out of the window before looking at Tommy as if to say: *Of course we are. We don't know anyone else who lives out this way, for goodness sake.*

'Something's going on,' Tommy continued. 'Something big. And to be honest, I really don't like not being able to work out what it is.'

As they came off the roundabout and onto the Ekerö road, Tommy took out his mobile and called Hans-Åke to let him know they were on the way. These days Hans-Åke conducted most of his business from home, which wasn't surprising as 'home' was a beautiful renovated nineteenth-century manor house with generous grounds and four sports cars in the garage.

The only response to Tommy's call was a pre-recorded message informing him that the subscriber could not be reached at the moment. He tried the landline, but there was no reply. That was unusual but not unheard of, and yet Tommy had a bad feeling. A premonition. To be perfectly honest, he was afraid. The Hammer was a major player, and these days major players had a tendency to end up dead.

*

A newly erected fence surrounded the entire property. No one answered when Tommy rang the bell, so he keyed in the alarm code,

18

opened the gate and drove through. The drive was covered in fallen leaves, and the bad feeling grew stronger.

He parked in front of the main entrance and let Hagge out. The dog ran up the wide steps, eager to see his friend. Tommy looked around. Apart from the slightly unkempt appearance of the garden, there was nothing out of the ordinary. Hans-Åke's oversized gas barbecue and deckchairs hadn't been taken in, but maybe he was hoping for an Indian summer. Tommy went up to the front door, where he found Hagge cowering and whimpering.

'What's wrong, boy? What's upsetting you?'

It was in situations like this that Tommy wished he was Sam Spade or Mike Hammer, or simply a cop, so that he could whip out his gun and feel the weight in his hand to counterbalance his pounding heart. Once or twice Hans-Åke had offered to get him a gun, but Tommy had declined. The police sometimes searched him before he was allowed to enter a crime scene.

For want of anything better, Tommy grabbed a boule from a box of garden games. Then he took out his key ring and found Hans-Åke's key. As soon as the lock began to turn he heard the sound of claws on parquetry. Fortunately he was on good terms with Hans-Åke's two pit bulls, Lisa and Sluggo, who also viewed Hagge as an authority figure.

The dogs are home.

The fluttering in his chest subsided a little. It was hardly likely that some thug—apart from The Hammer—would be in the house if Lisa and Sluggo had come scampering to greet him. He replaced the boule and opened the door.

Tommy had visited enough crime scenes to immediately register and identify the sweetish smell of excrement. Somewhere in this house there was at least one dead body. Lisa and Sluggo wound themselves around his legs, the muscles twitching beneath their skin. It wasn't until Hagge ambled in and the two pit bulls sat that Tommy saw the blood around their mouths.

He glanced around the hallway: nothing out of place. A curving double staircase led to the first floor; Hans-Åke had chosen a replica of the staircase in *Scarface*, but there was nothing to indicate that The Hammer had met the same fate as Tony Montana.

'Hello?' Tommy called out, even though he wasn't expecting a reply. 'Hans-Åke?'

Hagge limped towards the stairs, with Lisa and Sluggo following at a respectful distance. Tommy closed the front door behind him then sniffed, trying to work out where the smell was coming from, but without success. He thought the dogs probably knew, so he followed them up the red carpet of the left-hand staircase.

His heart began to race again, and for at least the hundredth time over the past few years he thought: *I'm too old for this*. He was no longer afraid of what might happen, but of what he was going to *see*.

The dogs disappeared along the landing and Tommy paused; the stench was stronger now. He inhaled deeply through his mouth, pulled himself together and set off after the dogs. He passed the billiards room and the guestroom where he'd stayed over on several occasions. Daylight was pouring onto the landing from the open door of Hans-Åke's bedroom. From inside he could hear Hagge whining piteously. Another deep breath, another mental squaring of the shoulders, then Tommy stepped across the threshold.

Hans-Åke's bed was approximately the same size as a garden shed, and sported black satin sheets. In the middle of the bed lay the big man, dressed in nothing but a pair of shredded underpants soaked in blood. He looked as if he was floating on a dark pool. Over his head was a blue plastic bag with the Nike logo, secured around his neck with silver duct tape. The body was covered with fresh and dried blood. Faced with the lack of food, Lisa and Sluggo had sunk their fangs into their master. His thighs were especially badly mauled, and the state of his underpants suggested they'd found a particularly tasty morsel in there.

A wave of nausea surged up from Tommy's stomach, but he was much too hardened to throw up. He'd seen worse things. Not many, but enough. It was the smell that was getting to him. He looked around the room, attempting to reconstruct what had happened, and saw an empty Rohypnol bottle on the bedside table.

The disgust moved aside to make room for sorrow when Tommy was confronted with the unavoidable truth. Hans-Åke, dangerous, funny, loyal, crazy Hans-Åke, had taken his own life.

The livid patches on the almost-naked body and the dogs' hunger indicated that this hadn't happened yesterday, or even the day before. On the desk lay a newspaper dated October 4, five days ago. Next to the newspaper was a note.

> To whom it may concern
> I, Hans-Åke Larsson, do hereby declare that I am going
> to my death of my own free will. I can't do this anymore.
> There is nothing but emptiness. I don't want to be here any
> longer. Silence, emptiness, darkness. Fuck. Stick a landmine
> on my grave.

Tommy couldn't help smiling at the final sentence. The note seemed to have been composed by a stranger in Hans-Åke's handwriting, but the real Hans-Åke had managed to peep through for a second right at the end.

Sometimes when they'd had a few drinks, Tommy and Hans-Åke had talked about 'life' and the best way to handle it. They had more or less shared the same attitude. It was all crap, which was why it was important to find enjoyment wherever possible. Hans-Åke was basically a simple man with simple pleasures. A few drinks, a decent film, a good fuck, a victory won. Tommy had never heard him brood over life's difficulties. *What happens happens.* But here he lay, floating in a black pool, gone forever.

Tommy turned to leave, unwilling to risk being drawn into whatever was going on, but he couldn't do it. He owed it to his friend to at least try to get some sense of what had dragged him down into the depths of despair. He pulled out one of the desk drawers, turned it over and removed the false bottom with the help of a pencil.

The notepad in the secret compartment was filled with symbols and abbreviations that would test the skills of a code breaker unless he knew the key. Which Tommy did. One convivial evening Hans-Åke had explained the whole 'system' as he called it. The following morning, his face ashen with the effects of a killer hangover, he'd said: 'Tommy, that system I told you about last night. Do you remember it?'

'I do.'

Hans-Åke had shaken his head sadly. 'Do you think you might be able to forget it?'

'I can try.'

'Please do. Otherwise I'll have to kill you.'

Tommy hadn't forgotten, in spite of Hans-Åke's genuine threat. He was now holding a detailed account of all Hans-Åke's most important business transactions over the past three years. Dates and locations of trucks and containers hijacked, the contents, who they had been sold on to, and the amount of money involved. Drug shipments received, how the pure drugs were to be cut and distributed. Who needed to be reminded of key points and how those reminders would be delivered. Tommy turned to the last six months.

The most spectacular thing he learned was that Hans-Åke had had a stake in a bullion robbery a couple of months ago that had been all over the media. Tommy ran his finger down the columns. He wasn't sure exactly who all the abbreviations referred to, but the letter 'X' occurred regularly, and thanks to this individual...Tommy brought the notebook closer to his eyes. Yes. He'd read it correctly.

4521 mha bib .//. tr00003

*

Twenty-nine days earlier Hans-Åke had bought *eighty kilos of ninety per cent pure cocaine* for the sum of ten million kronor in Värtahamnen. Those insignificant characters concealed three astonishing facts:

1) Eighty kilos of cocaine was a lot. It was rare for that amount to be sold in one single consignment.
2) It was impossible to get hold of cocaine that was ninety per cent pure unless you had serious contacts very close to the source.
3) Ten million was peanuts for a deal like that. Fifty might have been closer to the mark.

Tommy had had no idea that Hans-Åke was mixed up in something of this magnitude. He glanced over at the discoloured body on the bed. Had Hans-Åke found himself out of his depth? And who was this X who was capable of handling that kind of volume?

Maybe the ten million was just a down payment, with the rest due after Hans-Åke had distributed the coke to his suppliers on the streets. Tommy went back to the notebook to see if he could find confirmation for this more reasonable scenario. He stopped breathing when he saw: *hi 05 ho*

'You stupid fucker,' he said to the corpse. 'You stupid, greedy fucker.'

In spite of the fact that Hans-Åke had apparently been dealing with a player from the very top division, he had cut the ninety per cent coke down to forty-five per cent before selling it on. Even forty-five was an unusually high degree of purity and would command a high price, but what did X think about the fact that Hans-Åke was pocketing a few extra million on the side? Perhaps the answer was lying there on the bed.

But he took his own life, didn't he?

Before Tommy put the notebook back in the secret compartment, he used Hans-Åke's scanner to make a copy of the relevant page. He tucked the sheet of paper in his inside pocket, then stood there for a moment in front of the desecrated body, arms dangling by his sides.

'Goodbye, my friend.'

*

23

Tommy let Hagge into the car then drove a kilometre away from Hans-Åke's house. He turned onto a forest track then stopped, switched off the engine and wound down the window. The scents and smells of the forest filled the car; the breeze sighing through the treetops sent leaves spiralling to the ground and frolicked with those that had already fallen.

Tommy picked out a CD of Swedish Eurovision entries. He chose Jan Johansen singing 'Look at Me', then reclined his seat. He spent the next three minutes listening to the song and running through pictures of Hans-Åke in his mind, a series of memories of their years together. He did that instead of crying, and when Jan stopped singing he was able to breathe more easily, even though the final grotesque image still lingered.

Tommy looked into Hagge's dark, sympathetic eyes. 'Somebody did this. Somehow, somebody did this. Took Hans-Åke away from us. We can't just let it go, can we? Shall we call Henry?'

Hagge sighed and lay down with his head resting on his paws. Tommy scratched behind his ear and was comforted by the shudder of pleasure that passed through his companion's body. He took out his phone and scrolled through his contacts list until he found 'Don Juan Johansson'. He put on an ironic smile in order to help him summon up Tommy T, then pressed the call button.

*

When the police switched to the Rakel national digital communications system in 2004, making it impossible for outsiders to listen in to police radio messages, Tommy had sought out a more permanent contact than the occasional informants he was using at the time. Someone who could provide him with news from the field before it was tidied up and presented as a media pack.

After sounding out the terrain, Tommy had settled on Henry Johansson. This was partly because he was working for the National Crime Unit, but also because he had children by four different women and was paying maintenance to three of them. He was well-informed, broke and full of himself, which suited Tommy perfectly.

Tommy didn't really like Henry, but had a certain amount of sympathy with him. He was fifty-four years old and could have come straight out of the old Magnus Uggla song 'Fula gubbar'—'Ugly Old Men'. He dyed his greying hair, his fringe was a transplant from the back of his neck, he went to the gym, played squash and dabbled in extreme sports, all with the aim of trying to pull women who were thirty years younger than him.

But he delivered. Over the years Henry had sold so much valuable information to Tommy that it was hard to understand how he still had his job with the National Operations Unit, as the Crime Unit was known these days.

The signal rang out and Tommy cleared his throat, preparing to adopt the cocky drawl that his persona demanded. Henry answered almost immediately; he was going for 1950s hardboiled cop. Two roles meeting each other.

'Is that really you, Tommy?'

'Who else would it be?'

'They said you were dead.'

'Who did?'

'People.'

Tommy looked at Hagge and shook his head. At some point he was going to have to get to the bottom of how this rumour about his death had started, not least because he didn't like having to keep repeating that he was actually alive.

'It is me, and I'm not dead. I need to check something out. I'm a little short of cash at the moment, but I can offer you a juicy titbit in exchange.'

The 'juicy titbits' Tommy occasionally tossed in his direction partly explained why Henry still had his job. He was able to regurgitate them for his boss as the result of solid police work.

'How juicy?'

'One of Stockholm's top criminals is lying dead in his house, and nobody's found him yet.' Tommy hated referring to Hans-Åke like that, but *Tommy T* was doing the talking, and with someone like Henry it was important to stay in character.

'I'm listening.'

'Okay, but first of all I have one little question. I just need to know whether a whole lot of cheap, top quality cocaine has come onto the market recently.'

'One little question? So you're asking me if I can confirm that the Stockholm drugs squad has completely failed in its duty, since the suburbs are overflowing with cheap coke of an exceptionally high quality?'

'Do they know where it's coming from?'

'You mentioned a dead guy.'

Tommy briefly outlined the situation with Hans-Åke, and swore that he hadn't touched anything inside the house.

'Okay. Is that all?'

'The coke—who shipped it?'

'So you're asking me...'

'Enough, Henry. Just tell me.'

Henry snorted. Tommy didn't know where he'd got the idea of giving facts in the form of hypothetical questions—presumably from some movie. It was incredibly irritating. Henry sounded quite offended when he said: 'No point in asking when you already know the answer.'

'Are you sure?'

'Who else could it be? In those quantities?'

Tommy ended the call, then sat there gazing out of the windscreen, the phone still in his hand. A leaf-strewn forest track stretched before him like a shimmering promise or a veiled threat.

If it hadn't been for 'X' in Hans-Åke's notes, Tommy would have assumed that Colombians were behind the distribution, just as Henry had intimated. No one else had contacts with the producers in the jungle reliable enough to guarantee deliveries at that level. However, Tommy couldn't think of anyone who had the financial resources.

Could 'X' be a completely new player?

There was only one sensible place to start. He could kill two birds with one stone and pay a visit to his sister Betty and her son Linus if he was going to visit the suburb known as Gårdsstugan anyway.

Gårdsstugan

As they gather silver, and brass, and iron, and lead, and tin,
into the midst of the furnace, to blow the fire upon it, to melt
it, so will I gather you in mine anger and in my fury, and I will
leave you there, and melt you.

EZEKIEL 22:20

A modern myth tells us that the Great Wall of China is the only man-made structure visible from the moon. This is not true; the wall is too narrow and irregular. It would be more credible if Gårdsstugan were visible from space, so let us play with that thought. If an astronaut standing on our closest heavenly body were to take out a superpowerful telescope and focus on Sweden—northern Stockholm, to be more precise—what would he see?

If visibility was good enough, he might just be able to make out the contours of an X surrounded by greenery, as if some intergalactic pirate had marked the spot where he buried his treasure. However, let us assume that our astronaut is equipped with a high-tech telescope on a stand, and that he can zoom in. He will now realise that he's mistaken. The X is not in fact made up of two intersecting lines, but *four* lines that don't quite meet; there is a space in the centre.

He zooms in a little further and sees that the four lines are four gigantic buildings. He looks up from the lens and thinks there's a lot he doesn't know about Sweden.

*

The controversy around the remodelling of Slussen is as nothing compared to the storm of protest that blew up towards the end of the 1950s, when plans to build housing in the southern Haga Park area were announced. Action groups were formed, demonstrations took place, architects wrote articles in the press debating the proposal, and petitions bearing tens of thousands of signatures were handed in. No one disputed that additional accommodation was needed, but not *there* and not *like that*.

Admittedly the plot in question was uninhabited forest; Gustav III's copper pavilion, the Echo Temple and the Haga Palace to the north would not be touched, but were these historical and culturally significant structures supposed to live side by side with a *monster*? The available drawings and models showed four hyper-modern blocks arranged at an angle towards one another, twelve storeys rising above the treetops.

The protests grew louder, and Sune Granström, the architect, received death threats on more than one occasion. And yet the proposal went through, and when the final plans were presented, they depicted a mastodon of a building that was even bigger and even taller than the models that had provoked such fury. Then construction began.

Four blocks, each with twenty entrances. The twelve storeys became fifteen. Two thousand four hundred one-room, two-room and three-room apartments, with the odd four-room penthouse on the top floor. A total of six thousand people would be housed in Gårdsstugan. The same as Filipstad, but stacked on top of one another.

As the foundations were laid and the first concrete buttresses rose up into the sky, the protests fell silent. There was nothing more to be done. An opinion poll later concluded that the half of one per cent that the Social Democrats lost in the 1964 election was largely a consequence of Gårdsstugan. That was as bad as it got.

*

The name, which suggests a country cottage, is somewhat misplaced. Gårdsstugan no more resembles a cottage than a refrigerator resembles a cygnet. The choice was made partly because the social engineers had a predilection for that kind of name, evoking the mythical concept of the reassuring and cosy 'people's home' through the magic of letters, and partly because a cottage once stood on that particular spot. There was a manor house with a cottage for the groundsman and his family, approximately where door 18 section C is now located.

Gårdsstugan was ready in the spring of 1963, and in spite of the fact that it had become a symbol for the blind megalomania of the 'million program', it didn't technically form a part of that program, which was hustled through three years later. Gårdsstugan's insanity is completely its own, even if it shares that diagnosis with, for example, Grindtorp and Storstugan. The magic of letters once more.

*

The majority of those who moved in were what we would now call ethnic Swedes, although there were also quite a large number of Finns. The Hagalund rail depot needed staff, and plenty of Finns had the ability to repair and maintain trains damaged by the cold. Printers and workshops on the industrial estate also proved to be a draw. In addition there were students from the Karolinska Institute who rented one-room apartments on the lower floors, plus junior nurses from the hospital itself. Occasionally a doctor and his or her family would take one of the more appealing penthouses.

Over the years the Finns and Finland-Swedes came to form the largest minority in the blocks on the south side, designated C and D. When there was a party in the courtyard where the trees were still taking root, the Finnish pasties known as *piroger* were always on the menu, and the sound of tango music filled the air.

The northern blocks, A and B, were harder to fill. Because of a planning issue, it took a while for the drainage system to be completed. The excavators were still working when the residents of C and D moved in, which meant a delay in planting out the court-yard. While the south-siders were munching their pasties and swaying to the rhythm of the tango among small birch and pine trees, the northern courtyard was nothing more than a muddy rampart with the odd sapling sticking up.

The construction of a sports hall and football pitch to the west was postponed for a number of years because of this delay, and overall Gårdsstugan didn't turn out to be quite as immediately attractive as the civil engineers had hoped. In fact, you could say it gained a bad reputation pretty quickly. The chorus of critics from a few years earlier scented victory and began to shout from the rooftops, so to speak.

A series of articles catalogued the delays and attendant costs, frequently illustrated with images of the muddy northern section. The name Gårdsstugan acquired an aura of failure and modernist misery.

Eventually, however, the north side was also completed, and in order to compensate, or possibly as a PR stunt, the largest playground on any estate in Sweden was constructed. It was known as the Glade, and contained two or three examples of everything a child could wish for, plus two full-time caretakers. The papers had to report it, and people from all over Stockholm came to admire this wondrous sight.

However, quite a lot of apartments were still empty at the beginning of the seventies, and the next major change came with the coup d'état in Chile. Just as the Finns had set their stamp on the south side, so the Chileans would do the same on the north side. Once the Chileans had established themselves, the area attracted people from the rest of Latin America.

The significance of the Finnish / Chilean influences mustn't be exaggerated; they still formed the minority of the residents in Gårdsstugan, but nor can those influences be ignored. Throughout the ages people have a universal tendency to become polarised, to cling to their own special characteristics and to become 'we' opposed to 'them'. Certain mannerisms, slang expressions and business interests came to separate the north and south sides.

By the mid-nineties this polarisation had reached the point where parents from the south side refused to travel the three hundred metres to the somewhat run-down but still remarkable Glade in the north. They decided they could manage perfectly well with the fully functioning playground in their own area. Sometimes trouble flared between groups of youths from the opposing sides.

Things might have been different if there had been a common enemy, some gang of losers from Hallonbergen or Rissne who'd come down to mess around. Maybe then north and south could have joined together to defend the honour of Gårdsstugan from the rabble, but that didn't happen. Gårdsstugan was beyond everything else, and in the absence of a threat from outside, they created their own inside.

In 2016, when this narrative begins, the situation is relatively calm. You could say there is an air of resignation. The battles of the eighties and nineties have acquired a mythological status, and only the occasional skirmish disturbs the peace among the increasingly dilapidated blocks. Gårdsstugan has not benefited from the extensive renovations that have been carried out in similar areas. The rental payments or housing association payments are the lowest in inner-city Stockholm.

The façades have been painted and the locks on the outside doors have been renewed, but that doesn't have any impact on the *smell*. Some of it is down to mould or damp, but a prospective tenant cannot avoid the odour of structural fatigue in every apartment, as if the whole place was about to collapse, giving it all the appeal of milk past its best-before date. And if you manage to avoid the smell, the *feeling* is still there: 'No, you're not going to be happy here.'

*

Finally, a few words about the space in the middle where the four blocks meet, which our astronaut thought he could see. It's a square. 'Cottage Square', according to the maps. 'Shithole Square' according to the residents, and on this occasion they're not wrong.

The concept of 'a natural meeting place' is much loved by town planners and architects, and that was the original idea for the square. In the sketches from the 1950s you can see people happily wandering by with their shopping, sitting chatting on the benches, or enjoying the sun outside a café. That's not what happened, and it started with the wind.

During the planning and design phase, many factors were taken into account: growth, patterns of movement, the view from various points, everything relating to the sun's transit across the sky, how the light would fall—an important aspect back then. What no one took into account was the wind, and that was a big mistake.

As soon as the skeleton of the four enormous apartment blocks was finished and the architects met to discuss the square in more detail, they realised something wasn't right. The wind snatched the drawings out of their hands, and temporary structures were blown over. In a way that no one really understands to this day, the topography of the surrounding area combined with the fact that the four buildings stand at a ninety degree angle to one another meant that the square became the mouth of four gigantic air funnels. There might not be a breath of wind elsewhere, but it will be blowing a gale in Shithole Square.

Needless to say the cafés with outdoor tables were the first to disappear from the plans. A large number of benches were set out; no one ever sits on them. The square is just a place that people hurry across in order to get to where they have to go; no one wants to be there, which is why it has fallen into the hands of those who don't have anywhere to be.

The façades are covered in graffiti, and several shops stand empty, their broken windows roughly boarded up. The central feature, a proud fountain featuring an elf riding on a unicorn, dried up long ago and is filled with rubbish that whirls around with every gust of wind. Most of the streetlights have been smashed; no one is in a hurry to repair them.

People do meet here, but not in the way and at the times the planners had envisaged. Gabi's Grill, which bravely stays open until ten o'clock at night, has thick bars at the windows, and the ICA store, which is open until nine, has employed a security guard during the hours of darkness for a number of years now. Hardly anyone shops there anyway.

Linus

Linus Axelsson was standing on the balcony of the apartment he shared with his mother and father on the thirteenth floor of section fourteen, Block C. He clutched the aluminium railing, leaned over and allowed a gob of spit to drop to the ground before he looked up again.

It was a misty evening, and towards the south the lights of Stockholm sparkled like a magical possibility. He tried out a thought: *I am king of all I survey, everything I can see is mine,* and from his elevated position it worked pretty well. It wasn't the first time he'd thought that way—more like the hundredth. Or the thousandth. The difference was that tonight his fantasy could begin to become a reality, if everything went according to plan.

He heard a squeaking noise from the living room as his mother wheeled his father into position in front of the TV. Linus glanced over his shoulder and saw her lock the wheelchair before flopping down on the worn leather sofa, which creaked beneath her weight. Linus wanted to feel a rush of tenderness for her, but it was no good. She was just an object, albeit a slightly more mobile object than his father.

*

Linus was four years old when the family moved to Gårdsstugan so that his father could be closer to his work. He was a jockey, and Täby Racecourse was only fifteen minutes' drive away. He raced on other courses too, but Täby was one of the biggest.

He'd tried to get Linus interested in horses, but Linus thought the big animals were horrible. His father talked about the intelligence in their eyes; Linus couldn't see it. He saw only a cunning, latent aggression, waiting to find its outlet. And they stank.

However, Linus went along to watch the races now and again; it was exciting to see if his father would win, and sometimes he did.

Whatever happened, Linus was always relieved when it was over. He loved his father, and it made him nervous to see him at the mercy of the muscular beasts thundering along the track. Their heads must be full of hatred as they were whipped to achieve greater speed.

Then, when Linus was eleven, *Glorious Game* went down at Täby and his father ended up underneath, his spine broken at the third vertebra. The horse was unhurt.

When Linus's father came home after two months in hospital, there was essentially nothing left of him. He was a shadow of a man, stuck in a wheelchair and able to move only his eyes and mouth. His speech was slurred, and usually contained more drool than comprehensible words. The light had gone out in those bright, amused eyes, and Linus was horrified to realise that they looked a lot like horses' eyes.

Linus would have preferred it if the accident had left his father with severe brain damage, if the thing sitting in the wheelchair had been nothing more than an ill-chosen houseplant: something stuck in the corner that needed a little attention from time to time. As it was, his father's brain was intact while the rest of him was a wreck. He could do nothing for himself except breathe, swallow and make noises. Unfortunately it was sometimes possible to interpret these noises. The first sentence Linus managed to decipher was: 'Kill me.' Once he'd understood those words, he couldn't fail to understand when his father said them again. Which he did. Often. *Kill me.*

On one occasion his mother lost her temper when the wheezing plea came for the hundredth time. Didn't he realise that what he was asking for was a criminal act, that she'd end up in jail for murder, how could he be so selfish? From then on his father stopped asking her and focused on Linus instead, possibly because he was too young to face prosecution. This in turn meant that Linus did his best to avoid sitting with his father when his mother wasn't there.

*

35

Linus leaned over the railing again and peered down at the path through the bushes down below. Alex had said he would flash his phone screen three times when he was ready for Linus to come down. He heard laughter from the television; stupid people laughing at stupid things while other stupid people watched them. He felt a sudden urge to climb over the railing and jump, put an end to it all. Instead he crouched down, closed his eyes and visualised a lion, relaxing on the savannah and contemplating his surroundings with quiet dignity.

The excoriating anxiety in his body abated slightly, but he couldn't help drumming his fingers on the plastic grass covering the floor of the balcony. It was at moments like this that he wondered if he ought to start taking his medication.

*

Linus had had problems in school from day one—literally, the first day. During class registration in the soft play room, Linus had bounced around on his cushion, convinced he was a fire-breathing frog, until he crashed into a little girl and banged her head and she burst into tears. When the cushion was taken away from him he turned himself into a ball that rolled into a board with a display of pupils' drawings and knocked it over. That was his first day.

After that, things improved. His teacher was diligent, and made a point of feeding Linus's overactive imagination with tasks that didn't require quiet concentration. He was allowed to build, cut and stick, or run all the way around the outside of the building, and his energy only occasionally collided with that of other children.

The alphabet was a serious hurdle. Dealing with the letters one by one was fine; Linus was able to trace their shapes and learn to recite their names. Things took a turn for the worse when the isolated symbols he'd learnt were put together to form words. They literally began to *flow*. Linus could sit staring at the word DOG, and all he saw was meaningless lines that insisted on moving, as if they possessed the same internal life force as him. He would slam his fist down on his book to kill the words and make them keep still.

As reading became more important, so Linus's fuse grew shorter. The letters wriggled around on the page, there was a humming sound in his ears and his legs were itchy. He was often sent to another room for kicking the wall and disrupting the rest of the class.

As soon as Linus was given a task where he could think freely and work with his hands, he was a star. At the age of eleven he won second prize in a national newspaper competition where junior high school children were asked to create a representation of the United Nations. Linus spent a week constructing a globe out of an old telephone book and wallpaper paste. The continents were clearly visible, with tiny people on them. The point was that he didn't use papier-mâché, but the thin pages covered in names, names, names. Which he couldn't read.

His parents were delighted that he'd managed to achieve something that was valued within normal parameters, while Linus himself was disappointed not to have won. A week later his father came off the horse.

*

A few days after his father returned home as a vegetable, Linus's mother decided he couldn't just sit in the apartment. Together they managed to get him to the elevator despite a constant stream of whining protests, where only the word 'spew' was intelligible. Linus wished he had earlids that would perform the same function as eyelids.

When they reached the courtyard his father fell silent and concentrated on drooling instead. Linus walked behind his mother with his hands shoved deep in his pockets, staring at the ground and listening to the words on a loop inside his head: *Run away, never come back. Run away. Never come back. Run away.*

A burst of laughter interrupted the loop. Two boys from his class, Melvin and Tobias, were sitting on the steps of the climbing frame watching Linus's father, who had started jerking his head back and forth. Linus clenched his fists and gritted his teeth. *Run away. Never come back.*

The next day was devoted to outdoor activities. Linus was often given freer rein than his classmates and didn't have to take part in every task, but he did have to be around at break and lunchtime. It was chilly, a touch of dampness in the air, so the children gathered around a bonfire. Linus took out his flask of hot chocolate and his egg sandwich. By some magical process the egg tasted much better after a couple of hours in a plastic bag.

He drank his hot chocolate and ate his sandwich, his eyes fixed on a damp stick at the very edge of the fire. It was crackling and hissing, and he wanted to see the exact moment when it caught fire. Then he heard a gurgling sound.

It was coming from Tobias, who was rolling his eyes and holding his hands stiffly at an odd angle as chocolate trickled from the corner of his mouth. 'Linus's dad's like a total spastic!' he announced. 'Isn't that right, Linus? Is that why you're a spastic too?' The teachers were chatting a short distance away and didn't see what was happening as Melvin also started dribbling chocolate and making whimpering noises like Linus's father. Everyone laughed. Everyone except Kassandra.

Under normal circumstances Linus had a restless animal moving around inside his body, tickling his internal organs and trampling all over his nerves. Now the animal stopped moving, backed into its lair and waited. Linus replaced the lid on his flask, got to his feet and walked over to Melvin, who was still sitting there with his eyes rolling back in his head, and therefore didn't have time to react before Linus slammed the flask straight into his face.

Tobias shot to his feet and said something inaudible, which made more chocolate trickle down his chin. Before he could raise his hands to defend himself, Linus delivered a single blow to the temple with the flask. Tobias crashed to the ground as Linus turned to the others to see if anyone else wanted to continue the joke. No one did. In the background the teachers came running.

During the next few weeks Linus met two different psychologists and turned twelve. He had to do lots of tests and answer questions. They scanned his brain, took samples and carried out association exercises. They finally concluded that there was nothing wrong with his intelligence, but that he displayed ninety per cent of the characteristics required for a cast-iron diagnosis of ADHD.

For many people it can be a relief to find a name for their diffuse problems, and the diagnosis becomes a part of their identity. Linus wasn't one of those people. Maybe it was because of his father's condition, but Linus absolutely did not want to be the victim of some illness or syndrome. The neat combination of letters was like being condemned to walk around forever with a dunce's cap on his head. *Oh, you're one of those.*

The symbol for all of this was the plastic bottle of tablets that was handed to him by the psychologist. The label said *Concerta 27mg*.

'We'll start with these, then we'll see.'

'What will we see?'

'How you react to the medication, whether we need to adjust the dose.'

Linus rattled the bottle. 'Are they strong?'

'They're one up from the weakest dose, but as I said, we'll start with these.'

Another defeat. If Linus was going to be on medication he wanted the strongest, proof that his head was totally fucked up, but he'd been given the pathetic version instead. And he had no intention of taking them.

*

He felt very low when he got home. He sat down on his usual bench in the courtyard and took out the bottle. As he saw it, he had two choices. He could either chuck the tablets in the bin or swallow the lot. Presumably they didn't hand out drugs that were strong enough to kill a twelve-year-old, but you never knew. And did he really want to die? Maybe, maybe not. The tablets could be like a kind of Russian roulette—make the decision for him.

He heard footsteps behind him and quickly pushed the bottle into his pocket.

'What have you got there?'

Part of Linus breathed a sigh of relief, another part was on full alert. The voice belonged to Alex, an eighteen-year-old who lived in the same block. He'd done a couple of stints in residential care homes, and was involved in most of what went on around Gårdsstugan. People said he'd almost beaten another boy to death. Linus was relieved because it wasn't an adult who'd crept up on him, but the fact that it was Alex put him on his guard.

'Nothing,' he said, pushing his hands into his pockets as Alex came into view. His loose-fitting hoodie and Adidas tracksuit pants couldn't hide the bulging muscles, the result of many hours in the gym. The neck tattoo, the shaven head, the scar that ran down his cheek from below one eye. He was perfect. If Linus hadn't known him he would have wet himself; as it was a swarm of butterflies fluttered into life in his belly.

'Show me,' Alex said, holding out his hand.

If Alex said 'Show me' then you showed him. Linus passed over the bottle and Alex studied the label. 'You've got ADHD?'

'Yes.'

'And?'

Linus shrugged, and suddenly realised he was on the verge of tears. Crying like a baby in front of Alex was out of the question, so he stared at the ground and drew a pattern with the toe of his shoe. Alex thudded down beside him.

'Pull yourself together, for fuck's sake.'

Linus glanced at Alex. 'I don't want a fucking illness, okay?'

Alex sighed and glanced around. 'It's not an illness, you idiot. It's a diagnosis. It's something they *say* you've got.' He nudged Linus's shoulder with such force that Linus almost fell over sideways, then pointed to himself with both index fingers. 'Look at me. I've had every fucking psych diagnosis there is, apart from Alzheimer's. Do I look like a fucking loser?'

Linus stared at the heavy gold chain around Alex's neck, then shook his head. Alex gave him back the bottle and edged a fraction closer. 'Now listen to me, and listen carefully. This is how it is. When something happens, whatever it might be. When someone disses your dad or you get some fucking diagnosis you don't ask yourself: "What does this *mean*?" or "How does this *feel*?" That kind of crap is for losers. You ask yourself this: "How can I *use* this?" Get it?'

Linus turned the bottle around in his fingers. No, he didn't get it. What use could he possibly make of being stamped with a diagnosis of ADHD? 'I don't know what you mean.'

Alex rolled his eyes and flicked Linus's temple with his index finger. 'Think!' When Linus didn't say anything, Alex pointed to the bottle.

'Those tablets? Got amphetamines in them. They're not very strong, but you could easily get...twenty or thirty kronor per tablet. Five hundred for the lot, if you're lucky.'

'You mean they have the same effect as amphetamines?'

'Not on people like you and me, but on ordinary punters. Students who have to cram for an exam and don't dare go after the real stuff.'

Linus weighed the bottle in his hand. 'Five hundred?'

'With the right customers.'

'So how do I find the right customers?'

A broad grin split Alex's face. 'That, little man, you'll have to work out for yourself. I don't deal with that kind of crap anymore.' He got to his feet, lowered his voice and leaned closer. 'Have I given you a clue?'

He looked at Linus as if he'd said something funny, and Linus suddenly caught on. He smiled at Alex, nodded and said: 'Golly, thanks Baloo!'

Five years had passed since that day, and now Linus was waiting for Alex's signal. He'd disappeared for a couple of years, but had returned a few months ago and started dealing. It would be an overstatement to say Alex's advice had changed Linus's life, but it had certainly helped. From that day on he was always on the lookout for opportunities.

Linus's very first scam served as a good example. The day after his conversation with Alex, he spotted old fru Gummerus's wheeled walker outside door twenty-six. He stared at it, wondered: *How can I use this?*

An idea came to him. He shoved the walker into a shrubbery, took the elevator up to fru Gummerus's apartment, rang the bell and told her he'd just seen a gang of boys from the north side heading off with her walker. The old lady went out onto her balcony to check, and wailed in despair when she saw that the walker was missing. Linus felt so guilty that he almost dropped the whole thing, but then fru Gummerus asked the question he'd been hoping for: was there any chance Linus could get it back for her?

He scratched his head and told her these boys were nasty pieces of work, if she knew what he meant. It wouldn't be easy. He let her beg and plead for a while before agreeing to try. He almost added: 'If I don't come back, could you please let my mum know what's happened to me?', but decided that was probably a bit too much.

Then he went back down, took a stroll to the square and pinched a bar of chocolate from the store before he returned. He retrieved the walker from the bushes and smeared a little mud over his throat and one cheek. He ran all the way up the stairs to the tenth floor so he'd be out of breath when he rang the bell this time.

He told fru Gummerus a long story about how he'd risked his life to reclaim her walker, grimacing in pain at regular intervals. The old lady was very grateful and insisted on giving Linus two one-hundred kronor notes.

That kind of thing. Spotting opportunities.

The three flashes didn't come from the path, but from the open area where the carpet-beating rack was located. Linus pulled a face. Of course. Alex wanted to remind Linus that he was in Alex's debt. And he was, there was no denying it. Linus went indoors and walked through the living room, where his parents sat spellbound in the blue glow of the television, as if they were about to be beamed up to a spaceship.

In the hallway he pulled on his dark grey hoodie and his everyday Nikes. The Asics were reserved for running and running alone; he would never besmirch them by using them like any old pair of sneakers. They were *the sneakers*.

In the elevator he checked his reflection in the cracked mirror, which was covered in graffiti. There wasn't much about his appearance he wouldn't want to change. Two fat, fresh zits had bloomed on his forehead among the scars of old ones. His hair was lank and mousy, and had started to thin. He was *seventeen*. And his hair was thinning. There was something emaciated about his whole face, and in the dirty yellow glow of the overhead light his cheeks looked hollow. The only positive thing was his eyes. Big and blue, they shone like two beautiful mountain lakes among the ravages of a forest fire.

The elevator screeched to a halt. Linus stepped out and shoved his hands in his pockets as he scanned the area. This was routine behaviour. You don't dart your head around like a nervous sparrow; you simply allow your eyes to scan for irregularities. Everything seemed fine. He set off towards the carpet rack. He had to admit that he was nervous, which became obvious when he started to think about his gait. Was he walking the right way?

When he turned onto the patch and saw the glow of Alex's cigarette he realised he was almost stumbling along, and gave himself a mental gut-punch that made him lower his shoulders and slouch in a more relaxed manner.

'Okay?' Alex said, taking a last drag before crushing the cigarette underfoot.

'Okay. You?'

Alex didn't reply, and Linus was grateful for the gloom among the tall bushes. He'd met Alex in daylight a couple of times since his return, and something in his eyes had changed while he was away. There had always been a glint of humour in his expression, in spite of the fact that Alex was a hard man; that was gone now, replaced by a gravity, a dark intensity, that made Linus's legs feel wobbly. As if Alex *knew*. Linus had caught a glimpse of that look before the cigarette was extinguished, and it had been enough to give him the creeps already.

'Here,' Alex said, handing over something that Linus put in his pocket before feeling it.

Shit!

Linus had been expecting five grams, maybe ten, but the package he was clutching must weigh at least...

'A hundred grams,' Alex informed him. 'Ninety per cent.'

Every drop of saliva in Linus's mouth dried up, as if he'd been sucking a hairdryer. His resting pulse rate was twenty-three, but suddenly his heart began to race. He'd been expecting to start dealing the real stuff at long last, but this was serious. He couldn't keep his voice steady: 'What the fuck?'

'Is there a problem?'

'Yes, no, I mean, where did you...' Linus broke off. He'd been about to ask the question you definitely didn't ask if you wanted to be able to carry on tying your own shoelaces in the morning.

'What did you say?'

'Nothing.'

'Okay. All good?'

Linus knew his voice would betray him, so he simply nodded. Alex traced the line of his scar with his index finger and went on: 'A thousand kronor a gram. How cheap is that? You weigh it out, package it up, and Linus...' Alex took a step closer. 'You wouldn't fuck me around, would you?'

Linus had no idea what Alex was talking about, but whatever it was, there was absolutely no chance that he would fuck Alex around in any way whatsoever.

'It can be tempting with such pure shit,' Alex added.

Okay, now Linus understood. He certainly had no intention of cutting the coke and increasing the quantity still further. The weight in his pocket now felt like at least a kilo. He swallowed and asked: 'How much do I pay you?'

As if it were the most obvious thing in the world, Alex replied: 'A hundred thousand.'

'But what about me?'

'What about you?'

'What do I get? If there's a hundred grams and I'm selling it for…'

'Linus, Linus.' Alex placed a hand on his shoulder. 'You get nothing. Not this time. This is a test. Do you understand? If you can manage this, then you're *in*. Then we can talk about what you get.'

'But…'

Alex moved his hand to Linus's throat, squeezed hard and drew him close, breathing into his face. 'Linus. If you don't get the concept of payback, then you're finished. Dead. Okay?'

Linus nodded as best he could. Alex loosened his grip, and in a pleasanter tone he said: 'Do you realise what we've got here? What a source we've tapped into? Do you realise what this could become?'

No doubt Linus would appreciate the positives at some point, but right now he was paralysed by the impossibility of distributing the amount of coke in his pocket. The cokeheads he dealt with might relieve him of ten, maybe fifteen grams. But the rest?

'How long have I got?'

Alex spread his arms wide. 'As long as you need.' Linus felt a spurt of relief, until Alex added: 'But no more than two weeks. You know where I am.'

He backed away and turned around. Before he left he patted the carpet rack to remind Linus exactly why he was doing this for free.

Because it was payback time.

It had taken Linus a couple of weeks to get the sale of his medication under way. His friend Erkki had an older brother who was studying economics, and his parents were incredibly proud of him. A week or so after Linus's chat with Alex, Erkki's brother Riisto, complaining about an important upcoming exam, had shown Linus the pile of books he had to get through before then. It seemed like an impossible task to Linus; he would rather have tried converting a toaster into a computer.

When Erkki went to the bathroom, Linus slipped into Riisto's room and found him sitting at the desk with his head in his hands, staring at a book that resembled the phone books Linus had used for his UN project.

'What do you want, Linus? I just told you I have to...'

'You must get tired.'

Riisto rubbed his eyes; there were dark brown shadows beneath them. 'No shit, Sherlock.'

'Would it be easier if you weren't tired?'

'Of course it would—what the fuck are you talking about?'

Linus heard the toilet flush, and quickly said: 'I've got some pills you can buy.'

Riisto looked sceptical. 'Caffeine tablets—I mean...'

The bathroom door opened. Linus shook his head and whispered: 'Amphetamines' before backing out of the room, crashing down on the sofa and grabbing an Xbox control. He and Erkki went back to *Call of Duty*, and from the corner of his eye Linus saw Riisto standing in the doorway watching him. Linus lost concentration and got shot in the head by a sniper.

After half an hour Riisto came and joined them on the sofa. When they finished the next round he said: 'Erkki, go and buy me a couple of cans of Red Bull.' After a certain amount of negotiation and a bribe of twenty kronor, Erkki left the apartment. Linus preferred to stay where he was.

'So what have you got?'

Linus showed Riisto the bottle. Riisto turned it around as if that would help him understand its contents. 'What is it?'

'It contains amphetamines.'

'Yes, but what is it?'

'Try it. Thirty kronor for one tablet.'

Riisto grinned and nudged Linus with his elbow. 'Listen to you— our local dealer!' He tipped two tablets into the palm of his hand. 'Two for fifty, okay?'

'Okay.'

The test exceeded all expectations. A couple of days later Riisto came back for two more tablets. During the three days that remained until his exam he slept for a total of ten hours, but was firing on all cylinders and passed by a decent margin. The day after he got the results he approached Linus in the courtyard.

'Listen, I've got these friends...'

*

That's what happened. The friends had friends, and soon Linus had a regular market for all the medication he was prescribed. His school work went to hell and he finished up back in residential care, where he got to know a girl called Ulrika. She was the same age as him and with similar problems; she was only too happy to sell him her medication for two hundred kronor a bottle.

. After a year with no improvement in Linus's condition, the strength of his prescription was doubled, and the price went up to forty kronor a tablet. He'd hoped that Ulrika would also be prescribed stronger drugs that she would be willing to sell to him, but she sliced open her jugular vein with a pair of nail scissors, so that source dried up, so to speak.

The demand considerably outstripped the supply. A dozen students, mainly from the Karolinska Institute, who lived on the lower floors of the Gårdsstugan apartment blocks had standing orders as soon as a 'delivery' arrived—which meant as soon as Linus could pick up his prescription from the pharmacy. It was infuriating to realise that he could have been earning three or four times as much if only he'd had the resources.

*

That was when he first heard about a player who'd run a similar business twelve or fifteen years earlier from the laundry, which was now a solarium, in the basement of number thirty-six. Apparently this guy had looked like Frankenstein's monster, but he'd had a reliable source at Karolinska who smuggled out the drugs hidden in the towels the hospital sent to the laundry. Rumour had it that he'd killed a couple of people then got into some kind of dispute with the Latinos on the north side, and was never heard of again.

Linus had no chance of establishing a set-up like that, and if it was so easy to get stuff out of Karolinska, the students would hardly turn to him for their fix.

He tried not to think about the fact that this profitable enterprise of his was against the law, and that there were probably other players around. Until they turned up one day. Linus was doing his Sunday round, and had just delivered five tablets to a girl, a psychology student who apparently needed some help herself. When he stepped outside he was confronted by two guys in their twenties, and he knew almost immediately that he was in trouble.

Almost immediately. If he'd known *immediately* then maybe he would have managed to get away. It was their appearance that fooled his reflexes. They didn't look in the least like brothers. No hoodies, no sneakers, no cropped hair. Apart from the fact that one of them had a small rabbit tattooed on the back of his hand, they looked more like city boys—neat haircuts, pullovers, loafers. However, as soon as Linus appeared they each grabbed an arm and dragged him down to the cycle storeroom, where they explained very clearly that *they* were the ones who took care of the Karolinska students' 'substance needs' as they put it. Some of Linus's customers had mentioned that there were people at the institute who sold stuff for twice the price Linus was asking, but he hadn't given it any more thought. This was Gårdsstugan, a world of its own.

They rolled up their sleeves and took it in turns to hold him while the other slapped him across the face so hard that the insides of his cheeks were bleeding by the time they'd finished. They told him they were going easy on him because he was young and didn't know any better, but next time it'd be fists, or worse. They left Linus lying on the concrete floor in a mess of blood and snot. By way of a farewell gesture, one of them picked up a mountain bike and threw it down on top of him so that the chain sliced open his temple.

The same evening Alex caught sight of him sitting on the bench where they'd met just over a year earlier. Linus was feeling very sorry for himself, and when Alex asked what had happened, he told him the whole story. He wanted revenge.

'Okay,' Alex said. 'Two arseholes beating up a thirteen-year-old; that's not cool. What can you tell me about them?'

Linus's mouth hurt with every word he spoke, so he kept it short. 'City boys.'

'I know exactly what you mean. Bastards. I'm getting a little annoyed here. Anything else?'

Linus searched his memory. Their style and appearance had been so alien to him that he found it hard to recall any detail; they might as well have been Chinese. Then an image came into his mind.

'A rabbit. One of them had a rabbit tattoo. Here.'

Alex nodded slowly. 'Now we're talking. I'll check it out. Give me your mobile number.'

'What are you going to do?'

Alex smiled and looked quite excited as he ruffled Linus's hair and said: 'I'll be in touch.'

*

The next two days passed with no business transactions. The city boys had taken Linus's tablets, and he made a mental note not to carry his entire stock with him. Assuming he didn't give up altogether. Even if he'd had tablets at home, he wouldn't have dared go out on his rounds. He told his mum he'd fallen off his bike and asked her to phone the school to say he wouldn't be in, then he spent most of his time shut in his room.

He hated to admit it to himself, but he was scared. The incident in the storeroom had gone on for maybe ten minutes, but it had felt like being catapulted into a parallel universe. The fact that another person was standing there with the intention of doing him harm. Not just one blow, as he'd delivered with the flask, but a systematic beating with the sole aim of causing injury and breaking him down. Being on the receiving end had changed his view of the world; it was as if a huge barb was stuck fast in his body. So he curled up on his bed and stared at the Harry Potter poster he should have taken down a long time ago.

It was just after eleven on Tuesday night when Alex called and told him to come to the carpet-beating racks, because he had a surprise for him.

'What kind of surprise?'

'If I told you that, it wouldn't be a surprise, would it? Get here now.'

When Linus arrived, Alex was leaning on one of the racks smoking. There was a sports bag in front of him, and Linus assumed it contained the surprise. Alex pointed to the area where the shadows were deepest; Linus had no idea what was going on, and felt like an idiot standing there. He was seriously considering packing the whole thing in and doing something else with his life.

Like what?

He was working through a range of impossible options when he heard footsteps approaching. Alex said something, and the other person answered. Linus thought he recognised the voice, and moved a fraction closer without leaving the shadows.

'...could be massive,' Alex said.

'Why should I trust you? I don't know you.'

'No, but you know my brother. Come here, Linus.'

Linus had no choice but to obey. He stepped forward and saw that Alex was talking to Rabbit Boy. It was clear from his expression that he recognised Linus. 'What the fuck...' he said as he turned to face Alex and was met by the barrel of a gun.

'Take it easy,' Alex said, pressing the gun against the boy's right eye so that he was forced to close it. 'Linus—open the bag and take out the ball and the rag.'

'Do you know who I am?'

'I know exactly who you are. Someone with zero contacts apart from some loser on the psych ward. Linus?'

Linus scratched his hand on something as he rummaged around. Eventually he found a rubber ball about the same size as a tangerine, and a long rag. Following Alex's instructions, he pushed the ball into the boy's mouth, then held it in place by tying the rag at the back of his neck. Any protests were silenced.

Alex shoved the boy towards the rack, gave Linus a cable tie and told him to fasten the boy's wrists to the frame. The boy started making guttural noises, and tears poured down his cheeks. Alex slipped the gun into his pocket, then undid the boy's belt and pulled down his jeans and underpants. His backside glowed white like that of a fleeing deer, and twitched spasmodically.

'So,' Alex said pleasantly. 'Time for a little chat, wouldn't you say?' The boy nodded and a string of snot dangled down past the rag. 'The other day you and your mate gave my brother here a real beating. He's thirteen years old. He's only a *kid*. Is that the way people should behave towards kids, do you think?'

The boy shook his head. If Alex had asked for permission to kill his grandmother, he would probably have nodded in agreement.

'No. Exactly. You realise you've done wrong, so can you assure me that you'll never do anything like that again? You'll leave Linus alone, whatever he's dealing?'

Nod, nod, nod, and a groan that could possibly be interpreted as 'yes, yes, yes'.

'There you go, Linus. That's okay, isn't it?'

Linus swallowed and nodded too. He might have been thirsty for revenge earlier on, but he didn't like this, and he particularly didn't like the thing in the bag that he'd scratched his hand on.

Alex patted the boy's bare buttock. 'In that case, all that remains is to...You really did some damage to my brother. I'm not happy about that, not at all. That kind of behaviour can't go unpunished.'

He reached into the bag and pulled on a glove. The boy looked over his shoulder, his eyes widening with panic, and when he saw Alex draw out a half-metre length of rusty barbed wire, he shat himself. Excrement ran down his legs, the stench filling the air. He tried to scream, but thanks to the rubber ball, the only sound he could produce was an animal whimper.

Linus's lips began to tremble. 'Alex?' he whispered.

'Yes?'

'He gets it. That's enough.'

'Do you think so?' Linus nodded again, even more feverishly.

'I don't agree,' Alex said. Then he began.

*

Five minutes later the boy crawled away on all fours. His underpants and jeans were so filthy that there was a squelching sound as fresh blood seeped through from his backside. Alex threw the barbed wire into the bushes and dropped the glove into his bag. Linus was making a real effort not to throw up. He'd only seen the first blow; after that he'd closed his eyes and kept them tight shut until it was over. But the noises...He didn't think he'd ever forget them.

Only when Alex placed a hand on his shoulders did he open his eyes. Alex nodded in the direction of the boy and said: '*Now* he gets it. Guaranteed.'

Linus's teeth were chattering, and he couldn't get a single word out. Alex lit a cigarette and leaned against the rack.

'You can't just let things go. If you're going to do this, then you have to take that on board. If you let things go, then sooner or later they'll blow up in your face. Okay?'

Linus swallowed a lump of saliva that felt like broken glass, and nodded. Alex's lips narrowed to a thin line, and he shook his head. 'You don't really understand, but I can promise you...' He gestured towards the boy, whose legs were just disappearing from view. 'That little fucker...He was scared, he would probably have kept his head down for a few weeks, but then he'd have started turning it all over in his mind, remembering that a kid with big ideas was dealing on his turf. He'd forget, decide it was time to do something. But now...' Alex brushed his hands together. 'Now he won't forget. For the next few weeks, or even months...every time he sits down, he'll remember. It will stick in his mind, no doubt about that.'

He crushed the cigarette between his thumb and index finger. 'I'm not saying this is necessarily true, I don't think he was tough enough, but I might have saved your life. Possibly.'

Linus managed to prise his jaws apart sufficiently to say: 'Thanks.'

Alex smiled.

'Thanks is good, but there's something else you need to understand. I just did you a favour. There may come a day—in a month, in a year—when I ask you to return that favour. And you'll do it, because that's called payback. That's how it works, okay?'

Alex had held out his hand, and Linus had shaken it.

*

It had taken four years, and now Linus was standing in the very same spot with a hundred grams of ninety per cent pure coke in his pocket. Alex's predictions had proved accurate. Linus had been able to conduct his business in peace, and over time had expanded his enterprise to include Russian vodka and stolen goods from loading bays. He'd got himself a crew in the form of Henrik and Matti, and apart from a brief spell in residential care, everything had gone well.

Like all living creatures he had longed to grow, to take the next step up to the level where real deals were done and there was plenty of money to be made, but standing here clutching that package he wondered if he'd bitten off more than he could chew.

Question one: should he involve Henrik and Matti?

They were his crew, but they didn't share his hunger. Henrik in particular had a habit of losing his nerve in a difficult situation, and it didn't get much more difficult than this. Plus he wasn't sure Alex would like it.

Question two: so what the fuck was he going to do?

He didn't have any heavy users among his customers, just low-level idiots who hoovered their half gram then waited patiently for next weekend. Apart from the medication Linus supplied in between times, of course.

Assuming that what Alex had said about the purity was true, they would no doubt want to sample Linus's wares, but he'd be treading on Chivo's toes, and Linus had heard quite a lot about what the Goat—as Chivo was known on the south side—was capable of. Alex's performance with the barbed wire could have come from the Goat's repertoire. Linus sat by the rack for half an hour without coming up with a solution.

Find the opportunities.

On one level he was living the dream. A hundred grams of quality merchandise in his pocket—who'd have thought it? On another level he felt as if he was carrying a time bomb. Two weeks, Alex had said, and Linus was in no doubt that he meant it.

He thought Alex probably wouldn't kill him or even beat him up too badly if he failed, but he wasn't absolutely certain. Alex had changed, and Linus didn't want to find out what expression his displeasure might take these days. And what if Linus lost the coke? Social services had made unannounced visits on more than one occasion, poking around the apartment.

So. Point one: stash the goods in a place where even a specialist narcotics dog wouldn't find them. Point two: come up with a way of distributing them. Put that way, it didn't seem impossible. Linus got to his feet and set off home.

*

When he walked in through the door he heard a voice from the kitchen, and stopped dead. *Shit.* Uncle Tommy had decided to pay a visit. Linus had nothing against his uncle, quite the reverse, but given what he had in his pocket, this wasn't a good situation. Plus he was bound to have Hagge with him, and there was something spooky about that dog. It seemed to *know* things.

Linus grabbed a hoodie from the hallstand, shoved the package into the pocket and put it back where he'd found it. Claws clicked on the wooden floor, and Hagge appeared in the kitchen doorway. He paused and gazed at Linus in a way that sent chills down Linus's spine.

If he looks at the hallstand I'll scream.

But Hagge simply wagged his stumpy tail, lolloped over to Linus and allowed himself to be scratched behind the ears. Linus was so relieved that tears sprang to his eyes as he crouched down and whispered: 'You're a very good dog, Hagge!'

Hagge's expression clearly said: *Yes I am, but are you a good boy?* Of course it didn't. Yes it did. Linus was very much on edge, and it didn't help when his uncle emerged from the kitchen and said: 'So what have we here, then?'

Tommy's head was worryingly close to the hallstand. Linus had a sudden urge to fall at his feet, confess everything and solve all his problems at a stroke. *Yeah, right.* Instead he crawled along the floor as if to play with Hagge, who wasn't in the slightest bit interested. However, it did make Tommy move away from the hallstand and follow him. When Linus reached the living room he got to his feet and gave his uncle a hug.

*

Tommy and Linus had had a good relationship ever since Linus was little. After his father's accident, Tommy was one of the few people Linus could talk to, even though they didn't see each other very often because Tommy was a busy man back then. When Linus got into real trouble at the age of fifteen and social services were called in, Tommy was the only adult who didn't write him off as a hopeless case. After a spell in residential care he actually moved in with Tommy for a couple of weeks, but there wasn't enough space for this to be a long-term solution.

In addition, Linus was proud of his uncle. He might not be at the top of his profession anymore, but being the nephew of *Tommy T* still brought a certain kudos.

Needless to say, Tommy was unaware of the extent of Linus's activities. He only knew about the things that had come out a couple of years ago. He certainly didn't know that Linus was selling his medication, and Linus wanted to keep it that way. He wasn't sure if his uncle's goodwill would extend that far. And the coke? No chance.

*

One bonus of Tommy's visits was that Linus's mother pulled herself together. Normally she wandered around as if enveloped in a grey cloud, weighed down by a backpack filled with bitterness, but when Tommy turned up a glimpse of the old Betty was visible. Linus knew they'd been close when they were kids, even though Tommy was five years older than his sister. When Tommy told one of his stories, Linus's father would sometimes make a noise that resembled a laugh. So in spite of Linus's current difficulties, he couldn't help feeling a warm glow when the four of them were sitting around the table over coffee in the living room chatting like an ordinary family—apart from his father's gurgling, of course.

After a while Tommy turned to Linus. 'How's your motor vehicle course going?'

Linus shrugged. 'Fine.'

'How would you know?' Betty said. 'You're never there.'

His father gurgled in agreement, but it wasn't true. Linus turned up as often as necessary to maintain the façade that he was a keen student studying motor vehicle maintenance at college, and that he was aiming to become a mechanic. Occasionally he actually learned something.

'The other day we changed the timing belt on a Volvo V70,' he said. 'The drive belt's in the way; it was a bugger to get off.'

Betty glanced at Tommy to see if this was likely to be true. Tommy nodded. 'They can be tricky.'

After a while Tommy and Linus went out onto the balcony for a breath of fresh air while Betty cleared the table. Tommy leaned on the railing and gazed towards Stockholm, then said: 'I didn't know there was such a thing as a multi-track belt. Do you ever go to college?'

'Now and again.'

Tommy turned to face Linus. 'Are you dealing?'

Linus looked his uncle straight in the eye. 'No.' Tommy held his gaze for a few seconds, then nodded.

'You might have a friend who's dealing,' he went on after a moment. 'In which case you ought to tell that friend to lie very low. A new player's come onto the scene, and he's very dangerous.' There was almost a pleading note in his voice. 'And when I say very dangerous, I mean it. A lot of people have died. He's taking over. Or maybe there's more than one player involved.'

'Does this have anything to do with those suicides?'

Tommy grimaced as if he were in pain for a second. 'Yes. Among other things.'

Linus went and stood beside Tommy by the railing to avoid meeting his eye. His mind was racing. *A new player.* Maybe that explained why Alex had suddenly come up with such unbelievably pure coke. Was Linus actually working for the new guy?

Good or bad? *Very dangerous.* Bad if you messed up, good if you needed backup. Bad if you were against, good if you were for. Linus didn't know which he was.

'This new player,' Linus said. 'Does he sell...really pure stuff?'

He could feel his uncle's eyes burning into his cheek, but kept his attention focused on the city in the distance. He didn't like having to reveal so much, but he needed to know.

'Yes. Why do you ask?'

'Just something I heard.'

Tommy seized Linus by the shoulders and turned him around. Linus didn't have time to wipe off the smile that had taken over his face when he found out he was probably on the winning side. The dangerous side. Tommy saw the remains of the smile and tightened his grip.

'Linus. Earlier today I went to see one of my best friends. He'd taken a whole bottle of sleeping pills and wrapped a plastic bag around his head. He'd tried to get one over on these people.'

'Sorry for your loss.'

'So whatever you do...'

Linus shook himself free. 'Stop going on—I don't do that kind of thing.'

Tommy let his arms fall to his sides; he looked several years older. 'I love you, Linus. You know that.'

'Yes. So?'

Tommy's mouth moved as if he were searching for another way to make his point. When he failed to find it, he seemed to give up. His shoulders slumped and he leaned back against the railing. The two of them stood wordlessly, side by side, until eventually Tommy asked: 'The Colombians. Is it still Chivo?'

'How should I know?'

Tommy sighed. 'Linus, don't insult my intelligence. You'd know that anyway.'

'Yes.'

'Yes what?'

'Yes, it's still the Goat.'

*

58

When Tommy had left, after another long, pleading gaze, Linus stayed on the balcony thinking things over. His uncle obviously thought the Colombians on the north side had something to do with what was going on, but that seemed unlikely. Why would they break into an area they already controlled, offering a far superior product for more or less the same price?

But in that case, where was the stuff coming from? Linus didn't know enough to speculate. He thought the majority of the coke in circulation originated in Colombia, but he wasn't sure. There could be major producers elsewhere that he'd never heard of. *A new player.*

He would find out eventually, but right now he had a more urgent problem. He had to find a way of getting that hundred grams onto the market. He stared out over the courtyard and lowered his gaze to a covered kitchen window on the third floor of number eight.

He needed someone to talk to, someone who knew what he did, someone he could trust. Someone who could give him advice, maybe come up with a suggestion. As soon as he'd hidden the package he'd go and see her. Kassandra.

*

When Linus and Kassandra were little, they always hung out together in secret. There was something shameful about their relationship that couldn't withstand the full light of day or the scrutiny of their peers. Obviously they knew they'd have been teased if it emerged that Loopy Linus and Ka-ka-kassandra were hanging out, but it went deeper than that. They didn't even like each other. Kassandra thought Linus was hard work, with his excessive energy and frequent outbursts, while Linus thought Kassandra was a lazy cow. Sometimes he couldn't even be bothered to listen until she managed to finish a sentence.

They were ashamed because they were both aware that they were together because neither of them had anyone else to spend time with. They played in dark basements, on desolate industrial estates and in gloomy wooded areas, as if even they couldn't bear the light. Their games usually consisted of Linus doing something while Kassandra watched.

When Kassandra was thirteen and Linus had just started his medication business, she moved away from Gårdsstugan with her horrible mother and her even more horrible father. She and Linus spoke on the phone occasionally, but her stammer left Linus clutching the receiver and jumping up and down with impatience. He stopped calling, and before long Kassandra stopped too.

Shortly before Linus turned seventeen, Kassandra came back. Her father had killed her mother. She hinted that he'd abused her too over the years. Anyway, he was sentenced to life imprisonment, and social services organised a basic apartment for Kassandra.

During her absence she'd gone one hundred per cent emo. Black, frizzy hair streaked with pink, heavy on the kohl; clothes that made her look as if she was going to a funeral, but with a hint of wedding thrown in. Velvet and tulle, almost exclusively black and white. Occasionally she wore a top hat. When she and Linus bumped into each other in the courtyard, he didn't recognise her at first. When he realised who it was, he burst out: 'Jesus, you look fucking terrible!'

'So do you,' Kassandra replied calmly. 'Worst acne I've ever seen.'

There was no warmth in their conversation, just a statement of facts. However, they did give each other a brief hug, mainly to demonstrate that they were brave enough to do so these days.

'So have you stopped stammering?'

'K-kind of.'

Kassandra had been seeing a speech therapist, but the definitive improvement had come when her father was locked up. She insisted she wasn't traumatised by her mother's death, which had involved a whole bottle of Koskenkorva vodka and a kitchen knife. 'The standard Swedish murder,' as Kassandra said. She hadn't been home at the time.

She and Linus started hanging out again, and the change in their circumstances benefited both of them. Linus was more patient, and had more self-confidence now that he was running his business and had his crew. Kassandra was less lethargic now she'd found a mask to wear, a role to play. They weren't exactly a couple, but Kassandra was the first girl Linus slept with. He didn't find her particularly attractive; she was fat, with hundreds of self-harm scars on her arms and legs, and her breasts were white and doughy. But somehow they just did it, and it was nice.

Kassandra lived in a one-room apartment with a kitchenette; it was really supposed to be a student residence. The extractor fan was broken and the kitchen surfaces were covered with a layer of grease. If you picked up anything that hadn't been put away in a drawer, it left a sticky deposit on your skin. Kassandra didn't like daylight, so a thick blanket was draped over the only window, and the room was illuminated by a dozen or so small lamps.

Her furniture was all bought second-hand or rescued from skips. The whole place was pervaded with damp and a mouldy smell that Kassandra combated by burning incense. If you sat still and listened, you could hear cockroaches scuttling around in the kitchen cupboards.

Their situation improved significantly when Linus found a key to the roof of Kassandra's block. He brought over a couple of sun loungers and the two of them spent most of their time up there—unless they were going to have sex, which didn't happen very often.

If it felt good to stand on the balcony at home and imagine that he was king of all he surveyed, that was nothing compared with the roof. A gigantic flat surface with views in all directions, a space the size of at least two football pitches that was Linus and Kassandra's domain. Added to this was the sense of danger, because the edge was protected only by a knee-high wall. Linus's stomach flipped over whenever he looked down.

One evening when they were sitting on the roof drinking vodka and watching the sun go down behind the other apartment blocks, they'd promised each other that if they hadn't managed to get away from Gårdsstugan by the time they turned twenty, they would jump off the roof together. It was a tense moment, and they'd both felt shy and embarrassed afterwards. But they didn't take those promises back.

*

Linus dragged out the sun loungers, which he usually hid behind a ventilation shaft, and placed them next to the southern edge with a view of Norrtull and the Wennergren Centre. The temperature was only just above freezing, so they wrapped themselves in blankets that Kassandra had brought up from the apartment. Needless to say, they were impregnated with the smells of damp and mould. Linus had produced a bottle of Magic Crystal from his stock beneath the electricity cupboard.

Matti's uncle, who was a truck driver, bought the Russian vodka in Estonia for thirty kronor a bottle and sold it to Matti for eighty, Matti, Linus and Henrik then sold it on, mainly to young teenagers, for a hundred and fifty. They also had a couple of alcoholics among their regular customers, and usually gave them a discount for buying in bulk.

The bottles under the electricity cupboard were Linus's private stash. His condition put him at risk of becoming a serious drinker: the alcohol calmed his racing thoughts. Therefore he exercised self-discipline. On the odd occasion, he allowed himself to get really drunk—to relax and kind of reboot his system—but that would be it for a while. Never more than once a week. Otherwise he used his running to clear his mind.

He sank down on the chair, took a good slug of the oily, burning liquid and offered the bottle to Kassandra, but she shook her head. 'I have to be up in five hours.'

Kassandra got up at three o'clock most mornings and headed off to a basement on the Hagalund industrial estate where she made sandwiches for a range of commercial outlets. Wearing noise-cancelling headphones, she stood under harsh fluorescent lights at a stainless-steel bench with an array of trays containing tomato, cucumber, mozzarella, sliced ham and so on. She listened to Black Veil Brides and avoided thinking. Ideally, when she finished at nine o'clock she preferred not to realise she'd been at work. Sometimes this strategy was so successful that she was halfway home before she woke up, and didn't know where she was, what she was doing there, or who she was.

Goodbye agony.

Kassandra lit a Camel and leaned back. She gazed up at the clear, starry sky with her resting expression of sorrowful rage, as if she were constantly accusing some undefined entity.

'I've got something on the go,' Linus said.

Kassandra didn't turn her head. 'Okay. Something illegal, I presume.'

'Thousand per cent.'

'That's not possible.'

'Wait till you hear.'

He told her everything. She already knew about the incident with Alex and Rabbit Boy, so he didn't need to fill in the background. He told her about the cocaine, the quantity and the purity, what Alex had said, and the problem he was now faced with. When he'd finished, Kassandra didn't speak for a long time. Then she stretched out her hand. 'I need a drink.' She wiped her mouth and lit a fresh cigarette. 'I can help you.'

'How?'

'You'll have to take care of the distribution, but I can sort out the weighing and packaging.'

'What do you know about that kind of thing?'

'I watch TV, for fuck's sake.'

Kassandra took a deep drag on her cigarette, and her black-painted lips moved as she worked through her calculations.

'We need a couple of hundred small Ziploc bags, an apothecary's scale and a razor. One gram and half a gram packets. Maybe two grams as well—what do you think?'

'You know there's no money, right?'

'Not right now, but later—yes?'

'In that case you'll have to keep the stuff at your place.'

Kassandra shrugged. 'No problem. I don't have social services dropping in, like certain people I could mention.'

'How much will you want further down the line?'

She answered immediately, as if she'd already thought it through. 'Twenty per cent. Ten for the packaging and ten for storage.'

'I'm the one who'll be taking the biggest risks.'

'Which is why I'm only taking twenty.'

Kassandra helped herself to another swig of vodka. Linus tilted his head on one side and looked at her. Her pale cheeks had acquired a faint flush. 'I thought you were working tomorrow?'

'Maybe not. Shall we go downstairs and f-f-fuck?'

'Haven't got the energy.'

'What?'

Linus held out his hand to her. 'Raincheck?'

Kassandra actually smiled as she took his hand. There was a lot about her body that wasn't great, but Linus really liked her hands. They were small, delicate and warm, and even the dark blue nail polish didn't bother him. As he sat there now, holding her hand in his and seeing the sparkle in her eyes and the glow in her cheeks, he almost felt horny. The sense of a dizzying future played its part too, but he still couldn't face going down to her squalid apartment to roll around in her smelly sheets.

He was a little bit drunk, and right now everything seemed simple and full of promise beneath an endless sky full of stars, but of course it wasn't that straightforward. There was work to be done, a goat to avoid. *Chivo*. The very name sounded like a stabbing.

'Which only leaves the real problem,' Linus said. 'How the fuck do I sell a hundred grams without ending up in the bottom of Brunnsviken?'

'It's that guy who controls the market, isn't it—the Cow?'

Linus glanced involuntarily over his shoulder to make sure no one was listening. They were chirruping away about serious drug dealing without a care in the world, like birds in the forest, but referring to the Goat as the Cow was a step too far. That was a death sentence.

'It's the Goat, for fuck's sake. Chivo.'

'Okay, whatever. This is the situation—basic economics. You either find a different market, or you expand the esk…esk…Fuck! The *existing* market. The Goat has his customers. You need to attract new ones.'

Tommy

Even Hagge seemed downcast, shambling along with his head drooping like his master's as they headed towards Shithole Square. Tommy was finding it difficult to concentrate on the task at hand; the conversation with Linus bothered him. No: it really worried him. He'd always thought that things would somehow work out for Linus; he was intelligent and spirited, with a good sense of humour.

Tommy distrusted symptoms, psychologists and diagnoses. He felt that, apart from genuine illnesses and neurological conditions, everything else sat on a sliding scale. These days they threw a cluster of letters at behaviour that used to be called nervous or eccentric, or some other term that simply meant the person was a little bit different. It was more definitive now than it had been back then, and he wasn't sure it had improved anything.

Tommy didn't even see Linus as different, just unusually intense and impatient. He'd been exactly the same when he was young. He could see that Linus had a problem with reading, which was something he'd never experienced, and of course the ability to absorb information through words was undeniably important in today's society. But not essential. There were plenty of jobs that would be better suited to a bright, creative person like Linus than poking around with carburettors and catalysers or whatever the hell they were called.

Tommy had tried to steer Linus towards something involving design; he'd offered to fix up an internship with Swedish Television. He knew the motor vehicle course would never be enough for Linus, and that would leave him open to the risk of slipping into all the other stuff that was always on offer in a place like Gårdsstugan.

When Linus was caught breaking into a storage depot, all Tommy's worst fears were confirmed. Linus was on a downhill slope; Tommy just didn't know how far down he'd already gone. When Linus came to stay with him after his stint in residential care, Tommy tried his best to get him to open up, but Linus just laughed off his concerns and said the break-in had been a stupid one-off.

So how come Linus had the key to a basement storeroom filled with stolen goods and smuggled booze? Oh, he was just holding onto it for a friend. No, he couldn't name the friend—Linus was no grass. Maybe that was when he and Tommy began to drift apart, despite how hard Tommy tried to prevent it.

And now? In the worst-case scenario, Linus had started seriously dealing, and in the *very* worst-case scenario he was mixed up in the tangled mess Tommy was trying to sort out. If he'd been worried on his own behalf, he was now even more worried about Linus. Tommy was under no illusions. Even if somehow he managed to find something out and the series he wrote had an impact, the dealing wouldn't stop; at best it would die down for a while. His only hope was that this dying down would have some impact at the level Linus was on. It was a fraction of a chance of an unlikely possibility, but it was all he had.

At the height of his fame, with his network of contacts at its strongest and widest, he might have been able to do something to protect Linus. A word or two with the right people and Linus's source would have dried up instantly, or he would have been quietly protected. But that was then. These days the majority of those contacts were no longer the right people, because they were dead.

The wind struck him as soon as he reached the square. It was eight-thirty and everything was closed apart from the pizzeria, the fast-food kiosk and the ICA store. With his hair flapping around his scalp, Tommy crossed the square and stopped by the sculpture of an elf riding a unicorn, perched on a plinth in the dried-up fountain.

Several of the streetlights around the square were broken, and shadowy figures lurked in doorways and passageways. A man with eastern European features stepped into the light and made an enquiring gesture with his hand. Tommy shook his head and the man scowled. *What the fuck are you doing here, then?*

Tommy carried on around the fountain and crossed the north–south borderline. There were people hanging about here too, alone or in groups, sheltering by the walls in an attempt to escape the wind. Many looked Latin American. A young guy with long black hair tied back with a bandana covered in a skull design stood there playing with a butterfly knife.

Tommy scanned the faces he could see. He didn't recognise a soul. It was a few years since he'd visited Gårdsstugan for work purposes, and a generational shift appeared to have taken place since then. These faces belonged to kids eighteen to twenty years old. The one with the butterfly knife looked up. Hagge stopped. Tommy stopped. Without an opening gambit, going straight in and starting to ask questions was tantamount to suicide. Hagge tugged at his leash, wanting to return the way they'd come, and Tommy couldn't disagree with his instincts. Next time he'd come in daylight, and with back up.

*

At home in Traneberg, Tommy fed Hagge and mixed himself a whisky sour, then called Tomás.

They had met when Tommy was working on a report on anabolic steroids. Tomás was running a gym in Rissne, and he absolutely hated roids. Two childhood friends from Guatemala had fallen victim to a bad batch from Russia that had made their hearts explode—and broken Tomás's heart at the same time. If he saw any hint of a needle or a pill in his gym, he personally threw its owner out into the street or decked him on the spot.

Tomás was only one metre seventy-five tall, but what he lacked in height he more than made up for in breadth and strength. He'd been a very promising boxer, and boxing had saved his life. At the age of fifteen he and his two friends left their village to compete in the district championship, which Tomás won. When they returned home, the village had been burnt to the ground and his entire family had been killed by government forces because of suspected collaboration with the guerrilla movement. His friends had also lost their families, and together the three of them fled to Sweden.

That was over twenty years ago. Tomás had given up the gym and now ran a boxing club for young people. He still kept himself in shape. Something within him was constantly on the alert, waiting for the attack, and when it came he wanted to be fit enough to face it. He and Tommy had got along very well; when Tommy went to visit a somewhat seedier gym he had taken Tomás with him for support, and had engaged his services on several occasions since.

'*Diga?*'

'*Hola*, Tomás. It's Tommy.'

'Eh, Tommy! *Qué pasa?*'

Tommy smiled. At least one person who didn't think he was dead.

'All good. How about you?'

'Head up and feet down.'

Tomás had a predilection for expressions that he regarded as typically Swedish, and had taken great care to assimilate them into his conversation when he was learning the language as a teenager. Unfortunately many of them were dated even then.

'Listen, I need your help.'

Without going into detail, Tommy explained that he needed to do some research on the north side of Gårdsstugan. Tomás laughed.

'So you need a beefy Latino to watch your back?'

'Something like that. I'm a bit short of cash right now, but…'

'No problem. Pay me when you're on easy street.'

'Great. How about tomorrow?'

'What time?'

They arranged to meet in Shithole Square at one o'clock. They said goodbye and Tommy was about to end the call when he heard Tomás's voice again.

'Eh, Tommy!'

'What?'

'Somebody told me you'd fallen off your perch, but I said *nunca!* Not Tommy—no way!'

'Okay Tomás. See you tomorrow.'

Tommy had just fallen asleep with Hagge at his feet when his phone rang and *Don Juan Johansson* appeared on the screen. Tommy answered and spoke to someone called Henry, who was out celebrating the day's triumphs.

Tommy's tip-off had been worth its weight in gold. In the boot of Hans-Åke's car they'd found eighty kilos of forty-five per cent pure cocaine—one of the biggest busts in a long time. And that wasn't the best of it. The coke had been in a box from the ferry *Finnclipper*, which plied the route from Nådendal to Kapellskär, so now they knew which port to watch. Tommy couldn't write about any of this, of course—he hadn't even heard it.

Henry was both lyrical and drunk. To Tommy's surprise, the music in the background indicating that he was partying at Golden Hits, so maybe age had caught up with him at last. They said goodbye to the sounds of Harpo singing 'Movie Star'. Tommy put the phone down on the bedside table, then lay staring up at the ceiling. From time to time a wave of light washed through the room as a car passed by on Margretelundsvägen.

He considered calling Anita, but decided it was too late. After a life lived without limits, at some point she had done a complete one-eighty and begun to follow a strict routine, one aspect of which involved early nights. Tommy was alone with his thoughts.

One thing was clear: he trusted Hans-Åke's notes more than a cardboard box. The goods had come in via Värtahamnen. The astonishing aspect was that someone had sacrificed coke with a street value of millions on a plant that wasn't even watertight. There had to be some bright sparks among the cops who could see that the business of the box was ridiculous. Okay, so they would have to keep an eye on Kapellskär, but only a woodentop like Henry could believe that was the right place.

Sadly, Hans-Åke's death and the subsequent discovery in his car was all a part of the same plant. Tommy's best friend had died so that someone could lay a false trail.

But he killed himself, didn't he?

Hans-Åke's dead body floated towards Tommy in the darkness, hovered over him like a silent threat. It happened to me. It could happen to you. The smell of death filled Tommy's nostrils and he stopped breathing as he was lifted up and became part of Hans-Åke, became Hans-Åke, was lowered down and lay dead in his bed, waiting for the dogs to come and desecrate him with their teeth.

X?

Tommy's eyes flew open and he gave a start; Hagge let out a small grunt of protest.

At the beginning of Tommy's career, older colleagues had talked about the so-called 'Mr X' who had operated in Stockholm in the 1960s and 70s. It seemed likely that he had been a petty crook called Leif Stenberg, who was anything but mysterious, and Tommy had thought the designation exaggerated. Now, bearing in mind what had happened to Hans-Åke, it seemed provocative, like something a child might have made up. The crazy scientist Doctor X. Who the hell could call themselves X and hope to be taken seriously?

Someone who can get dozens of people to take their own lives, and waste millions on a stupid prank.

Forces in the darkness, a continental shift in the silence.

Linus

Kassandra's comment on the market was sensible. *Find a different market or expand the existing one.* The first option was out of the question. The thought of wandering over to, say, Sundbyberg to start dealing with no idea of how the land lay, whose toes he might be treading on...no chance.

Ideally he would manage to entice some fresh customers without touching Chivo's. He had to start by assessing the market, checking out the terrain. Legwork. That wasn't a problem. Legwork was what had held Linus together without the help of chemicals.

*

It had begun when he was fourteen, and like so many things that come to define our lives, it happened by pure chance.

He'd been in a bad way, finding it impossible to sit still for more than two minutes at a time. Even though his brain was exhausted by the tag-team thoughts inside his head, he couldn't sleep. He spent the nights playing *Call of Duty* or *Battlefield* online on his Xbox.

One day a punter approached him in the courtyard. The punter knew about Linus's business enterprise, and had managed to convince himself that Linus had instant access to Subutex, *right here right now.* When Linus told him he was wrong, the guy pulled a knife.

Linus backed away. The punter followed, waving the knife around. Linus turned and ran. He flew across the courtyard and the punter, who was in poor shape but high on some kind of upper, took off after him. However, Linus was faster. After only a few hundred metres the punter crashed into a waste bin and went down.

Linus kept on running. He rounded the corner of the building and continued north towards Haga Park. It was summer, and the greenery whizzed by. His feet hardly touched the ground, and when he reached the path leading up to the copper tent, he increased his speed. He wasn't exactly dressed for running in his jeans and a long-sleeved T-shirt, and sweat stuck the fabric to his body, but it didn't matter. For the first time in he didn't know how long he felt *free*.

Ever since that day, Linus had been a runner. He got himself a pair of Adidas sneakers that he'd been wanting for ages, because they were more…gangster. He researched articles about running shoes online, and eventually settled on Asics Gel Nimbus 15s. They were expensive, but he had the money. They turned out to be perfect, and he'd stuck with them.

In his closet, as proof of time gone by and distance covered, there were two pairs of AGN 15s, two pairs of AGN 16s and one pair of AGN 17s, all worn out. His current AGN 17s would last a few months; he was hoping for a new generation by the time he needed to replace them.

He ran ten kilometres four or five times a week, often more. Those were the only times when his mind quietened down. He would fantasise about running forever, his feet drumming on the surface beneath them, eyes fixed straight ahead, arms pumping, until Death came alongside him. Wearing a pair of Nike Airs. Fucking amateur.

Linus's ability to sit still improved, he calmed down, and best of all, he was able to sleep at night. When he occasionally logged into his Live account and teamed up with his old contacts, they wanted to know what he'd been up to. He told them he'd started long-distance running, and received many verbal variations of LOL over his headphones. 'Of course you have,' someone said. 'And I've taken up weightlifting.'

*

Legwork was literally Linus's thing, so he decided to knock on every door, talk to as many as possible of the three thousand residents on the south side of Gårdsstugan, check out the lie of the land. As for the north side…Linus might be stupid, but he wasn't suicidal.

One slight problem was that Chivo also controlled the south side; his people were able to come and go as they wished. A couple of Swedes ran things for a while before Chivo; after they vanished without a trace, the Goat came galloping in. It was said that the badly mutilated arm that was found on the shore of Brunnsviken belonged to one of the Swedes, which contributed to the fact that the Goat was able to graze freely.

Linus couldn't even consider the north side. Chivo had eyes everywhere, and his men would be watching Linus as soon as he passed the ICA store. The Latinos came to the south side only in the line of business, so it ought to be possible to suss things out unnoticed.

But how? He couldn't ring somebody's doorbell and say: 'Excuse me madam, I was wondering if you'd be interested in a little coke?' He needed some kind of cover. He thought for a while, then came up with a possible solution. It wasn't cool and it was beneath his dignity, but maybe those were points in its favour. He took a five hundred kronor note out of his stash in one of his old running shoes, then set off to buy biscuits.

*

'Hi, my name's Linus and I play for the Haga Boys football team. We've qualified for a tournament in Germany, and we're trying to raise funds by selling biscuits. Would you like to buy some?'

The woman, in her fifties, didn't look as if she had a coke habit, but Linus had to say something, and he needed to practise his spiel. The woman's eyes narrowed as she looked at the half-full ICA bag at his feet.

'What kind of biscuits?'

'All kinds—chocolate, vanilla, lemon.'

'Which chocolate ones do you have?'

Linus rummaged in the bag and produced a packet of Ballerina with chocolate filling. 'There you go.'

The woman looked suspicious. 'But those are just ordinary Ballerina.'

'Yes, but we get them at a'—Linus leaned forward and lowered his voice—'*very* reasonable price.'

'So how much are they?'

'Fifteen kronor a packet.'

'Hmm. I'll take two.'

Linus handed over two packets and received a twenty and a ten kronor note in return. This meant he was eight kronor down on the deal. First amendment: raise the price to twenty. He hated bad business, regardless of the commodity.

The woman was about to close the door, the biscuits clutched to her chest, when Linus said: 'Anything else?' The woman frowned. 'What do you mean?'

'I was just wondering if you might be interested in anything else. I might be able to get it for you.'

'Like what?'

'You tell me, and I'll see what I can do.'

Not for a moment did Linus allow the mask to slip. He was a keen footballer, doing his best to raise funds. The woman thought for a moment, and Linus realised she wasn't a future customer.

'Do you have any ice cream?'

'I'm afraid not.'

'Dog food?'

'Sorry, no. But you have a nice day now!'

The door slammed shut. Second amendment: tighten things up. If he could see that someone was the wrong type or clearly not interested, he needed to keep it brief. And twenty kronor a packet. One krona profit. Yabba. Dabba. Doo.

*

Linus got his first bite when he rang the twenty-fourth doorbell: an overweight guy aged about thirty, who looked as if he'd dragged himself away from a two-day session of *World of Warcraft*. Pale, unshaven, dark shadows beneath his eyes. He listened wearily to Linus's biscuit spiel, slowly shaking his head. The door began to close by the time Linus reached 'tournament in Germany', so Linus jumped straight to 'Anything else?'

'Like what?'

'Anything you like.'

The man peered out into the stairwell, then wiggled his index finger through a hole formed by the thumb and index finger of the other hand. 'How about that?'

'No, not that. But anything else.'

The man leaned forward and whispered: 'What have you got?'

'Maybe I ought to come in.'

It transpired that the man, whose name was Göran, was a developer of indie games and pretty well-heeled. In his living room there were two large screens linked to serious computers, humming away and filling the air with electricity. Linus explained what he had, and how much it would cost. Göran didn't believe him.

'*If* what you say is true, which I very much doubt, then I'll take five grams off you. But I need to try a sample first.'

'Of course,' Linus said, plastering on a smile. *Shit*. He should have thought of that. He was going to have to stand a loss during the set-up phase, pay for the samples out of his own pocket. He told Göran he'd be back the following day at the same time.

'One more thing,' he said before he left. 'Do you buy from Chivo?'

Göran snorted and shook his head, the wattle of fat beneath his chin wobbling. 'I wouldn't even shove the crap he sells up my arse if I...' He stopped and a horrified expression came over his face. He stepped forward and grabbed Linus by the arm. 'You don't work for him, do you?'

'No, no, calm down.'

'You promise?'

Linus removed Göran's hand from his arm. 'I promise, okay?'

Göran didn't seem entirely convinced; he nodded, but his lower lip trembled.

'And Göran? This is the start of something new. I can promise you that too.'

*

By the time Linus finished for the day he'd acquired three new customers, plus one of his old pill-poppers who wanted to try something different. They had all been as sceptical as Göran when Linus told them the price, and in the end he was doubting himself. When Alex had said a thousand kronor a gram and ninety per cent purity, it had been presented as a cold fact, but when every prospective customer reacted as if Linus had offered them the lease on a cheap apartment in the heart of the city, he began to have his doubts.

What if Alex was pulling a fast one? Linus had never snorted coke; he had no way of judging the quality of the merchandise. And yet something told him Alex was on the level. Linus had to assume everything was okay. When he got home, he texted Kassandra: *get anything done?* He'd just sent the message when there was a knock on his door.

He let his mother in, then went and lay on his bed. As always her eyes scanned the room like a Cruise missile, searching for a target to land on. This time it was the ICA bag.

'What's in there?'

'Biscuits.'

Betty picked up the bag and examined the contents. Fourteen packets remained, thirteen had been sold. Linus had raised the price to twenty, then twenty-five. He'd put in five hours' work and made a profit of thirty-eight kronor.

Betty's lips pursed, then parted as she spat: 'Stolen, of course.'

Linus gave her the receipt he'd placed on his bedside table for precisely this eventuality. Betty studied it, clearly at a loss.

'I buy biscuits. Then I sell them. For a bit more than I paid.'

'Why...Why are you doing that?'

77

Linus gave her a warm, only slightly condescending smile. 'To earn some money. Obviously.'

Betty looked at the receipt, then at Linus, then at the remaining biscuits as if they were elements of a rebus she couldn't solve.

'College rang. You haven't been in for two days.'

'No, I know. I'm going in tomorrow.'

'Why haven't you been there?'

Linus sat up, adopted an unhappy and helpless expression, and spread his hands wide. 'Because I've been selling biscuits. Because I don't have any money. Because I don't get my student allowance.'

Betty's jaw tightened and she blinked. Linus knew she was ashamed of the fact that they were so short of money they had to use Linus's student allowance, and only gave him a few hundred a month. She took a step towards him and looked as if she was about to say something loving. But they were long past that kind of thing. She simply said: 'But you're definitely going in tomorrow?'

'Absolutely, Mum. I promise.'

Linus rarely said 'Mum', and Betty stood there motionless for a few seconds as if she was drinking in the moment so that she could savour it later, when she was sitting on the balcony with a glass of Baileys. She nodded and left the room. Linus's phone pinged. Kassandra.

Got all the stuff. Starting now.

Okay. Everything was moving along nicely. Tomorrow he'd wander into college, see if there were any openings there. He knew a couple of kids who snorted, but he wasn't sure if they'd be able to afford what he was offering. Worth checking out though.

It had been a good day, all in all. His unconventional approach to broadening his client base had worked pretty well, and with a bit of luck he'd be able to shift ten grams tomorrow. It would be a pain if he had to carry on the same way; he hoped his new customers would be so delighted with the quality of the stuff that they'd come crawling back to the source in no time.

Linus. The source. Not bad.

He changed into his running gear and reverently removed his shoes from the closet. He put them on with exaggerated care. He stood up and bounced gently, enjoying the almost weightless flexibility of the shoes. A good long run, then sleep—recharge his batteries ready for tomorrow. That's how a serious player rolls.

Tommy

Tomás was already perched on the edge of the fountain when Tommy arrived in Shithole Square just after one. Dust and grit swirled in the wind, but Tomás sat with his hands resting on his massive thighs, the picture of calm. As soon as he saw Tommy his face lit up and he got to his feet.

'Tommy T!' he said. 'The legend is here!'

Tommy and Tomás might have been something approaching friends, but their relationship was based on the premise that Tommy stayed in character, playing the hard-boiled and blasé version of himself that went by the name of Tommy T. Tomás probably wouldn't have wanted anything to do with the soft-boiled, insecure person Tommy really was. They shook hands.

'Sorry I'm late.'

'No problem. I've been checking the place out. Where's Hagge?'

'He's off sick today.'

'Nothing serious, I hope?'

'No, no—he's just a little out of sorts.'

Hagge had a melancholy streak that could sometimes tip over into depression. He would lie in his basket, his chin resting on his paws, eyes dark with sorrow. He would refuse to do anything, and if Tommy tried to cheer him up, he responded with deep sighs. Today was one of those days.

Over the years Tommy had noticed a slightly worrying correlation between Hagge's bouts of depression and days when everything was going to go badly wrong for Tommy. If Hagge did have a limited ability to see into the future, then Tommy hoped it had failed him this time. There was a great deal at stake.

'Lunch?' Tomás suggested, gesturing towards the pizzeria on the north side of the square.

'Absolutely.'

Pizzeria Primavera had opted for Mexican décor. Sombreros on the walls, cacti in pots and black and white photos of Pancho Villa. The place was licensed to sell alcohol, and behind the bar a few bottles of mescal were on display, each containing a worm. The pizzas had names like Azteca, La Bamba, Oaxaca and Subcomandante Marcos, which was heavy on the jalapeños.

The Mexican atmosphere was disrupted by an Addams Family pinball machine near the door, plus a mirror ball in front of a DJ booth in one corner. On weekend evenings the place changed its identity and became the budget nightclub Prima!

Tommy and Tomás both ordered an Acapulco to eat in, plus another to take out, then sat down opposite each other. While they waited they ran through possible courses of action depending on what they found on the north side. All these plans required the presence of Tommy T, and at times like this Tommy often missed cocaine.

During his years in the sun the drug had helped him to keep his eyes on the prize, create the blinkers that allowed him to keep ruthlessly moving forward without glancing to either side, which was exactly what was expected of Tommy T, the tough guy. These days he felt increasingly like an ageing actor, staggering onto the stage to give his signature role before a dwindling audience.

Their pizzas arrived. The waiter nodded to Tomás and gave Tommy a curious look. *'Buen provecho.'*

'So what's your take on the situation?' Tommy asked after thirty seconds or so, by which time Tomás had shovelled down half his pizza.

'Interesting. It feels as if...how should I put it...There's a lack of focus.'

'What do you mean?'

'There's a sense of apathy. No energy.'

'Why might that be?'

'I've no idea. We'll have to ask. I've brought the tape.'

Tomás patted his jacket pocket before turning his attention to his pizza once more. He was convinced that most things could be sorted out with duct tape, and having seen him in action, Tommy had to agree.

If Tomás was right about the atmosphere on the north side, then it must have something to do with Chivo. He normally kept a firm hand on the reins, but 'a lack of focus'—that suggested he was losing his grip. In which case, a minor revolution was on the way.

Five minutes later Tomás had finished his pizza and eaten half of Tommy's. They paid, took the box containing the third pizza, and left. Tomás nodded towards two boys shivering on a bench outside the ICA store.

'Look at those two, for example. They're not keeping an eye on things. They've got no attitude. They're just sitting there as if they're...'

'Crying over spilt milk?'

Tomás grinned. 'I wouldn't have said that, but you're right.'

They crossed the square and went through the opening leading to the north side. The boys on the bench watched them go, but did nothing.

*

Very little remained of what had once been the largest playground on any estate in Sweden—only the shadow of a wreck, with all the attraction of a broken promise. The two caretakers were cut to one after twelve months, and seven years later that job disappeared too. Left to its own devices, the Glade began to deteriorate. Anything that could rust rusted, anything that could rot rotted, and the vandals took care of the rest.

In spite of the lack of resources, the Glade was still a part of the Swedish system to the extent that it couldn't be allowed to become a danger to children. As soon as an attraction started to fall apart, when the nails began to stick up and the wooden planks began to crumble, it was removed without being replaced by a new one. The things that had been the most enjoyable were the first to go. Older residents could remember hours of fun on the swing carousel and the witch's hat, but they were long gone. Only the boring objects remained: a rusty metal structure, the entertainment value of which was unclear, a few slides and simple climbing frames; a couple of sandpits.

A boy of about fourteen was sitting on the edge of one of the sandpits staring vacantly at his mobile phone. From time to time he glanced around; when he caught sight of Tommy and Tomás, his thumb stopped moving across the screen and his expression grew wary.

'Hi there,' Tomás said in Spanish. 'Shouldn't you be in school?'

The boy pulled a face and answered in Swedish. 'I don't understand.'

'We need a word with Chivo,' Tommy said. 'Any idea where he might be?'

The boy shook his head, his eyes drawn to his phone. 'Don't know anyone by that name.'

'Isn't it cold sitting here,' Tommy went on, 'when you could be indoors? We've got pizza here. Freshly made pizza.'

The boy couldn't help looking at the box. He wasn't sufficiently hardened to be able to ignore the sight or the aroma, but all he said was: 'So?'

Tomás leaned closer. 'As you're sitting here on guard duty...' With a single movement he took the phone out of the boy's hand and straightened up. 'Maybe you're in need of a snack?'

'What the fuck...' the boy said, getting to his feet.

'Calm down, son.' Tomás whistled when he checked out the mobile—a new gold iPhone. 'It's only a temporary exchange. Give him the pizza, Tommy.'

Tommy held out the box, but the boy refused to take it. A childish, pleading tone crept into his voice: 'Give me my phone!'

'Listen to me,' Tomás said. 'I'm borrowing your phone to stop

83

you from calling anyone. And if you just nod or point in the right direction...'

The boy's hand moved to his back pocket. 'Then what?'

'Then you get this pizza. You sit down and eat it in peace. And before you've finished, I give you your phone.' Tomás pointed to the hand, which had now reached the pocket. 'And you...no. No.'

The boy looked into Tomás's face and saw the weight and wisdom of a Native American chief. He allowed his hand to drop, and nodded in the direction of the Diablo Negro Gym, which was housed on the ground floor of a block fifty metres away. Tomás nodded. 'I should have guessed.'

The boy sank down on the edge of the sandpit and Tommy offered him the pizza. This time he took it. He opened the lid and wrinkled his nose. '*Mierda*—Acapulco! Why Acapulco? Pineapple, for fuck's sake!'

Tommy shrugged. '*Buen provecho.*'

*

A Lexus with a sticker from the gym in the rear window was parked by the door. Tommy unscrewed the radio antenna from the roof and inserted it into the valve on one of the back tyres. The air began to hiss out. They went inside.

The Diablo Negro Gym lacked any kind of ornamentation. No machines, no bells and whistles, just free weights and dumbbells on stands. Benches, mats and an enormous mirror. The bare cement walls were impregnated with an odour of sweat and screaming. Two men with Bluetooth earphones stood side by side in front of the mirror, moving heavy dumbbells up and down in a homoerotic dance. Tomás nodded to a thick-necked individual who was standing behind the counter leafing through a copy of *Flex*, then headed for a back door hidden from the entrance.

The guy looked like the clichéd image of a hardcore lead in an action movie: square face, crew cut, tension in his lips. He looked up as Tommy approached, and blinked suspiciously.

'How much is a year's membership?'

'You're joking, right?'

'Absolutely. Is that your car outside?'

'Why? Are you from the tax office?'

Tommy was tempted to say yes and run with a different routine, but he chose the simpler option. 'No. I saw some kids messing around with it.'

The guy's lips tightened a fraction more. He slammed down the magazine, said 'Shit!' and ran out of the door. The Bluetooth twins were so absorbed in their own reflections that they didn't even notice Tommy hurrying towards the back door, which was now ajar. From inside came noises that suggested torture, and Tommy frowned. Definitely not Tomás's style, and not something Tommy wished to be associated with.

He walked into a mini-gym of around fifteen square metres. It contained only two benches with Smith machines and the accompanying weights. On one of the benches lay a mountain of a man covered in tattoos. Tomás was standing behind his head.

There was another door next to Tommy, solid steel with an impressive lock. That was where the noises were coming from, but Tommy now realised it was a movie rather than real life.

'Would you mind closing the door?' Tomás said.

The guy on the bench was lying perfectly still, holding the bar with his arms straight. As Tommy edged closer, he could see why. Tomás had wound several lengths of duct tape around his neck and the bench, so he couldn't move. He couldn't replace the bar, because Tomás had taped down the slots. He'd also pulled the bench forward a few centimetres. If the guy let go, the bar would come crashing down on his throat. Tommy counted four twenty-kilo and two ten-kilo weights. The guy's arms were trembling, and he wheezed through his constricted airway: *'Hijo de puta, voy a matarte...'*

Screaming and sobbing and heroic music came from behind the steel door, voices shouting in a language that sounded like Arabic.

Perhaps someone was enjoying an IS execution video.

'How's Chivo?' Tommy asked in a friendly tone of voice. The guy's forehead was one of the few parts of his body that wasn't covered in tattoos, and it was pouring with sweat as he replied: '*Voy a coger tu madre en el culo.*'

'What's he saying?'

Tomás took a couple of ten-kilo weights from the rack by the wall. 'He sends his best wishes to your mother,' he said as he slipped one weight onto the bar.

Panic and hatred shone in the guy's eyes as he looked from Tomás to Tommy. When Tomás added the second weight, most of the hatred disappeared. The bar dropped towards his throat. Tomás grabbed it and helped him to straighten his arms again.

'Something's wrong with Chivo,' Tommy said. 'What is it?'

No reply. Tomás let go of the bar, went over to the wall and picked up another ten-kilo weight.

'*Vale, vale! Coño.*' Tomás lifted the bar once more. The guy coughed, mucus running from the corner of his mouth. 'Chivo doesn't talk. To anyone. To strangers.'

'Why not?' Tommy persisted.

'Someone talks to people. Then suicide.'

'Who?'

The screams intensified, someone begged for their life in English. Laughter that sounded live broke through. Until now whatever was going on in the inner room had drowned out the guy's curses, but if the movie or whatever it was came to an end, they would have a problem.

'Who's making people kill themselves?' Tommy repeated as Tomás allowed the bar to sink a fraction. The guy's muscles rippled with the effort he was making, his tattoos moving like an animation.

'No one. Knows,' he said through clenched teeth. 'Everyone. Says. Different. Faces. Everyone. Who's seen. Is dead.'

'Okay. Does he have a name?'

'Equis.'

86

Tomás drew two intersecting diagonal lines in the air with his index finger. X. So this evasive X talked to people, then they took their own lives. And he had different faces. What kind of a person was this?

Tommy nodded to Tomás, who wound the duct tape around the guy's wrists and then around the bar. His eyes widened in fear and he began to pant as the bar, which now weighed one hundred and thirty kilos, slowly sank. He inhaled, ready to let out a scream, but before he could make a sound, Tomás had placed a piece of tape over his mouth. Then he removed the weights, freed up the slots and replaced the bar.

'What a session,' he said to his victim. 'Well done.' He leaned forward and whispered something. The guy stopped trying to free his taped hands, and Tomás smiled at him. Then they left.

The owner of the gym had returned to the desk. As Tommy and Tomás headed for the door, he scowled at them.

'Who are you?'

'We're from the council,' Tommy explained. 'We're carrying out an evaluation of leisure activities available to young people. We'll be back.'

*

The boy by the sandpit was finishing the last slice of pizza. Tommy and Tomás went and sat on either side of him, and Tomás gave him back his phone. Tommy took out a five-hundred kronor note, folded it up and concealed it in the palm of his hand.

'What do I get for this?'

'I don't know what you're talking about.'

'What have you got?'

'You're *pasma*, right?'

'Do we look like cops?'

'Yes.'

'Listen, my pal here could pick you up, turn you upside down and shake you until whatever you've got comes tumbling out...'

The boy glanced at Tomás, who nodded to confirm that this was indeed a possibility.

'…or you could just sell it to me. Coke? Point five of a gram?'

The boy looked around, lowered his voice and said: 'Point three.'

'Expensive.'

'Times are hard.'

Tommy held out the note. It disappeared into the boy's pocket in a second, then he handed over a small foil packet.

'Just one more thing,' Tommy said. 'How's Ernesto?'

'Out of the picture. He'll be dead soon.'

'Why?'

'What do you mean, why?'

'Why will he be dead soon?'

'Fucked if I know. Smoking, maybe?'

'I don't understand.'

'The C-word. Cancer.'

*

They left the playground and went into a doorway. Tommy took out the foil packet, licked his finger, dipped it in the powder and rubbed it on his gum. 'It's crap,' he said. 'Hardly a tingle. Chivo's not a player in this.'

'So who's this Ernesto?'

Tommy screwed the foil into a ball and shoved it behind a radiator. 'Ernesto ran things around here fifteen or twenty years ago. He was a major player in the Revolutionary Armed Forces of Colombia—the People's Army—before he came to Sweden. Best contacts you could possibly imagine. Then something happened that got him an eight-year sentence. He was out in six, and Chivo had taken over. That was when I met Ernesto. Nicest guy you could meet, and as cold as ice. He had a certain amount of difficulty adapting to the new situation.'

'You can't teach an old dog new tricks. So what do we do now?'

'If there's anyone who knows what's going on, it's Ernesto, and I know him. So now we buy flowers.'

They bought a mixed bunch at Mafalda's Florist's, which like all the other stores around the square had bars on the windows. When Mafalda found out the flowers were for Ernesto, she said: *'Ay, pobre-cito'*, added a few extra blooms and sent her best wishes.

*

'You've given me far more help than I expected,' Tommy said when they were back outside in the square. 'Particularly as I can't pay you. And Ernesto...either he'll talk or he won't.'

Tomás raised an eyebrow at the huge bouquet, which made Tommy look like an over-enthusiastic suitor. 'I thought you were going over to Värtahamnen too? Semtex-Janne?'

'Yes, but...'

'Dangerous.'

Tomás gazed across the square, where the wind was blowing even more viciously now. A couple of young boys hurried past, bent almost double, their hoods pulled so tightly that their faces couldn't be seen at all.

'I've been thinking,' he said. 'There's a lot of stuff in the papers and online about young people today, the problems they have, the fact that so many of them have joined gangs by the time they're twelve. But there's not much about the alternatives, the activities that offer something different.'

'Like your boxing club.'

'Now you come to mention it...If someone wrote a couple of decent articles—someone who could write—then more kids would find their way there and be given a chance, right?'

'I can't promise anything—it's up to the news editor. But I can certainly promise to do my best.'

'Okay, let's go.'

They set off in silence towards the north side, the wind snatching at the paper around the flowers. After a moment Tommy asked: 'Do you really think I can write?'

Tomás tutted his disapproval. 'Don't fish for compliments, Tommy. It's not attractive.'

'I don't care. I'm old and I need encouragement.'

'You're the best, Tommy, and you know it.'

'*Gracias.*'

'*De nada.*'

*

They stepped out of the elevator on the twelfth floor and were greeted immediately by the smell of sickness and death. Tommy recalled from his previous visit that all the apartments from the eleventh storey upward were occupied by Ernesto's friends and relatives, while he himself lived in one of the superior four-room apartments on the fifteenth floor. Somehow he'd arranged it so that the elevator didn't go all the way to the top, so Tommy and Tomás continued up the stairs.

A door opened and a big man with a big moustache appeared, grabbing hold of the railings at either side of the stairs to block their way. Tomás looked at Tommy, who shook his head. Apart from the fact that he didn't want any trouble, he knew that the Moustache Man's aura—that of a dimwitted coffee farmer—was misleading. His name was Miguel, but he was known as Muerte, and was one of Ernesto's bodyguards. Tommy remembered that Miguel had been having problems with his teeth, and had planned to have several removed and replaced with crowns.

'Hi Miguel,' he said, pointing to his own front teeth. 'Looking good!'

Miguel frowned and drew back his head as he stared at Tommy. Then his eyes narrowed and he nodded.

'Not too happy with them,' he said. 'Bit itchy.'

'Would it be possible to see Ernesto?'

Miguel shook his head. 'Bad day today. Very bad day.'

'Another day, maybe?'

'Most days are bad days.'

'I'm sorry to hear that. Please tell…' Tommy searched through his almost unfailingly reliable memory for names, and found Ernesto's wife sitting at a table next to Hitchcock's wife Alma Reville. 'Tell Alma that she has my sympathies.' He handed over the flowers. 'These are for both of them. There's a card with my number on it—if he wants to call me.'

*

'You think he's really sick?' Tomás asked as they headed for the car.

Tommy nodded. 'I don't know how many murder attempts Ernesto's survived. He's been stabbed, he's been shot, he's had a bomb planted underneath his car and another sent in the post. And that's just in Sweden. You don't get to be a major player in the Revolutionary Armed Forces of Colombia by shuffling papers around; I know he cheated death more than once in Colombia. And in the end that fucking disease has got him.'

'The smallest tuft of grass can trip the…'

'Tomás? You're one of the smartest people I know, but those expressions…'

'You tell bad jokes. That's your thing. Expressions are mine. We all have our roles to play.'

That was the first time Tomás had ever indicated that, like Tommy, he was maintaining a façade. Tommy wasn't sure if it was reassuring or worrying. They got in the car.

*

'How the hell do you make people kill themselves just by talking to them?' Tommy asked as they pulled out into Essingeleden.

'Karin, my first girlfriend here in Sweden…'

'Seriously, Tomás.'

'I am being serious. She had an unbelievable ability to make me feel worthless.' He drew his index finger across his throat. 'I was well on the way.'

'But she had plenty of time to work on you, presumably.'

'Six weeks, then I fled, hell for leather.'

Tommy had forgotten that expression even existed. When Tomás died he ought to donate his brain to the National Archive so they could extract a sample of early-twentieth-century colloquialisms.

'Okay, but this person, if we assume it is one person—Equis— seems to be able to achieve his goal in just one meeting. And what's all this about different faces? That makes it sound like several individuals. I can just about accept one, but a whole group I've never heard of? I don't get it.'

'You're out of the loop, Tommy. You'll just have to beard the lion in its den.'

'Lion? What lion?'

'Mehdi. You need to talk to Mehdi.'

The thought had occurred to Tommy. Within reasonable limits, Mehdi probably wouldn't mind giving him an update on recruitment and movements, but Tommy would rather not ask. Nothing made him feel old and past it like talking to Mehdi.

'It goes against the grain. I'm sure he's got valuable information, but it goes against the grain.'

'Nothing ventured, nothing gained.'

Tommy sighed. 'There's no end to them, is there?'

*

Semtex-Janne was an expert safebreaker who had worked his way up and no longer dealt with the explosive that had given him his name, except when he was importing it legally for his construction business. He was also a full-blown psychopath, a pressure cooker with a shiny surface that could explode without warning. He was one of the few people in the criminal world that Tommy was actually afraid of.

Tommy's knowledge of what was going on in the suburbs might have been superannuated, but when he arrived in Värtahamnen he was back on home turf. If Janne was still around, then he and his henchmen were running the show, and nothing happened without his knowledge.

Tommy parked in front of a large storage depot; a Ferrari with a metallic paint job stood gleaming in the afternoon sun, giving a clear indication that Janne was still in the game.

The two men climbed the steps and knocked on the door.

'Who is it?'

'It's Santa Claus,' Tommy replied. 'But I don't suppose there are any good children here.'

'There are. Come in.'

Janne had a number of depots around the docks, all filled with the legitimate goods he imported. They acted only as transit stops for anything slightly more dubious.

The room Tommy entered was crowded with stuff that Janne had, for some inexplicable reason, hung on to. A small digger with different-sized scoops, three huge flat-screen TVs, still in their boxes, a rubber dinghy, several electric mopeds. Piles of brand new winter tyres, a couple of wetsuits along with the requisite scuba diving equipment. Four lit chandeliers hung from the ceiling and a stuffed elk stood in one corner. Among other things.

Janne emerged from his office in jeans, a T-shirt, and a jacket that looked expensive but didn't fit. In spite of his high-end cars and designer clothes, he could never quite shake off an air of Kivik Market.

'Tommy! It's been a while! And I see you've brought some muscle with you. You're not scared of Uncle Janne, are you?'

Tommy introduced Tomás as his accountant, which made Janne laugh and slap his thigh.

'Always the joker, Tommy. Guess what? I was thinking of giving you a call.'

'And why didn't you?'

'I heard you were dead. Come on in. Bring your accountant—I

93

can find him some calculations to keep him amused.'

Tommy prided himself on his ability to read people, but when it came to Janne he hadn't a clue. Janne's smile could be hiding a plan to electrocute him then chop him up into tiny pieces, but it could equally be a sign of genuine warmth. Out of the corner of his eye he saw Tomás scanning the place for potential threats. Tommy glanced at him and he shrugged.

Janne's office was a scruffy storeroom with a concrete floor, into which Janne had crammed an exclusive white leather sofa and armchairs, and a glass coffee table. Janne took an armchair; Tommy and Tomás sat down side by side on the sofa.

'So why were you going to call me?' Tommy asked.

Janne rubbed his hands together and leaned forward. 'The thing is, I've been thinking of writing my autobiography, but as I'm not a man of words, I need someone who…Well, someone like you. Like Zlatan and whatsisname.'

If Tommy had made a list of a hundred reasons why Janne might wish to contact him, this wouldn't have been one of them. 'What… what made you think of that?'

Janne scratched the back of his neck and looked troubled. 'My daughter…'

'Jeanette.'

'That's right, Jeanette. She's getting married in the spring. To a *doctor*. It's going to be fantastic. And he comes from one of those families—names with *af* and *von* in them, all that sort of nonsense. And then I thought that her father—yours truly—that maybe there should be some kind of…'

'Memoir?'

Janne clicked his fingers and his face lit up. 'That's exactly what I mean—you're a man of words. A memoir. Something like that would…well, you know.'

'I get the idea, but if I wrote about everything you've done, it wouldn't be…'

Janne waved a dismissive hand. 'No, no. Not *that*. The other stuff.

I've done plenty of other stuff as well.'

'I don't mean to criticise, but that would be like writing about Zlatan without mentioning football.'

The tone of the conversation had been so relaxed that Tommy had misjudged the situation. A shadow passed over Janne's face and in an instant the other Janne appeared, the one who was responsible, so Tommy had heard, for a number of mutilations and executions involving concrete shoes.

'What are you saying? Are you suggesting I'm not worth writing about?'

Before Tommy could find the words to smooth things over, Tomás came to his rescue.

'I think it sounds like a brilliant idea. You said it yourself on the way over—Janne's life is like a book, that's what you said. You have to be able to bring out the positive side of a person.'

Tommy nodded in a way that he hoped was sincere, but there was no trace of joviality in Janne's voice when he asked: 'So what do you want? Why did you come here?'

'There's been a delivery. A massive delivery. Virtually pure cocaine. Which came in to Värtahamnen. Have you heard anything about it?'

Janne looked deep into Tommy's eyes, leaning even further forward to get as close as possible. 'I know nothing. Nothing at all.'

*

'That didn't go too well,' Tomás said when they were back in the car. 'Why did you have to say that about Zlatan? I thought you were smarter than that.'

'The curse of the journalist. I can't resist a wisecrack. And it doesn't really matter.'

'You've lost me.'

'First of all: there's no chance a delivery like that could arrive here without Janne knowing about it.'

'But you already knew that.'

'Yes, but I didn't know he was involved. Janne's vain. There's no chance he'd sit there and say "I know nothing", as if something was going on here behind his back. He'd hint that of course he knew, but he couldn't possibly discuss it with me. Which means he's definitely: a) involved, and b) scared.'

'Not entirely watertight.'

'No, but probably true.'

'So what now?'

'Now I'm going home to feed Hagge. Do you want a ride?'

'No, just drop me off at Slussen.'

*

Tommy pulled up by the bus stop and waved goodbye to Tomás after promising to pass on a few thousand when he got paid for the series. He sat in the car thinking for a while until a bus sounded its horn right behind him. He made an illegal U-turn and headed back towards the docks.

He passed Janne's storage depots and kept going until he reached the dock offices. With a bit of luck Susanne would be on reception. She was the one he got along best with, because she was the one he knew most about. Or vice versa. As soon as he opened the front door he spotted her blonde mane of hair behind the desk, and called up her file inside his head. *Summer cottage, problems with the water supply, husband with Sifo Engineering, daughter in the USA.*

Susanne's face lit up when she saw him. 'Hi Tommy.'

'Hi Susanne.' He didn't say anything else for a few seconds, and Susanne tilted her head on one side and raised her eyebrows. He gave an apologetic smile. 'You didn't think I was dead, did you?'

Susanne drew back her head, a hint of a double chin appearing. 'No, why?'

'No reason, I just…how's Milla getting on in Washington?'

'Brilliant. She's just been picked for the district team.'

People were sometimes astonished at Tommy's ability to remember details of their lives, but most operated like children. Anything that was obvious to them was obvious to everyone.

The district team in…

Susanne's bleached hair covered the Capitol building like a veil, and from that veil tumbled a girl with braided brown hair and in her hands she was holding a…

'No injuries?' Tommy asked. 'Basketball can be pretty brutal.'

'Not so far, touch wood.' Susanne tapped her desk. Tommy tapped the counter.

'Good to hear. Listen, I was wondering…'

'Of course you were.'

'Has a big ship come in from, say, the northern part of South America during the last month or so?'

Susanne clattered away on her keyboard. 'Drugs?'

'Maybe.'

'There are very strict checks in place these days.'

'I know, but still…'

Susanne was scrolling down a list.

'Mmm…Mexico?'

'Probably not.'

'I've got a couple from Brazil—coffee, sugar and airbags.'

'Sounds like a poem. Can you give me the dates and the shipping companies?'

Tommy made a note of the details. 'Anything else?'

'An oil tanker from Venezuela, but that's hardly…'

'Can a tanker get in here?'

'No, they anchor offshore and smaller tankers go out to them. Not exactly practical if you're trying to bring something in.'

'Give me the information anyway.'

When Tommy had written everything down, Susanne said: 'That's all, folks.'

'Okay, thanks Susanne. By the way, did you manage to sort out that problem with the water company at your summer cottage?'

As Tommy drove back to Traneberg, he tried to make sense of the random facts he'd picked up during the day. Someone (or more than one person?) known as Equis had persuaded a large number of major players to take their own lives over the past few months. By *talking to them*. This same Equis had also organised a massive cocaine delivery which was being distributed through Janne. The suicides had destroyed organised crime groups, and the cocaine had caused the market to crash. Equis was taking over, and everyone was scared. How had Equis managed to get hold of enough cocaine to break the competition?

Geographically speaking, Venezuela was the most likely option. After the death of Chavez the government machine had fallen apart, and corruption had exploded. There was an established route from Colombia, through the jungles in the south to the docks in the north.

But an oil tanker? If Tommy was right about the quantity involved, then a tanker was the worst possible idea—no falsely registered containers, no direct contact with the port itself. Transferring that amount via a smaller ship under the watchful eye of the port inspectors…No, it couldn't be done.

Brazil? Also unlikely. The mechanism of the state was more stable there, plus it was a longer journey than from Colombia. He couldn't imagine anyone taking the risk.

So what was left? Tommy could be barking up the wrong tree, of course. The links in his chain of evidence were mostly speculative. The image of a barking dog made him think of Hagge, and he put his foot to the floor.

Hagge raised his head when Tommy got home, then allowed it to sink back down. Tommy lay down on the mat beside him and scratched behind his ears. 'Do you want to go for a walk, boy? Or are you hungry?'

Tommy wasn't sure how much Hagge understood of what he said, but even less intelligent dogs were capable of grasping words like 'walk' and 'hungry'. This time there was no reaction. Hagge merely continued to gaze at Tommy with that same gloomy expression.

'Everything's fine. I'm home now. I missed you.'

Only when Tommy lay down did he realise how tired he was. Playing Tommy T for a whole day took its toll; he couldn't afford to let the façade crack. He wished he was like a Raymond Chandler hero, rock hard all the way through. Then again, who knew, maybe Philip Marlowe became a twitching wreck as soon as his author took his eyes off him.

Tommy grabbed a cushion from the sofa and pushed it under his head. Then he fell asleep with his hand resting on Hagge's warm back.

*

When he woke up, it was dark in the apartment. Hagge hadn't moved, his eyes two pinpoints of light reflecting the streetlight outside the window. The luminous hands on Tommy's watch showed him he'd been asleep for two hours.

Something had woken him. A sound. Ping. His mobile phone: a text. He stayed where he was, with his head resting on the cushion. It was probably Ove, wanting to know when the first article would be ready, what kind of photos and graphics would be needed. Ove usually called, though. Maybe it was Janne, keen to discuss the glorious details of an imaginary life. Tommy groaned. Then he gave a start and sat up.

Ernesto!

Ernesto was his best chance of tracking down a genuine lead. Tommy reached into his pocket and took out his phone; the screen had already gone dark. He brought it back up. The message, from a withheld number, made him inhale sharply even though it consisted of only three words and a sender.

Get on Snapchat. X

Linus

The operation was underway, and the first deliveries had been made. The previously sceptical Göran had gone crazy after Linus offered him a taster. Said he'd never had such good stuff, and had produced ten five-hundred kronor notes. He would probably relieve Linus of a considerable amount of his stock in the future.

One of the idiots in school was sufficiently well off to buy a gram, and he also had a friend who was keen to give it a try. Linus had created a new address folder on his phone marked *Ballerina*. At the moment it contained five numbers, and this evening he was planning to visit more apartments with his biscuits.

Right now he was sitting in Kassandra's kitchenette. It was much nicer since she'd given it a good clean, got rid of all the grease. A new start, she'd said. Paving the way for their new business. Linus had to admit she'd set everything up like a real pro.

The window was covered even more meticulously than before, but because Kassandra hadn't been a fan of daylight anyway, the fact that no one could see in wouldn't attract attention. She'd put in a hundred-watt bulb, which bathed the objects on the table in a cold, white glow.

The small digital scale she'd bought measured the weight down to hundredths of a gram. She'd been to Clas Ohlsson and purchased a couple of hundred small Ziploc bags and a box cutter. The package from Alex had been neatly sliced open, and in the middle of the powder sat the only item from Kassandra's own possessions: a gold-plated coffee spoon that was a part of a set of six she'd received as a christening present from her horrible maternal grandmother.

'Is there anyone in your family who *isn't* horrible?' Linus had asked.

'My gran on my dad's side, but she died of a heart attack when I was eight. I think her death was down to years of psychological abuse from my grandfather.'

There was only one other thing on the table: a small jar containing a cockroach. Kassandra had caught it a couple of days earlier and placed in the screw-top jar to see how long it survived. It was now sitting here in the capacity of chief security officer. The only part of the insect that was moving in the cramped space was its antennae, waving in the air as if it really was on the alert for potential danger.

As Kassandra placed a small amount of powder on the scale, Linus picked up the jar and studied the cockroach. Its black, segmented body was like a precision calibrated watch mechanism that had temporarily stopped.

'Why is it alive?' Linus asked.

Without looking up from her task, Kassandra said: 'They've always lived, and they always will.' She scraped a fraction of the powder off with the knife, then tipped the rest into a bag.

'But *why*?' Linus persisted. He tipped the jar to one side, but the cockroach didn't move. 'It's got no food, no air, no sex, no fun, no space. It's got nothing, and yet it's alive. Why?'

Kassandra shrugged. 'Maybe because it doesn't have a choice. I mean, look at your dad. He's still alive.'

'But he wants to die.'

'So he says, but I wonder what would happen if you came at him with this knife. Would he be so keen then?'

Linus drifted off into a fantasy. The razor-sharp blade, his father's wrinkled neck, the spurting blood as he sliced into the jugular vein. No. He went back to the good old pillow over the face, even though he knew he'd never actually do it.

'Then again, what's the difference?' Kassandra mused as she prepared the next bag. 'We distract ourselves. We watch movies, have sex, go for a run, eat pasta. But *why*? Is there anything we want to achieve? Is there any reason why we do the things we do? No. In the end we're just like the cockroach. The difference is that it doesn't need the distractions. It's enough in itself. It's God.'

'Isn't it depressing to be so deep?'

'I am depressed, Linus. I've got the paperwork to prove it.'

Linus nodded towards the coke. 'Have you ever tried anything like that?'

'Yes. You?'

'No, I daren't. I'd get addicted right away. Don't you want to sample the goods?'

Kassandra straightened up and pushed back a strand of pink hair that had fallen over her face. 'Can I?'

'Only a tiny bit. I'm curious. Göran said a couple of things, but he's not as…what's the word…articulate as you.'

Kassandra looked at Linus, then at the cockroach. She looked at the cockroach for a long time. Then she pulled an *okay-what-the-hell* face and used the blade to scoop up a very small amount of the powder. 'Okay, cheers.' She bent down and inhaled it through her right nostril.

A few seconds passed. A few more. Linus had begun to suspect that Göran was messing him around and that the stuff wasn't top notch after all, when Kassandra let out a long, shuddering breath that suggested absolute terror or sheer pleasure. Her eyes opened wide, then half-closed; her mouth chewed thin air and her body collapsed, relaxed as if all the tension that kept it moving during her everyday life had simply gone away.

'Jesus,' she whispered.

'Isn't it any good?'

Kassandra moved her head from side to side and touched the piercing—a skull—in her right nostril.

'Isn't it any good? It's totally fucking…' She rolled her eyes so that only the whites were visible.

'Come on, Kassandra. You sound like Göran.'

'Okay, okay.' She ran her hands over her face. 'It's completely… it's like…a fantastic winter's day with blue sky and snow and birch trees and children on sleds and all that shit. And the sun, the sun just *shining* on the snow, it's as if all of that, all at once, just explodes in your whole body, in your head…'

'Could you be a little more quotable?'

'It's like…the most mind-blowing orgasm, only better.'

'Thank you.'

Kassandra was more or less back to normal, apart from the dilated pupils, which combined with the thick kohl around her eyes made her look like an over-stimulated ghost.

'Amazing. Incredible.'

'You're not going to get hooked, are you?'

'No chance. I'm with you—it's too dangerous. But…wow.'

As if to confirm Kassandra's review, Linus's phone pinged. A message from a punter who wanted to be known as Rockstar, and who'd bought half a gram to try it out.

Fantastic chocolate biscuits! Two more packets?

It had been agreed that all communication should be couched in terms of biscuits. So Rockstar had tried it, reacted in the same way as Kassandra, and now wanted another two grams. Linus texted *OK* and picked up two one-gram packets. He could deliver them while he was on his Ballerina rounds. He gestured towards the table and said: 'You've set this up really well. Carry on weighing out the rest. I've got a feeling it's not going to be hard to shift.'

Kassandra fixed her eyes on him and took his hand. 'Can't we go into the bedroom? I'm so…Or just sit and chat, tell each other funny stories? I know a really good one. There was a Frenchman, a Russian and Ulf Lundell…'

'Sorry, I have to go. But we've got a good thing going here.'

'They decided to see who could drive the fastest…'

As Linus headed for the door, Kassandra was still babbling away. Linus had heard the story before. It ended with Ulf Lundell having a close encounter with an airbag.

*

Linus went home and picked up the bag of biscuits; he'd decided to carry on from where he'd left off the previous day. Dusk was falling, and the streetlights that weren't broken had come on. He was just about to leave the path through the bushes when he saw something that made him stop and crouch down.

Cerdito, one of the newest and youngest members of Chivo's gang, was passing the apartment block. 'Little Piggy' probably wasn't the nickname he'd have chosen for himself, but it suited him very well. He was the same age as Linus, and gave the impression of an overfed mummy's boy as he wobbled along. His face was round, with cheeks that looked as if they were stuffed with a day's supply of food, like an overgrown hamster. He had little piggy eyes and an upturned nose; the name was inevitable.

Linus wasn't actually scared of Cerdito himself, even though appearances had to be deceptive; Linus knew what kind of things Chivo's gang members had to do in order to be accepted. No, it was what his presence meant. Linus's heart started beating faster as Cerdito entered the building where Linus had hooked Rockstar yesterday. The guy had sworn that he'd never bought from Chivo, but who could trust a punter? Did the north side already know what Linus was up to? And if so, what the fuck was he going to do?

He realised he wouldn't be able to keep his business a secret forever, but he'd counted on having enough time to build up a solid client base so that he became valuable, and therefore worthy of protection from Alex and those above him in the supply chain. The way things were right now, no one would lift a finger to help him.

His chest contracted, he couldn't breathe. He'd heard about Chivo's methods. Apparently he often turned to a good old favourite: the victim's hands would be secured behind his back, then he would be suspended from a hook and left there until the shoulder muscles burst, or the experience was enlivened with the use of a blowtorch.

When Chivo was after information, he usually stopped when he'd got what he wanted, otherwise no one would ever talk. But what made him really happy was when there was no information, and it was simply a case of administering punishment. Then he could carry on for however long he wanted, and no part of the body need be spared. What use is a tongue if you have nothing to say?

If Chivo was on to him, then Linus could only hope he was interested in finding out who Linus's supplier was. On the other hand, betraying Alex wasn't a pretty thought either. He would have to endure as much as possible, offering up his injuries as evidence that he'd tried to keep his mouth shut. Not that that would be enough…

Please God let it be a coincidence, please God don't let them…

'What the fuck are you doing down there?'

The door had just closed behind Cerdito, but Linus still jumped at the sound of Matti's voice. He straightened up and rubbed his forehead. 'I just…low blood sugar, I think.'

'Or you've been drinking?'

'Maybe that too.'

Matti grinned and nodded, then he caught sight of the ICA carrier bag and his expression darkened. 'A solo enterprise?'

'No, no. One for all and all for one, you know that.'

'So what are you doing?'

Linus couldn't think straight, and had to give Matti the same story he'd told Betty, even though he knew Matti wouldn't buy it. Their vodka business was ten times as profitable. Matti listened patiently until Linus had finished, then said: 'Okay. So what are you really doing?'

'I've just told you.'

'Do you think I'm a fucking idiot? Am I supposed to believe you're going around selling biscuits like some ten-year-old? Not that any ten-year-olds would be stupid enough to do that here.'

'Think what you like.'

Before Linus could stop him, Matti grabbed a packet out of the bag and broke it open. Biscuits tumbled out all over the ground. Matti shook his head, more in sorrow than anger. 'What the fuck is going on? One more time: what are you doing?'

'Maybe I want to stop.'

'Right, and I'm going on a date with Rihanna. Who is it who's got your back? *Talk* to me, for fuck's sake.'

The fear of what Cerdito's appearance might mean had scrambled

Linus's brain, but now he'd had time to recover and could see the way out. He stared down at the ground, looking embarrassed. 'Okay, I'm a useless idiot. I stole four boxes of this shit and now...'

The lines of concern disappeared from Matti's face. 'I like your style. Not. So how much will you make?'

'A couple of hundred.'

'So that's a hundred for the kitty. Pathetic.'

The kitty was their joint stash of money—Linus, Henrik and Matti. If anyone did any business on their own, the agreement was that half went into the kitty. Linus kept his eyes fixed on the ground, poked around with his toe. 'Don't say anything to Henrik, okay?'

When he looked up, Matti's expression had changed again. His eyes narrowed and he poked Linus in the chest. 'I still don't know if I believe you. Selling biscuits like some little...No, I don't believe you.'

'It's the truth, Matti. I'm really short of cash at the moment, and the opportunity was just there, and...'

'Do you swear?'

'Yes.'

'Do you swear on brotherhood and friendship?'

'I swear.'

Lying to Matti didn't make Linus feel any better than lying to Tommy—in fact he felt worse. They were brothers, they had each other's backs. But he had no choice. Alex hadn't said anything about telling anyone else, and it was bad enough that he'd involved Kassandra. Plus...

Plus!

...he couldn't stay in one place like Kassandra's cockroach until he died of misery and a lack of oxygen, could he? The smuggled vodka, the thefts from loading bays or trucks—that was small-time stuff. Matti held out his right hand, palm upward, fingers bent inward. 'Paws?'

Linus held out his right hand, palm down, fingers bent inward to link with Matti's. They both squeezed. 'Paws.'

That one little thing. They'd invented it when they were about ten years old; they'd decided the three of them should greet one another 'bear-style'. It seemed unlikely that bears really greeted one another that way, but it had become a joke, a parody of the Latinos' complex hand gestures, and had stayed with them. But it was infantile, ridiculous. Linus was a player now; he couldn't afford childish games.

The sound of a door opening made him turn around. Cerdito emerged and Linus made a snap decision. He stepped towards him, where there was more light. Cerdito looked him up and down. Linus nodded. Cerdito screwed up his face in a way that made him appear even more piggy, then gave Linus the finger before heading back the way he'd come.

'What was that all about?' Matti asked.

That was about dealing with fear. Linus's lungs expanded and his heart rate slowed. Cerdito's reaction hadn't said *aha, there's the little fucker.* He hadn't widened his piggy little eyes or smiled nastily. This was just the usual unpleasantness from north to south. They didn't know what Linus was up to.

'Marking our territory,' he informed Matti.

'Chivo must be shit-scared now. He'll be saying: "The bears are running the south side, I'd better stay away."'

'I have to go.'

'To sell biscuits?'

'Yes.'

Matti stared at him for a long moment, then he sighed. 'Okay, what's the spiel?'

'Haga Boys football team. Fundraising to get to a tournament in Germany.'

Matti grinned. Linus's instant response seemed to have convinced him that maybe his friend was telling the truth after all, and his tone had softened when he said: 'Happy hunting.'

*

'Have you spoken to Cerdito?'

'Who?'

Linus searched Rockstar's face for any sign of lying or unease, but all he found was the same blank stare Kassandra had displayed. The good stuff was still in his bloodstream.

'Doesn't matter. Two grams, right?'

'Mmm.'

A hungry light flared in Rockstar's eyes when Linus produced the bags. Judging by his twitching fingers and glassy-eyed expression, it seemed unlikely that he was planning to take a break before his next hit. He dug four five-hundred kronor notes out of his pocket and handed them to Linus, who contemplated the grubby, crumpled balls of paper and said: 'In future...'

'Mmm, mmm?'

'A bit tidier, yes? Rolled up. Maybe an elastic band.'

'Absolutely, absolutely, absolutely. Sorry, sorry. Listen...'

There was a pleasing aspect of dealing that hadn't been quite so evident when Linus was selling his medication: the power. His customers had been keen to get their pills, but it wasn't a disaster if they had to wait. This was different. Linus held the keys to the kingdom of heaven, and it was up to him whether the gates would be unlocked. The punters knew that, and treated him like St Peter. Nice.

'Yes?' Linus smoothed out the notes as best he could.

Rockstar was clutching the bags as if he were dangling over an abyss and they were his lifeline. He glanced furtively around and lowered his voice. 'I've got two friends, if you know what I mean.'

'And you're sure of them?'

'Completely sure. Have you got anything?'

'Maybe. Do they live here?'

Rockstar shook his head energetically. 'No, no, no. In town. In town. Both of them. They're brokers. Both of them.'

'What, like insurance brokers or something?'

A spastic smile passed over Rockstar's face. 'No, no. Stockbrokers. Stockbrokers.'

'You mean city boys?'

Rockstar nodded his head with enthusiasm. 'That's right. That's what they are. City boys.'

'How do you know people like that?'

Rockstar looked offended; his lower lip jutted out, but then he remembered who he was talking to. 'Went to the School of Economics.'

'And now?'

The question appeared to confuse Rockstar. His eyes darted all over the place before he tentatively answered: 'Now...I don't go there anymore.'

'No—what do you do now?'

'Do I...Do I have to say?'

'I like to know who my customers are.'

Rockstar glanced over his shoulder at a cupboard in the living room. 'Viagra. Cheap generics. Bring them in from Thailand. Sell them for cash. Online.'

'You mean people send you *cash*?'

Rockstar nodded towards the notes in Linus's hand. 'I've got a PO box.'

'So we're colleagues. Can't you sort out your own shit?'

'I can sort out my own shit, but not shit like this,' Rockstar said, holding up the fist concealing the bags Linus had given him. 'This is out of my league. Way out.'

'Okay. I'll see what I can do.'

'About what?'

'I'll see if I can help your friends.'

When he'd left Rockstar's apartment, Linus sent a text to Alex: *Can we meet?* The reply arrived by the time the elevator reached the ground floor: *20 min.* Linus headed for the carpet-beating rack to wait.

*

Linus pushed the packets of biscuits to one end of the bag, spread it on the ground then sat down on it, his back resting against the frame to which Rabbit Boy had been tethered four years earlier. He thought about the various substances that were in circulation. Even Rockstar was running his own little business. Dick pills. Betty took three different tablets—one for her heart, one for her blood pressure, and something else. Linus's father was given both injections and liquid medication to keep him alive against his will. And that was all *legal* stuff.

Then there were all the other things that stayed under the radar and changed hands in the shadows. If you wanted to get high, or low, get a hard-on, pump up your muscles or just zone out. All that money circulating so that people could acquire substances that would change them. That was the essence of the deal, when you thought about it.

A feeling of pride came over Linus, and he gave himself a mental pat on the back. Apart from the vodka, he wasn't dependent on anything that could make him go crawling to a supplier—despite the fact that society saw him as a freak who *needed* medication. He'd beaten those bastards. Broken them.

His hatred towards society was deep-seated and diffuse. Apart from Johanna, his teacher in junior school, he'd never met any adult in a position of authority that he'd liked or trusted. Some had tried to help him but gone about it all wrong; others had simply wanted to put him down, make sure he knew his place. The police belonged to the latter category. Since his arrest and his stint in residential care, Linus loathed the cops with such venom that it was almost like an allergy. The mere sight of a uniform or a squad car made his stomach turn over and his skin start itching.

'Okay?'

Linus hadn't heard Alex approaching. He leapt to his feet, because sitting down seemed disrespectful, and said: 'Okay. I just wanted to ask you a question.'

'How's it going?'

'Fine.'

'Good.'

Alex's responses were mechanical, as if he was operating on

autopilot. Something else was occupying his mind.

'I was wondering…Is it okay to sell to people outside Stugan?'

'You can sell wherever you like, but it's your problem if you fuck it up. There are no eyes outside Stugan.'

Linus gratefully seized the opportunity to ask: 'Eyes?'

'There are always eyes around here.'

'So someone's got my back?'

'What's wrong—are you worried about something?'

Yes, Linus was worried about Cerdito, but decided it was best not to say anything; he didn't want to come across as weak. 'No, everything's fine.'

'Everything's fine?'

'Mmm.'

Alex lingered, and in the silence that followed Linus thought it was worth asking another question. 'One more thing…Is it okay to send stuff in the post?'

For the first time a glimmer of interest sparked in Alex's dark eyes. Or maybe it was scorn. 'You think you're the first person in the world to come up with *that* stroke of genius?'

'I just…'

'They use dogs and they do spot checks, but if you want to risk losing a delivery worth a few thousand, then carry on. As long as you can cover the cost.'

'I didn't say I was going to…'

Alex placed a hand on his shoulder. 'Linus. As far as I'm concerned you can go and stand next to the E4 with a sign around your neck if you feel like it. Once again—as long as you can come up with the money when it's due, and never, ever…'

'I know, I know, I know.'

Alex's grip tightened, and Linus gasped with the sudden pain. 'Are you interrupting me?'

'No, sorry, I just, sorry. I know.'

'What do you know?'

'That I didn't get it from anybody. That I found it.'

'In the bike storeroom. In a saddlebag.'

Alex nodded and let go of Linus's shoulder. Silence once more. Alex's face closed down, and Linus stood there looking at the swoosh logo over his heart. He didn't dare walk away until Alex gave him permission. Seconds passed. Someone yelled something in Finnish from a balcony, and a small animal scuttled by in the bushes. When Alex finally spoke, his eyes were fixed on something far beyond Gårdsstugan's apartment blocks.

'I'm getting closer.'

'Closer...to what?'

As if Alex hadn't heard Linus's question, he added: 'Tonight. I'm going to meet him. Tonight.'

'Who?'

'*Him.*'

There was no trace of Alex's normal, rock hard tone in his voice; he sounded almost ecstatic, and his expression was terrifying in a completely new way as he turned his eyes on Linus. 'I might get to... taste.'

He kept on staring at Linus, and all Linus could manage was a cautious: 'Congratulations,' which brought Alex back to reality. He nodded and left.

Linus stayed where he was, with his biscuits and his confusion. If being handed a hundred grams of ninety per cent pure coke had made him feel as if he was in the deep end of the pool, unable to touch the bottom, now he was in the sea. The bottomless ocean, with only the horizon in all directions.

*

He arrived home to the worst possible scenario. Katarina, the district nurse, was waiting to leave, and Betty wasn't back yet. She'd probably won a voucher or some other crap and got stuck in the bingo hall. As if it was Linus's fault, Katarina stood up and said: 'Good, you're home. I'll leave you to it.'

Linus would have happily given her the two thousand kronor he had in his back pocket to persuade her to stay, but he knew that would lead to tricky questions. Helplessly he watched as Katarina manoeuvred her square body towards the front door, and then he was alone with his father. A gurgling that could be interpreted as his name was coming from the living room.

Linus took off his jacket and shoes in slow motion, listening for the elevator or footsteps on the stairs. Betty was a bingo addict—how unsexy was that?—and if she was in the right frame of mind she could sit there until the place closed at ten o'clock, having gambled away all the money they didn't have.

The gurgling came again. Linus went into the kitchen, turned on the tap, filled a glass with a thin stream of water, then drank it as if it were the finest malt whisky. Not that it helped. It wasn't the sight of his father that Linus found hardest to bear; it was his presence; his thoughts.

He realised this was irrational, if not completely insane, but he could feel his father's thoughts filling the apartment. The found their way into every corner, like the smell of burnt hair. If Linus had been out he knew, the second he stepped in through the front door, if his mother or Katarina had taken his father outside. He knew the thoughts weren't there, knew he had a breathing space until his father was installed in his corner again, and the thoughts began to billow out once more.

It wasn't that Linus heard what his father was thinking, he wasn't that crazy, but he felt the thoughts like a pressure, or a constantly present smoke that he couldn't help inhaling when he was in the apartment. So he might as well pretend to hang out for a while with the man responsible for his existence.

The television was off, the room illuminated only by a dim floor lamp. Sitting in his dark corner, his father looked like something from a horror movie, the malformed figure who would get to his feet at any moment, grab a knife and start slashing. The idea didn't scare Linus; in fact he found it quite reassuring, because it afforded his father a

113

weird dignity that he didn't actually have.

Linus sat down on the sofa, picked up the remote and switched on the TV. *Idol* was on. An overweight guy with a beard was giving his all to the final note of an Adele song, then he stood there wearing a panic-stricken smile as he waited for the judges' verdict.

Linus couldn't understand how anyone could put themselves through that. Night after night, being either praised or humiliated in front of millions of people just for the chance of travelling around shopping malls signing autographs for seven-year-olds. They always said they had a dream, and it certainly seemed like a dream to Linus: disconnected, meaningless; usually terrifying. The judges weren't impressed by Fat Boy. Not 'authentic' enough. His father grunted in a way that Linus knew meant he was dissatisfied.

'Shall I change channel?' His father moved his head a fraction from side to side. Linus changed channel anyway. A debate. People with opinions, standing at a long table. A louder grunt from his father. The faces weren't familiar to Linus. He thought a couple of them were party leaders, but he hadn't a clue which party, or what that party stood for. He couldn't have cared less. Nothing would change for Linus whoever was in charge. From the inarticulate noises beside him, he was able to distinguish: 'Out! Out!'

'Absolutely. Out with the lot of them, that's what I say.'

'Wit-o! Wit-o!'

'You want me to switch it off?'

'Mmm-M!'

Reluctantly Linus complied. The room became silent and dark. He sat there with his hands between his thighs listening to his heartbeat, to his father's wheezing breaths, to his own, thoughts jangling the room like static electricity.

I might get to…taste.

What the hell could make a hard man like Alex look so smitten? Something he was going to taste, something…

'Iino?'

Linus turned at the gurgled version of his name. 'Do you want a

114

drink of water?' His father's head moved from side to side. 'No? So what do you want?'

'Oo-ook.'

'Try again.'

His father grunted and made a huge effort, his lips trembling as he said: 'y-y-ook.'

'Look?'

'Mmm!'

'What do you want me to look at?'

'Mmm…mmm…eee!'

'You want me to look at you?'

'Mmm!'

Linus sighed, swallowed, and shifted his gaze. He didn't know how long it was since he'd last looked his father in the eye. It might be years. Unconsciously at first, then consciously, he avoided them: those wells of sorrow that threatened to drown him. Now he did as his father asked, and found a steady contemplation that wasn't at all hard to bear.

The rest of his father's face was contorted in an expression of paralysed terror, but in the middle of this mask of horror were a pair of calm, clear eyes looking at Linus. The corners of his father's mouth turned up in a smile, and he said: 'Iino…Iino.'

A lump grew in Linus's throat. 'Yes, Dad?'

His father let out a long, pleasure-filled 'Mmmmmm…' as he held Linus's gaze.

Linus was on the verge of tears, and he couldn't let that happen, so he tried to work out what this reminded him of. It was like something that had happened before, or something he'd seen before.

Darth Vader.

That was it. When Darth Vader is about to die, and Luke Skywalker takes off his helmet and mask and sees his father's face for the first time. The breathing apparatus covering his mouth, the hard, disfigured face, and those warm, clear eyes. Linus managed to convince himself that it was the similarity with this scene that had moved him, and succeeded in holding back the tears. His father's eyes moved to the chest of drawers. 'F...f...ch.'

Linus thought he knew what his father wanted him to fetch. There were a number of framed photographs on the chest of drawers: Linus at various ages, his parents' wedding photo, among others. The largest took pride of place; it had been taken when his father won a race that Betty and Linus had watched. His father was in the middle dressed in his jockey's silks, with his arms around Betty and eight-year-old Linus. The three of them, beaming like the sun that shone down on them. A happy, close family.

The lump in Linus's throat grew bigger. He couldn't sit here next to his father looking at that photograph without breaking down completely, so he swallowed hard, stood up and said: 'Another time. I've got stuff to do.'

He stroked his father's hand, then remembered and stroked his hair instead. His father was still gazing at him with those clear eyes. Linus glanced at the cushions on the sofa.

Two minutes, that's all it would take.

In six years, he'd never wanted his father to live so much. In six years, he'd never been so close to killing him. He went to his room and locked himself in.

Tommy

Tommy had a habit that he just couldn't shake, even though he'd been in the business for thirty years. As soon as anything he'd written was published, he would buy the paper to see what his article looked like in print. He once mentioned this to some fellow journalists—from a purely hypothetical point of view, of course—and they insisted they never bothered about their work once they'd filed. So either Tommy was unusually self-obsessed, or they were lying.

It was a gloomy day in the middle of October. The glory of the autumn colours had faded, and dampness hung in the air beneath an overcast sky as Tommy headed for the newsagent's with Hagge. The dog had emerged from his depression, and made a number of brief stops to sniff an interesting lamp post or to have a pee. It always seemed to Tommy that he did these 'doggy things' in an absent-minded way, more out of duty than desire, as if he were ticking boxes. *Yeah, yeah, lamp post. Sniff, piss…yeah, yeah.*

The two women who took it in turns to work in the newsagent's were the only ones who knew Tommy's secret. When he opened the door he was pleased to see Karin, who teased him less than her colleague. She smiled and came around the counter.

'Hi Tommy, hi Hagge.'

She crouched down and Hagge ambled over and licked her hand, glancing up at Tommy as if to say, *see, this is what's expected of me.* Karin stroked his head gently and said: 'I read what happened. Horrible.'

Tommy picked up a copy of *Stockholmsnytt* and smiled when he saw that Ove had given his article top billing. Half the front page, continued on pages four and five. His smile stiffened when he saw what the headline writer had come up with: GANGLAND ANGEL OF DEATH. Bosse, no doubt; he was particularly fond of the word 'death'.

However, the layout was good, and the piece was illustrated with a graphic showing the geographical spread of the suicide epidemic and a picture of...The remains of Tommy's smile disappeared as he recognised Hans-Åke's house behind the body bag being loaded into an ambulance

'Yes. Horrible.'

Hans-Åke was mentioned in the text but, as Tommy had read his farewell note, he'd written that this death probably wasn't related to the wave of suicides. Bosse clearly had a different opinion.

'Do you know more than you wrote?' Karin asked.

'About what?'

'About this...Equis.'

Tommy's article was largely a rehash of old material. The new information was that the suicides had been prompted by one or more people *talking* to those who would soon take their own lives, and most importantly, he had given a name: Equis. Even if people didn't know it meant X, it had an ominous ring to it.

'Yes,' he said. 'Yes, I do.'

'Go on.'

'If I told you, I'd have to kill you.'

Tommy was pretty sure that the cocaine delivery was part of the picture, but he didn't have enough solid evidence to write about it yet. He was meeting Mehdi later; he'd wanted to wait until his own article had been printed, show he was firing on all cylinders again. That was one reason why he was especially pleased to be on the front page. As if Karin had read his mind, she grinned at his last comment and said: 'You ought to do something about your by-line. Take a leaf out of Mehdi's book.'

Tommy turned the pages until he found Mehdi's opinion piece and a picture of Mehdi himself in a black T-shirt that showed off his biceps. The image was twice as big as Tommy's—not to mention that a red jacket and some seriously bad photoshopping made Tommy look like a superannuated ringmaster.

'One day you'll be old too, Karin,' he said, putting the newspaper on the counter with a bar of chocolate.

Tommy strolled home. Back in the day he used to hold court at Café Opera, treating everyone to Bollinger after a particularly successful scoop, book, review or TV appearance. Nowadays he celebrated with a bar of chocolate, which he ate as he walked. In a way he preferred it, and Hagge was able to join in too. That was another un-doggy thing about Hagge; he loved chocolate, and it didn't seem to do him any harm. He always got the last square.

Tommy was halfway to Traneberg when his phone made a sound he didn't recognise, a drop of water falling into an echo chamber. The Snapchat icon showed that he had a message. He sat down on a box of road grit and touched the little ghost.

What he saw shocked him so much that he almost missed the screen dump. The picture was only there for five seconds—it would be gone forever if he didn't press the buttons in time. He took a deep breath, then brought the image back up. It showed Hans-Åke sitting in his bed with the plastic bag over his head. *Sitting.* Still alive. The window behind him was black, so it must have been evening or night. In a couple of minutes he would suffocate and fall back into the position in which Tommy had found him. Equis had read his article and wanted to correct a factual error. Hans-Åke was definitely a part of the suicide wave.

Hang on a minute…

Tommy pinched the screen to zoom in on the dark pane in which the bedroom was reflected. He could see Hans-Åke's massive body, stoically waiting for death, and a few metres away from him, with a camera held up before the face…

The sound of an echoing drop came again; Tommy gave a start and almost dropped the phone.

This time he saw a man in a white T-shirt lying in a dumpster, surrounded by broken computer monitors. An old-fashioned Mac desktop had been smashed over his head, the screen smashed so that his face—nothing more than a bloody mass—was visible. Tommy was about to take a screen grab, but paused when he saw what was written on the man's T-shirt, presumably in his own blood: SCREEN DUMPER.

As Tommy hesitated, the image disappeared. Equis didn't want his pictures kept. Tommy might well have succumbed to paranoia if he hadn't read up about Snapchat. He now knew that the person who sent the image received a message if the recipient took a screen dump. Tommy went back to Hans-Åke, to the reflection in the window.

Is that you?

The man—he assumed it was a man—was holding a phone in the camera position in front of his face. The lighting was poor, and he was out of focus. It wasn't possible to say much about his appearance, except that he had fair hair and appeared to be of medium height. Even so, it was pure gold. He had named Equis in his article, and now he had something more to add. He got to his feet and hurried home to run the image through Aperture, dragging Hagge along behind him.

*

Tommy was no expert, but after an hour he'd managed to clean the enlarged image so well that new details had emerged. He was ninety-nine per cent certain it was a man, based on the posture, the build and what could be seen of the face.

The sharper contours and improved contrast made two things stand out. Firstly, the person who'd taken the picture was wearing thin gloves, and was holding the phone in a clumsy, awkward way, as if it were an unfamiliar object and he wasn't sure how to handle it. The other thing was more difficult to pin down. There was something wrong with the parts of the face that Tommy could make out. The ear didn't sit right in relation to the rest of the features, and the mouth was rigid—almost as if he'd undergone botched cosmetic surgery.

The gender was the only issue that had been resolved; in fact new questions had been raised. Why had Tommy received the picture? Why send a picture in which Equis himself could be seen—if that was him? Tommy was convinced that the reflection wasn't an oversight.

Equis realised that Tommy would take a screen dump, clean up the picture then use it in an article, for which he could demand a substantial fee. But why had Equis revealed himself?

*

Tommy opened a blank document to begin an article in which he could use the image, but after five minutes without the important introductory sentence popping into his head, he went and sat down in his armchair, gazing around the living room in search of inspiration.

He neither loved nor loathed his apartment. Like so much else in his life, it was merely something that fulfilled a purpose. He'd bought it after the death of the previous owner, a lady who'd lived there all her life, and he'd kept it exactly the same as the day he'd moved in. Pale green kitchen cupboards from the 1950s, an ancient gas cooker, and wallpaper with a faded floral pattern that was barely visible, as Tommy's bookshelves covered the walls.

Money had run through Tommy's fingers back when he was really raking it in, and these days he owned only a few objects that bore witness to the fact that he'd once been pretty well off. A Rocket Milano espresso machine was tucked in an alcove in the kitchen. It took five minutes to prepare a cup of coffee from scratch; Tommy had often thought of getting himself one of those fancy new capsule machines, but he'd never got around to it. There was something meditative about going through all the different steps in the process, plus it would feel as if he was giving something up.

Tommy might roll his eyes at people who spent time and energy on home décor, but he also envied them. It would be nice to have a lovely home, in theory, but he wouldn't know where to start. On one occasion he'd gone into Svenskt Tenn in a moment of temporary insanity and spent almost ten thousand kronor on a Josef Frank designer footstool. It sat there in front of his sagging, shabby armchair, like a peacock in a chicken factory. He could almost feel it turning away from the rest of the room in disgust.

Tommy could have spent a million in Svenskt Tenn and filled the apartment with designer furniture and the finest rugs; it would have looked less like a home and more like a warehouse full of stolen goods. Words were his forte, not style.

*

When Tommy was in a skittish mood, he would say his training ground was the popular family magazine *Hemmets Journal* rather than journalism college.

'It all started in my grandmother's outside toilet…' he would say as he stood at the bar in Café Opera, surrounded by admiring men and the odd woman. In his grandmother's outside toilet there had been a pile of copies of *Hemmets Journal*, and Tommy would sit there for half an hour or more reading 'Crime of the Week'. There was something fascinating about those photographs of ordinary people, rooms with circles and arrows to show the location of bloodstains or where a weapon had been found. The idea that everyday life could suddenly erupt into violence, those dark, secret forces at work inside us all.

When he was eleven years old he'd tried writing a detective novel, but had got bored and edited his account so that it read like a report on a real case—à la *Hemmets Journal*. That was the truth. He'd never had any formal training but had learnt by doing, and that had started with HJ.

Tommy leaned back in his armchair, closed his eyes and returned to that toilet with its smell of shit and peat; he tried to recall the sense of a story that captured his imagination, made him lose track of time.

*Hans-Åke has only a minute left to live…*no, no.

*The reflection in the window pane…*too wordy.

*October fourteenth, 19:42…*if only there had been a clock in the room.

*He's known as Equis, the man who…*pull yourself together, Tommy.

He knew from experience that there was no point in trying to force something. If it came, it came, and if he had a deadline, it *always* came. He got up, went over to the window and looked down onto Margretelundsvägen. Three hours until he was due to meet Mehdi, and then it would be evening.

The feeling came over him. Loneliness. He'd learnt to cope with it, even appreciate it, but sometimes there was a great emptiness inside him, and a silent veil settled over a world he rarely shared with anyone. Hagge was a good friend, but he wasn't a *witness*, someone with a mind like Tommy's who could look at him and confirm his existence; you needed another human being for that. Fortunately Tommy had just such a person. He called Anita, and she answered almost right away. 'Hello? Yes?'

Anita loved to talk, but not on the phone. She'd said it was because she got a funny sensation, as if she was speaking to a severed head. Their conversations were usually restricted to arranging a time and place.

'Okay to meet up?' Tommy asked.

'Absolutely.'

'Tonight?'

'Yes.'

'Yours or mine?'

'Mine.'

'Good. See you later.'

'After seven.'

Before Tommy had the chance to ask if he should bring anything, Anita had ended the call.

When Tommy was writing his book on trafficking, Anita's name had come up on a number of occasions, and he'd managed to get her to agree to meet for a chat. He'd never really worked out what her role was in the convoluted business of young girls from Eastern Europe being lured to Sweden with false promises.

On the one hand she seemed to act as a kind of den mother, taking care of the girls and occasionally having one or more of them staying at her place. On the other hand she was tolerated by the pimps, which suggested that she was in it up to her neck and was probably earning a fair amount of money. She oiled the machine; maybe she was one of the really bad people. Or maybe she was a good person doing her best in a system that was rotten to the core. Tommy didn't know.

He'd stopped viewing his friends and acquaintances through any kind of moral lens a long time ago. He liked them or he didn't. And he liked Anita. She was damaged and sharp, tender and cynical. Incomprehensible. And she was a Hitchcock fan.

She was also a prostitute, but when she met Tommy she was forty-three and seeing only the occasional client in her apartment 'for old times' sake'. They tended to be older men; five hundred kronor for a hand job and a chat. Maybe she had a client this afternoon and that was why she'd said after seven.

They'd never slept together. When the subject came up at the beginning of their friendship, Anita had said she'd be perfectly happy to go to bed with Tommy, but that it would change everything; he would become one in a long line, so to speak.

Tommy had only mentioned it to check if *she* wanted to do it. He wasn't interested; he'd known that for years. He wasn't gay either, as far as he knew. Just not interested. He'd never had sex. It wasn't something he talked about, because he knew it would cause an enormous fuss. People were fixated on sex. Anyway, he had been able to reassure Anita on that point, and thus avoid becoming one in a long line. He liked being unique.

*

In the early nineties, St Erik's Bowling Café was a real nest of vipers. Not in the same class as casinos like Oxen or Monte Carlo, but pretty impressive for a place that didn't have a liquor licence. Not that that made any difference. You could buy just about anything both over and under the counter, then withdraw to the private café area and have a lovely time.

Tommy had been there often and spoken to members of the lower echelons of the criminal fraternity, but had never worked out why St Erik's, with its orange plastic stackable chairs and fluorescent lights, had become a meeting place. As with so many other things, he assumed it had just happened.

After a couple of raids the place went bust. It closed for a while, then reopened under a new regime. A Bosnian-Croatian guy by the unfortunate name of Dragan gave the club a total makeover with renovated lanes and disco bowling, which gave him the right to sell beer. Along one wall was the dubious combination of a bar and a children's play area. As far as Tommy was aware, Dragan didn't have a stain on his character. He drove away the old clientele as soon as they tried to creep back. He had a Terminator-stare that he could switch on in a second, and that was enough to frighten away small-time crooks.

Mehdi was standing by the reception desk chatting to Dragan. When Tommy arrived, they both turned their heads and gave him a funny look. Tommy spread his arms wide and pointed to his chest. 'I'm alive, okay? I'm alive!'

'I know that,' Mehdi said, 'but Dragan had heard otherwise. He was pretty surprised when I said I was meeting you.'

As far as Tommy was concerned, this was the first indication that Dragan had contacts in the underworld, since that seemed to be where the rumour of Tommy's death had started. They shook hands. 'Okay, let's get this straight, Dragan: who told you I was dead, and what exactly did he say?'

'Ronny. A cop who comes here to play.'

'I don't know him. So what did he say?'

'That you'd written the wrong thing about the wrong person and you'd been...dealt with.'

'And who's the person I'm supposed to have written about?'

'Someone they were after. Someone they didn't know.'

Mehdi joined in the conversation. 'The guy Tommy's writing about now? The new guy?'

'How am I supposed to know that?' Dragan said; the Terminator made a brief appearance.

After Mehdi had apologised and Tommy had changed his shoes, they went to choose their bowling balls. Mehdi went for a black sixteen, the heaviest, while Tommy settled on a dark blue ten. He'd been surprised when Mehdi suggested a couple of games.

Bowling was the only sport Tommy was reasonably good at, and he assumed Mehdi knew that. Maybe Mehdi was even better, and wanted to take the opportunity to crush Tommy in yet another area. Then again, that wasn't like him. Given Mehdi's position and reputation, he was astonishingly modest.

'Clever,' Mehdi said, swinging the ball as if it were a kettle bell. 'If that's what he's doing. Issuing a warning in advance, so to speak. Good piece, by the way. *Equis*. Nice. Any contact?' When Tommy didn't answer right away, Mehdi raised his eyebrows. 'You have? Congratulations! Have you actually spoken to him?'

'He sends pictures. On Snapchat.' Mehdi stopped dead and nodded slowly. 'What?' Tommy asked.

'I was talking to this guy—pretty high up. While we were standing there he got a message—you know, that sound. On his phone. I remember thinking: *Snapchat*. Isn't Snapchat for twelve-year-old girls? But that explains it. What kind of pictures does he send?' Tommy gave Mehdi a look, and Mehdi put down his ball and raised his hands. 'Okay, okay. Sorry. I'm not fishing, I'm just curious. Do you want to go first?'

It was a few months since Tommy had played, and he didn't feel the optimum synchronicity—when the alley, the ball, the arm and the swing come together as one, and there's only one way for the ball to go. However, he made a good start and sent the ball off with a screw that made sure it hit the front pin in exactly the right spot. Strike.

Tommy's personal best performance was two perfect games one after the other. He averaged six or seven strikes per round, and the rest spares—with the odd exception.

Mehdi had a completely different style. Two rapid steps forward, then he flung the ball in a dead straight line with the force of a battering ram. There was a crash and eight pins flew up in the air. The remaining two stood there trembling, as if they feared the next onslaught. To Tommy's surprise, Mehdi clenched his fist and said: 'Yesss!' Maybe it was going to be a pleasant afternoon after all.

Mehdi killed the two standing pins with an equally ruthless attack and another 'Yesss'. Tommy turned his ball around in his hands and asked: 'This top-shelf coke that's circulating—do you know anything about it?'

Mehdi shook his head. Tommy's heart sank, but it turned out the headshake wasn't meant to convey a lack of knowledge, only despair at the phenomenon itself. 'It's everywhere. A thousand kronor a gram. It's insane.'

'What, the same price across the board? And isn't it supposed to be ninety per cent pure?'

'Like I said, it's insane. It's taken over completely, and there seems to be an unlimited supply.'

Tommy let fly, achieving the same perfect arc as the last time. All the pins went down, and a bright red X glowed on the screen above.

'Tommy, you're the *man*,' Mehdi said. His ball veered to the left and took down only five pins. No *Yesss* this time. After six rounds Tommy had twice as many points as Mehdi, and still had one spare to cash in.

'I've been thinking,' Mehdi said. 'How do we carve this up?'

Perhaps that was the reason for choosing the bowling alley. Mehdi was modest, but he was also smart. Maybe he knew how skilful Tommy was, and wanted to get him in a good mood before they started talking about dividing up the cake. Tommy was undeniably in a good mood, but he'd have to be ecstatic to let Mehdi have something unless he was forced into a corner.

'Any suggestions?'

'You write about everything you know, I write about everything I know. You take the suicides, I take the coke.'

'Tricky. Given that there's a connection.'

Mehdi gritted his teeth, throwing a film-star jawline into relief. Two steps, and this time he achieved his first strike. He stood there for a couple of seconds staring at the X; he even forgot to say 'Yesss'.

'All right, Tommy. I'll stick to the effects—the kids, the dealing, that kind of thing. Okay?'

'Okay. Thanks. Just one question.' Mehdi's expression said *don't push it, Tommy.* 'On a personal matter—is this coke circulating in Gårdsstugan?'

'Yes. Personal reasons?'

'Exactly. Personal reasons.'

'Okay.'

Tommy's performance deteriorated over the next few rounds, because he was finding it hard to concentrate. He really didn't want Linus to be involved. Just before the final round, he said, 'I can give you something. You know Chivo?'

'Yes, he's in the dark on this. What do you know?'

'That he's in the dark. It was really difficult to find that out.'

'You could have asked me.'

'And would you have told me?'

Mehdi grinned and sent his ball flying. Another strike; it wouldn't help him even if Tommy missed completely with his final ball, but at least it made Mehdi happy . He started humming.

Tommy had hoped to learn more from the meeting, but realised it was impossible if he wasn't prepared to give Mehdi any further details, now they both had their fingers in the same honeypot. The information about the geographical spread of the coke, the sheer quantity involved, was very useful though. Mehdi got ready for his next throw, still humming, and now Tommy recognised the tune.

'What are you humming?' he asked.

Mehdi shook his head. 'Just something I heard. Gang members out in the suburbs, they whistle, they hum. I guess it's a hit. Do you know the name of it?'

'I do. It is a hit. Written by Peter Himmelstrand for Jan Sparring.'

'Himmelstrand? The guy who used to be a journalist?'

'Yes. It's called "Somebody Up There Must Like Me".'

'Wow. I suppose it must have been sampled or something.'

'Yes. Or something.'

Tommy almost sent his last ball into the gutter. 'Somebody Up There Must Like Me.' It couldn't be a coincidence. The song had haunted him all his life, since the first time he heard it as interference over police radio. His body moved on automatic pilot as his brain was fully occupied with trying to find a line between what was happening now, and the Brunkeberg Tunnel.

*

Tommy's love affair with police radio began when he was seventeen. He'd already started writing, sold a couple of articles to a local newspaper, and was the editor of the school journal. He secretly bought the magazine *FIB-aktuellt*, because it contained the toughest crime reports. The naked girls didn't appeal to him at all, and maybe that was when he realised he wasn't interested in sex. Bare skin, tits, bums—so what?

In May 1975 the magazine ran an article about crime reporters and police radio. Most had it on all the time, subconsciously filtering the stream of information and suddenly paying attention when something useful came along. If you wanted to be on the spot at the critical moment, then the radio was indispensable.

Via a schoolfriend who was an amateur radio ham, Tommy managed to get hold of a second-hand Handic 007 FM-scanner, with the accompanying crystals, aerial and amplifier. He would never forget finding the right frequency for the first time, the excitement of sitting in his bedroom listening to authentic calls about things that were happening *right now.*

His excitement soon turned to frustration. He knew the police used number codes to refer to different types of crime and other incidents, but he hadn't grasped the extent of these codes. He could work out which car was going where, but what was 'a twelve' or 'a possible thirty-one'?

Tommy plucked up courage, called *FIB-aktuellt* and asked to speak to Billy Dahl, the writer he liked most. He was in luck. Billy was at his desk for once, and able to take his call.

'Billy Dahl.'

He sounded every bit as impatient and harassed as Tommy had expected, but Tommy took a deep breath and said: 'Good morning, sorry to bother you, my name is Tommy Torstensson and I'm a great admirer of your articles.'

'Yes?'

'Erm, I'm doing some writing too, or at least I'm trying to, and… I've got myself a police radio.'

'And?'

Tommy's palms grew sweaty, and his tongue was sticking to the roof of his mouth. He'd never felt so crushed. The only thing that stopped him from putting the phone down was the knowledge that he'd never become a journalist if he gave up as soon as he met an obstacle. He took a deep breath and said: 'I want the codes.'

'What?'

'The police call codes.'

There was a brief silence and Tommy waited for the click as Billy hung up. Instead he heard a burst of laughter. He was glad Billy couldn't see him, as his cheeks flushed bright red like hotplates. The laughter changed to a cough, and Billy spluttered: 'You want the codes. How old are you?'

'Seventeen. But I've already written several articles.' Tommy couldn't help adding: 'I want to be like you.'

Billy cleared his throat. 'I don't think you should do that, Tommy Torstensson. Have you managed to tune into the right frequency?'

'Yes, but I don't understand what they're saying.'

'You do realise this is illegal if you're planning to distribute the information?'

'Yes.'

'Yes. So you're asking me to collaborate in a crime you're planning to commit.'

Tommy hadn't seen it that way, but of course what Billy said was true. His courage almost failed him, but he kept his voice steady. 'That's right.'

Another silence. 'Have you got a pen and paper?'

Tommy would never understand why Billy Dahl spent five minutes of his valuable time reeling off the forty most important codes, which he naturally knew by heart. Tommy scribbled away until he had two A4 pages filled with numbers and corresponding violations, and cramp in his hand.

'Then there's a whole load of crap you don't need to bother about—mostly traffic-related.'

'Okay. Thank you. Thank you very much.'

'Hmm. And listen—if you get anywhere with all this...'

'Yes?'

'Use the by-line Tommy T. It has more of an edge. Good luck.'

Tommy put down the phone and stared at his notes. He was so happy he felt like screaming. Not only had he got the codes, he'd got them from *Billy Dahl*. Billy Dahl had said his name, Billy Dahl had spoken to him for ages. Spoken to *him*. Tommy T.

When he sat down at the radio with the pieces of paper in front of him, it was as if the world opened up to him. Cars were being stolen, people were fighting, stores were being robbed, children went missing and were found. There were domestic incidents in apartments, criminal damage was done. Tommy learned half the codes on that first day, and ten more the next. The more unusual ones, like 39, *violence against a police officer* and 40, *armed perpetrator, approach with caution*, took a little longer.

*

He had the police radio to thank for his first scoop. After a week of intensive listening in the afternoons and evenings, he had adopted the professionals' approach and simply left the radio on while he was doing his homework, reading or chatting to friends on the phone.

His mother and father tolerated it as they tolerated most things that stemmed from a genuine interest. Betty liked to sit in his room and listen. Sometimes she would ask: 'What are they doing now? What's happened?' She was twelve years old and thought her big brother was wonderful. Tommy put up with her.

It was three weeks after he'd been given the codes. Tommy was at his desk studying for a physics exam and listening with half an ear. The evening had been quiet so far; the most exciting incident was a confused old man who'd wandered off and been found in a playground.

Tommy was trying to learn the formulae for electrical conductivity when he picked up a call. A possible 31, a break-in, was in progress at Carl Larssons Väg 42 in Södra Ängby, patrol car to attend. Tommy actually lived at Carl Larssons Väg 28; number 42 was less than a hundred metres away. He grabbed the bag containing his notepad and camera, which was always at the ready, and took off.

As he ran down the street he dug out the camera and looped it over his shoulder, ready to shoot. Which was lucky—just as he reached the house the garden gate flew open and a man fled. Tommy fired off a series of shots. Only when the man was so far away that there was no point in trying to take any more pictures did Tommy realise what he'd had under his arm. Tommy had thought it was a bag of stolen goods, but in fact it was a dog. He walked over to the gate and heard the sound of crying. He knew exactly what Billy Dahl would do. He stepped into the garden without waiting for an invitation.

A woman in her fifties was standing halfway between the house and the gate, wringing her hands. Tommy took a quick snap before asking: 'What's happened?'

The woman looked up at him, her eyes red and swollen with weeping. 'Sture took Bibi.'

'I gather Bibi's the dog—but who's Sture?'

'My husband. My ex-husband. When I got home I saw that the

lights were on even thought I knew I hadn't left them on and I could see there was someone in the house so I went to the phone box and called the police then I came back and he ran out and he hasn't even taken her lead and she hasn't had anything to eat today and she always sleeps at my feet...' The woman stopped, her mouth opening and closing like a fish on land, then she asked: 'Who are you?'

'Tommy T. I'm a journalist.'

The woman pointed in the direction of Tommy's house. 'Don't you live over there?'

'That's right.' Before she could come up with any more objections, Tommy took advantage of her distressed state to plough on. 'I'm so sorry—how come he's taken Bibi?'

A police car arrived three minutes later, but during that time Tommy had learnt that it was all down to a toxic divorce. Custody of the dog had never been clearly spelled out, and now the ex-husband had taken matters into his own hands. Tommy made a note of that phrase: *Taken matters into his own hands.*

When the police asked Tommy who he was, he said he was just a concerned neighbour. Then he went home to write.

*

Tommy realised what he'd witnessed wasn't suitable for a heavy article, but sometimes *FIB* published lighter pieces—idiots trying to rob a bank with a screwdriver, someone who'd smuggled a rattlesnake into the country in a cello case. The dognapping would be good to practise on.

He spent all evening writing, and the next morning he handed in the film for quick development. He continued to work on the text, making sure to include details like the dog always sleeping at the woman's feet, her despair as she stood there wringing her hands, clutching Bibi's lead. A *red* lead.

The photographs came out really well. The man sneaking out of the gate with the dog tucked under his arm looked like a classic villain from a comic movie, and fitted perfectly with the tone of the article. The picture of the woman wasn't so good, plus of course she wasn't holding the red lead that Tommy had made up.

To cut a long story short, he contacted Billy Dahl again, went into the magazine's editorial office and handed everything over. They decided to publish, and paid Tommy a fee of three hundred kronor. The comical impression of the dognapper was heightened by the fact that they put a black strip across his face.

*

Tommy carried on listening to the police radio that had given him a way into the industry. After a few years he upgraded to a better model with a wider range.

The first interference occurred on February 28 1986 at 23:25. At that time Tommy was freelancing for several publications, and was earning enough to rent a two-room apartment on Birger Jarlsgatan. He was on his feet as soon as the first call came: a shooting at the junction of Tunnelgatan and Sveavägen.

He turned up the volume and pulled on his jacket, grabbed his bag. A second call indicated that a murder had taken place, and Tommy's pulse quickened. He had the chance to be the first journalist on the scene, and murder was the cream of the crop. He was on his way out of the door when a loud crackling, like a broadcast from far, far away, drowned out the police voices.

Somebody up there must like me.
Somebody who gives me all I have.
Why...

The interference disappeared and Tommy had no more time to wonder about it, because an agitated voice yelled: 'It's the Prime Minister!' Tommy ran.

*

The next occasion was June 23 1991 at 23:03. Tommy now had a contract with the newspaper *Stockholmsnytt*; he did a few jobs on the side and had been able to buy a three-room apartment. The call was a code 20, assault / violence. Tommy had no intention of following it up, but then he heard the location: the junction of Tunnelgatan and Sveavägen. As he gathered up his things, the interference came again.

Life's been good to me
I've been given so much
I can hardly remember going without anything…

The first time it happened, Tommy had found out that it was Jan Sparring singing a song written by Peter Himmelstrand. When he spoke to police officers who'd been out that night, all but one had shaken their heads. The patrol that was first on the scene had experienced a brief interference from the song, but that was nothing to worry about, was it?

When Tommy had told Peter Himmelstrand himself at the Publicists' Club, Peter had merely coughed his smoker's cough and said that Jan Sparring, being a religious nut, had wanted to change the lyric to '*He* who's up there must like me,' but Peter had flatly refused. *Somebody* or nothing. That was all he had to say on the matter.

The assault in itself was nothing unusual. A gang of skinheads had attacked some poor guy from the Lebanon with such violence that his skull had almost been fractured when they banged it up and down on the memorial plaque to Olof Palme. Tommy couldn't afford to be sentimental. The location made it a saleable article.

*

The last occasion was May 19 2009 at 22:34. Almost all police calls were now sent out via the digital system known as Rakel, and police radio was no more than a memory. Tommy's star was fading, and he was about to move from Birger Jarlsgatan to Margretelundvägen. He left the radio on for old times' sake, even though there was only the odd call from cars that hadn't switched over yet. When the interference came there wasn't even a call; it just came through the rushing sound of the static.

Why are things so good for me?

How little we understand...

Tommy wasn't doing anything special, so he decided to take Hagge for a stroll, see if anything was going on. As soon as he stepped out onto the street he saw the blue lights of a patrol car parked on Tunnelgatan. As he got closer he saw a woman with a little girl in a stroller walking away from a police officer she'd obviously been talking to.

The woman was strikingly beautiful, but there was something hard and determined about her expression. Tommy thought she was married to a reasonably well-known footballer. The child was a pretty little thing, but her eyes were empty. Tommy knew the officer who'd taken the report and was now putting away his notepad.

'Hi Micke—what was all that about?'

'Nothing for you to write about.'

'No, no, I promise. I'm just curious.'

Micke scratched his chin with a ballpoint pen. 'It's all a bit weird. First she loses the kid and goes crazy, then she finds her locked inside the Brunkeberg Tunnel.'

'Had she left the kid in there?'

'It's not impossible, but she claims otherwise. And why would she leave her daughter, then have hysterics?'

'People have done stranger things. By the way, have you ever heard a song called "Somebody Up There Must Like Me"?'

'No—is it new?'

'It's old. Very old.'

*

Anita's three-room apartment on the ground floor of a three-storey block from the 1950s in Bergshamra was simply and tastefully decorated, always clean and tidy, the walls impregnated with the smell of candle wax. No one could have guessed her profession from this environment. Tommy's right shoulder was aching from the bowling, so after he'd taken off his coat and shoes, he sat down on Anita's bed, intending to ask her for a massage. He noticed a couple of things that provided clues to her job.

The contours of a body were just visible on the satin sheet, and on the bedside table was a roll of kitchen paper and a pair of thin gloves. Clearly Anita had had a visit from a client with the preference Johnny Bode sang about: *Jerk me off with a pair of white gloves on*. Tommy wasn't what you'd call kinky, but there was something about sitting in the space recently vacated by 'Uncle Sven', as Anita referred to him.

He went into the living room and sat down on one of the two white leather armchairs flanking a glass coffee table with three lit chunky candles. When it came to interior design, Anita's taste was similar to Semtex-Janne's, but the things that looked out of place in his storage depot were a lot more appealing here. She came and sat in the other armchair and rested her chin on her hand.

Through his job Tommy had met a great many female prostitutes and a few males, either to write about them or to fish for information. Certain clients could become talkative once they'd ejaculated, and would talk about matters they wouldn't normally reveal. He knew several women in their thirties who looked older than Anita at fifty-two. She had a clarity in her gaze that her colleagues usually lacked. This was partly down to her character, but it was mainly because she'd been clean for years. Nothing extinguished the light in a person's eyes quicker than a heroin addiction.

'How was your day, darling?'

This was a game they played, pretending to be an old married couple with a great fondness for each other. Anita's role-play wasn't all that convincing and her tone was a little too sharp, but she insisted she enjoyed it, so they kept doing it.

'Well, sweetheart, it feels as if I'm putting together three jigsaw puzzles at the same time, and I haven't a clue which pieces belong to which puzzle.'

'Do you want to talk about it?'

'Have you got any whisky?'

Anita raised her eyebrows, which were plucked and redrawn in the style of Marlene Dietrich. Asking her if she had any whisky was like asking Fidel Castro if he had a beard. Tommy scratched the back of his neck. 'Okay, okay, stupid question. Macallan. Seven years old.'

Anita got up and opened the cocktail cabinet. The light came on, illuminating shelf after shelf of whiskies, starting with Famous Grouse and ending with bottles that were more of an investment. The finest were worth around twenty thousand kronor.

'Macallan,' she said with a sigh as she poured a generous measure. 'Would you like *ice*?'

'No, that's fine.' Anita handed over the glass as if it were a bag of dog shit, then poured herself a smaller measure of a brand with a name only a native Scot could pronounce.

The flickering flames turned the liquid in Tommy's glass to gold. 'So why do you keep this if you dislike it so much?'

Anita sat down. 'For people like you.'

'There isn't anyone else like me, is there?'

'No, there isn't, my darling. Now let's hear it.'

Tommy told her. Everything. The wave of suicides, Hans-Åke, Janne, Chivo. The Snapchat messages he'd received and what Mehdi had told him, plus 'Somebody Up There Must Like Me' and its spread through the suburbs.

'The Jan Sparring song? The one you heard on the police radio?'

'Yes. And now we come to the final chapter—so far. Three years ago when I was on holiday, a body was found in the Brunkeberg Tunnel—a retired cop who'd been tortured then hung in chains from a ventilation grille.'

'I remember that,' Anita said slowly. 'Wasn't it something to do with the Colombians?'

'That's what people thought—because of the tie. But it was never confirmed.'

'The tie?'

'He didn't die from the torture. He died because they slit his throat then pulled his tongue out through the hole. It's called a Colombian tie. But then you have to ask yourself what a retired Swedish cop could have done to annoy the Colombian mafia, if that's who it was, to such an extent that they do their very worst? And in Sweden! It's not unheard of, but it's very, very rare.'

'Aren't you scared?'

'That incident doesn't necessarily have anything to do with what I'm working on now.'

'But you think it might.'

'I do. So yes, I am scared.'

'So why keep going?'

The eternal question. Why keep digging, putting his life in danger, when the only outcome was a few articles? Tommy didn't have a good answer, so instead he asked: 'Why do you keep seeing Uncle Sven? You don't need the money.'

'What else would I do? That's what I'm good at—fucking, blow jobs, hand jobs.'

Tommy wished he hadn't asked. As soon as Anita felt under pressure she became bitter and crude in order to silence whoever was attacking her. Somewhere inside Tommy there was a prim little miss who didn't like to hear Anita talking that way, but he simply said: 'So it's habit. Same for me.'

'Mmm. But Uncle Sven isn't going to pull my tongue out through my throat.' Anita got up to refill her glass. As she was passing Tommy she tweaked the tip of his nose. 'Did I detect a hint of jealousy there?'

Tommy twisted free, rubbed his nose and saw the image of those white gloves in his mind's eye. 'It can't be entirely pleasant.'

'*Entirely pleasant.*' Anita pulled a face as she mimicked his high-flown language. 'It's nothing. Like hammering in a nail or squeezing an orange. It's just something I do. And at least he's grateful. Is anyone grateful for what you do?'

'Good point.'

They sat opposite each other in silence, watching the candle flames as they sipped their whisky. Tommy didn't dare push it any further. After a while Anita tucked her legs under her body and fixed her gaze on him. 'Tommy?'

'Yes?'

'Don't you think we should...combine our fortunes?'

Tommy let out a snort. 'Wow—it's not every day you hear that expression. Even Tomás would...'

'Tommy—I'm serious.'

'Right. Okay. Sorry.' Tommy took a good swig of his whisky. The thought had occurred to him in the past, but now Anita had come straight out with it, his head was suddenly empty. All he could think of to say was: 'So what about Uncle Sven? And the others?'

Anita's expression darkened and she looked like a schoolteacher who was about to rap a particularly recalcitrant pupil over the knuckles with a ruler. 'I'd stop. Obviously.'

Without knowing why, Tommy felt he needed to play for time. 'And Hagge? You don't like him.'

'I never said I don't like him. I said I sometimes feel uncomfortable when he looks at me.'

'How can you like him if he makes you feel uncomfortable?'

'Tommy, you're a coward.'

Tommy swallowed. He did indeed feel like a coward right now, and as he was used to being pretty courageous the sensation was exhausting, as if he were running an internal marathon. *Combine our fortunes.* It wasn't exactly a proposal, more a practical suggestion that they should share things. Life, for example.

'I...' Tommy stared up at the ceiling, at Anita's little chandelier, which made him think about the cop hanging from the grille in the Brunkeberg Tunnel, which in turn gave him the argument that could buy him more thinking time. 'I don't want you to get dragged into what I'm involved in right now. It's too dangerous. Then...I'll definitely consider it.'

'But do you *want* to move in?'

'To be honest...the whole idea terrifies me.'

Anita's voice was far from steady as she said: 'Charming.'

Was he really doing this? Yes, he was. Tommy was astonished to see himself rise from his armchair and drop to his knees in front of Anita. He took her hand and kissed it, then said: 'Anita, my dear, dear friend. I think the world of you. I absolutely don't want to be without you. If we have to combine our fortunes in order to stay together, as far as you're concerned, then...that's what we'll do. Probably. I need to think. But the last think I want is to lose you.'

Anita gave him a sideways glance and said: 'Better.'

*

After Anita had changed the sheets they went to bed and spooned until she fell asleep. Tommy lay with her left breast cupped in his hand, feeling her heart beat against his fingertips. The words *I love you* had almost slipped out during his little monologue, but he was very much aware of the currency of those words. If they were used indiscriminately, then they lost their meaning. The biggest words of all must be saved until they were completely true, and that wasn't yet the case.

Or maybe it was. What did Tommy know about love? Very little. He'd devoted so much of his life to loving himself that the love between human beings was an abstract concept as far as he was concerned. Maybe what he felt for Anita was in fact love, and maybe he wouldn't know that until he actually uttered the words.

A candle on the bedside table cast the shadow of Tommy's head on the wall when he raised himself up on one elbow. He looked at Anita's back, where scars and burn marks formed a disconnected narrative of the life she'd once lived; he knew next to nothing about her past. He silently formed the words *I love you*. A shiver ran through his body and he listened to Anita's calm, steady breathing before he ventured a barely audible whisper: 'I love you.'

The shiver came again, a feeling in his chest and stomach like standing at the top of a mountain pass: the wonderful view, the

141

terrifying prospect of a fall. He rolled over onto his back and closed his eyes. *Yes. Maybe. Probably. Almost certainly.*

Sleep refused to come. After half an hour he got up and pulled on Anita's silk robe. On the way to the kitchen he switched on the light in the hallway and caught sight of his reflection. What he saw was Sweden's worst transvestite.

The frilled robe was too small for him, revealing his greying chest hairs and his belly. The beginnings of a double chin, bags under his eyes, the thinning fringe that needed cutting. The person in the mirror should be deeply grateful that a woman like Anita wanted anything to do with him.

He saw a closed door behind him. He turned and looked at it. An ordinary internal door in an ordinary apartment. The curious thing was that Anita's three-room apartment was really only two rooms for Tommy, because he'd never been into that third room and had no idea what was behind the door. When he'd asked, Anita had said it was *her* room and he wasn't allowed in.

He respected her integrity, and therefore he didn't even know if the door was locked, because he'd never tried it. Now he took a step towards it. If he was going to move in at some point, then surely he ought to have seen the whole place? What could Anita be so unwilling to share with him?

He reached out, then lowered his hand. It was Anita's choice. Betraying her trust—or rather breaking a taboo—wasn't the best way of starting a life together. A *possible* life together.

He sat down at the kitchen table and opened up Anita's laptop. For many people the computer was their secret room, but of course Anita's room was elsewhere. She'd given Tommy her password long ago: Vertigo58. Like Tommy she was a fan of Hitchcock films, and her favourite was *Vertigo* from 1958. He typed *brunkeberg tunnel police officer* into the search box on Google. The case had attracted so much media attention that all the top results contained the information Tommy was looking for.

The man who'd been found hanging in chains from meat hooks

inserted beneath his shoulder blades was called Svante Forsberg. Forty years' service. Tommy clicked on a photograph; he didn't look like a nice person. He had a hard, square face and cold, dark eyes. It was easier to imagine him as a perpetrator than as a victim of the torture, which had been exceptionally brutal. He had no fingers left, no eyes, no teeth, no sexual organs. It would have been impossible to identify the body if the police hadn't made the link with an abduction two days earlier.

Tommy glanced through an article that gave more details. The last time Forsberg had been seen before he turned up in the tunnel was at Saludden campsite outside Trosa. He been there in June and July in a silver-coloured caravan. The model was known as 'the Egg'. It wasn't clear how much time he'd spent living in the caravan, which had disappeared.

One day when Forsberg was leaving the campsite, a dark blue Volvo V70 pulled up beside him in the car park. According to witnesses, three men with a 'southern European appearance' jumped out and eventually managed to bundle him into the car, which later turned out to have been stolen in Södertälje.

According to the forensic pathologist, it was likely that the torture had gone on throughout the entire period between the abduction and the discovery of the body—forty hours or more. Traces of ephedrines that had been used to keep him alert while it was going on were found in Forsberg's blood. Tommy couldn't help shuddering.

Towards the end of the article the writer mentioned that it had been an unfortunate summer for Saludden campsite; there had been very few visitors when Forsberg was taken. A month earlier four caravans and their occupants had mysteriously disappeared from the site.

Tommy was about to search for more information about these missing caravans when a sound made him glance up. Anita was leaning on the doorframe without a stitch on, her long bleached-blonde hair falling over her shoulders. Discoloured patches on her arms bore witness to carelessly administered injections in the past.

She gazed at Tommy, sitting there in the glow of the computer screen wearing her robe, and said: 'Kinky. I'm just wondering what you're looking at.'

With the glow of the hallway light behind her, she was framed by the backlit down on her skin. Tommy closed the laptop and said: 'I love you.'

Linus

It took Linus five days to sell his hundred grams, even though he'd only knocked on a third of the doors. He hadn't reckoned with his customers' enthusiasm for the product. Almost everyone who made a purchase contacted him within a day or two, wanting more.

Göran, his very first customer, was so thrilled that after snorting two grams he immediately asked for another five. He was manic when Linus arrived, and Linus suggested he should maybe take it easy. Göran insisted that everything was under control, he was just going to let a couple of friends try out the goods. Linus didn't believe him.

When Alex called that evening, Linus had a hundred thousand kronor neatly rolled up in a plastic bag and hidden away in the box where he kept his old Lego bricks. He'd had to put in two thousand of his own money to cover the samples a few prospective customers had insisted on.

'Okay?' Alex asked.

'Okay—all done.'

'And the cash?'

'Sorted.'

'Good. How much do you know about cars?'

'A bit. Why?'

'Come down to the car park. Block three. Second floor. Bring the necessary.'

Before Linus had time to ask whether 'the necessary' meant money or tools, Alex was gone. To be on the safe side, Linus put the money in a sports bag along with a few basic car tools.

He wasn't wild about carrying so much money, so he slipped a hammer in his pocket with the shaft sticking up before he set off for car park three. His palms were sweating; his glance darted with ill-advised nervousness across his surroundings.

As he opened the door of the multistorey car park his paranoia ramped up. Too many movie scenes with the drugs, cash, car park combo. He kept his right hand behind his back, resting on the shaft of the hammer, and wished it was a gun.

When he reached the second floor and saw Alex waving, he almost broke into a run. However, he managed to control himself. Once he'd handed over the money he was safe: he wanted it to happen *right now*, before the sound of screeching tyres told him everything had gone to hell. Alex grinned as Linus came towards him, hips moving like a race walker.

'What the hell's wrong with you? Ants in your pants?'

'Uh,' Linus said. He wanted to add something cool, but nothing came to mind, so he said it again. 'Uh.'

'Very profound.' Linus held out the plastic bag. Alex looked away and said: 'In the boot, idiot.'

Linus almost apologised, then gritted his teeth and opened the boot. He lifted the covering on the spare tyre and pushed the bag into the space. Alex glanced at him and nodded. Linus hoped he would ask how things had gone so that he could tell Alex about his genius idea with the biscuits, but instead Alex said: 'Something wrong with the battery. It's not charging.'

'Sounds like the alternator.'

'Or the carbonator. Or the catamaran. Fuck knows. The battery isn't charging. I want it to charge. Okay?'

Only now did Linus take a closer look at the car, which was a 2008 or 2009 Ford Fiesta. Red, for fuck's sake. About as far from a gangster's wheels as you could get. Linus opened the bonnet and tried to loosen the connections with a spanner, but everything was covered in rust and impossible to shift. He sprayed on a generous amount of 5-56 and leaned on the windscreen while he waited for it to do its work.

'How did the meeting go?' he asked.

'What meeting?'

'With...him.'

Alex stared at him, and Linus made a huge effort not to look away. The fact that he was fixing Alex's car gave him a small advantage, so he held Alex's gaze for a little longer than he would normally have done. Alex's expression softened and he shook his head.

'Guess what? He's from here!'

'From Gårdsstugan?'

'Mmm. He was the one operating in the laundry—you remember.'

'When people disappeared?'

'That's right.'

When Linus started selling his medication, he'd heard a few stories about the business being run from the laundry ten years earlier. The firm did some of the laundry for Karolinska Hospital, and a contact on the inside smuggled out drugs that were due to be disposed of. They were hidden in sheets and towels, ready to be sold on.

The guy in charge had a horrible appearance, and anyone who got in his way simply vanished. He'd branched out and started dealing crap that couldn't possibly have come from the hospital. Chivo's star was beginning to rise at that time, and one day Laundry Boy vanished too. End of story. Until now.

Linus managed to loosen the alternator and lifted it gently, taking care not to damage the wires. The connections were rusty too; maybe that was the problem. He sprayed on a good dose of 5-56 and waited again.

'He disappeared too, didn't he?'

'Yes, but now he's back.'

'Where's he been?'

Alex snorted. 'He didn't exactly sit down and tell me his life story.'

Linus turned his attention back to the alternator. He unscrewed the connections, polished them up with an emery cloth until they shone like new, then reattached them. As he leaned in to replace the alternator, he casually asked: 'So what does he look like?'

'I don't know.'

'You don't know?'

'No. I don't know.'

Alex's tone made it clear that the discussion was over. Linus wondered how you could meet someone without finding out what they looked like. There were several possibilities, but maybe this was just Alex's way of saying he had no intention of telling Linus, because it was certainly valuable information. Linus straightened up. 'Okay, give it a try.'

Alex got into the driver's seat, started the engine, then looked at Linus and spread his hands wide.

'There's a light on the dash with a picture of a battery,' Linus said. 'Is it showing now?'

'No.'

'Was it showing before?'

'Yes.'

'Okay, good. That means it's working.'

Alex switched off the engine. When he got out of the car he was holding a package, which he dropped in Linus's bag. 'Same amount. You get thirty.'

'Thousand?'

'No, *hundred*, you idiot. Thirty *hundred*. That's what people say, isn't it?'

'So...you do mean thirty thousand?'

Linus hated to appear so unsure, but he needed things clearly spelt out so there wouldn't be any hassle. Then again, if there was hassle, what could he do? Alex looked at him as if he were five years old and said slowly: 'Yes, Linus. Thirty. Thousand. Kronor.'

'Nothing extra for the car?'

With the balance fractionally restored, Linus gathered up his tools and closed the bonnet. Should he try to tip the scales a little further by pointing out that you wouldn't see 50 Cent driving around in a red Ford Fiesta? He decided that would be tempting fate.

He picked up his bag, ready to leave and start dealing with renewed enthusiasm now he was getting a share of the profits. There was only one question he wanted to ask, even though he didn't know what the question meant.

'Did you get to...taste?'

Alex's reaction was unexpected. Linus had been afraid that he would get angry or wave him away, but instead his eyes widened and a blissful look came over his face, like someone remembering perfect sex or the best trip ever. He nodded towards Linus's bag and said: 'This crap we're dealing, Linus. It's nothing. *Nothing.*'

*

When Linus emerged from the car park with the coke in his bag, he felt less paranoid than when he'd gone in. Once he was outside, he could run. The bag wasn't heavy enough to slow him down significantly. As he headed for Kassandra's apartment, he thought about what Alex had told him. One detail was particularly intriguing: the fact that the top guy came from Gårdsstugan. It was possible to start in this dump and climb to the top of the coke tree.

The crap we're dealing, it's nothing.

Who the hell was this guy? He had top quality coke that he was selling for peanuts, and apparently he had something else that made it seem like nothing. Linus was on the fringes of a mystery, and that was both terrifying and exciting. It was something *different*.

He'd been walking along with his head down, and when he looked up he stiffened. There was a police car parked outside Kassandra's block. His thigh muscles twitched as his body got ready to run, but then he realised that the car was empty. No doubt the cops were upstairs hassling some poor bastard who'd hit his poor bastard wife.

The very thought that the uniforms could march into any apartment and do whatever they wanted lit a searing flame of hatred in Linus's breast. In spite of the fact that he was carrying a hundred grams of coke and ought to keep a low profile, he reached into his bag and took out a screwdriver. He walked slowly past the police car, making a deep scratch in the paintwork. The flame died down a little and no longer threatened to consume his heart. He put the screwdriver away and made for Kassandra's place.

*

She looked rough. Her hair, which was normally fluffed up like a pinkish-red lion's mane, was lank and greasy, and her eyeliner was smudged. She wasn't wearing any foundation, and even though she had only half as many zits as Linus, her skin was badly marked for a girl.

Linus closed the door behind him. He was about to make a cutting remark, but her eyes were so sad that he simply said: 'How are you?'

'I'm just so tired, Linus. So fucking tired.'

'Are you sick?'

'Of course I am. I've been sick all my life.'

Linus went over to the kitchenette, took out the coke and placed it on the table. The packaging was the same as before, several layers of plastic film tightly wrapped around the contents. Linus ran his finger over the surface. 'This time we make some money. Six hundred for you.'

'And twenty-four for you.'

'Yes.'

'Fine.'

In spite of Kassandra's general state, Linus was irritated by her lack of enthusiasm over the fact that their business was now launched. 'Is something wrong?'

'Only everything.'

'Has something happened?'

'Only nothing.'

Linus was keen to get on with dealing, but Kassandra had to do her bit first. The way she was behaving now, she wouldn't even be able to slit open the package. 'Are you working tomorrow?'

'Don't remind me.'

'Can't you just give up? I'll shift this lot in a few days, then there'll be more. You'll be earning four times as much for far less work.'

Kassandra shrugged. 'And?'

'What do you mean, *and*? We're talking about…quality of life here.'

Kassandra's smile was so sad it was closer to a grimace. 'There's a picture,' she said. 'Of clinical depression. It's like this. You're lying on a bed. On a table two metres away is a pill. If you take the pill, the depression will go away. But that means you have to get up from the bed. And walk over to the table. And you can't do it. It's not worth the trouble.' She poked at a dishcloth that should have been thrown away six months ago. 'So...quality of life? No.'

'Cool picture. Obviously you ought to get up and take the pill.'

'You don't understand, you really don't. You could tell me I'd earn ten times as much for working five minutes a day, but in order to do that, I need to *live*. And there's the problem.'

'Seriously—you're thinking of killing yourself? Forget it!'

Kassandra shook her head. 'Why don't you get it? Suicide is the same as that pill. Not. Worth. The. Trouble.'

'Jesus, listening to you is depressing me. Can't you...'

'What, Linus? *Pull myself together*? Certainly. Can't you *calm down*? We're both sick, Linus. Just in such different ways.'

'Are you taking your medication?'

'You've seen my box of meds. I'm on twelve pills a day. I'm a fucking walking pharmacy. Without those pills I wouldn't be standing here. I'd be lying on the bed, shaking. And for you of all people to ask if I'm taking my meds—it's a fucking joke.'

'Well, I'm a fun guy, you know that.'

'Yes, Linus. You're a fun guy. That's what I like about you. Now move so I can get started.'

She shuffled over to the table and began to set out her equipment. Linus had never seen her in such bad shape. In spite of the fact that he found her listlessness irritating, he couldn't help being moved by the bottomless sorrow in her eyes. He placed the palms of his hands on her spotty cheeks and kissed her equally spotty forehead.

'Does that make you feel anything? Anything at all?'

'No. But thanks anyway.'

*

Linus went down the stairs, his bag of tools clanking. His relationship with Kassandra was so horribly fractured. On the one hand he thought she was the ugliest, most difficult girl in the world, and the recollection that he'd slept with her almost made him feel sick. On the other hand she was his closest friend, and they were bound together by their situation. He wanted to help her get out of here, he wanted to give her a better life. *He* could walk over to the table and pick up that pill for her, even if he was barefoot and the floor was covered in broken glass.

He didn't understand how he could simultaneously feel like slapping her in the face and taking her in his arms to chase away her demons. There was always an underlying frustration when he was with Kassandra.

He pushed open the door and stepped outside. After only a couple of steps he heard a voice in the darkness: 'Could we have a look in your bag?'

Two police officers, a man and a woman, emerged from the shadows. The man had the usual cop-face: studied indifference. The woman was the same height as her colleague and presumably a dyke, judging by how butch she looked.

'No,' Linus said, and kept on walking.

The man grabbed his shoulder. Did they learn that grip in cop school? The grip Linus hated more than anything else in the world. Its purpose was to make him feel small, to convey *I can do whatever I like to you.*

The woman wrenched the bag from his hand. 'We asked nicely. But you didn't answer nicely.'

'There have been a number of break-ins,' said the man, who seemed slightly less of a dick, 'so anyone carrying a bag...Well, you understand.'

'Tools,' the woman said, showing her colleague the contents of the open bag. She turned to Linus, looking even more like a hard-faced dyke, and asked: 'How do you explain the fact that you're carrying these around?'

'A couple of spanners and a can of 5-56—just what you need for a break-in,' Linus said.

'I asked you a question.'

'And I gave you an answer that shows you're an idiot.'

The woman pushed her face close to Linus's. Her breath stank of rancid hamburgers.

'Oh, so you're one of those. A little tough guy.' She poked him in the chest with her index finger. 'Let's see what's in your pockets.'

The hand. The index finger. Enemy planes flying across the borders, invading the territory just because they're cold. Anti-aircraft fire. The planes exploding in balls of fire. Linus had to summon up every last shred of self-control to stop himself from doing something stupid as the man locked his arms and the woman rummaged in his pockets. Wallet, keys. She checked his ID, dangled the key ring. 'Keys to what?'

'Your arsehole.'

Linus felt the man twitch and knew he'd almost laughed, which made the woman even more furious. She was probably in love with him but had no chance because she was such an ugly dyke—and it hacked her off. She threw the keys into the bushes, held up the wallet and said: 'I think we'd better check you out.'

She led the way to the car, carrying Linus's bag, while the man followed with Linus. There was no real conviction in his grip now; this was her show. She'd just unlocked the door when she stopped dead, took a flashlight out of her belt and switched it on.

'What the fuck...! Look at this, Staffan.'

The deep scratch running the length of the car didn't exactly help matters. Staffan dragged Linus closer, his grip tightening once more. The woman looked at Linus, the bag, the car. Then she took out the screwdriver and shone the beam of her flashlight on it, examining the flakes of paint that had stuck to the tip.

'So, Linus. I'd say you're in quite a lot of trouble. Get him in the car.'

The man pushed Linus towards the back seat and did that thing Linus had never understood, placing his palm on top of Linus's head.

Presumably it was another demonstration of power, another grip. *I've got your head, your thoughts, you are mine.*

The man closed the door and got into the front seat. The woman sat beside Linus in the back and picked up a laptop. Her hands were shaking, her jaw line was set. If steam could have come out of her ears, it would have done. She started tapping away at the keys, then paused for a moment before slamming the computer shut. 'You know what? This is a fucking waste of time. I can't be bothered. We'll do it this way instead.'

Before Linus had the chance to defend himself, she delivered a rabbit punch to his kidneys. The pain paralysed the right-hand side of his body and made him double over. She seized his right wrist and bent his little finger back.

'Margot, for fuck's sake…'

'That's right, for fuck's sake,' Margot replied, bending his finger until it almost broke. 'They've got to fucking learn some time.' Linus took a deep breath, getting ready to yell, but Margot placed one hand at the back of his head and the other over his mouth. 'You say nothing, okay? It's your word against ours. You don't have a chance. Get it?'

Linus tried to bite her, but she removed her hand and smacked him across the ear. 'Get it?' A pulse of agonising pain shot from his little finger up to his shoulder, and tears sprang to his eyes.

'Margot, for fuck's sake,' Staffan said again, before getting out of the car. Linus gathered as much saliva as he could muster and spat at Margot's face. The anger in her eyes changed to uncontrollable rage, and anything could have happened if Staffan hadn't opened the door on Linus's side and pulled him out. Linus ended up on his back on the tarmac.

'I hate you!' he shouted. 'I know your fucking names! I'm going to kill you!'

The police car shot away. Linus's wallet lay on his chest, but they'd taken his bag and tools. As he dragged himself to his feet to search for his keys, he heard the sound of a nearby window being closed, then locked.

Are there eyes?
There are always eyes.

*

Linus found his keys and limped home. He'd banged his hip when he was dragged out of the car, and his little finger was smarting as if he'd held it in molten wax. Apart from that, he was very pleased.

He hadn't *bowed down*. Okay so there'd been a tear or two when Margot almost broke his finger, but it wasn't like boo-hoo crying, just sheer pain. She hadn't managed to take him down, not even a tiny bit, and he was the one who'd won. If there had been eyes and ears, he hoped that outcome would be reported to whoever was in charge.

And he'd been so lucky. If they'd stopped him when he was carrying the money, or—even worse—the goods, they wouldn't have been content with their mediaeval dispensation of justice. No, Linus would have been back in the system, and this time the punishment would have been a lot more serious than a spell in residential care. He smiled as he approached his own apartment. Okay, so he'd lost his tools, his hip was aching and his finger hurt like hell, but he still felt like a winner. Talk about looking on the bright side...

Maybe it was the adrenaline rush that had made him feel so positive, because by the time he stepped into the elevator, his mood began to deteriorate. In the mirror he saw the same spotty rat-face the police had seen, and thought they could treat like dirt. The hatred came rushing in.

Staffan and Margot. Staffan and Margot.

He placed them in the worst scenes from his downloaded horror films. Staffan got the needles in the eyes and the sawn-off foot from *Audition*, while Margot tried out for a number of roles, eventually finishing up in *Cannibal Holocaust*. Impaled on a wooden pole, in through her arse and out through her mouth. He left her hanging there.

When he opened the door, Hagge was looking at him with a

horrified expression, as if he could see inside Linus's head, where Margot was still twitching on her pole. He crouched down and held out his hands; Hagge shuffled forward and licked his little finger. Linus felt a brief burning sensation, then the pain eased.

What is it with that dog?

Voices from the living room. His mother and Tommy. The rustle of notes. No doubt Betty had gambled away the housekeeping in another bingo binge, and Uncle Tommy had stepped in. It had happened before. Linus straightened up and crept into his room.

*

One day when Linus was fifteen years old and hanging around Gårdsstugan, he spotted a decorator's van with the back door left ajar. Never one to miss an opportunity, he grabbed six rolls of wallpaper.

When he got home and opened up one of the rolls, he discovered that he was in luck. The wallpaper looked expensive—it was thick, covered in a dark red, velvety material shot through with gold thread. He and Matti spent half a day putting it up, and when it was done Matti put his hands on his hips and said: 'A real gypsy den.' Matti was proud of his Roma heritage, so Linus took it as a compliment. Kassandra thought it looked like a brothel.

Linus hadn't even told Kassandra what he himself saw. If the walls were the skin of the room, then the wallpaper meant that Linus was *inside* that skin, and the gold thread was the network of blood vessels. When he lay on his bed, he was enclosed in a cocoon of tissue. It was calming.

The room had two windows. One faced Norrtull, but from the bed only the sky was visible. The other was at the foot of the bed and was actually a poster of Mila Kunis. This window—or rather windows—comprised her left eye and her right eye. Wide-open and shimmering green, they were peepholes into an alien and beautiful world. Kassandra often teased him about the poster—*total teenage boy cliché*—but she just didn't get it.

It was all about the fact that Mila Kunis was one hundred per cent unattainable. She represented something from which a boy like Linus was totally excluded. For the time being. But he'd taken his first step towards the door. Soon he would take more. He would knock. And the door would open. He now realised that Mila's predecessor Harry Potter had served the same purpose: a window onto a different, magical world.

He lay down on his bed and linked his hands behind his head. He winced as the pain in his finger kicked in, and he placed his right hand on his chest instead. He needed to make plans. The most important question was how to take a step closer to the centre of the action.

Rockstar had passed on a couple of grams to Erik and Johan, his friends from the School of Economics, and they'd been as excited as everyone else who'd tried out Linus's goods. In two days a larger group was due to meet at the White Room; they wanted Linus to come along and 'spread a little happiness'.

It wasn't like a fishing expedition; the students could become regular customers. And yet he wasn't sure. He'd never been to a place like that, he didn't know the codes or the layout. Easy to go wrong, tread on someone's toes, get in the way of a hard blow to the back of the head.

Mila Kunis looked encouragingly at him. The White Room was a big step up for a kid who trailed up and down piss-reeking stairwells dealing the odd gram. He heard a knock on the door, then Uncle Tommy's voice: 'Can I come in?'

Linus banged his hand on the bedpost as he got up and couldn't stifle a gasp. He wasn't in the mood for an interrogation, but he unlocked the door anyway.

Unlike Betty, Tommy didn't scan the room before he sat down on the desk chair. Linus perched on the bed, making a huge effort not to show how much pain he was in. Tommy gazed at Mila Kunis and said: 'I might be thinking of...settling down.'

That was the last thing Linus had expected. 'You're getting *married*?'

'No, but I might be moving in with someone. Maybe.'

'With Anita? The one who used to be a whore?'

Tommy looked offended. 'Why do you say that?'

'Because it's a fact. Has Mum gambled the housekeeping away again?'

Tommy stared at him for a long time. A few years ago that look would have made Linus crumble, apologise, explain that his hand was really hurting, but not anymore. He wasn't that easy to break—he'd proved that today. When Tommy had finished staring, he took Linus by surprise yet again. Linus had expected Tommy to start nagging him about the coke, but instead he asked: 'Have you ever heard a song called "Somebody Up There Must Like Me?"'

'Not as far as I know. Why?'

'It goes like this…'

In spite of the pain in his hand, Linus had to smile when Tommy started humming a tune that sounded as if it came from the stone age. His uncle looked distinctly uncomfortable, sitting there with his hands clasped together.

'Never heard it,' Linus said. 'Is it some kind of old folks' favourite or what?'

For some reason the comment seemed to reassure Tommy. He pointed to Linus's swollen finger. 'What happened?'

'I fell.'

'You fell.'

'That's right. I fell.'

Even if Linus had thought that Tommy might be able to do something, it was still his word against the cops', so there was no point. Tommy raised his eyebrows. 'Is it broken?'

'No, just like sprained or something.'

Tommy dug into his pocket and brought out a blister pack of tablets. He pushed out two and placed them on the bedside table.

'What are those?'

'Codeine. For tonight.'

'Do you always walk around with a pack of codeine?'

'Yes. Just in case.'

Tommy got up and stroked Linus's hair. Linus let it happen because it felt nice, a brief pause, a softening among the hardness. 'Look after yourself, my favourite boy.'

'Mmm. Tommy?'

His uncle stopped halfway to the door, and it just happened. Linus's façade was cracked, and the words simply seeped out. 'The guy who's supplying. He's the one who used to operate from the laundry.'

'You mean the pill-pusher? But that was ten years ago.'

'I haven't said a word.'

'I understand. And I'm not going to ask how you found out, but please, please Linus...'

'I know. I know. I know.'

When Tommy had gone, Linus swallowed one of the codeine tablets, then curled up with his hands tucked between his thighs. The difference between a brother—a *player*—and an extra was that a brother was self-sufficient. He didn't need anyone's help or advice, didn't need to spill his guts to anyone or have a bit of a cry.

He hated to admit it, but he wasn't a brother yet. The business at the White Room was too big for him; he was better suited to the stairwells of Gårdsstugan. He ignored Mila Kunis's reproachful gaze and allowed himself to sink into a fog of codeine. In a way it felt good to know his place. He closed his eyes, and the song Uncle Tommy had mentioned came into his mind. He began to hum.

Tommy

After saying goodbye to Linus, Tommy took the elevator down to the ground floor then strolled over to the former laundry, with Hagge trailing along behind him. It was after ten o'clock, with that particular suburban darkness that comes from a combination of tower blocks, tired shrubbery and broken streetlights. A darkness that has room for most things, as long as they're neither elegant nor expensive.

A cement staircase led down to the basement, which now housed the Las Palmas solarium—a Canary Islands tan for a fraction of the price, and no hassle with luggage. Tommy peered in through the barred window; he could just make out a reception desk and a curtained-off changing room.

He hadn't found out about the pill-pusher in the laundry until the business had been shut down and the person in question had disappeared. That was around the time when Ernesto got out of jail and found that Chivo had taken over. It wasn't impossible that there was a connection there.

The trail had been cold, nothing that might lead to an article, but Tommy had undertaken a little research anyway. He'd learnt that the laundry was used as a kind of testing ground to see if certain individuals were ready to work: rehab patients, psychiatric cases and chronic invalids. If they could cope with the laundry, then theoretically they were suitable for other jobs that then turned out to be non-existent.

Tommy heard footsteps approaching. He turned and saw a man of about his own age walking a lively dachshund pulling on its lead. As soon as the dog caught sight of Hagge, it made a beeline for him. Hagge was unimpressed by the short-legged creature.

When the light from the solarium sign fell on the man, Tommy saw that he wasn't in the best shape. Broken blood vessels covering his nose and cheeks suggested a fondness for alcohol; whether that was fine malt whisky or home-made wine in plastic bottles was a matter of conjecture. However, he had friendly eyes that seemed unscathed by the booze, and he nodded to Tommy as the dachshund sniffed at Hagge.

'Hi,' Tommy said. 'Do you happen to know when the laundry that used to be here closed down?'

'Let me think, it was…' The man's eyes widened and he took a couple of steps forward. 'Well, I'll be…Tommy T!' His attitude made Tommy think he wanted to get as close as the dachshund had to Hagge; fortunately social conventions constrained him.

'Is something going on, Tommy?' The man glanced around as if something might in fact be going on right now, then he looked back at Tommy with the expression Tommy knew so well. The expression of someone faced with a celebrity, an authority figure, a person in the know.

'Could be. Can you tell me anything about that business with the pills?'

The man nodded. 'Is there a connection with what you're writing about at the moment? This Equis?'

'No, no, this is a different matter. But it would be good to know.'

'He used to sell Rohypnol, Xanax, that kind of stuff. Subutex too.'

'Did you ever buy from him?'

The man didn't take offence—Tommy T was asking! There were some advantages to being famous. 'No—wet goods are more my style, if you get my drift.'

'Have you any idea what he looked like?'

The man moved a few inches closer, and Tommy was able to confirm that the wet goods in question smelled of whisky.

'That's an interesting question. No, I've no idea. And shall I tell you why?'

The dachshund had stopped sniffing at Hagge and was now pressed against his master's legs, head drooping. Hagge often had that effect on other dogs, as if his nonchalance made them realise the meaninglessness of a dog's existence.

Tommy let the man have his moment. 'Go on.'

'I saw him twice, and both times he was wearing one of those bala…bacla…what are they called? Like a ski mask where only the eyes are visible.'

'Why?'

'Apparently he was badly burnt or something like that. People said his face was scarred.'

'What happened to him?'

Another step forward—was the man really going to start sniffing him? The minimal airspace between them was filled with a miasma of whisky. 'Chivo,' he whispered. 'That's what they say, anyway. Chivo got rid of him. Brunnsviken.'

Tommy nodded and crouched down to pat Hagge, taking the opportunity to move away.

'Will I be in the newspaper?'

'I don't think so—this is just deep background. But thanks anyway.'

The man didn't seem too upset, and Tommy knew why. He had a story now—how he'd given Tommy T important information, chatted to Tommy T and his dog. Over time the story would probably grow, until eventually he'd helped Tommy shake the entire underworld to its foundations.

'Just one more thing,' Tommy added. 'Have you heard a song called "Somebody Up There Must Like Me"?'

'Jan Sparring? Sure. It's a while ago, though. And I'm afraid it's not really my kind of thing.'

*

Tommy was out of sorts when he got back to Margretelundsvägen. He fed Hagge, then mixed a whisky sour and sat down in the armchair. The only useful information he'd gathered all day had come from Linus. It seemed unlikely that a pill-popping former psych or rehab patient would have climbed to the top of the food chain, but that was what appeared to have happened.

Somebody up there must like me.

Definitely, if that were the case.

He took out his notepad and wrote down what he thought he knew so far, worked out a provisional timeline.

X turns up around 2000, dealing medication, upsets Chivo, disappears. Returns years later, imports a huge shipment of coke with the help of Janne. Makes sure that a large number of top players vanish or kill themselves apparently by talking to them. Communicates via Snapchat.

The campsite? Ernesto? The cop in the tunnel?

He checked the time; just past eleven. He called Don Juan Johansson.

'Yes, Tommy?'

'Good evening to you, Henry.'

'Cut to the chase.'

As so often when he contacted Henry in the evening, he could hear music and voices in the background. This time, however, it wasn't familiar old favourites, but some modern racket. A heavy bass line and tortured synth strands that made him think of smoke, strobe lights and headaches.

'I need your help. What do you know about Svante Forsberg?'

'The cop in the tunnel? I never met him, but of course there was a lot of talk when it happened.'

'And?'

'A good guy. Went in hard, but got things done. A great loss to the police service when he retired.'

'Okay. And the unofficial version?'

'You're asking me to spread gossip about a conscientious police officer so that you can blacken his memory?'

Tommy was sick and tired of Henry's insistence on bigging up every little piece of information he gave out, but as was his habit, he merely said: 'Yes please.'

'Bastard.'

'In what way? Corrupt, or…?'

'No, just a bastard. The kind of guy you don't want to be around. The worst vibe you can imagine. Petty villains crapped themselves when he turned up, and some of his fellow cops were scared of him.'

'Any possibility he could have been involved in something major? The Colombian mafia, for example?'

'That was mentioned, of course, because of the tie. But nobody really believed it. What's this about, Tommy?'

'I promise I'll tell you more when I know more.'

'In that case I promise to tell you what I already know. Goodnight, Tommy.'

Before the connection was broken, Tommy heard a young woman's voice shouting over the music: 'Heenry! Boooring!' Where did he get the energy?

Tommy tapped the notepad with his pen. The next thread to follow was the guy in the laundry. How he'd ended up there, where he'd come from. Even if Tommy had lied to the man with the dog, it was a long shot. However, sometimes you could score a goal from a long shot, even if you weren't Zlatan.

When he lacked inspiration Tommy liked to watch a film he knew by heart so that his thoughts could run free as they associated with the images on screen. This evening he opted for *Vertigo*. He inserted the disk in the Blu-ray player and sank back in his armchair as the hypnotic opening titles whirled around, culminating in *Directed by Alfred Hitchcock*. He gave a contented grunt, as if a pleasant assumption had been confirmed.

It was over halfway through the film—Kim Novak had reappeared with a new hairstyle—when his phone rang. The display told him it was Anita. He picked up and said, 'Hi sweetheart.'

'Hi—what are you doing?'

Tommy held the phone towards the TV, where a section of Bernard Hermann's characteristic score was playing, and heard Anita laugh. When he brought the phone back to his ear, she said: 'How many times have you seen that film?'

'Thirty, maybe. You?'

'Enough to recognise the music. I have a question for you.' Tommy sat up straight. He still hadn't reached a decision about combining their fortunes, so he was relieved when Anita asked, 'What is it with Kim Novak? I mean, she's supposed to be so beautiful, but she looks like...'

As Anita searched for the right words, Tommy interjected: 'A glorified dental hygienist?' which made her guffaw. *Tommy T, always ready with a quip.*

'Thank you,' she said when she'd recovered. 'Best laugh of the day.'

She fell silent. Tommy watched as Kim Novak emerged from the bathroom, once again transformed into her previous self. The dental hygienist with bling. When she spoke again, Anita's voice was hesitant. 'What you said to me before. Those three words. Nobody's ever said that to me before. Not for real. There's just been a whole lot of fucking...'

Anita had clearly backed herself into a corner and now needed to fire off some foul-mouthed missile in order to rebalance, but Tommy got in first: 'I've never said those words to anyone before.'

There was a silence as Anita disengaged the missile. Eventually she said: 'That's a good combination.'

'It's a very good combination.'

Now it was Tommy's turn to say something, to tell her that he wanted to give her the gift of laughter every day instead of just now and again, that he wanted to say those words again. He couldn't do it. Fortunately Anita didn't push him; she simply said: 'Goodnight, my darling.'

'Goodnight, my sweetheart. Sleep well.'

*

Only when the film had finished, when the images had faded and the music had fallen silent, did Tommy realise that something had been nagging away at him, possibly inspired by Kim Novak, who changed her appearance and pretended to be two different people.

He went over to the computer and brought up the enlarged picture of the person who might possibly be Equis, reflected in the window of Hans-Åke's bedroom. The strange position of the ear, the rigidity of the mouth. As Tommy studied the figure with his new idea in mind, he became more and more convinced that the person was wearing a mask—an unusually lifelike kind, but definitely a mask.

He googled 'lifelike', 'rubber' 'silicone' and 'mask' and found several companies that manufactured exactly what he was looking for. The most exclusive, which was based in Los Angeles and also worked for Hollywood, was called Realflesh. A series of short videos showed some of the masks they supplied.

The cost was between eight hundred and a thousand dollars, and they were horribly realistic. In a couple of the videos Tommy would never have guessed that the person was wearing a mask, and the reveal was very unpleasant. Tommy compared the Snapchat picture with the thirty-three models advertised by Realflesh, but couldn't find the right one.

If he was correct, then this explained what Chivo's gorilla had said: *Everyone says different faces.* Maybe Equis had a stock of masks and could change his appearance at will. And what had the man with the dog said? *one of those bala…bacla…what are they called? Like a ski mask…*

If the guy in the laundry was the same as the guy in the Snapchat picture, then he'd improved the way he hid his disfigured face. Tommy drummed his fingers on the desk. The inspiration was there now, his synapses working like eager spiders, casting threads between disparate phenomena.

Mask. Balaclava. Colombia. The Revolutionary Armed Forces of Colombia (FARC). Cocaine. Suicide.

It was worth a shot. Tommy entered the search words in various combinations without getting a useful hit. He tried again in English, with the same disappointing result. Lots about FARC's smuggling methods, the balaclavas they wore, their recruitment procedures and the suicide of one of their leaders.

Tommy's high-school Spanish, enhanced by a couple of adult education courses, wasn't the best, but he decided to give it one more try: *suicido, cocaina, farc*. He found an article in the Medellín-based newspaper *El Colombiano* about a number of suicides in the upper echelons of a cocaine-smuggling family organisation that had been in competition with FARC.

The piece was dated November 2008, and as Tommy skimmed through it he felt his pulse begin to quicken. He found an online dictionary and looked up the words he didn't know; there were quite a lot of them. His ignorance of the grammar was also an obstacle, but after a while he thought he'd grasped most of the content.

The organisation that had lost six of its top players to suicide had been in conflict with FARC over an area in the jungle where two big cocaine producers were operating. There had been a number of skirmishes during the past twelve months, and several people had been killed.

Nothing out of the ordinary there, but then came these inexplicable suicides. There was no indication that the individuals concerned had been forced to take their own lives, but their deaths had caused the organisation to collapse, leaving the field wide open for FARC. And what really made Tommy's heart race: the suicides were related to someone known as *el diablo rubio*, the blond devil. He had met some if not all of the victims before their demise.

The newspaper had even published a picture of the person who was thought to be the blond devil. He could be seen in a grainy black and white photograph along with three others, all wearing balaclavas. They were standing in front of a wall of jungle vegetation holding their guns up in the air.

Tommy zoomed in and stopped breathing. The picture was too pixelated to reveal anything about the blond devil's face, but the hand clutching the gun was concealed by a glove, the grip awkward as if the fingers were deformed.

He brought up the Snapchat picture and placed it next to the image from the jungle. The awkward grip on the mobile phone, the awkward grip on the gun. Tommy was pretty sure it was the same person.

He shut down the computer and sat for a while with his head in his hands as his pulse returned to normal. He really, really needed to talk to Ernesto now.

Linus

Running on the roof was more of a relaxation exercise than real training. The area measured a hundred and fifty metres by twelve, so each lap was around three hundred and ten metres, since Linus couldn't run right along the edges. He'd completed ten circuits and was intending to do ten more. His finger was still aching, but that didn't affect his ability to run. His feet, encased in his Asics, flew over the concrete. He was on his way into the state where his conscious thoughts were replaced by something closer to sleep.

Kassandra was sitting on her sun lounger wrapped in a blanket, listening to Antony and the Johnsons through a Bluetooth speaker. Every time Linus passed her she shouted out a brief, obscene chant. She'd come out of her depression and was now in a mildly manic phase. She'd spent all day cleaning her apartment, and had decided to relax for a while.

It was late afternoon, and the first stars were twinkling in the sky above Gårdsstugan. Beneath Linus's feet were eight of his customers in their apartments, one or two of them probably high on his latest delivery. He'd shifted half of the hundred grams in two days, and in spite of his previous doubts he'd decided to try his luck at the White Room later.

Those who do not grow are dying—who'd said that? If he simply stood on one spot marking time, or rather stuck with the fifteen customers he'd acquired so far, he'd be like Kassandra's cockroach—which was still alive—and slowly suffocate. Or be outmanoeuvred by some newcomer with bigger balls.

Growing meant expanding, and if he could get a foot in the doors near Stureplan, then the sky was the limit. Linus looked up at the stars, floated up from the cracked concrete roof and made the Milky Way his new round.

He passed Kassandra, whose latest chant brought him back from space and made him aware of a vibration by his hip. He took out his phone and kept running. One of the disadvantages of dealing was that you had to be available, preferably 24/7. The display showed *Yeti*, his code name for Alex. The Abominable Snowman. Linus stopped.

'Yes?'

He took a few rapid breaths to oxygenate his blood; he didn't want to pant while he was talking.

'You sound weird—having a lie down with the girlfriend are we?'

'No. Running.'

The sound on the other end of the line was tinny, as if Alex was using the loudspeaker function. Linus thought he could hear another voice in the room.

'Listen, a mate of mine's having problems with his car. The brakes have locked, so he's got some new...what are they called...'

'Brake pads.'

'That's it. He just needs someone to fit them.'

'Okay, no problem. Seven hundred.'

'What?'

'I want seven hundred for the job. That's half of what a garage would charge.'

'Okay, fine. As long as you don't want it up your arse in kind.'

'Up your arse, in that case.'

'What did you say, Linus?'

Linus took a deep breath and said in a clear, firm voice: 'I said it might be worth seven hundred to see you get it up the arse.'

'Ha. Ha. Let's just take it easy here.'

'I'm a good worker. You don't need to put me down. Stop doing it. If you want to give me another hundred grams, that's fine. I can shift it in a couple of days.'

Muted voices, then Alex came back on the line: 'I'm told you're funny, Linus. That's lucky for you.'

'Who says I'm funny?'

'Car park, half an hour.'

When Linus turned around he saw that Kassandra was standing

just a couple of metres away, staring at him with a mixture of horror, disbelief and admiration.

'Was that Alex?'

'Yes.'

Kassandra shook her head. 'Do you know what you're doing?'

Linus slipped the phone in his pocket and carried on running. He had no chance of achieving the desired dreamlike state now; he had too much to think about. A new balancing act, new opportunities. By standing up to Alex when others were listening, he'd grown quite a lot. Plus he was upping his game by going to the White Room tonight. All he needed now was a couple of employees as well as Kassandra, and he was on his way to becoming a player. There were no clear boundaries, but when you got there you just *knew*.

And he *knew*. That he was on the way. Those who do not grow are dying, and he felt as alive as he could possibly be. He ran on, aiming a couple of jabs at the stars.

I'm coming, just you wait and see.

*

When Linus arrived in the car park after going home to collect the tools he'd stolen from Biltema the previous day, Alex was waiting next to a rusty Mercedes with a guy Linus had never seen before. He was about the same age as Alex, in his early twenties, with sharp, pock-marked features and deep-set, miserable eyes. Nike trackers and a hoodie a size too small, emphasising his muscles. Cropped hair. Alex introduced him as Sergei.

'Russia?' Linus asked.

Sergei pulled a face. 'Ukraine.'

Linus didn't bother with the news, but he was aware of some kind of dispute between Russia and Ukraine. He refrained from further comment and turned his attention to the car. Fifteen years ago it had been a luxury vehicle, but it hadn't been looked after, and now it was a wreck, covered in rusty patches and dents that had been 'fixed' by someone clueless. Linus raised an eyebrow and said: 'A bit more gangster than Alex's wheels.'

Sergei smiled, revealing teeth that were in the same state as his car. 'Fiesta Man.'

Linus glanced at Alex, who met his gaze with half-closed eyes and an expression that said: *I know what you're doing. Be very, very careful,* which Linus had every intention of doing. He'd marked his territory, and that was enough.

When he'd jacked up the car and removed the wheel, he asked Sergei: 'Are you in the same business?'

Sergei nodded. 'Täby.'

'Täby? Isn't that just smart houses and directors and all that kind of crap?'

'No.'

Sergei made Linus feel uncomfortable. Couldn't he manage an actual sentence? His accent was very strong, so maybe it was a strategy to hide his lack of linguistic expertise. Or maybe he was just a cold bastard.

'Grindtorp. Storstugan. Same as this shithole,' Alex informed him.

'So it's a good market?' Linus asked as he unscrewed the old brake pad, which was completely worn down. Without a shred of enthusiasm, Sergei replied: 'Fantastic.'

Obviously Sergei wasn't the sociable type, so Linus worked on in silence, taking care not to hurt his finger. When he'd almost finished the second wheel he decided to ask one more question: 'So how do you two know each other?'

'Work,' Sergei said as if it were self-evident, as if he and Alex worked in the same office and were in the habit of chatting by the coffee machine.

As Linus was tightening the last wheel nut, something really weird happened. Sergei started humming a tune, and after a few seconds Alex joined in. Linus recognised the song Uncle Tommy had asked him about; it had stuck in his mind for some reason. Somebody somewhere likes me. He lowered the jack, removed it and got to his feet.

'What was the name of that song again?' he asked. Alex and Sergei stopped humming. Presumably they hadn't realised they were doing it.

'No idea,' Alex said. 'Why?'

'So why were you humming it?'

'I just heard it somewhere.'

'From *him*?' Alex and Sergei exchanged a glance. When they didn't say anything, Linus refused to give up. 'Was *he* the one who thought I was funny?'

Alex placed a hand on Linus's shoulder and squeezed. 'Little Linus. Don't push your luck, okay? Otherwise it'll jump up and bite off your cock.' Alex pressed hard with his thumb, finding a nerve that sent a spasm through Linus's body.

Sergei had taken out a thick wad of notes. 'Seven?'

'Five,' Linus said. 'It was a straightforward job. Mates' rates.'

Sergei smiled, possibly at the ridiculous idea that he and Linus would ever be mates.

*

It was dark as Linus walked home, the shadows even deeper around the door of his apartment block, where the streetlight had been broken during his absence. For some reason he was on his guard. He took an LED torch out of his bag and shone the beam around him. He had five grams in his pocket, which increased his tendency to paranoia—the hand reaching out to snatch the coke. However, there was no sign of anyone. He opened the door.

The three figures waiting in the stairwell looked as if they came from the north side. One of them pointed a gun at Linus, who realised he was in serious trouble. The LED torch saved him. The man with the gun raised his free hand to shield his eyes from the sharp glare. He took a step towards Linus and said: '*Culo!*' Linus hurled the bag of tools at his head, hurled himself through the door and ran.

He was still wearing his running shoes, and immediately broke into a sprint. There was no chance that any of those three would be as fast as him, but they were armed, and he couldn't outrun a bullet. His only hope was that they wouldn't dare shoot with so many people around.

He was ten metres from the door when he heard it crash open. He crouched down as much as he could without losing pace and veered to the right. He heard running footsteps behind him, someone swearing in Spanish. Good. This was a race, not an exercise in shooting a moving target.

As he ran he tried to think through his options. Keep running. No, there were three of them and they'd be able to cut him off at some point. Plus they might decide to use the gun when they realised he was too fast. Kassandra? No, he was pretty sure they didn't know about her involvement, and even if he was well ahead at the moment, he didn't want to lead them to her. The multistorey car park? A good choice if Alex and Sergei were still there; if not, he would be trapped in an enclosed space.

Which left the simplest answer, every criminal's automatic reaction: to put as much distance as possible between himself and the pursuer. Find somewhere to hide, assess the situation. Linus leaned forward a fraction, engaged top gear and left Gårdsstugan, heading for Haga Park.

He didn't risk glancing back until he'd covered another hundred metres. One of his pursuers had given up; the other two were crossing the brightly lit car park.

His earlier run on the roof hadn't taxed Linus's resources. He could run all the way to the airport if necessary.

Jump on a jumbo jet, hang out in Bangkok.

He let out a strange sound, somewhere between a laugh and a sob. He had nothing left but his flight. There was no goal, he had nowhere to go. As long as he kept on running, he was safe.

Onto well-lit tracks through the park, through groves of trees where damp leaves stuck to the soles of his shoes, across wet lawns, shimmering like grey silk by the light of the half moon and the stars, all with one single purpose: distance. As much distance as possible. He didn't even know if they were still chasing him.

As he passed Gustav III's pavilion he slowed down and listened. He couldn't hear a thing, but he sped up anyway until he reached the Echo Temple. He sat down in its shadow with his back resting against a pillar, peering in the direction from which his pursuers would appear. After five minutes he allowed himself to relax.

He was in no doubt that it was Chivo's guys who were after him, because they knew about his business. If they caught up with him they'd put a stop to that business, one way or another. The stepladder up to the stars had been broken in two, and Linus's place now was underground, living or dead.

He let out a sob. He couldn't go home. Not ever. They'd be watching his door, waiting for him. And if he somehow managed to get home, he'd never be able to go out.

A cold wind sneaked in beneath his thin jacket, licked the sweat on his back and made him shiver. Two people came walking along the path from Haga Palace, and Linus shuffled behind the pillar. He started shaking—was it fear or cold? He peeped out and saw that the couple were holding hands, but he was still so paranoid that he stayed hidden until they were out of sight.

There was only one thing to do. With trembling hands Linus took out his mobile and scrolled down to Yeti. Alex answered on the third ring.

'Yes, little Linus?'

'They're after me. Chivo's guys. They were waiting for me in the stairwell, but I managed to get away.'

Judging by the noises on the other end of the line, Alex was in a car—maybe Sergei's Mercedes.

'Okay—what do you need?'

'Fuck knows. Help of some sort.'

'You need help now?'

Linus's head drooped. It was unfortunate that he'd chosen this particular day to mark his territory as far as Alex was concerned. All he could do was back-pedal and completely abase himself.

'Yes, Alex, I need help. Please help me, Alex. I don't know what to do.'

'Hold on.'

Linus heard muted voices; he couldn't work out what they were saying, but it sounded like Alex and two other people. Alex came back: 'Where are you now?'

'At the Echo Temple in Haga Park.'

'Okay, we'll be there in ten.'

Linus was so relieved that all he could do was let out a long sigh. He thought Alex had ended the call, but he was wrong. 'What did you say, Linus?'

'Thank you. Thank you, Alex.'

*

After ten minutes Linus was shivering. He jogged on the spot, slapped his arms to keep warm. He would have preferred to run, but he didn't dare leave the temple in case he missed Alex, or Chivo's guys were still around.

After another ten minutes he sent a text: 'Where are you?' His teeth were chattering as he pressed Send. He clutched the phone, staring at the screen and jumping up and down as he waited for an answer. None came. Five minutes later, he called again. No reply. Ten signals rang out before he gave up. What the fuck had happened? Alex was available 24/7; he *always* picked up.

Had Chivo caught up with him too? Was this the night when the north side launched a concerted attack to wipe out the competition? Were all escape routes finally closed? Linus felt like crying. He shook his head and slipped his phone in his pocket.

There was one last chance: Uncle Tommy. It was a seriously bad idea, but it was all he had left. Tommy would never swallow some sob story about big boys being out to get Linus; he would have to tell him more or less everything, and that would be the end of his business.

Tommy would make sure of it.

Linus gave a start as his phone vibrated. He pulled it out and read the message. It wasn't from Alex, but from Tinnie, one of his customers. 'Three? Now?'

Three grams right away. Tinnie was one of his most enthusiastic clients and had already relieved him of six grams. The last time Linus had visited, he'd just sold his camera online to fund his habit and was on a slippery slope. He wouldn't last forever, but he clearly still had resources.

Ten minutes, Alex had said. That was now forty minutes ago. Linus tried calling again—no reply. He couldn't understand what had happened, but he had to consider other options. He put the idea of Uncle Tommy on ice for the moment. Tommy was his last resort.

He was on the run now, and the first thing you need when you're on the run is cash. All he had in his wallet was the five hundred he'd got from Sergei, and that was useless. He thought for a moment, then texted Tinnie with frozen fingers: 'Okay, but you need to take five.'

The reply came in seconds; the desire was clearly there. 'OK!' The idiot had even gone to the trouble of adding a manic smiley with its thumbs up.

Five thousand. That was something, at least. Linus was back at the airport, a last-minute ticket to anywhere. Hanging out in Bangkok, in cheap bungalows. In which case he would need a passport. He didn't have a passport, he'd never had any reason to acquire one. What about Europe? Greece—you didn't need a passport for Europe, did you?

Linus knew these were nothing but meaningless fantasies. He was freezing cold, and he was thinking about hot countries as a starving person thinks about food. He needed to get hold of those five thousand kronor, then he could plan the next step. But first he had to go back to Gårdsstugan.

*

Fortunately Tinnie lived in number eight, on the opposite side of the courtyard from Linus. As Linus made his way over there, he didn't care if he was behaving like a sparrow. His eyes were darting all over the place, scanning the area, his head twitching from side to side, backward and forward, his body ready to run at any second.

But there was no sign of any Latinos. He took a detour so that he skirted the perimeter of the playground hidden by the shrubbery, making sure he wouldn't be visible from the door of his own block. He reached number eight without any indication that he'd been seen.

There are always eyes.

Linus stiffened and glanced up at the block. Did Chivo have eyes on the south side too? Not impossible—highly likely, in fact. Maybe a pair of eyes was watching him right now behind one of those darkened windows, maybe a hand was picking up a phone right now.

Linus scurried over to the door. If there were goats' eyes here on the south side, then at least they couldn't see through walls. He pulled open the door and listened before stepping inside and switching on the light, his little bird's heart hammering away in his chest. No one. Nothing.

Goats' eyes.

He laughed then put a hand over his mouth, forcing himself to keep quiet. Tinnie lived on the third floor, and Linus crept up the stairs with his hand still covering his mouth. He crouched down as he passed the windows; no one must see where he was going.

He used to sneak around the stairwells like this when he was a kid, pretending to be a spy. The same movements, except that what had been a game back then was now deadly serious. He tried to tell himself that it was only pretend, that he was just playing, but it didn't work. He was so fucking scared.

He'd feel better once he was inside Tinnie's apartment. Maybe he could ask to stay the night? The scruffy living room suddenly seemed attractive. He rang the bell, still on the alert for the slightest sound from downstairs; could he hear footsteps approaching from outside? When Tinnie opened the door he slipped in without even saying hi.

'Shit,' Linus said as Tinnie locked the door. 'What a fucking night!'

'Sorry,' Tinnie said. 'I'm so sorry.'

Linus looked up. Tinnie's normally puffy right cheek was swollen, and the skin around his eye was discoloured. In a second Linus realised what was going on. He'd been so desperate that he'd missed an obvious risk.

One of the guys who'd been waiting for him earlier in the evening stepped out of the living room, and when Linus spun around to make his escape, he felt the barrel of a gun in his back.

'*Hola, coño,*' he heard. 'No more running.'

'You said…you said you'd never had any dealings with Chivo,' Linus whispered to Tinnie, who was standing there with his head down, constantly repeating: 'Sorry. I'm so sorry.'

That was the last thing Linus managed to say before he lost the ability to think. There was no way out of here. This was ground zero.

'There's someone who wants to meet you,' the voice behind him said. Linus didn't even understand what that meant; his brain had stopped working. Like some physical manifestation of his internal state, a hard object slammed into his temple and flung him into a red sea that became black before he hit the floor.

*

Linus was ripped out of unconsciousness by a wave of pain that coursed through his arching body. His eyes flew wide open and he found himself face to face with the person he'd pictured so often but never met.

Apart from the goatee beard, Chivo didn't bear much resemblance to a goat. His face was round with a low forehead, and his black hair was tied up in a ponytail that snaked around his neck and hung down over his chest. With some war paint he would have been the epitome of an Indian warrior from some old cowboy movie. Apart from the eyes. A movie Indian needs big, wise eyes. Chivo's were tiny, black and ice-cold.

Chivo removed the peeled electrical wires from Linus's knees, leaving behind small darkening wounds and the smell of burnt body hair. Linus was sitting naked in a chair, his hands tied behind his back and his ankles tightly bound. His belly was a porous sack filled with fluid, and when he tightened his anal sphincter to avoid soiling himself, a bolt of pain shot through his head, so powerful that it made him want to throw up. He gasped and took a deep breath. His head wanted to sink towards his chest, back down into the forgiving darkness.

'No, no,' Chivo said, applying the wires to his thighs. A burning shoal of sticklebacks raced through Linus's body, throwing him off the chair. He lost control of his muscles and warm, liquid excrement ran down his left leg. He was so scared that he twitched and whimpered uncontrollably, lying there on the concrete floor.

Chivo waved a hand in front of his nose and gestured to one of his men. Linus couldn't work out what was happening; it felt as if the guy was putting clothes on him—pants anyway. Was it over? So soon? Then he understood. He was now wearing an adult diaper.

'We'll be here for some time,' Chivo explained. 'We can't have you crapping all over the place.'

Linus was lifted back onto the chair. He couldn't help himself; the tears began to flow and he snivelled: 'Please, I'm only seventeen.'

Chivo grimaced. 'You might want to save that. Until you're hanging up there.' He jerked his head, and there it was. A large hook was screwed into the wall two metres off the ground. The hook. The floor beneath was stained with a range of bodily fluids.

Until now the danger in which Linus had put himself had been an abstract concept, a vague *I need to be really careful*. The hook and the discoloured floor were real danger and real horror gathered into one concrete point.

'Okay, so this is where we're at. I'm not intending to kill you. After a while on the hook you'll be begging me to do just that, but I'm not going to. So you don't need to worry about that. Mmm...'

Chivo placed his index finger on his lips as if he were considering the next point in his lecture, checking that he hadn't missed a key point before continuing: 'Then it's up to you how permanent your injuries will be. If you understand. Do you understand?'

Linus nodded. He understood. He'd understood perfectly in Tinnie's hallway, before his brain was short-circuited.

'Good. Then we'll start with a simple question. How many customers do you have?'

'Only a few.'

The wires were pushed into his thigh with such force that they pierced the skin. Linus's body went rigid, and this time he took the chair with him. His shoulder hit the unforgiving floor, and a different kind of pain ran down his arm. Chivo pushed the wires in again, and Linus scraped the skin of his knee as his leg scrabbled over the rough surface. There was a crackling sound inside his head as if his synapses really were short-circuiting. The chair was picked up, Linus was placed on it once more. Blood was trickling from his thighs. Chivo held up the wires.

'My friends here. Plus and Minus. They like honest, precise answers. So let's try that again.'

'Fifteen.'

'Fifteen. How did you find them?'

'I sold biscuits.'

Chivo began to lower the wires, and Linus yelled: 'It's true, I sold biscuits and asked if there was anything else they wanted, and sometimes there was!'

Chivo raised the wires, then his eyebrows. For a second something like a genuine emotion passed across his face, as if he'd heard it all and seen it all, but now, against all expectations, he'd heard something new.

His three gorillas were sitting on a shabby sofa idly watching something that looked like soft porn, strangely enough. Soft focus, no sexual organs. Maybe that was why they were so bored. 'Did you hear that?' Chivo said. 'He sold biscuits.' The grunts he got in response suggested they found this roughly as interesting as the half-naked bodies on the screen.

'*Coño.* I could have used you. Too bad I have to destroy you. And who's your supplier?'

'Of the biscuits?'

Any trace of warmth was gone, and Chivo held up the wires again. Linus gritted his teeth, tried to prepare himself. The wires pierced his thigh further up. He managed to stay on the chair, but the electric shock was far worse when it wasn't alleviated by a physical pain. Sweat poured down his face.

'Next time it will be little willy,' Chivo said, pointing to Linus's crotch. 'Who. Are. You. Dealing. For?'

Linus took a deep breath and yelled 'HEEEEELP!' with such force that it felt as if something had burst in his throat. Chivo recoiled, dropped the wires and put his hands over his ears. Linus inhaled again, but before he could make a sound a pair of hands stuck a wide strip of duct tape over his mouth.

Chivo's expression was thunderous as he shook his head and tipped it from side to side, as if he were trying to shake water out of his ears. When he picked up the wires, Linus closed his eyes.

Chivo applied the wires to Linus's cock, to his belly, to his temples. When the tape was ripped from his mouth his tongue felt as if it had turned to mucus, and he could only gurgle like his father.

His hands were tucked under his armpits and he was lifted from the chair, his head lolling helplessly. His eyes saw through a red, liquid veil, everything was shapeless until a new pain took over. His arms were bent up behind his back and he felt as if his shoulders were being dislocated. He was on The Hook. He tried to scream, but he had no control over his vocal cords, and the only result was snot spurting out of his nose.

There was the clink of metal, a hiss and then a click. The tone of the hiss changed, and a streak of blue penetrated the mist. It took a few seconds, but Linus managed to raise his head enough to see Chivo standing in front of him with a lit blowtorch.

'Mmm,' Chivo said. 'Do you want to try that *I'm only a kid* thing again? Otherwise we'll give this a go, then I want answers.'

Linus gurgled, tried to say that he could have his answers now, could have had them a while ago if he'd been allowed to speak, but his tongue, vocal cords and lips refused to cooperate, because his entire body was a burning, agonising mess. As Chivo moved closer with the blue flame Linus couldn't even cry; he just shook his head feebly.

His brain was so scrambled that when he heard a crash, he actually thought it was the sound of pain as the blue flame seared his skin. But the flame was still a few inches away, and it stayed there. Chivo turned his head towards the closed metal door, and his gorillas leapt to their feet.

Another crash, and the door flew open. Two people tumbled into the room holding a barbell loaded with weights, which they'd used as a battering ram. They dropped it on the floor, cracking the concrete. Linus peered at the two figures and blinked. Managed to open his eyes a little wider. The electricity must have done something to his head, because the people who had forced the door were Barack Obama. Times two. The President of the USA and his twin brother had come to rescue him.

The gorillas reached for their guns, but stopped in mid-movement when a third person entered the room. Barack Obama number three, but instead of a barbell he was carrying an assault rifle in his gloved hands. His fingers were bent around the stock at strange angles as the barrel swept from side to side. No one moved; it was as if everyone was suddenly caught up in a game of Statues.

The first two Obamas picked up the guns lying on the table and frisked Chivo, who had dropped the blowtorch, extinguishing the flame. Covered by the Obama with the assault rifle, they pushed Chivo into an armchair.

Linus felt as if his arms were being ripped from their sockets. He chewed air for a few seconds before coming out with a slurred version of: 'Help…me.' The Obama with the rifle turned to him, reached into his pocket for a mobile phone, and took a photograph. Then he gestured to the other two, and together they lifted Linus down. One of them said: 'Have you started wearing diapers, for fuck's sake?'

Linus swallowed saliva mixed with blood. 'Alex?'

The Obama who was Alex turned to the one with the rifle and asked: 'No witnesses, right?' The other one shook his head and Alex pulled off the rubber mask that covered his entire head. Sergei did the same.

'Ta-da,' Alex said. 'The cavalry has arrived.'

'I waited. You didn't come.'

'No.' Alex lowered his voice and nodded to the Obama who was still Obama. 'He wanted to see what you could cope with.'

'You...you *knew*?'

'Don't get hung up on that now.' Alex glanced at the hook, grinned and patted Linus's burning shoulder. 'Get it? *Don't get hung up on that.* Good, eh?'

'Fucking hell...'

'Ssh,' Alex said, glancing at Obama, who was advancing on Chivo and his gorillas. 'You came through with flying colours. One hundred per cent, in spite of the diaper. I'm impressed. I think he is too.'

He took out a butterfly knife and cut the bonds securing Linus's wrists and ankles. The relief of having his arms in front of him, of not hanging from the hook, was indescribable. Linus took a few breaths of freedom, then asked: 'Is that *him*?'

Alex nodded, watching Obama as he positioned himself in front of the four men. Linus could see only the back of his head, covered with Obama's short, greying hair. His mask was more carefully secured than Alex and Sergei's had been, and presumably stuck on to follow the movements of the face.

'Hi,' Obama said in a soft, high voice. He pointed to the three gorillas with the assault rifle. 'You've been stupid. So I'm going to kill you. Later. Just so you know. Then you'll be gone. Alex?' Alex hurried over, and Obama handed him the rifle. 'There you go.'

There was no mistaking the pride in Alex's expression as he accepted the rifle and the responsibility. Sergei took out his own gun and sat down on a chair, providing backup. Obama turned to Chivo, whose armchair was a short distance from the others. Chivo pressed his body against the back of the chair, as if every centimetre further away from Obama was a bonus.

'And you...' Obama pulled off the mask. Linus couldn't see his face, just strands of mousy hair and a slender neck. Chivo's features contorted into something that also resembled a mask, a mask of pure horror as the man leaned towards him and continued: 'You and I are going to have a little chat.'

Tommy

It was after one o'clock and Tommy was in bed when he heard the sound of a drop of water falling into an echo chamber. His phone cast a greenish glow on the ceiling. Tommy switched on the bedside lamp and sat up. Hagge, who was lying at his feet, pricked up his ears and gave him a curious look.

'It's okay, boy. I just have to…'

Tommy opened a drawer and took out his glasses and a small Ixus camera. He didn't know why Equis was so sensitive about screen grabs when it was equally possible to photograph the screen manually. Maybe it was just a matter of form, and of course the quality was adversely affected when the image had passed through two filters.

He placed the phone on the floor and zoomed in, then bent down and pressed the Snapchat icon. He managed to take two snaps of the screen, but didn't have time to look at the picture on his phone before it disappeared. He pulled on his robe, went over to his laptop, downloaded the image onto Aperture, then clicked on it.

Semtex-Janne. And judging by his expression, he wasn't too happy. He was holding up his right thumb to show that everything was great, but the gesture was at odds with the troubled look on his face. In his left hand was a remote control, but not the kind that's used to operate a camera.

He was in the storage depot where Tommy and Tomás had visited him. At his feet lay a rectangular metal box with the lid open. The box contained countless packages wrapped in plastic. Hundreds and hundreds of kilos of what had to be cocaine. Maybe as much as a tonne.

Certain things Tommy had observed in Janne's storage depot had led him to certain suspicions; those suspicions were now confirmed. He went and sat on the edge of the bed, picked up his phone and scrolled down to Ernesto's number. With a sweaty thumb he wrote:

'Know how the coke came in. Parasite. Meet up and talk before I write?'

He sent the message, then lay down and stared up at the ceiling. Why the hell had Equis sent him that picture? It gave away his entire operation, his method. A metal container, known as a parasite, attached to the hull of a ship. If his aim was to dump Janne in the shit, there had to be an easier way.

Admittedly the picture had come from a hidden number, but it must have been taken by someone who was involved. And who else could force a hard man like Janne to provide pictorial evidence that would be enough to put him away for life? It had to be Equis, and it made no sense at all.

The phone buzzed. Ernesto. 'Tomorrow at 10.'

Tommy stayed where he was with the phone resting on his chest. Maybe he would finally get some answers. He could feel his heart beating through the screen, faster than normal. He was in deep waters now, deeper than ever. Huge, unseen monsters were moving around in the darkness beneath him, capable of swallowing him in a second.

He was going to have to contact the police before long. He couldn't write an article until he'd shared all relevant information with them, and they'd given him the go-ahead. Otherwise he'd end up in jail. Obstructing such a huge investigation by revealing something in advance would also mean that no one would ever talk to him again. Plus he needed protection. He had no funds to pay for protection, so the police were the only ones who could provide it.

The more Tommy thought about it, the more he began to feel the urge to delete the image from both his camera and his hard drive, pretend he'd never received it.

Why, why, why did you send it?

Lying there on a bed that no longer felt safe and secure, he realised he was furious with Equis for putting him in this dangerous situation. And it didn't matter if he deleted the image. Equis *thought* he had it.

Why? Why?

The question went around and around in Tommy's head until he fell asleep on top of the covers, then tossed and turned so much that at four o'clock, Hagge got up and went to his basket.

*

Tommy woke up with palpitations. He sat up, his eyes darting around the room as his heart fluttered and buzzed. Then he heard his mobile; he was still clutching it to his breast, and the vibration had created the illusion of an impending heart attack. He looked at the screen: Betty.

'Hi—it's a bit early to be...'

'Tommy, Linus has gone missing.'

Her voice was thin, filled with anxiety.

'What do you mean, missing?'

'You know what he's like, he's always up to something, but he's always, *always* come home when he said he'd be home and now he hasn't come home, he's been out all night.'

'Have you tried calling him?'

'Of course I have. I just found out he hasn't been home and I've called and texted, but there's no reply, what shall I do?'

'Have you contacted the police?'

'What would they do? Nothing. They'd just say "wait and see, he'll be with a friend", but I *know*, Tommy. I *know*.'

'Okay. I'm on my way.'

Tommy ended the call and got to his feet. He wasn't quite as worried as Betty. When Linus was living with him he'd sometimes decided to go for a thirty-kilometre run in the middle of the night, when things got too much for him. Maybe he'd done something similar now.

The brief, unsettled sleep had left its mark. His brain felt slow and woolly, as if it were wrapped in insulating material. He needed a decent espresso before he did anything.

He was halfway through the process, tipping the freshly ground coffee into the filter, when he heard that drop of water once more. He grabbed the Ixus and placed the phone on the floor.

He pressed the Snapchat icon, but this time he glanced at the screen before he took a photograph. Although in fact he didn't take a photograph. As soon as he saw the picture he gasped and dropped the camera. He tore off his robe and got dressed as fast as he could, then ran out of the door without even saying goodbye to Hagge. The tears began to flow as he raced down the stairs.

Linus, Linus...

2. Inside

The Unicorn and the Goat

Like every other place where people live, Gårdsstugan had acquired its own mythology over the years, a loosely connected collection of images and stories that were as integral to the soul of the buildings as their balconies, elevators and apartments, if not more.

Certain images were pure fantasy: embryonic creations that had somehow avoided being stillborn because of the power of suggestion they carried. For example, everyone 'knew' that in a basement between main entrance doors 54 to 58 there was a gigantic unfinished swimming pool where rainwater and groundwater had gathered over the years. It was now home to all kinds of aquatic organisms, which were completely white due to the lack of light. The secret military tunnel between Gårdsstugan and Karolinska Hospital had never been found, nor had the gang of feral refugee children who lived in tents on the roofs. They used ropes to abseil down the building and got into people's apartments through the windows.

Those were the phenomena that existed only in the imagination of the residents. There were also the stories. Some were likewise pure invention: the ghost who lived in an apartment on the fifth floor of number 72, and only showed himself when the moon was on the wane, or the rabid German shepherd that had bitten four small children to death in the playground in the early 1980s.

Other events had actually taken place, then gradually been expanded and embroidered upon until they were more like fiction. One such incident was known as 'The Massacre in the Square'.

The criminal activity that forms the hub of this narrative was already beginning to grow in the 1970s, although on a much smaller scale, because cocaine had not yet become just about everyone's flight from reality. In simplistic terms, the Finns on the south side sold smuggled booze, while the Chileans on the north side peddled stolen goods, so the Swedes who wanted to play could choose their team.

They usually chose their fellow Scandinavians, and everything was sweetness and light.

For reasons unclear, a conflict arose between the two groups, a conflict that escalated and climaxed in June 1977, when two gangs, one from the north and one from the south, came together in the square to resolve the matter. No guns were involved, but there were plenty of knives and makeshift cudgels.

A vicious fight broke out, and one person from each side lost their life before the police arrived ten minutes in and put a stop to the melee. One of the dead had fallen into the fountain in the middle of the square. The police arrested a number of the combatants and dispersed the rest. Three individuals were later found guilty of manslaughter. That's it: the whole story. But once again, over the years the collective imagination has turned this tragic but essentially banal occurrence into the stuff of fairytale.

In this world, *seven* people died. Seven. Throats cut; thrown into the fountain, turning the normally clear water red. The jets shooting out from the hands of the elf also turned red, and a bloody mist covered the square during the *two hours* the battle lasted.

For several weeks' afterwards, the residents of Gårdsstugan found blood in their tap water. Rivulets of blood continued to leak from the fountain, trickling across the square, blood seeped up through the drains in people's showers. This is what everyone knows and still recounts about the massacre of 1977.

*

During the early hours of October 23 2017, another chapter was written in the bloody history of the square, a chapter which would soon become a part of the tale that had begun forty years ago.

There were only three eyewitnesses and, since their accounts are largely in accord and have not yet been strewn with the glitter of fantasy, we can accept them as credible.

Dawn was still a couple of hours away, and the square was

illuminated only by a few unbroken streetlights at 05:25 when the three witnesses, from different viewpoints, saw Enrique Morales, better known as Chivo or the Goat, enter the square from the north side. They probably wouldn't have paid much attention if it hadn't been for the fact that he was carrying a long aluminium stepladder.

All the witnesses knew who Chivo was, even if they professed ignorance about the precise details of his business activities. To see a person like Chivo marching across the square in the hours of darkness with a ladder was guaranteed to attract attention, if not direct action. The witnesses therefore slowed down so they could covertly watch what Chivo was up to. Chivo himself seemed unaware that anyone else was around, and the closest witness claimed that he had seemed 'totally out of it'.

Chivo walked up to the edge of the fountain and opened up the ladder. With shaky, uncertain movements he began to climb. By this stage all the witnesses had stopped dead. None of them could work out what the hell he was doing.

Until the moment when Chivo reached the top platform of the ladder, the witness statements are identical; from then on they vary slightly. One claims that Chivo spread his arms wide, another that he whispered 'ayúdame'. This may be regarded as of minor importance, because all three are in agreement about what happened next.

Chivo leaned back as far as the stepladder's balance would allow, then hurled himself forward. As soon as his feet left the aluminium platform, the unicorn's horn penetrated his chest and emerged just below his left shoulder blade, leaving him hanging there.

His intention may have been to pierce his heart so that death would come as quickly as possible, with some degree of dignity. However, things didn't quite work out that way. The horn entered to the right of his heart, breaking two ribs, and punctured his left lung.

Until then the operation had been conducted in complete silence, but now it was as if Chivo had woken from a dreamlike paralysis. He began to wave his arms and legs, and guttural, gurgling cries forced their way up from his throat, along with a considerable amount of blood, which dripped down into the fountain. Chivo braced himself against the unicorn's head and tried to push himself off the horn, but it was hopeless. He moved a couple of centimetres before his strength deserted him, and he slid back down with a squelch.

For the first time the three witnesses caught one another's eye as best they could in the darkness. *Shall we…? Should we…?* Nobody moved, but as Chivo's struggles died away, they all took out their phones. Two called the emergency services, one started filming. A minute or so later, it was over. Chivo may not have achieved a direct hit, but enough arteries around the heart had been damaged to produce the desired effect. Chivo was dead, and his induction into the mythology of Gårdsstugan could begin.

Linus

'You find someone who's alive and pretend it's you. You are a collection of disparate pieces. You were made. Your brain is lying there thinking. Coming up with ideas. Making sounds. Sometimes words. Saying things. Lying in its darkness and saying things. It means nothing. Only the darkness has meaning. You are nothing. Only the darkness exists.'

Linus didn't know how long the lesson had gone on. Time had lost its linear quality and turned into drops falling towards a surface and spreading in all directions. The only thing he could hold on to was the sky, slowly growing lighter over the Järvafältet nature reserve where he and Barack Obama stood facing each other as the lesson poured into Linus's head.

He was in a blessed state, because the torture had made him receptive to the truth about the human condition. While he was hanging on the hook, he'd been able to observe himself from the outside, see what he really was. A piece of meat with the ability to experience pain. Nothing more. Soon this physical realisation would be painted over with bright colours by the brain; its function was to produce meaning where none existed. However, there was still time for instruction. That was the explanation he'd been given.

He looked up at the dawn sky and saw an insignificant backdrop of atmosphere, concealing the endless darkness behind it. In the same way, the brain evokes illusions to make us forget that we are nothing. Self-confidence, ambition, nostalgia. All merely ghosts, as insubstantial as the clouds, produced by the brain in order to allow us to go on living.

Barack Obama fixed his gaze on Linus's and came a little closer. Linus could see the edges of the mask around his eyes, a mismatched flap against the pale skin beneath.

'You see,' Obama said. 'Now you see.'

Linus nodded. 'Yes. I see.'

Obama grabbed the mask, clenched his fists and pulled upward. The mask came away with a sucking noise. His face was horribly distorted as the glue released its grip. With one last jerk he yanked the mask off and dropped it on the grass.

Under any other circumstances Linus would have screamed when he saw Obama's real face, but that was no longer an option, because now he was empowered by the knowledge he had just been given. What was before him was, on a deeper level, still only a mask, still a painted background placed in front of the darkness.

The true face was less a face, more a badly healed wound with a pair of unfathomably deep eyes looking out. Countless large and small scars from wounds that had never been stitched, from burns that had never been salved, areas of discoloured or flaking skin, cavities exposing chipped bone. One injury stood out among the rest like the cross at Golgotha. A two-centimetre wide scar that must once have been a gash down to the bone ran from the outer edge of each eyebrow to the corners of the mouth, dividing the face into four triangular sections. The two lines intersected beneath a flattened nose. The letter or the symbol 'X' had been carved into the face. A pair of hands were placed on Linus's shoulders and a voice said: 'Come into the darkness.'

Up until that moment, Linus had thought he'd been absorbing the lesson. On some fluid level, X's words and presence had made him hurtle down towards the deepest imaginable understanding of the speciousness of life and identity. But that was merely *imaginable*. It turned out to have been the treacherous brain, busily eradicating its own significance.

Something else was happening now.

What had been intellectual insight seconds ago had become physical conviction. The scenery was ripped away, and Linus was swept into the darkness where he had actually been all along. It had an incalculable volume and a certain warmth. He reached out and his fingers touched something cheerful and sticky with a hint of life, like internal organs in the making.

God. I am inside God.

His legs gave way and he fell into a pair of arms.

*

When Linus opened his eyes he found himself lying on X's lap. The disfigured face was bent over his and didn't bother him at all. Revulsion would have been absurd—like being disgusted by the palm of his own hand.

Alex and Sergei were standing on either side of X. They were staring at Linus, their expressions completely unreadable. On one level Linus was in the Järvafältet nature reserve, on another he was still in the darkness. He had no content, no substance. If someone had told him to dance he would have danced, if someone had told him to take his own life, he would have done it. None of it mattered.

Like a religious celebrant, X made a movement with his hands, palms up, and said: 'Fall down.'

As if their skeletons had been whipped away, Alex and Sergei fell to the ground and landed on the soft grass. They crawled over to X and rested their heads on his thighs, faces upturned and close to Linus's. Their breathing was rapid and shallow, as if they were gripped by a powerful sense of anticipation, and Linus began to breathe in the same way without knowing why.

The sound of bass notes vibrated through X's body and passed on into Linus's skull. It was that ancient song Uncle Tommy had hummed, 'Somebody Up There Must Like Me'. Something began to ooze out of X's deformed nose. A black substance, too dense to be blood or snot, too shapeless and runny to be flesh. The substance stretched out into a glutinous string with a shining droplet on the end.

Linus opened his mouth to receive it.

Tommy

Tommy found Betty on the balcony, clutching the rail as she scanned the area with red-rimmed eyes. He stroked her back, then positioned himself beside her so that their arms were touching. Raised voices from the square found their way along the façades and reached the balcony: an inarticulate hum.

'There's something going on in the square,' Betty said. 'I daren't go down there. What if it's to do with Linus?

'It isn't.'

'How do you know?'

'I got a message. From the paper.'

If Tommy had been focusing on his professional role, he would have been in the square right now, following up on what had happened to Chivo. But 'Tommy T' had become blurred and the real Tommy, who cared more about his sister than a scoop, was emerging more clearly.

'Show me.' Betty held out her hand.

'What?'

'Show me the message.'

Tommy hesitated before giving her his phone. Even though Snapchat deleted pictures after five seconds, the image of Linus's tortured body suspended from a hook was seared onto Tommy's retina with such clarity that he couldn't quite grasp that it had disappeared from his phone.

'Don't you believe me?'

'I believe you'll say whatever you think I need to hear.'

'So why can't you trust me?'

Betty shook her head and opened his message folder.

Tommy had always been Betty's main authority figure. When she was a little girl she would go to him rather than her parents if she had a question. She wouldn't have married Göran if Tommy hadn't given his enthusiastic blessing. And they were very happy. Tommy could never have foreseen what would happen to Göran.

So Betty's refusal to accept that he knew best was unusual. She normally swallowed his sanitised version of the truth as a toothless man slurps his soup.

'Who's Chivo?' Betty asked, eyes narrowing as she read.

'Don't you know?'

'If I knew I wouldn't ask, would I?'

'He runs things on the north side. Ran.'

'Could Linus be involved in these…things?'

'No. Not on the north side. That's impossible.'

'How can you be so sure?'

'I'm sure. Trust me.'

Tommy used those last two words to Betty in special cases. They were an emergency brake, something absolute and irrevocable. When Tommy said *trust me*, it meant he was putting his authority on the autopsy table. She could slice and carve as much as she wanted, there was nothing suspicious to be found. This time they achieved the desired effect. Betty's shoulders dropped and she let out a long sigh that turned into a sob as she handed back the phone. 'But where *is* he?'

Tommy hadn't lied; he was convinced that Linus had nothing to do with Chivo's business. However, he'd omitted to mention that he was equally convinced that there was a connection between Chivo's death and Linus's disappearance. He just didn't know what it was.

'How has Linus seemed lately?' he asked.

'Same as usual. Stressed.'

'Anything a little bit different? Has he done anything he wouldn't normally do?'

'No. Or rather yes. Sold biscuits.'

'What kind of biscuits?'

'Just—biscuits.'

'Okay, let's try this one more time. Are you telling me Linus has been going around selling biscuits?'

'Yes—to earn a bit of money. The problem is, we have to take some of his...'

'I know, I know.'

Tommy left his sister and went into Linus's room. On the way he passed Göran, sitting in his chair in the living room. A repetitive gurgle indicated that he wanted to say something, but listening required a patience that Tommy just didn't have at the moment.

The idea of Linus trotting from door to door like a boy scout selling biscuits was as believable as the children's author Barbro Lindgren suddenly deciding to write about true crime. Tommy snorted when the first thing he saw was an ICA carrier bag half-full of packets of...biscuits. He opened a packet of Ballerina lemon cream wafers. They were definitely biscuits. He took a cautious nibble. They tasted like biscuits. He squeezed each packet; they seemed to contain exactly what they were supposed to contain. Ordinary fucking Ballerina biscuits, because of which Linus had been tortured and suspended from a hook. No chance. A spasm of pain squeezed Tommy's heart, and he rubbed his chest. No pain radiating down his arm, so probably not angina. Just good old fear.

Linus, Linus, what have you got yourself mixed up in?

Regardless of what Linus's teachers and others thought, Tommy knew his nephew was smart. He'd used the biscuits as a smokescreen to hide something else, something so serious that it had won him the honour of being tortured.

There was an hour to go before he was due to meet Ernesto, and in the absence of other leads to follow, he might as well pick up on the story of the day: the Unicorn that killed the Goat. He sincerely hoped the tale would have a happy ending.

*

A light drizzle had begun to fall when Tommy left the apartment block; it was more like a damp thickening of the air, but combined with the cold and the overcast sky above the concrete façades, the atmosphere was the very epitome of Swedish suburban gloom, and Tommy couldn't help being drawn into it. He buttoned his jacket up to the top, pushed his hands deep in his pockets and headed for the square. A thin film of moisture draped itself over his face, and his heart sank.

You get dragged in, then you get dragged down.

Nostalgically he thought back to the way things had been before he got that damned phone call from Ove Ahlin, chief news editor at *Stockholmsnytt*. Sitting in his armchair with a Weightwatchers ready meal, Hagge's head resting on his feet as he watched 'Antiques Roadshow'. Right now it seemed like paradise lost.

His phone was full of missed calls. From Tomás, who presumably wanted to discuss the article about the boxing club, from Janne with his ridiculous memoir, from Ove, from Anita. People who wanted something from him. In his phone all these calls and messages were neatly listed; in his head they were bouncing around like red-hot pinballs made up of stress, fear and a guilty conscience, and he felt like giving the whole machine a good kick, knocking it over. Packing the whole thing in. Crawling back to his armchair.

If it hadn't been for Linus.

Linus was the one necessity that forced him to keep playing, keep those balls moving. Yes, balls. It was a multi-ball game now, and he hated it. He was too old, too tired for the split vision that the exercise required, and free play was an unimaginably distant prospect. Forget the metaphors. Carry on walking.

*

There was a large crowd of people hanging around the square, where one benefit of the drizzle was that the constant wind had a harder time whipping up the dust.

A police armed-response-unit vehicle and an unmarked van that presumably belonged to the National Forensics Centre were parked next to the fountain, which was cordoned off with blue and white tape. Chivo's body had been taken down and removed. A couple of CSIs in white overalls were having a discussion just inside the tape. Tommy peered up at the unicorn, where the pale dawn light exposed the fresh discolouration.

The message from the paper had been short and to the point: 'Chivo's killed himself in the square at Gårdsstugan. Impaled himself on a statue. Can you take it?' Tommy hadn't replied.

He ambled around the square, where several police officers were talking to residents who didn't seem too pleased to have attracted their attention. A larger group was standing outside the store, gathered around a well-built guy who was busy writing something on a notepad. It took Tommy a few seconds to recognise Mehdi, who had dressed to suit the environment in a hoodie and tracksuit bottoms— the kind of transformation that would look absurd if Tommy tried it.

The group dispersed as Tommy approached, and Mehdi turned around, looking irritated. When he saw Tommy, he shook his head.

'Shit, Tommy. Talk about the wolf frightening away the sheep.'

'I don't feel much like a wolf. And they didn't look much like sheep either.'

'You know what I mean. You look like a cop.'

'Fuck that—what are you doing here?'

This came out with unnecessary aggression. Mehdi frowned and looked hurt.

'You didn't take it, so I did. Is that a problem?'

'No. Sorry. It's just...'

Mehdi's expression softened and he nodded. 'I know, this is your turf. So why didn't you take it?'

'Personal reasons.'

'Same as before?'

'What?'

'When you were bowling. You asked me if the top-class coke was being distributed here. You said you wanted to know for personal reasons.'

'Impressive memory. Yes, same as before.'

'And?'

'What are people saying?'

Mehdi glanced at his pad and unconsciously moved it closer to his chest, as if Tommy really was a wolf, hungry for sensation, who might grab it in his jaws. Tommy held up his paws to show that he had no such intention, either on the immediate physical or the journalistic level.

'It's yours, I'm not going to touch it. But I need to know. For personal reasons, as I said.'

'Is someone close to you involved in all this, Tommy?'

'Yes. But I'd appreciate it if you'd leave it there.'

Mehdi scratched the back of his neck with his pen. 'Okay, so it's equally crazy and straightforward. Chivo turns up with a stepladder. Climbs the ladder, throws himself onto the statue, twitches for a while, dies. End of story. No apparent coercion, nothing.'

'And before that?'

Mehdi pushed his tongue beneath his top lip, and for a moment he looked like an Iranian taking snuff—very unusual. Tommy had clearly touched on a vital part of the story, which Mehdi was reluctant to share. He glanced at Tommy, then said: 'Okay. Apparently something went down at Chivo's office beforehand.'

'At the gym? What kind of something?'

'Something bad, if I can put it that way.'

'Go on.'

Mehdi sighed and he gazed up at the sky as if to say *look how I'm sacrificing my own interests to help out a colleague in need, make a note of that in your big book.*

'There was a van. Three…Barack Obamas got out, one heavily armed. After a while shots were heard. Three guys were thrown in the back of the van. One was led out. The van drove off. Then Chivo comes along with his ladder, and the rest you know.'

It took Tommy a few seconds to work through what Mehdi had just told him and form a picture of the course of events. When he'd finished, all he could think of to say was: 'Barack Obama?'

'Yes. Barack Obama.'

'Three?'

'Three.'

It was obvious that Mehdi had no intention of giving away anything more, so Tommy decided to change tactics: give him the feeling that, at the end of the day, they were on the same team.

'The bodies,' he said. 'What do they do with all the bodies?'

'Sorry?'

'Seriously, Mehdi. You must be thinking the same way as me. The suicides...But they haven't all taken their own lives. Lots of them have simply disappeared. More than twenty people. And not one single body's been found.'

'I guess they're good at hiding them. Maybe they burn them, drop them in deep water, how should I know?'

'Not that *many*. It just doesn't happen. There's always someone who messes up, some unforeseen complication. And then the body turns up, or parts of it. One or two, okay. But not more than twenty. So what the hell are they doing?'

If the question hadn't engaged Mehdi before, it did now. He gazed pensively around the square as if he were looking for the missing bodies. Tommy made the most of the fact that he was distracted to ask: 'And the van? Stolen?'

Mehdi nodded slowly, and Tommy sensed that he was already beginning to formulate a story based on the unconfirmed suicides. Tommy left him to it, said goodbye and headed for the north side.

'Hey, wait a minute! Where are you going?'

'I promise, it's yours,' Tommy said over his shoulder.

Mehdi caught up with him. 'It's not that I don't trust you, Tommy, it's just that...'

'...you don't trust me.'

Mehdi had nothing to add, and they walked towards the Diablo Negro Gym in silence.

*

After a minute or so Mehdi got out his phone and took a few pictures of the crowd and the fountain. Then he turned it around and snapped himself and Tommy, asking belatedly, 'You don't mind, do you?'

'Haven't you got a photographer with you?'

'Yeah, Danne. He's somewhere around. No, this is for Insta.'

'Instagram.'

'Mmm.'

As they set off again, Mehdi's fingers skittered across the screen like a water spider on the surface of a pond. Mehdi was *active on social media*. Instagram, Twitter, Facebook and no doubt other platforms that Tommy had never heard of, since he was *passive on social media* and didn't even have a Facebook account.

Tommy considered asking Mehdi to take down the photo he'd just posted. A brief glance had told him that it showed a suitably serious Mehdi in the foreground, and behind him a crumpled extra who might possibly be allowed a comic monologue if the audience got bored. Mehdi put the phone away and asked: 'How's it going with Snapchat?'

'I get sent pictures.'

'I'm not going to ask what kind of pictures, but why?'

Tommy had asked himself the same question. He'd failed to come up with a sensible answer. He'd ruled out the idea that someone other than Equis was sending them, so what did that mean?

One possibility was that Equis wanted a witness, someone who could appreciate the significance of what he was doing and spread the word among the great unwashed. Tommy hoped that was the case, even it if did mean he was playing John the Baptist to a psychopath, because the other possibility was much worse. What if the Snapchat images were part of a bigger game, where Tommy was simply one of the pieces, unable to see the whole board from his limited viewpoint? It all boiled down to the only answer he could give Mehdi: 'I don't know.'

*

The gym was also cordoned off with blue and white tape, and it was clear that others had already been asking around. Among the thirty or so woodentops gathered outside the main entrance, Tommy spotted a reporter from the rival evening paper, plus one from a morning paper, and a photographer. A police car was parked next to the Lexus with the gym sticker, and another one had just arrived.

This was no longer Tommy's story, it was just something he wanted to know. When the door of the police car opened, he saw his chance. The man who unfolded himself from the driver's seat was almost two metres tall, his name was Göran Wivallius, and Tommy had had dealings with him on several occasions. He was an experienced officer, often among the first on the scene at major incidents.

As Göran moved towards the tightly packed group by the entrance, Tommy materialised at his side. 'Hi Göran. Can you confirm that this is the location of Chivo's so-called office?'

Only now did Tommy realise that Göran had a Bluetooth headset in one ear: he was clearly in the middle of a conversation. He waved at Tommy to shut him up, cupped his ear and said: 'Sorry, I didn't quite catch that.' Tommy stuck close behind Göran as he pushed his way through the crowd, lifted the tape and entered the gym.

Göran strode through the empty venue, continuing his conversation. Tommy was able to pick up only the odd word, but it seemed to be about the search for the van. The door to the back room was open, and Tommy waited while Göran went in. He heard muffled voices, brief greetings. Tommy crept forward and noticed that the remains of the duct tape were still on the barbell following his previous visit. A couple more steps and he was able to see into the room beyond the steel door.

Two people in protective clothing were crawling around the floor, which was stained with bodily fluids, while a third was busy with something over by the wall. Göran, who was standing just inside the door in order to avoid contaminating the crime scene, suddenly caught sight of Tommy.

'What the fuck!' he yelled, grabbing hold of Tommy's upper arm.

At that moment the CSI by the wall stepped back and Tommy saw it. The Hook. It looked exactly the same as the one in the photograph he'd been sent. The texture of the wall was also the same. Linus had been hanging from that hook just a few hours ago.

Göran dragged Tommy away, yelling that he'd thought Tommy was a professional. His grip tightened to the extent that it would definitely leave bruises.

'Sorry, Göran. I had to do it.'

'Right. And I have to make sure you never come anywhere near a crime scene as long as I have any say in the matter.'

'Listen, I can walk by myself.'

'Yes, so I've seen.'

Göran hustled Tommy to the door and shoved him under the tape with a final 'fucking idiot' before storming back inside. Tommy spotted Mehdi—and wasn't he wearing a smug smile? It disappeared as soon as his eyes met Tommy's. He turned to Dan Schyman, his photographer, and started issuing instructions. Tommy let them have their fun. He rolled his shoulders as if to shake off all the stares attaching themselves to him, then walked away from the gym.

Three guys were thrown in the back of the van. One was led out.

If Tommy's reconstruction was correct, Chivo had got hold of Linus and tortured him, then Linus had been rescued by Equis, who had taken him away. Tommy hardly dared contemplate how involved Linus must be to have earnt such a punishment and such a redemption. One thing was clear: this wasn't about biscuits.

Assuming that Linus was now being held by Equis, it seemed fortunate that Tommy was now on his way to see the only person who could tell him about this elusive figure. It was ten o'clock. Tommy hurried towards Ernesto's apartment block.

*

In the elevator on the way up to the twelfth floor, Tommy felt something change colour inside him. The unpredictable lighting technician in his head switched on a whole bank of new spotlights, so that the stage which was Tommy himself was bathed in a different atmosphere.

An hour ago he'd been sick with worry over Linus, while at the same time he'd felt an overwhelming desire to sink down into his armchair with his tail between his legs. The worry was still there, but now it was combined with something he hadn't felt for a long time: the desire for revenge. *I'm going to show those bastards.*

Mehdi, for a start. He reminded Tommy of that dachshund that had been sniffing around Hagge. Nose everywhere, all the time. Down with the kids, out in the field, on the spot, up on Facebook, while Tommy was…shambling along. He knew Mehdi was a VIP at Riche; he would stand at the bar regaling a sparkling audience with his stories, and never had to go home alone if he didn't want to. In short, he was a slightly better version of Tommy himself a few years earlier. And that hurt.

Added to this was the humiliation of being thrown out by Göran. Everyone watching. *Jesus, would you look at that—Tommy T being slung out like some old drunk!* He would reinstate himself, he would break the lot of them, he would…

The elevator stopped with a bump and a squeak. Tommy stepped out and was met by that indefinable smell of death. When he reached the thirteenth floor, Miguel was waiting. He didn't look happy. 'You're late.'

Tommy checked his watch. 'Seven minutes.'

'Being late means you're stealing time from someone else. Maybe you know how Ernesto feels about people who steal from him?'

'My apologies. It won't happen again.'

Miguel moved aside and jerked his head to indicate that Tommy could go up. As Tommy passed him, Miguel seized his sore upper arm and pushed his face close to Tommy's. 'Ernesto is vulnerable to the risk of infection. Are you sick in any way?'

'No. This is just the way I look.'

*

On the top floor Tommy rang the doorbell. There was no name on the letterbox, because the postman wasn't allowed up here. The door was opened immediately by yet another bunch of muscles. Tommy had never seen him before, so he simply said: 'I'm here to see Ernesto.'

'And who are you?'

'Tommy. Tommy Torstensson. Tommy T.'

'Which is it?'

'Tommy T.'

'Any proof?'

Tommy had thought that Ernesto would have wound up his business now he was ill, but the muscle and the meticulous security told a different story. He took out his wallet and searched for his press card, which he hoped would convince the Vin Diesel clone.

Before he had time to produce the card, a woman's voice said: 'Come on in, Tommy. *Está bien*, Mario.'

Alma was standing in the hallway. She was so thin and frail next to Super Mario that it looked as if he could break her in two with his index finger, but Tommy knew she was made of the toughest stuff imaginable.

She and Ernesto had met as teenagers, and she'd been with him in the jungle during the guerrilla conflicts, which over time had turned into a kind of tribal war. Their group was one of those that came out of it comparatively well, largely due to Alma's tactical skills in battle and her clarity of vision in camp. She knew who could be trusted and who should be given a drink and a bullet to the back of the neck.

She was also as hard as juniper wood. After an ambush in which Ernesto had been seriously injured, she had spent three days dragging him twenty kilometres along a dried-out riverbed until they reached a village where he could receive treatment. Ernesto had told Tommy all this with a flame of pride flickering in his eyes.

Tommy shook her hand. It was as cold and bony as a bird's foot. There was nothing friendly about Alma, and age had hardened her features even more. The wrinkled skin draped over her skull made her look increasingly as if she really was made of the juniper wood that formed her spiritual make-up.

'How is he?' Tommy asked.

'You'll see. He's looking forward to your visit.'

'He was very reluctant until he was forced into it.'

'Say that in a different way.'

Alma's Swedish wasn't perfect in terms of either pronunciation or vocabulary, but it wasn't her style to say *I don't understand*. She would put the responsibility on the person who'd spoken the incomprehensible sentence, and order him or her to rephrase it.

'I made him want to see me,' Tommy said, emphasising every word.

'No. He wants to see you now.'

Tommy followed Alma to the oak door of Ernesto's office. Tommy remembered it as a stylish room with antique furniture, South American works of art and rugs impregnated with the aroma of cigar smoke. He had assumed that Ernesto was bedridden, but that didn't seem to be the case.

Alma tapped on the door. '*Mi amor? Tommy está aqui.*' Something that sounded like: '*venga, venga*' came from inside the room. Alma pushed open the door and nodded to Tommy.

*

The smell of death Tommy had noticed in the stairwell had been stronger inside the apartment, and now he was at its epicentre. Curiously enough, the smell became less unpleasant when it was strong, when it was the thing itself rather than a terrible foreboding.

The room Tommy recalled as pretty overcrowded had now been transformed into its direct opposite. There was virtually nothing in here. The walls were bare and white, there were no rugs to soften the parquet flooring, and the only furniture was the armchair in which Ernesto was sitting, plus a footstool in front of it. All that remained of its former glory was the aroma of cigar smoke. Tommy's footsteps echoed as he walked in. Alma closed the door behind him.

Ernesto had been a powerful man—not as big or muscular as Miguel, but sturdy enough for Alma's trek along the riverbed to become the stuff of heroic songs. Right now she could have put him on her back and jogged along with no difficulty whatsoever.

It was hard to believe how much of a person's body could be gnawed away from the inside before it gave up the ghost. Ernesto looked like a skeleton with an almost transparent coating of skin. He was wearing a short-sleeved white shirt, revealing arms like pool cues. A tartan blanket was wrapped around his legs, and there was a drip stand beside him with a tube attached to a cannula in the crook of his arm. Tommy went over and took a limp hand.

'Hello, Ernesto. What's happened to all your chattels?'

Ernesto moved his head sideways, indicating that he didn't understand. His Swedish was better than Alma's, but either he hadn't heard the question, or he didn't understand the word *chattels*. Tommy clarified: 'Furniture. Where's the furniture gone?'

'Storage unit. In Kista.'

Tommy had been asking about the reason for the furniture's absence rather than checking on its whereabouts. Ernesto presumably knew this perfectly well, because there was a twinkle in his eye as he said: 'Sit.'

Tommy settled down as best he could on the footstool, his rump spilling over the sides thanks to all those ready meals. This felt like an audience, which was no doubt the intention. They sat opposite each other in silence for so long that Tommy had to shift his position to avoid getting cramp. Eventually Ernesto spoke: 'Reduction.'

'Sorry?' Tommy leaned forward. 'Reduction?'

'Mmm.' The loose skin beneath Ernesto's chin wobbled as he nodded. 'Reduction. Clearing out, you know? Death will take everything. Nothing will be left. Nothing. So I'm practising. Getting used to it.'

'Okay. I get the idea, but it doesn't seem as if you've exactly scaled down your business interests.'

'How did you find out?' Ernesto demanded. 'The parasite?'

Tommy wasn't prepared to reveal his one-way communication with Equis until he knew where Ernesto stood, so instead he told him about the detail he'd remembered as being significant only after Equis had sent him the photograph of the cocaine delivery.

'I called on Semtex-Janne,' he said. 'I knew the coke was being distributed, and I knew it must have come in via Värtahamnen. I saw the wetsuits and the rubber dinghy, put two and two together.'

'The stupid bastard left them out?'

Tommy had no desire to sign Janne's death warrant, so he quickly added: 'No, no, they were among a load of other crap, but I was already thinking along those lines, so...'

Ernesto raised a weary hand. 'Why are you protecting him?'

'I'm going to ghostwrite his biography.'

In the hope of diverting Ernesto from the thought of what punishment Janne's carelessness warranted, Tommy launched into an account of the glowing memoir that was to contain everything except Janne's criminal activities. He even name-checked Zlatan and David Lagercrantz. When he'd finished, Ernesto stared at him for a few seconds, then burst into laughter so deep and protracted that it seemed life-threatening in his current state. Spasms shook his thin body, and the air was expelled from his lungs in a series of wheezing thrusts.

When he'd finished laughing he wiped the tears from his eyes, then bent down with an enormous effort and picked up a silver case from the floor. He took out a cigar and a gold-plated Ronson lighter. While he cut and lit the cigar with slow, ritualistic movements, Tommy thought once again about the extensive organisation and top-quality contacts that were needed for the parasite.

The production of the cocaine, packing it into the metal container he'd seen in the photograph. Transportation to the docks in Venezuela. The divers, attaching the container to the oil tanker with an electric magnet. The voyage across the sea, with a captain who either did or didn't know what was going on. It was more likely to be an ordinary seaman who was involved. The arrival offshore, outside Stockholm.

The release of the container before the ship was inspected, presumably via the remote control Janne had been holding in the photograph. Then more divers, loading the container onto the dinghy. Storage. Distribution.

So many people, so many strands, so many points where one or more individuals could decide this was too much trouble, why not just take the lot and buy a South Sea island and a private army with the money. But no. Stockholm's local politicians had a great deal to learn from the discipline and dedication running through Equis' import operation.

Ernesto took an ashtray out of the silver case and placed it on the blanket covering his legs. He took a long drag, his frail eyelids quivering with pleasure as he closed them. Then he peered at Tommy through the smoke. 'What is it you want to know?'

'Everything.'

'We don't have time for everything. I've got three months to live— at the most. So you're going to have to be a little more specific.'

'Who is he? I'm assuming he's the same person who was operating from the laundry. Were you involved? I mean, I know that was on the south side...'

Ernesto gazed at Tommy for a long time. It was impossible to read from his face what was going on in his head. Three months. In Tommy's experience, those who were dying had an urge to *tell*. To create a coherent narrative of their life, with the aim of giving it something that resembled a meaning.

Then again, Ernesto wasn't like most people, so maybe this was his own idea of reduction, offloading a narrative just as he'd got rid of his furniture. Maybe that was what made him start talking.

*

'I don't know where he came from,' Ernesto began. 'He mentioned Huddinge at some point, but that's all.'

'Huddinge as in the hospital or the place?' Tommy asked.

'As I said. One day he was there. In the laundry. My activities on the south side were limited, but I made sure I kept myself…updated. The guy was dealing pills. He had a source at Karolinska Hospital who sidelined medication that was going to be thrown away, and hid it among the sheets that were sent to the laundry.

Tommy knew all this from his earlier interest in the laundry, but he hoped this was just the start and chose not to interrupt Ernesto.

'I don't know if you remember, but it was the Mikkonen brothers who were pulling the strings on the south side at the time, and they weren't the kind of guys you messed around with. So I assumed the pill-popper's—no, pill-pusher's—career would be short-lived.'

Ernesto frowned and looked at his cigar as if it was responsible for his error. Tommy had a vague recollection of the Mikkonen brothers as old-school villains, their knuckles permanently skinned. The slightest suspicion that you were even thinking of crossing them, and you woke up in a white room with concussion and a broken jaw.

'Okay.' Ernesto tapped the ash off his cigar; he had yet to take his second drag. Maybe he just liked the aroma, the atmosphere of his former life that it evoked. 'So the Mikkonen brothers hear about what's going on. Send someone. He doesn't report back. So they go down there themselves. Then…' Ernesto spread his hands wide.

'Gone?'

'Vanished. Both of them. I don't remember their first names. I find it hard to remember foreign names. Antti? No. Don't know. But they'd disappeared. Without a trace.'

'So what happened to them?'

Ernesto ignored Tommy's question. 'So now I'm interested. There's…' Ernesto clicked his fingers next to his temple and found the word: '*potential* here. I send in a scout. Is there any interest in distributing better merchandise than out-of-date medication? There is. We arrange a meeting.'

Ernesto sank back in his chair and finally took that second drag, which led to a coughing fit. Tommy quickly took the cigar from him so that Ernesto could concentrate on coughing and bringing up mucus with his hands free. When it was over he waggled his fingers impatiently. Tommy gave him back the cigar and said: 'You're going to kill yourself.'

'Listen to me. I've smoked cigars all my life, I've never drunk very much, and where does the cancer decide to strike? My liver. Unfair, no?'

Tommy shook his head, but refrained from comment. Fairness was a complicated concept in relation to Ernesto's previous lifestyle. However, Ernesto wasn't the type to brood on his misfortunes, so he continued.

'He looks terrible. He wants to keep his mask on when we meet, but I say no. I want to see the face of someone who's going to be my partner. So he takes off the mask. *Coño*, what a…pizza face. I saw a lot in Medellín, but this…More wounds than flesh. And right across, like this…' Ernesto drew two intersecting lines across his face with his index finger. 'Deep, deep scars that form an X.'

'Equis…' Tommy breathed.

'*Exacto*. Equis. I don't react at all. I'm like: all my friends look like this. My whole family looks like this.'

Ernesto let out a bark of laughter, but managed to stop it before it turned into another coughing fit. He held his stomach and grimaced in pain before going on. 'We get on well. Mutual trust. That's important. So we go into business together. Successful business. No messing. Respect. Good money. For a couple of years.'

Ernesto nodded to himself, a sadness in his eyes as he recalled a golden period in his working life. At the risk of interrupting the flow, Tommy just had to ask: 'And the Mikkonen brothers? Did you find out what happened?'

Ernesto shook his head. 'No idea. I heard about another guy too, some big player from Finland. Same thing. Gone.'

'Did you never wonder?'

'Nothing to do with me. He kept his side of the deal, I kept mine. How should I know? Maybe put the body in one of the industrial washing machines, run it with lye? Should work. Works in barrels.'

Tommy chose not to ask how Ernesto knew lye worked in barrels. Ernesto had always relied on the fact that he could speak freely to Tommy, but probing for details was impolite if nothing else. Tommy let it go.

'Okay,' he said. 'So a few good years working together. And then?'

'Then.' The corners of Ernesto's mouth turned down in disgust. 'Then Chivo came along.'

At that time Ernesto had been in the early stages of the investigation that would eventually put him behind bars, so he'd had no choice but to lie low. The young goat saw his chance, and offered to be the new supplier for the guy in the laundry. He refused. Whether this was out of loyalty to Ernesto or because he didn't trust Chivo wasn't entirely clear.

'So they came,' Ernesto went on. 'Five. No doubt they'd heard about the Mikkonen brothers. My eyes on the south side reported back to me. I got three guys together. We waited. They carried the laundry guy out to a car. He was a mess. A real mess. Into the trunk. Nothing we could do. We followed them. To Brunnsviken. They'd tied a rope around him, and attached a...'

Ernesto made circular movements in the air with his cigar, glowing sparks falling to the floor. 'What's it called? A tractor...not the whole wheel...not the tyre...?'

'A rim?'

'*Exacto!* A wheel rim from a tractor. To weigh him down. They threw him in. Careless. Too close to the shore. They carried him out onto the jetty. Threw him in. Then. We heard screams. Not very loud, but screams. Still alive. Chivo and the others. Laughed as he sank. They left. We waited a minute. Then we moved fast. Dived in. Cut the rope. Dragged him out.'

Ernesto's breathing was becoming shallower, his sentences more disjointed. He closed his eyes, took a couple of deep breaths, then waved a dismissive hand.

'Long story short. Guy gets treatment. At home. Survives. I think: can't stay here. Get in touch. With people. In Colombia. My people.

Send him away. Then I go to jail. Seven years. Don't hear much. Apparently he does well. He's an asset. That's all I know.'

Tommy thought of the grainy photograph from the jungle, the major players in the rival faction who were persuaded to take their own lives. *An asset.*

Somehow Ernesto managed to put out the cigar, sinking so deep into the armchair that it looked like a monster in the process of swallowing him. The narrative had taken its toll, and Tommy would have to hurry if he was going to get any more out of him.

'And now? What happens now?'

It was a long time before Ernesto spoke, and his voice was so weak that Tommy was afraid he was dying right there in front of him.

'I came out. He came back. He has his contacts. Back there. Current. I have mine. Old guard. Together...' Ernesto linked his fingers, his hands trembling, '...good business. Respect. Opportunities.'

Tommy looked at the shrivelled old man's body that seemed so alien to concepts such as respect and opportunities. 'Why do you do it, Ernesto? If you have so little time left, why do you carry on?'

A smile passed over Ernesto's sunken lips, and the faintest spark was lit in his eyes. 'What do you think I should do, Tommy? Play bingo? Enough now. Can you fetch Alma?'

'One last question. Do you know where he hangs out? Where can I find him?'

Ernesto blinked a couple of times, then laboriously hauled himself upright so that he could lean closer.

'Tommy. Listen to me. You don't go *near* him. All these years. Everything I've done. I've never met such a dangerous person. He's insane. He's...evil. He's the Devil. *El Diablo, entiendes?* Stay away from him. Far away.'

Linus

Close. I'm close now.

Even as Linus hovered on the cusp of two states he knew that he was closer than he'd ever been, without being able to define what exactly he was close to.

His vision cleared and all he could see was green and blue. A field, the grass cut very short, stretching to the horizon where it became blue sky. When he looked down he found that the distance between his eyes and the grass was no more than half a metre, because he was on all fours. The hands with which he was supporting himself had taken on the appearance of paws, fully equipped with claws.

Strong smells in layers drifted into his nostrils. Burnt flesh, cows and other animals, the stench of death and rusty metal. His sense of smell had been enhanced by several hundred per cent because he was now largely cat: a big cat, a predator. The feeling was amazing, as if he'd cast off an ugly, false shell in order to become what he really was. *Close.*

'Linus.'

Notwithstanding his metamorphosis, he knew that the two syllables uttered behind his back referred to him, so he spun around. In doing so he discovered firstly that his thigh muscles were incredibly strong, and secondly that he had a tail to help him balance. He was, to all intents and purposes, a cheetah.

If his own transformation seemed oddly natural, then the sight that met him when he turned was something very different. Before him stood a child, a boy maybe five years old, with clear, brown eyes. To the left of the boy stood a bear, to the right the Joker as played by Heath Ledger.

'Come with me, Linus.'

The child spoke with a child's high voice, but with the authority of a very old person. There was a temporary short circuit in Linus's brain. He wanted on the one hand to obey immediately, and on the other to fall backward and laugh, waving his paws over his tummy like a character from Winnie-the-Pooh. This was *too much*.

A surge of joy and strength flooded his body, and in his animalistic confusion he rejected both of those options in favour of the one that was now his soul, his essence: he began to run. The acceleration made possible by the explosive power of his leg muscles was unbelievable. In two seconds he'd reached a speed way above what he could ever have achieved as a human being, and he just kept going faster and faster. He flew across the grass, barely feeling the ground beneath his feet.

Everything he had previously thought of as enjoyable or satisfying disappeared like flakes of ash in his wake. A delicious pizza, an orgasm, a successful break-in, a bundle of money. Nothing. Simply isolated events and objects. He was running across the endless field in his perfectly calibrated, immensely powerful body, and he wanted to go on forever and ever.

When he'd been running for a while and slowed down to a tempo that was still faster than a human being could attain, the odour of cattle grew stronger. He followed the scent trail and something came gliding along from the horizon: an old-fashioned caravan attached to an equally ancient Volvo. That was where the smell of cattle was coming from, mingled with a whiff of dog and cat.

A new feeling took over. It started like an itch in the roots of his teeth, became a metallic taste in his mouth, then grew into a red film of blood lust coating his tongue. *Pets. Bite. Eat.*

He could smell people as well, two people, but if they got in the way of his prey they would also end up between his jaws; he knew he could easily deal with them. His tongue shot out and he licked his lips as he ran, eyes closed with pleasure.

When he opened his eyes again, there was something sitting on the grass between him and the caravan. He slowed down, then stopped. It was a tiger. A jet-black tiger. Linus raised his head and sniffed the air, but couldn't pick up its scent. The tiger's being was different in kind from the other phenomena in the field.

The tiger looked at him, got to its feet and walked slowly towards him. In spite of the fact that the hunting instinct still had him in thrall and he could actually see his intended prey, a little beagle lying under the caravan, some other instinct made him back off. With his tail between his legs and his head down, Linus edged away from the caravan. The tiger was his superior in a way that couldn't be measured in terms of strength or speed. It was…something else. After a few more steps Linus turned and fled.

His human brain was becoming accustomed to its wrapper of animal instincts, and as Linus ran towards the horizon he asked himself this question for the first time: *What is this place?*

The last thing he remembered was Järvafältet, the glutinous droplet that had fallen into his mouth, a dizzying sensation of tumbling across a border then awakening to this new reality, where all his previous worries and pleasures were irrelevant. He wanted to stay here. Whatever this place was, he wanted to be here in his newly discovered true body.

He looked up at the clear blue sky: a sudden sense of *spot the difference*. Something was missing. He moved around in a full circle, his eyes scanning the dome of the heavens, and discovered that there was only one thing missing, something so self-evident that everyone simply takes its presence for granted. The sun. There was no sun, just a sky that seemed to glow with an internal light of its own.

A new scent entered his nostrils, the burnt smell he'd picked up earlier; he spotted a human figure on the horizon, and at that instant the tiger was there once more, blocking his path. He turned and ran in a different direction, only to be swiftly cut off again. This happened at shorter and shorter intervals, until he realised what the immeasurably more powerful animal was doing. It was *herding* him. Back to his starting point.

*

'Finished?'

Linus was sitting on the ground, head down in front of the child, whose arms were folded over his skinny chest. The bear was regarding him with a distinct lack of interest, while the Joker could do nothing but smile with his exaggerated upturned lips.

Linus tried to form words with his new tongue, and found to his surprise that he was able to do so. 'Where are we?'

'A place,' the child replied. 'A place I made a long time ago.'

'Made?'

'Yes. I was in a bad place. So I made a good one.'

'Why is there no sun?'

'I didn't know much about the sun when I made this place.'

'But how…'

'Quiet,' said the child and, as if he'd pressed a button, Linus's jaws closed of their own accord.

By this stage he had understood that just as he was a cheetah here, Sergei was a bear and Alex was the Joker. Which meant that the child must be the man with the scarred face. Who had created this place and decided what should happen—who was allowed to speak and who was not, for example.

'It's like this,' the child said, sitting down on the ground and drawing his knees up to his chin as if he really was the little boy he appeared to be. 'There can only be two. So you have to choose. Who you want to get rid of. Or if you want to be the one who goes.'

Linus didn't have to choose. Before he'd had time to grasp the full implications of what the child had said, the bear who was Sergei leapt at him with astonishing agility. While he was in the air Linus saw that his claws were made of some shining metal with needle-sharp points, before they landed on his head. The Joker merely smiled.

*

Linus's newly acquired instincts sent a command to his resting legs and he flew backward at an angle, and upward. The bear passed so

223

close to his face that he felt a draught of air on his snout. Judging by the speed and weight, he knew he would have been dead if it had struck him. He landed on all four feet and saw the bear tumble to one side, caught off balance by the glancing blow Linus had delivered. Linus didn't hesitate. His hind legs, which had just landed, immediately sprang back as if the grass were a trampoline, and he stretched to his full length as he sank his teeth into the thick skin at the back of the bear's neck.

A stream of wonderful flavours gushed into his mouth. Sinews, muscles, nerves and, underlying them all, the life-giving shimmer of blood. A thrill of pleasure ran all the way to the tip of his tail and everything went black before his eyes in a moment of sheer bliss. Then pain: he landed flat on his back. Sergei had made the most of his inattention to retaliate, and although the blow was a little off, it was enough to hurl Linus several metres. His head was ringing as he struggled to focus, seeing nothing but a mass rushing towards him—a shadow determined to engulf him in eternal darkness. He rolled to one side, got back on his feet and ran a few steps.

One more time, from the top.

He and Sergei stood on all fours, glowering at each other. Sergei's unacceptable exploitation of the element of surprise had failed. Now they both knew what was at stake. Unfortunately the bite to the back of Sergei's neck hadn't pierced a major artery, but his fur was dark and wet. Linus skittered sideways; Sergei's gaze followed him.

It was all about not being hit by that enormous paw. One blow and it would be over. If Linus didn't die instantly, he would be helpless when the bear came at him with those vicious jaws. Linus circled around Sergei, bared his teeth and hissed.

The current situation was, perversely, every bit as wonderful as when he'd been running across the field. Despite the fact that he was in danger of being killed by a bear, Linus felt no fear. Extreme tension and total concentration, yes. But no fear. He was here. He was *present* in a way he hadn't been for as long as he could remember. And he couldn't remember.

Sergei grunted and lunged towards him, but Linus baulked with ease. And again. The bear was surprisingly fast, given his physical bulk, but Linus was faster. Sergei shook his head, let out a roar and held up a paw as if he were asking for a high five.

'Come and fight, you fucking coward.'

Linus drew up the corners of his mouth like a hyena. He'd already forgotten the possibility of human speech. Hearing Sergei's voice from that furry mouth was almost funny, but he couldn't allow himself to lose focus given that he was essentially facing an angry bear with knives for claws. Maybe Sergei was related to Wolverine, without actually having the soul of a wolverine.

And maybe Linus's bite had done more damage than he'd thought. After a few minutes—some circling, some half-hearted attacks—Sergei's head began to droop. The grass was stained with his blood, filling Linus's nostrils with a metallic bloom. The growing frustration in Sergei's body quivered in the air. Linus sat back and licked his right front paw, looking away from his opponent with a feigned lack of interest.

From the corner of his eye he watched as Sergei gathered himself. Linus waited until the very last moment, then leapt straight up towards the sky. Sergei's knife-claws ploughed furrows in the grass where Linus had been sitting a second earlier. Linus spun around and opened his jaws wide. He sank his teeth once more into the back of Sergei's neck, simultaneously extending his claws to swipe at the bear's eyes, then twisted away before Sergei could strike back.

One of Sergei's eyes was punctured, and Linus was chomping on a piece of flesh filled with oxygen-rich, venous blood. The child was behind him, watching with his head tilted on one side, while the Joker stroked one eyebrow idly with a butterfly knife.

Sergei swayed where he stood. Linus bit his rump, his back. Let him bleed for a while before burying his teeth in the aorta. Sergei was no longer capable of fighting. Linus locked his jaws around the life-giving artery, jerked his head back and tore it apart. Blood spurted from Sergei's body with every heartbeat.

They left the bear behind them, a brown mound on the green grass. Linus dropped a stone into the well of his conscience and listened for the devastating splash. It never came. The stone simply fell and fell. Wild animals have no capacity for guilt. They do as their nature dictates.

Alex was walking beside him twirling the butterfly knife with a dexterity that wouldn't be possible in the ordinary world.

'The body,' Linus said. 'What will happen to Sergei's body?'

Alex waggled his tongue in a manner that Linus recognised from the movie, and adopted the Joker's tone of voice: 'Acid rain falls. From time to time. It cleans the place up. Takes everything away.'

'I saw a caravan. How can that be here?'

'No idea.'

The boy, who was a short distance ahead, said over his shoulder: 'That's Lennart and Olof. I don't let the rain take them. They're nice. I go and visit them sometimes.'

Ahead of them, there had been a subtle change in the horizon. If the line between sky and grass had been a single pen-stroke earlier, it was now more like a line drawn with a felt marker, growing thicker until Linus realised it was a wall. A wall of darkness.

As they continued to walk, the line became a broad black band rising slowly from the ground. Linus couldn't work out its width or height. The closer he got, the bigger and more undefined it became. It was the end of the world, the edge beyond which nothing exists.

Alex explained quietly that sooner or later they would have returned to the ordinary world, when the effects of what they had swallowed wore off. However, it wasn't a pleasant experience. The process was gradual, and the period when you had one foot in each world was painful. Linus should be glad that he wouldn't have to go through it: that they had a companion who could lead them to the exit.

The exit.

The black wall was filling more and more of Linus's field of vision.

It brought with it a sense of fear and dread that reminded him of when he'd really seen Gårdsstugan for the first time. Until that moment his world had been limited to whatever he had in his hands or could see right in front of him. The playground, the nursery, the sandpit. But when he was four or five he had looked up and *seen* the height and width of the buildings, fully understood how many people lived their lives behind those windows. Fear. Dread.

Gårdsstugan was nothing compared to the wall towering above him now. His predator's heart was fluttering like a little bird's, the fear shot through with strands of sorrow. He didn't want to leave this place, leave his heightened senses and his strong, supple body, didn't want to go back to rat-faced Linus.

An impulse urged him to turn and run, race across the field with his paws drumming on the surface of the endless grass until he faded away or was consumed by the rain. However, he quashed the impulse. Just as the boy had made Linus's jaws close when he wanted him to be quiet, so he was no doubt capable of locking his paws, stopping his heart, making his head explode.

The boy was standing close to the wall. Alex went to join him, with Linus ambling along behind. The Joker took the boy's hand in one of his and held out the other to Linus.

Was he supposed to walk on his hind legs like some circus act? 'I'll follow your scent,' he said.

The boy seemed about to object, or to issue a command that Linus would have obeyed immediately, but instead he shrugged, said 'Good luck' and stepped into the wall with Alex on his heels. Linus gazed out across the field for one last time: the freedom that comes with having no limits. Then he padded into the darkness.

*

It didn't matter whether his eyes were open or closed. The darkness was complete, and when he looked back, despite having gone only a metre or so he saw nothing but dense blackness, as if a blackout

227

curtain had dropped on the edge of the field.

He sniffed the air and picked up the Joker's scent of sweat, unwashed clothes, make-up and rotting teeth. As he walked he used his senses of smell and hearing and attempted to create a picture of where he was now. If the field had been hard to grasp because of the lack of orienteering points, the darkness was worse. His hearing told him nothing. He could have been in a space of cosmic dimensions or a narrow soundproofed corridor.

Smell was marginally more helpful. Faint, distant scents—but not too distant. The space was large, but not endless. There were people here. Some living, some dead. He picked up shower gel, cleaning products, blood. And smoke. Far away Linus thought he could make out the glow of a cigarette that grew brighter when someone took a drag, then faded away again. He sneezed and continued to follow the Joker's trail.

The boy's scent was hard to define. He smelled like a child, a pleasant mixture of earth and vanilla, but there was an underlying tone of something much less appealing. Glowing iron, stagnant water, ash. *Hatred.* The boy's body was impregnated with the smell of hatred.

That particular odour drifted away, and was not replaced. Linus didn't know how long it was since he'd entered the darkness, but realised he was walking on two legs when he tripped over something on the ground and fell. He raised his head and shouted: 'Alex?'

While he was pondering he had been stripped of his guise as a cheetah, and his exceptional sense of smell was gone too. His human voice was swallowed up by the blackness, and there was no reply. He fumbled around—what had he landed on? Marble?—trying to work out what had made him stumble. A body. A cold, motionless body. A corpse. Linus battled a wave of nausea. His human nose was good enough to tell him that the corpse wasn't exactly fresh. He shuffled away and his hand touched another motionless body. He managed to get to his feet. The stench of death was everywhere, as if he was the only living person in a mass grave.

228

Person. I'm a person now.

He ran a hand over his stomach and found that he was wearing his normal clothes. He reached into his pocket and took out his mobile. No reception, but the torch was working. He held the screen above his head and shone the beam all around him. What he saw made him stagger backward; he almost fell again when his heels met dead flesh.

The image of a mass grave hadn't been too far off the mark, although it wasn't actually a grave. Linus was surrounded by dead bodies, scattered across the black, marble-like surface. The light from his phone wasn't bright enough for him to determine how many—twenty, thirty, maybe more. Some had had their throats cut, some had gunshot wounds in their heads, and they all had something about their appearance, clothing and physique that Linus had learnt to recognise as...criminal. Here they were. All those who had disappeared.

'AAAALLLEEEEX!'

Linus couldn't do anything about the panic in his voice. He was lost in the darkness, in the killing field, and as he moved the beam around he expected one of the bodies to rise up with black, empty eyes and say *welcome* and then the other bodies would rise up and he would be surrounded by rotting...

A movement on the outer edge of the circle of light. Linus's teeth began to chatter. *They're coming.* But the figures who stepped over the dead were not of their company. It was Alex and the scarred man whose name Linus didn't know. X. They were holding hands like the best of friends.

'Turn off the light,' X said. 'Something might see you.'

The phone almost slipped out of Linus's sweaty grasp as he fumbled for the button on the side. He found it and the darkness returned.

Something might see you.

He managed to push the phone back in his pocket. A hand groped its way over his arm, then seized his right hand and squeezed it. 'Idiot,' Alex hissed, dragging Linus along with him and sending arrows of pain shooting up his damaged shoulder and chest muscles.

They hadn't taken many steps away from the collection of corpses before Linus was able to make out something ahead of them. A rectangle; narrow, yellowish. After a few moments he could see that it was the outline of a door frame, with light beyond it. As he formulated the thought the door was opened by the man in front.

After so long in the darkness, Linus was blinded by the daylight that attacked his eyes. That was why he didn't see that there was no floor on the other side of the threshold. He fell half a metre and wobbled when his foot splashed down into wet mud. He almost lost his balance, but managed to stay upright. He looked back.

The door he'd just come through was part of a caravan. It wasn't a big caravan, in fact it was the smallest he'd ever seen. It was silvery-grey, and the shape reminded him of an egg. Behind the rectangular doorway with the rounded corners, the darkness gaped. He ran a hand over his face and turned away.

I think I've had enough now.

Much of what he had assumed to be true about the world and himself had been upended over the past few hours. His head felt overheated, like when the computer has too many windows open at the same time. The fans were full on and the motherboard was melting. He needed to switch off.

He looked around, his eyes half-closed. A few shabby wooden buildings, a mini-golf course where weeds had forced their way up through the cracks. There were two more caravans, paint flaking and covered in rust patches. They appeared to be on what was—or had been—a campsite. Parked among some bushes was a white van in which Linus might possibly have travelled earlier. He couldn't remember.

X opened the back doors of the van and said: 'We have work to do.' Linus urged his legs to get over there and help, but they refused to move. Sparks flew from the motherboard as incompatible images and processes were forced to run at the same time. Linus's field of vision was filled with white dots.

'Sorry...Can I take a little...break?'

The man looked at Linus, standing there swaying. He gave a brief nod and pointed to a cabin about ten metres away. It was the biggest building on the site, but it was in equally poor condition. Above the door hung a faded sign that said: *Office*. Linus staggered over to it. The room contained nothing but a sofa and a couple of armchairs. A small radiator was spreading a little warmth and a burnt smell.

Linus glanced over his shoulder and saw X and Alex drag the body of one of Chivo's gorillas out of the van and carry it towards the egg-shaped caravan. *Enough now*. Linus closed the door behind him and flopped down on the sofa. He took out his phone, intending to set an alarm. He checked the time.

If he'd retained any capacity for logical thought, his brain would have protested when he saw that *four minutes* had passed since they'd been in Järvafältet nature reserve. Four minutes during which he'd run and run on that other field and had fought with Sergei; had walked towards the darkness and through the darkness. But his brain was empty. He fell asleep.

Tommy

Sometimes Tommy got himself confused with Hagge: believed for a brief moment that he was his dog. He longed to get back home to his basket and his food bowl. Longed to rest his head on his paws and think doggy thoughts. Sometimes Tommy imagined he was dead. What was normally a diffuse, passing sensation had been exacerbated by the rumour that had turned his demise into a fact: Tommy T was dead.

As Tommy wandered towards Norrtull from Gårdsstugan, the two concepts drifted together and became one. Tommy T was dead, and Hagge was the one walking along here. Rationality kicked in as always and told him it wasn't true, but that didn't matter; it *felt* true.

Tommy stopped and was almost run over by a cyclist in neon lycra, a missile made of flesh that came flying along the pedestrian walkway, touched Tommy's jacket and flew on without slowing down. The cyclist was wearing a headset and had a little screen on the handlebars.

Melancholy

That was the word for what Tommy was feeling, a melancholy so strong and persistent that it was comparable to having died and become a dog. A miserable dog.

Tommy turned and looked back at Gårdsstugan. The morning's rain had passed, and the chequerboard of windows shone in an October sun with so little heat that it could have been an LED lamp. Six thousand people packed into four blocks that formed a cross, as if the man he knew as X was a culmination of the whole place, its soul boiled down into the figure of a lone psychopath. *I am Gårdsstugan.*

In Tommy's current state, everything seemed overwhelming. The desire for revenge that had surged in him was already spent. Many years ago, things had been very different. Back then, anger or ambition would have driven him relentlessly for days, weeks, until the job was done. These days such feelings popped their snouts above the slough of melancholy only briefly, then sank back down.

Tommy sighed, pushed his hands deep in his pockets and continued on his way into town. He felt so tired and sad he was almost enjoying it. He fantasised about dumping all his bedroom furniture and replacing it with a huge basket full of blankets and cushions. He would crawl in and curl up and let the gears of the world grind on without any input from him.

The sound of a drop of water falling into an echo chamber prompted him to lift his nose out of his mental refuge and reach into his pocket for his phone. He pressed the Snapchat icon. The sun was falling at an awkward angle over the screen, and he lost a couple of valuable seconds before he was able to make out the shot. It showed Linus lying on a sofa, nothing else. Then it vanished.

Tommy closed his eyes, wanting to preserve the image. The most important piece of information was that Linus almost certainly wasn't dead. Tommy had seen enough dead bodies in his time, and that wasn't a dead body. The hand clutching a mobile phone in the picture was an exhausted hand, not a hand in the throes of rigor mortis.

What else? He tried to visualise the room in which the photograph had been taken...Nothing—he'd been so focused on Linus. The sofa was upholstered in some kind of chequered fabric. Linus was asleep on a chequered sofa somewhere. The question Mehdi had asked still applied: Why? Why had he received this picture?

It was hard to believe it had been sent out of any desire to allay Tommy's fears. It seemed more likely that X wanted Tommy to know that he had Linus, and also that he understood what Linus meant to Tommy. But in that case, what was he hoping to achieve? If there'd been a sign on the floor in front of Linus that said *Stop writing or else* then Tommy would have stopped writing. But there was no exhortation, no threat. Just an image documenting the situation.

Tommy dug deep into his chest and discovered that the picture had done nothing to disperse the slop of melancholy splashing around in there. However, a red-hot point inside his head, just above his right eye, had stopped burning. He called Betty. 'Hi, it's me. Linus is alive.'

Betty gasped. 'Have you spoken to him?'

'No, I got a photograph. He's asleep.'

'What do you mean, a photograph? Who from?'

'From the person he's with.'

'But who's he with, I don't understand, who's sending you…'

'Betty, he's alive. And he's asleep. That's all I know right now.'

After some more back-and-forth along the same lines, Tommy said goodbye and promised to call Betty as soon as he knew more. He put his phone away and carried on walking. As he was passing the Wennergren Centre, a dubious-looking man came weaving towards him through the bare trees in Bellevue Park. Tommy felt a sudden urge to ask if he could sell him a cigarette, but pulled himself together and turned off for Roslagstull.

A little kick of nicotine would be very welcome—a little kick of anything, in fact. The desire scratched around in his mouth as he tried to grab himself by the hair and lift himself out of the slop that was making it so difficult for him to think.

Huddinge.

Ernesto had said that X came from Huddinge, and bearing in mind what Tommy knew about X's character, he probably meant the hospital. Open unit or closed? Given the lack of leads, he might as well look into a historical one. It might prove pointless in terms of the search for Linus, but Tommy wouldn't have become a journalist if he hadn't cultivated the desire to see the bigger picture, find connections.

It's something that exists in all human beings from an early age. Give us a pile of round, triangular and square bricks, show us a board with corresponding holes. How many children—or adults for that matter—can resist placing the bricks in the right holes, just because we can? We want to create order in what we see before us. For Tommy, the desire was so strong that it had become his profession.

He wasn't satisfied with knowing half of X's story when there was an opportunity to find out the rest. He had a foot in the door at Huddinge, a hold over someone. Actually, that was putting it mildly.

He had an iron grip on Albin Palm, registered psychologist.

*

Albin's name had come up when Tommy was working on his book on trafficking. Tommy's interviews with Anita had turned into conversations, and she'd mentioned a psychologist who worked, via an interpreter, with girls who'd had a breakdown because of the situation in which they found themselves.

'He's some kind of good Samaritan, is he?' Tommy had asked.

'No, no. If he manages to fix them up so they can go back to work, he gets paid.'

'What a bastard.'

Anita had smiled. 'As usual, it's not that simple. He's stopped a number of girls from taking their own lives. In a couple of cases, I know he's persuaded the pimps to let them go home. I'm not saying he's a good person, but he does as much good as he can in the circumstances. And he gets paid for it.'

'He's like you.'

'Yes. But without my charm.'

*

This had definitely proved true when Tommy eventually managed to wheedle a name out of Anita and arranged a meeting with the person in question, under the pretext that he was writing an article about the prison service.

Albin Palm was possibly the driest and most colourless person Tommy had ever met. From the dull shoes to the balding head, he was a thirty-year-old with the aura of a disillusioned pensioner. His suit was a size too big—or his body was a size too small; thin lips, small eyes, slender hands, skinny shoulders and a voice that was barely audible above the hum of conversation in the Espresso House café where they met.

The pimps Tommy knew were mostly big tattooed guys who worked out, with violence simmering in their eyes and voices that discouraged opposition. Albin was their polar opposite. Maybe that was why the girls felt able to talk to him.

Tommy got straight to the point and explained that the business with the prison service was just a pretext, and that he knew all about Albin's lucrative sideline. He wanted to find out more, and if Albin was cooperative then Tommy might give him a pseudonym in his book .

Albin's already stooped figure slumped even closer to the floor, and his double espresso rattled against the saucer when he attempted to pick it up. 'What do you want to know?' he asked, giving up on the coffee.

'How you got into it. What you do, where you do it, how much you get paid. The lot.'

'That's out of the question.'

'It's not your decision. If you tell me everything, I can disguise you so that no one will recognise you, and you can carry on working. Huddinge, isn't it?'

'*They* will recognise me. I'm the only one who does this. And then the girls won't have anyone.'

Tommy gave a wry smile. 'Are you trying to tell me you do this for purely altruistic reasons? You fix these guys' defective investments and you get paid for it—that's what this is about.'

Albin closed his eyes as if he were in pain. His eyelids looked so thin and fragile that Tommy felt a pang of sympathy.

'You're a hard man,' Albin said.

'No, no, I have a heart of gold. Just like you.'

Albin picked up his cup in both hands and knocked back the contents. Then he began to talk.

It had started when a prostitute who'd murdered a punter had come to him for a course of therapy. Once he'd managed to help her overcome her suicidal tendencies, she'd begged him to see a friend of hers. He'd met the other woman outside working hours, one thing had led to another, and before long he was the person the pimps rang when one of their girls was feeling particularly bad.

'It just happened,' Albin said. 'Terrible places. Terrible people. At first I didn't want the money, but they forced me to accept it. A few thousand. I wish I'd given it to charity or something, but I didn't. I didn't.'

When Albin eventually decided he wanted out because he could no longer cope with the sight of those young women with their aching bellies, locked in shitty rooms, he was threatened. He was in too deep to withdraw. So he carried on. Took the money. Carried on.

Tommy had to lean across the table in order to hear the last few sentences, which were uttered in a whisper as Albin covered his little face with his slender hands. Albin sat like that for a while, then took a deep breath, straightened up and said with a certain amount of dignity: 'I'm a dead man walking. If you want to shoot the final arrow, then be my guest.'

Was that a reference to St Sebastian? If so, Tommy didn't think it was entirely appropriate.

Nevertheless, he said, 'Okay.'

'Okay? What do you mean, okay?'

'I'll leave you out of it. But there's one thing you have to understand.'

The eagerness with which Albin received the news that he was about to be let off the hook made Tommy wonder if he'd made a big mistake. All the more reason to drive home what he was about to say to the suddenly alert Albin.

'I'm doing you a favour. Not including your story in the book is a loss. I'm losing something. And one day I might want something from you in return. I might not, but if it happens, you will give it to me. Are we agreed?'

They were agreed.

As Tommy continued to work on the book, it had become clear from conversations with consumers and vendors that Albin wasn't quite as blameless as he'd portrayed himself. For example, he'd held

237

out for more money, and on several occasions he'd groped the girls he was treating. Nothing major, but he was no arrow-pierced martyr.

So Tommy had no problem at all in picking up the phone four years later.

*

Cigotek—come on in for free advice on e-cigarettes!

The digital display board showed a girl in boxing gloves giving an oversized cigarette a roundhouse kick. Tommy peered into the store through the barred window. A couple of people were sitting at a rickety table blowing out smoke that instantly disappeared; the whole thing felt more like Amsterdam than Stockholm. He opened the door.

Ten minutes later he was back on Valhallavägen with an e-cigarette in his hand and a bottle of liquid nicotine in his pocket. The assistant had explained that he needed to let the solution sit in the atomiser for a few minutes before he began to suck. The ghosts of cigarettes from days gone by hovered over his tongue and palate as he wandered towards the Eastern Station.

He passed the florist's on the corner and was heading down to the subway when yet another impulse made him turn on his heel and go up to the restaurant. He often used to lunch there in the nineties, and he noted with satisfaction that nothing had changed since then: the same 1960s décor around the circular opening above the foyer, the same tablecloths—the same waitress, for God's sake.

Tommy opted for a beer and an egg sandwich with anchovies. When his order arrived, he took a sip of his beer, pressed the start button on his e-cigarette, took a deep drag and was overcome by a coughing fit that made the other diners turn and stare at him. He was a little more careful from then on, taking shallower puffs. He kept his head down and blew the thin clouds of smoke at his knees so that he wouldn't upset anyone.

It worked. The vaporised nicotine solution exorcised the ghosts,

238

and the desire to smoke faded away. He felt better until he caught sight of himself, hunched over like a repentant sinner as he tried to hide what he was doing. The e-cig had none of the dubious glamour of a real cigarette, and on top of everything else he felt pathetic. Tears pricked his eyes, and he realised he was about to cry.

For fuck's sake, Tommy! Get a grip!

He blinked and took an angry bite of his sandwich. He had to struggle to get the food past the lump that had formed in his throat. He was off balance, that was all there was to it. He had never, ever cried in public, and he had no intention of starting now. A swig of beer, another bite. Okay.

When he'd finished eating he felt a little better, until he made the mistake of picking up his phone and checking out Mehdi's Instagram account. The first thing he saw was the selfie Mehdi had taken earlier. The caption read: *Checking out the suicide on the statue with legend Tommy T in tow.*

Tommy didn't know how deliberate Mehdi's choice of words was, but if he'd had to guess, he'd have said: one hundred per cent. *Legend* sounded good, but in fact it was a intimation of obsolescence. A legend belongs to the past, and the validity of the description was questionable. As for *in tow*, there was no room for confusion. He'd been unambiguously dissed, as Mehdi would have said.

Tommy zoomed in on his own face and found that it exactly matched the epithet Mehdi had used. He looked old, tired, puffy and scruffy. Grey. In tow, as if there was a rope somewhere just out of shot that Mehdi was using to haul the legend along in his wake. Tommy switched off his phone and leaned forward, elbows resting on his knees. The Legend.

He stared down at the black stone floor and felt death coming closer. He'd done his thing and lived his life; all that remained now was the process of winding down, dwindling until he was considerably less than a legend. Someone who'd once existed, but not anymore. That was all.

'Hi, what are you doing here?'

Tommy looked up; maybe he had begun to weep without realising it, because his vision was blurred. The outline of the pale figure in front of him was surrounded by a diffuse halo. Tommy rubbed his eyes and the vision crystallised into Anita in an ivory sweater. She stroked his cheek. 'Are you crying?'

Tommy shook his head. As if a plug had suddenly been pulled out at the bottom of his chest, the emotional sludge poured out of him, leaving behind a wonderful space that slowly filled with light. He'd never bumped into Anita in town before, and the fact that it had happened at this moment seemed like fate.

'Okay,' he said.

'Okay what?' Anita asked as she sat down opposite him.

For once Tommy had difficulty finding the right words. 'Our fortunes,' he said. 'Combining. Everything. I want to. I really want to. If you still want to.'

Anita slowly shook her head in a way that presumably meant 'yes'. She picked up Tommy's e-cig from the table and twisted it around in her fingers. 'What made you decide?'

'I'm dying,' Tommy said. 'And I want to stop.'

Linus

Linus had once seen a promotional film for the illusionist Carl-Einar Häckner. He was wearing an evening suit and walking along a dirt track between two fields. In one hand he was holding a black balloon on a string. He didn't have a head. The balloon, however, had hair and was wearing a hat, but it didn't have a face.

That was how Linus felt as he stumbled along forest paths near Kymlinge—as if his mind had been separated from his body, and was hovering a short distance above his shoulders, controlling his movements through telepathy. The knowledge he had acquired from the torture and the lesson remained. He was nothing in this world and everything was pretend, a game he had to play.

He didn't even feel any guilt at having killed another person—admittedly in the guise of a bear, but Sergei would never again do business in this world, as far as Linus understood. And yet it didn't drag Linus down, because there was no real or significant body to drag down. His sinews and muscles ached from the electric shocks and the spell on the hook, but it was all happening somewhere else. Inside the balloon, everything was fine.

It was dizzying and wonderful at the same time. He'd loathed his body ever since puberty. The fact that he'd insisted on having the light off whenever he slept with Kassandra wasn't just because of her doughy flesh. He didn't want to see his own protruding hip bones, skinny thighs or narrow, hairless chest; his physique was every bit as off-putting as Kassandra's rolls of fat.

None of that mattered now. The marionette he was guiding between wet branches was simply something he had to live with. He felt no shame, no fear. In his heart he was a cheetah, and that was the essence of him. He had seen it, felt it, lived it.

He'd had only three hours sleep, and perhaps that was contributing to what he was feeling now, but it was hardly critical. *Look at that body! The temperature is only a couple of degrees above freezing, and it's stumbling along in soaking wet shoes, a T-shirt and a thin jacket. It's bitter weather, but am I cold? No. I cannot feel the cold because I am nothing.*

Linus emerged from the trees by the fence surrounding Kymlinge station, the subway platform that had never been used. He, Henrik and Matti had talked about an expedition to check out the place where the ghost train Silver Arrow stopped to pick up the dead, but they'd never got around to it. Linus trailed the fingers of his left hand over the fence as he followed it in the direction of Hallonbergen. His frozen fingertips tingled, but it was as if it was happening at distance. In his right hand he was carrying a plastic bag, the contents of which were worth half a million. That was a simple fact. In one jacket pocket he had a glass jar worth more than that; in the other, a gun. It was cool.

X had placed both objects in front of the table, pointed to the gun, a small Sig Sauer, and said: 'Instead of running away.' Then he'd pointed to the jar and its contents: 'If you *have* to run away.'

Linus's feet slapped on the ground as he walked, evoking the summer by humming the season's most irritating song; apparently Justin Timberlake had that sunshine in his pocket and that good soul in his feet. Whatever.

*

'Say something.'

Kassandra had been staring at the package on the kitchen table for thirty seconds. Linus was sitting opposite her, wrapped in a blanket. The cold and pain had caught up with him when he eventually got into the warmth, and his T-shirt and jeans were drying on the radiator. While Kassandra was sorting out his clothes, he'd slipped the Sig Sauer into a drawer in the hallway that she never used.

Kassandra's silence was starting to get on his nerves, and he repeated: 'Go on, say something.'

Her heavily kohled eyes made her look like a panda as she levelled

242

her gaze at him and said: 'This is something else.'

Linus shrugged his aching shoulders. 'What are you talking about—it's just a matter of quantity. It's the same thing, just ten times as much.'

'No. With that amount it turns into something else.'

Linus picked up the package, which was slightly larger than a brick. A burning sensation shot through the muscles of his upper arm, and he dropped the package on the table with a thud.

'It's a kilo. An object. A thing. Something we have to deal with. And we'll get a hundred and fifty thousand for our trouble. Which means thirty for you.'

At last Kassandra seemed prepared to consider the enterprise from a commercial point of view. She frowned. 'What, so you're only on fifteen per cent now?'

'No, thirty. We sell for five hundred a gram.'

'*Five hundred?* That's ridiculously cheap for quality like…'

'That's the way it is.'

Kassandra folded her arms and shivered. 'It's horrible, Linus. It's really horrible. How can you not think that?'

'I told you. Because it's not important. Because this world doesn't matter.'

*

He'd told Kassandra everything, as far as he could remember. How he'd been set up, tortured, suspended from the hook. The rescue mission, and what happened next: the field, the fight with Sergei. The journey through the darkness, the abandoned campsite. Kassandra had listened without interrupting, her panda eyes blank. Maybe she'd overdosed on some kind of tranquilliser.

'Nothing you want to ask?' he'd said with a hint of irony when he'd finished.

'Yes. Why aren't you dead?'

'What do you mean?'

'Everyone else who's been given this…lesson, if that's what you're calling it, has taken their own life. Why haven't you?'

The question hadn't even struck him until Kassandra asked. He tried to recall the lesson, what it actually *was*, and all that came to mind was a darkness, and the knowledge that this darkness was everything, while he himself was nothing. He remembered this insight flooding his body with a physical certainty when X placed his hands on Linus's shoulders.

'Because he didn't let me.'

'What? The lesson is the lesson, as I understand it. Everyone learns the same thing, the thing that I've known for a long time, if you don't mind my saying so.'

'No. There are different *ways* of knowing.'

'Right. So you're like a Buddhist now, are you?'

In the past Kassandra's sarcastic tone of voice would have enraged him or flattened him, but he knew what he knew, even if he couldn't put it into words. Before she could make any more cynical comments he'd brought out the package and put it on the table, which shut her up very effectively.

*

Now she was sitting with her arms folded, staring at the package in horror as if it was a cobra, poised and ready to attack. Suddenly something happened. The aura around her changed as if a dimmer switch had been turned up. She relaxed, unfolded her arms and actually smiled as she said: 'You're right.'

'About what?'

'About the fact that it's not important. Do you know what I've started to do?'

'No.'

Kassandra made the index and middle finger of her right hand into two little legs, walking across the table. 'I've started going up onto the roof. All the way to the edge.' The fingers kept on walking until the flaking, black-painted nails were hanging over the edge of the table, the fingers themselves swaying. 'I shuffle forward one centimetre at a time until my feet are about halfway over...'

'For fuck's sake, Kassandra.'

'Wait. The point is that I find the spot where my weight is perfectly balanced. One puff of wind is all it would take to make me fall forward. Then I stand there and wait. *That's* what I've started to do.'

'Weren't you the one who said that suicide is as meaningless as living, and that's why you wouldn't do it?'

'It's not suicide. I'm just giving the universe the opportunity to take my life.' Kassandra weighed the package in her hand. 'And you shouldn't complain. I just thought about it, and it's given me some perspective on this crap.'

'I don't want you to keep doing that. I don't want you to die.'

'I can stop. If you promise me something. Again. Do you remember?'

'What?'

'We said we'd jump together if we haven't managed to get away from here by the time we're twenty.'

It was a long time since Linus had thought about the promise made in an over-stimulated and drunken state, and it no longer felt relevant. The realisation that existence lacked any kind of meaning had made him more determined than ever to stay alive. He didn't understand it, but there it was.

He didn't want Kassandra to put herself in mortal danger. Why not? He didn't know that either. With this new way of seeing, all reason had become blurred because there was no solid base. Everything was fluid. However, since this also meant that words were no more than sounds uttered into the silence, it was perfectly simple for him to look Kassandra in the eye and say: 'Absolutely. We will. I promise.'

*

They turned to the logistics. Shifting a thousand grams was going to take more than an afternoon. Kassandra said it took her about two minutes to make up a one-gram bag, so she would need over thirty hours just to weigh the stuff out.

'We'll make four-gram bags,' Linus decided. 'At that price it won't be a problem.'

'Okay, so ten hours then. But how the hell are you going to sell two hundred and fifty units?'

Linus grinned. 'Units— that's good. Sounds more businesslike. Swanning around in a suit, discussing transactions in units. Brilliant.'

'That's not an answer.'

'I'll talk to Matti and Henrik.'

'Linus.' Kassandra leaned across the table and held out her hand. Her sleeve rode up, exposing a network of thin scars on her forearm. She grabbed Linus's hand and squeezed it hard. 'You're treating this as if it's a matter of selling a few bottles of cheap booze. You do realise this is something completely different, don't you? Like I said. This quality, this amount. You'd have to be up for…first-degree murder for it to be a more serious offence.'

'I'm below the age of criminal responsibility. And I haven't been caught dealing drugs before.'

'I don't think that would cut it in this case.'

Linus wasn't interested in discussing the matter any further. He looked around the room and spotted the cockroach in the jar on the windowsill. He picked it up and waggled it back and forth. The insect slid along the bottom of the jar, its antennae waving in the air. Linus laughed. 'Jesus—is it the same one?'

Kassandra nodded. Linus held the jar as close to his eyes as he could without losing focus, and studied the little black thing—this precision mechanism with the apparently unquenchable flame of life. It was so pathetic, yet at the same time so horribly worthy of respect. He understood it now. No problem whatsoever. He only had to look at himself, and he was looking at the cockroach. He put the jar back on the windowsill and gestured towards the package on the table.

'Like you said. They're units, to be portioned up and sold. That's all.'

Kassandra shook her head. 'We're in the dark, Linus. I've nothing against that, but we are in the dark.'

'I've seen the darkness,' Linus said. 'And this isn't it.'

Kassandra gave a supercilious smile, as if he'd said something pretentious. His jacket was draped over the back of the chair, and he had a sudden urge to take out *his* glass jar and show it to her, but he quelled the impulse. The glutinous black substance didn't look impressive, and it was his secret. He knew exactly what he was going to do with it, and it didn't involve Kassandra.

Justin Timberlake could have the sunshine in his pocket. Linus had an entire world in his.

*

After his father's accident Linus had begun to spend more time hanging out in the courtyard because the apartment felt musty and… sticky. Both his parents had been active, outgoing people, and were ill-suited to the roles of carer and cripple. The air became suffused with sorrow and bitterness, so Linus was drawn downstairs and outside.

He gradually started hanging out with two other boys who had their own reasons for being there. Henrik was in the class above Linus at school and Matti was in the class below, but he'd had to repeat a year. He and Linus were eleven and Henrik was twelve. They must have seen one another when they were younger, maybe even played together, but it wasn't until they were exiled from their respective families that they became friends and bear-brothers.

Matti's father was something of a celebrity in Gårdsstugan, but for all the wrong reasons. When Matti was five years old, the family's poodle had peed on the floor because Matti's parents were too drunk to take it for a walk. In a rage, the father had hurled the dog from the balcony on the ninth floor.

That alone would have guaranteed a certain notoriety, but the dog had landed on a seven-year-old girl who was skipping with a couple of friends. She crashed to the ground, breaking her collarbone and sustaining permanent brain damage. The dog died instantly.

The incident was reported in the newspapers and gave rise to a vicious hate campaign on Flashback. The combination of animal cruelty and an injured child inspired detailed posts about what the writers would like to see happen to Jokkum, Matti's father. They made a point of finding out his name and using it frequently.

Regardless of public opinion, the drunkenness and lack of malicious intent counted as mitigating circumstances. Jokkum was sentenced to one year in jail. He served two months before he was beaten to death in the common room.

You might have thought the news of his demise would put a stop to the hate campaign, but no. It simply shifted focus and directed itself at Matti's mother, the whore who had fucked the bastard. Phone calls, letters, stalking, words whispered through the letterbox all combined to reduce her to a quivering lump of fear who needed a handful of pills to get out of bed and a bucket of booze to get to sleep.

By the time Linus and Matti started hanging out, the campaign had long since moved on to fresh targets but Matti's mother still hardly dared show her face in public. The only person she saw—apart from Matti—was her brother, when he was home from his trans-Europe trucking run. She spent most of her time in the apartment, smoking with the blinds closed. Matti couldn't stand being in there with her.

Henrik's situation was very different. It took several years before Linus began to understand, and before Henrik had the language to explain why he sought refuge outdoors.

Both his parents worked at Karolinska Hospital: his mother in the canteen, his father in the maintenance department. They had met at a staff party and soon produced two children, Henrik and his sister Liisa, two years younger. Henrik didn't know what went awry after that, or if there had always been a problem.

They went to work and got home at five-thirty. His mother

cooked tea while his father read the paper. The family ate. Then his parents watched television until they went to bed at eleven. That was it. The first time Henrik talked about his home life, Matti had almost punched him as he sat there on the climbing frame looking miserable.

'What the fuck is wrong with you?' Matti said. 'You've got the fucking dream family there! Linus's father's a vegetable and my mother's a nutcase and you just…*boo hoo, my mummy and daddy go to work and come home and watch TV!'*

On that occasion, Henrik had been unable to explain any more clearly. Head down, shoulders drooping, he'd left Linus and Matti on the climbing frame and gone home to his Perfect Family.

Over the years, Linus came to understand better. One day he and Liisa happened to bump into each other on the way to school. He'd never really talked to her before, and after the endless seven-minute walk he was determined never to talk to her again. She was the most depressing ten-year-old he'd ever met. She was like a *fish*.

The slightly bulging eyes showed no emotion, and barely even blinked. Her hair was straight and dull. She hardly said anything, and what she did say was spoken in a monotone, as if she was unfamiliar with human language. It was hard to imagine a red heart beating in her body, warm blood flowing through her veins.

Linus had never seen her around except when she was walking to and from school, so presumably she spent most of her free time at home. It had turned her into an amphibian, a fish on land.

Eventually he met Henrik's parents, and they had exactly the same aura. By that stage Henrik had a greater capacity for abstraction, and the word he used was *cold*. It was so cold at home. Even in the winter he had to get out of the apartment in order to avoid freezing to death.

*

The three boys were brought together by the fact that something was lacking in their lives; the reasons were different, but the result was the same. They were all unhappy at home, and created a new 'family' together. Another common denominator was that they received very little money from their parents—Linus and Matti because there wasn't any, Henrik because his mother and father believed he had everything he required.

They needed a business, and suitable premises. Linus was already selling his medication, and had contacts. Matti had his truck-driving uncle who could supply this and that, while Henrik had a place they could use.

Every apartment in Gårdsstugan had a storage facility in the basement. On top of all the other weird stuff about Henrik's family was the fact that they never visited theirs, because there was nothing in it.

'What?' Linus had said. 'Surely you must have *something*. Some old…I don't know…kitchen chair? Ugly picture?'

'No. Mum and Dad only have things that are necessary. They use them until they're no good anymore, then they throw them away.'

'But what about your old toys?'

'I didn't have many. They sold the ones I did have when I grew up.'

Matti laughed and gave Henrik a playful shove. 'That's so depressing! Say what you like about my mother, but my Moses basket is still mouldering away down there.'

Henrik shrugged. 'Not mine. I don't even know if I had one.'

'No,' Matti said. 'You probably had to sleep on the floor. And eat gravel.'

'Maybe,' Henrik said, without a hint of a smile. 'Shall we take a look?'

'Have you got a key?'

'I have.'

*

The room was indeed completely empty. The floor was covered in a thick layer of dust, and the fluorescent ceiling light was equally dusty. The boys stood with their hands in their pockets visualising how the six square metres could be used, what the place might look like. As if on cue they each chose a corner and sat down, gazing at the space and at one another.

'It works, right?' Linus said.

'Absolutely,' Matti agreed.

Twelve cubic metres of air currently filled with dust motes dancing in the light, but twelve cubic metres that belonged to them. That same afternoon they found a rug in the junk room, where residents could leave unwanted items, and over the next few days they searched dumpsters and abandoned storage facilities until they had a place worthy of three bear-brothers. Needless to say, they called it the Den.

The Den was furnished with a two-seater sofa bed, an armchair, a corner table with a small Bluetooth speaker, plus a seaman's chest with a bad case of woodworm. A standard lamp with a large shade spread a soft glow after Matti ran a wire from the ceiling light, which was never switched on again. It was snug and it was perfect.

Since the Den was directly linked to Henrik, they decided it wasn't a good idea to use it for storage, in case problems arose. They found a smaller facility that no one was using, and made it theirs by fitting a sturdy padlock to which each of them had a key. Once the business got going, that was where they kept the smuggled booze and cigarettes, and anything they managed to lift from various loading bays.

Linus ran the medication side of things alone, but put some of the profits into the seaman's chest, which was also secured with a padlock. Matti and Henrik did the same when it came to their solo projects. They were bear-brothers, they were the kings of Gårdsstugan.

At the same time, they knew they were really only minor players. When they were fourteen and fifteen respectively, they made a half-hearted attempt to raise their game by giving themselves tattoos. They looked online to find out how to do it, but as none of them was artistically inclined, they went for a hastily executed triangle in blue ink on the upper arm. At least it confirmed the fact that they belonged together, that they had one another's backs.

Linus's stint in residential care inevitably led to an interruption in their activities, and when he and Henrik went up to the high school and Matti began an apprenticeship with a firm of electricians, they drifted apart. They were still brothers, and each of them knew that the other two would be there no matter what, but their business enterprise and the intensity of their companionship was put on hold. All three missed those golden years—lounging around in the Den, slightly pissed, listening to music and counting their money as they made increasingly crazy plans for their brilliant future. The feeling that anything was possible. They missed that feeling.

*

Henrik and Matti had replied straight away when Linus texted to say that he had something good on the go, could they meet up? Absolutely. Where and when? When Linus wrote *Primavera in an hour* he received a frowning emoji from Henrik, and one he'd never seen before from Matti: a question mark dripping with blood. Linus replied: *It's cool. Trust me.* He wasn't big on emojis; as an ironic gesture he added a grinning devil giving the thumbs up.

He understood their concerns. Under normal circumstances, three boys from the south side going to Primavera would be like asking to be beaten up. But these were not normal circumstances. Chivo had met his end on the unicorn's horn, and his crew were lying dead in the darkness between two worlds. The stage was empty at the moment, so it was important to show up: join the new cast.

The main role would no doubt go to Alex, who had contacts on the north side and whose father came from Uruguay. His real name was Alejandro, but he'd stopped using it since it was taken over by a TV hand-puppet in the shape of a Chilean monkey. With X's backing he would pick up Chivo's fallen mantle and take over his business—which, after the show of strength in the gym, was entirely achievable. Rumour spread like the wind, and being linked to X was the best possible testimonial.

That wind was probably also whispering Linus's name, which meant he could probably go to Primavera without undue risk.

Probably. But that was the plan: to establish himself on the north side. Create a presence: snap up both leading and supporting roles before anyone else got wind of a casting call and turned up for auditions.

*

Linus had been to Primavera once before, with his mum and dad when he was ten years old. There was no problem for a normal family back then: the territorial restrictions applied to people in the business, plus teenagers. Linus knew nothing about any of it at the time, he just thought it was cool to go to a pizzeria.

He didn't remember much about it, apart from the fact that there was some kind of cowboy-based décor, his pizza had been a little too spicy, and he'd played on an Addams Family pinball machine with his dad: a good day.

Linus stopped by the carpet-beating rack, took out his phone and looked up at his window. He stopped himself before he made the call. If there had been any chance of his father answering, he would have done it. The memory of the pinball game had softened him. But his father couldn't speak, and his mother's hysteria would come gushing down the phone. He couldn't deal with that right now, he needed to stay focused. He slipped his mobile back in his pocket and headed for the square.

*

There was no sign of the Latinos who usually hung out around the ICA store. In fact the square was more or less deserted, as if the police tape around the fountain was acting as some kind of deterrent although the cops themselves were nowhere to be seen. One exception: a kid aged about ten or eleven, taking photos of the fountain with his phone. Linus went over to him. 'Hi. Why are you doing that?'

The kid gave a start and looked suspiciously at Linus. He decided Linus was neither a cop nor a danger. 'Haven't you heard?'

'Heard what?'

'Chivo—you know Chivo? He came running into the square this morning, jumped straight up in the air and…' The boy struck his chest with his fist. 'Splat! The horn went straight through his heart. Can't you see the blood?'

Linus looked at the discolouration on the unicorn's forehead and snout. He reckoned the distance between the ground and the horn was around three metres. 'That was one hell of a jump—I mean like a world record. How did he manage that?'

The boy shrugged. 'He was completely crazy, of course.'

'Why?'

The boy looked around, less to check that no one was listening than to make the point that he was about to drop some serious info. Linus smiled. Someone in the kid's family had to be in the business for him to be so familiar with the body language at such a young age. The boy lowered his voice, leaned closer and said: 'The Mask had spoken to him.'

'The Mask? What, like Jim Carrey?'

The boy sighed, indicating that it was really beneath his dignity to talk to an idiot like Linus, but he placed a hand over his face, fingers spread like the monster in *Alien*, and said: 'The Mask—he has different faces. Masks.'

'And is he dangerous?'

'Are you kidding? He's like the most dangerous person in the world. If you meet him, you're toast.'

'Okay. I'll be careful.'

'You do that,' the boy said with an indulgent smile as he returned to his photography. Linus continued on his way.

*

A smell swept over him as he opened the door of the pizzeria and a hollow wave of hunger surged through his stomach. He hadn't eaten for twenty-four hours; he'd kept going on his body's meagre reserves and sheer willpower. Now there was food within reach, his hunger made its presence known.

Henrik and Matti were cowering in an alcove in the back corner, trying to be invisible. Linus took his time, scanning the restaurant casually, like a real brother. It was just before twelve, and the lunch service hadn't started. Apart from Henrik and Matti, there were only a couple of alcoholics sitting by the window, making a single beer last as long as possible.

When Linus's gaze reached the corner by the counter, his composure cracked a little and his lips curled upward in a smile. The Addams Family pinball machine was still here. Unbelievable. It must have discovered the secret of eternal life. He reached into his pocket and found a ten-kronor piece, but going straight for Lurch and Morticia instead of Henrik and Matti would be uncool. They waved and he went over to their table.

He endured the bear-paw greeting and slid into the alcove. Henrik checked his phone and said: 'I have to be back in forty minutes. I had to leave fifteen minutes early to get here. The lunch break doesn't actually start until...'

'Okay, you're in a hurry. Matti?'

Matti shrugged. 'I took a long lunch.'

'Can you just do that?'

'We'll soon find out.'

Of the two boys, Matti was the one who'd changed the least. He'd just grown a few inches since he was twelve; he was a head shorter than Linus, but significantly more muscular. His wayward brown hair hung down over his forehead, and his expression was smart and alert. He was the player who swooped in and helped himself before the others had worked out what was going on.

Henrik looked more like Linus, with a long, narrow face and mousy hair waxed into a slicked-back style that emphasised the spots on his forehead. He'd managed to get onto the sociology course at Täby, where the kids in his class came mainly from well-off homes, and now he was trying so hard that it was painful to watch. The

255

Morris sweatshirt and the slicked-back hair couldn't compensate for the tense desolation in his eyes—Gårdsstugan eyes. His fingers moved restlessly over the screen of his mobile on the table. Linus pointed at it. 'Something important?'

'No, I just…'

'Then leave it.'

Henrik looked up, frowning at Linus's authoritative tone of voice. Before he had time to object, Linus said: 'Have you ordered?'

'No,' Matti replied. 'Bit short of cash at the moment, so…'

'Order whatever you want. On me.'

Matti peered out from under his fringe and grinned. 'Is this from selling *biscuits*?'

'That's right. It's from selling biscuits. Have a beer.'

*

While they were waiting for their pizzas, the restaurant began to fill up. In spite of his hunger, Linus felt a warm glow in his belly when a couple of guys who'd been part of Chivo's crew walked in and immediately looked away when they saw him. They obviously knew who had his back.

If you meet him, you're toast.

Linus decided this was a good time to show Henrik and Matti how the land lay, so he shouted: 'Hey!' and beckoned the two guys over. They exchanged a look before answering the call. Henrik sank down in his seat and whispered: 'Have you lost your fucking mind? I don't want to go back to college with…'

'Shut it.' Linus glanced at Matti, who seemed dubious but interested. The guys came up to the table, pushed their hands into their back pockets and nodded to Linus. Job done. They were a few years older, with neck tattoos and gold chains. The fact that they'd even acknowledge his existence for any reason other than to beat him to a pulp would have been unthinkable twenty-four hours earlier.

But power is not power until it has been exercised, so Linus nodded in the direction of the pinball machine. 'Does it work?'

The guy who looked the hardest, and whose tattoo reached all the way up to his earlobe, nodded cautiously while checking out Henrik and Matti, like a hunter seeking out an alternative prey when the animal closest to him is in the off season.

'Good,' Linus went on. 'In that case I only need a ten.'

Power or not, it's all about knowing where the boundaries are. For example, Linus didn't hold out his hand. That would have been impressive, but the risk wasn't worth taking at this point. The guy looked Linus in the eye, and Linus held his gaze. They stared at each other as silent questions and answers ricocheted in the air and information was exchanged as if over super-fast wi-fi, until the guy nodded and said: 'You'd better find one, then.'

Not ideal, but Linus gave no indication that his opponent had played an impressive shot. Instead he nodded, his expression rueful. He took out his phone. 'In that case I'll give Alex a call, see if he's got one. What's your name?'

The guy's eyes narrowed and his lips tightened. He was weighing up his options. His colleague had already made up his mind; he produced a ten-kronor piece and placed it on the table. The hard man let it happen, still staring at Linus, who picked up the coin with an indifferent nod of thanks before turning to Henrik and Matti, ignoring the gaze burning into the side of his head.

'I'm starving,' Linus said. 'I ordered two, but I think I could eat three.'

Henrik and Matti had nothing to say; they had been struck dumb by the murderous intent coming their way from the end of the table. Linus slowly turned back, looked the guy up and down, raised his eyebrows and said: 'Was there something else?'

'No. Not at the moment.'

'Okay. See you around.'

Linus focused his attention on his friends once more. After a few seconds he heard a snort, and the guy walked away. Game, set and match.

A minute or so later the pizzas appeared, and Matti decided to accept the offer of a beer. Linus gave Henrik a hundred-kronor note and asked him to go and get the drinks.

'What the fuck? Are you going to start bossing me around too?' Henrik said.

'Yes, I am. But right now the fact is you're the only one who's eighteen. So you're the only one who can buy booze.'

'So you say jump and everybody says how high?'

'That's not how it works. Come on, Henrik.'

Even though Henrik had said he was in a hurry, he took his time getting to the bar. Linus was under no illusion that his newly acquired status carried any weight in the real world, and being turned away would be a real slap in the face. No doubt Chivo would simply have clicked his fingers for someone to come rushing over with a beer, but Linus wasn't there yet.

Neither Henrik nor Matti had commented on the showdown with the Latinos; they had simply stared open-mouthed at Linus until the pizzas arrived. Linus rolled up his capricciosa and took a big bite. Matti placed a hand on his shoulder and said: 'Okay. How the hell did you do that?'

'Stuff's happened.'

'Is this to do with Chivo?'

Linus nodded. 'I was there. He had me picked up, tortured me. Hung me up on the hook. And then someone rescued me.'

'Who?'

Linus gave Matti a long look. 'Who do you think?'

Matti pulled a face and shook his head. 'No, no. No, no, no. Not a chance.'

Henrik came back from the bar and slammed a glass of beer down in front of Matti so that it splashed over the edge. 'Not a chance of what?' he wanted to know.

'Linus.' Matti gestured towards him with his whole hand as if he were a circus attraction. 'Linus just told me that the guy with the faces or masks or whatever rescued him from Chivo.'

'I'm with him now. That's just the way it is.' Linus took another huge bite as Henrik slid into his seat, stared at his Acapulco, swallowed a couple of times, then he too shook his head. 'I feel sick. I can't eat that. What the fuck do you think you're doing, Linus? I thought those guys were going to make mincemeat of us.'

'Didn't you hear what I said? I'm with *him* now.'

Henrik pushed the pizza away. 'I don't know what you're talking about.'

Matti hadn't reacted quite as badly as Henrik, and had already polished off a quarter of his Subcomandante Marcos with a couple of swigs of beer. He flapped his hand in front of his mouth and said to Henrik: 'You can't have missed this—the guy who's taking over? Everything. Those who are against him either kill themselves or disappear. And he's pushing the purest coke anyone's ever seen. Linus's uncle's written about it, for fuck's sake.'

'I haven't read the papers. I've got so much work to do...'

'Shut up.' Matti turned to Linus. 'You say you're with him—what does that mean?'

During Matti's little lecture, Linus had managed to finish his first pizza, taking the edge off his hunger. He would be able to enjoy the next one. He leaned across the table and signalled to the others to do the same. When they were close enough to hear him whisper, he said: 'It means. Among other things. That I have the best backing. You saw the Latinos. And it means. That I have *a kilo*. Of the coke Matti mentioned. And it means. That you should be very glad you know me.'

After a brief silence, Linus expanded on the quality of the goods and financial arrangements. They would get a hundred each of the sale price per gram, and were permitted to add on no more than a hundred themselves. So they were looking at a possible profit of two hundred thousand. Silence. Then Henrik got to his feet. 'I have to go.'

'Sit down. Didn't you hear what I said?'

'Yes,' Matti chipped in. 'Sit down.'

Henrik flopped back down, gazed gloomily at his uneaten pizza and said: 'It sounds great, but...well, I'm in college now.'

'Why?' Linus asked.

'To get an education, of course.'

'Why?'

'I don't know—so I can go to university, maybe?'

'And then?'

'Get a job. Like normal people do.'

'As what?'

Henrik shuffled uncomfortably, still glowering at the pizza as if it were to blame for his lack of clarity with regard to his future. Linus knew that Henrik had no idea *why* he was studying; it was just something that his mother and father had made him do, in their ice-cold way. And his grades were crap.

'Let's go over this one more time,' Matti said. 'You say ninety per cent purity, you say five hundred a gram, and do you know what I say to that? I say *bullshit*. It's impossible to get hold of that kind of quality, and if it was possible, it would cost...I'm not sure, but at least two thousand a gram. At least.'

'Well, that's the way it is,' Linus informed him.

'I'll believe it when I see it.'

'You will.'

*

When Linus had eaten his second pizza and his stomach felt as if it was made of modelling clay, he told the others to go to the Den and wait for him. Henrik was still moaning. In the end he agreed to skip the rest of his classes for the day, but only because it was cool to meet up again. That was the *only* reason.

Linus gave them a minute's head start, then followed them, checking to make sure they weren't watching to see where he went. When Matti asked where Linus was storing the barely believable shit,

Linus had told him not to bother his pretty little head about it.

He didn't want to involve Kassandra, partly because he wanted to protect her—keep her out of any possible trouble—and partly because he thought it was a good leadership technique to keep the two branches separate. And the worst and most important reason was because he didn't want Henrik and Matti to find out about his relationship with Kassandra.

Henrik had never had a girlfriend, but Matti's girlfriend Julia belonged to the very highest echelon of Gårdsstugan society. She was the kind of girl people turned around to look at, drinking in the way she walked, wondering if the back view was as attractive as the face they'd just seen. Introducing Matti to fat emo Kassandra would be asking for gibes and sneers, and Linus couldn't afford that anymore.

Henrik and Matti disappeared into Henrik's apartment block, and Linus moved quickly across the courtyard. In the elevator up to Kassandra's place he thought about his current situation, where he could no longer *afford* certain things. He wasn't a minor player now; he didn't have to take the crap raining down on him from above, but nor was he a major player able to dictate his own terms. He was in the middle, where it was all about not losing face.

Kassandra started babbling when he told her he'd come to collect the coke, called him an idiot. He tolerated it from her, but only from her. Maybe it was a good thing—we all need someone to call us out, make us think. He thought. Then he asked: 'Have you got an old backpack or something?'

More babbling, but in the end she dug out her school backpack. It was black, scruffy, and covered in badges with slogans like: *Meat is murder*, *Reclaim the streets* and *Strangle the last priest with the entrails of the last king*. She'd made the last one herself. Linus pushed the package into the bag and zipped it up.

'What if someone takes that off you?'

'Nobody's going to take it off me.'

'How can you be so sure?'

Linus retrieved the gun from the drawer in the hallstand and tucked it into the waistband of his trousers. 'Nobody's going to take it off me.'

Surprisingly enough, Kassandra didn't say anything about the gun. She just went very still, then nodded and said: 'So that's where we are.'

'That's where I am. I don't know where you are.'

She took his face between her hands and kissed him gently. Linus closed his eyes. There was nothing wrong with her lips—quite the reverse. They gave him a moment of blissful peace during this jagged day. Their lips parted, she rested her forehead against his and said: 'I'm with you.'

Linus felt good as he left the apartment block. The sun was peeping through a gap in the clouds, the pizza had settled in his stomach and his lips recalled the kiss. He had a kilo of the finest coke on his back, a gun in his waistband and another world in his pocket.

He remembered standing on his balcony just a couple of weeks earlier, hands clutching the railing as he gazed towards the city, longing for it to begin. Now it had begun—with a vengeance. He had the stuff, he had the traction. At last he was on his way.

*

There was something odd about the atmosphere when he arrived in the Den. Linus had expected his crew to be sitting there like burning candles waiting for Daddy to come home with the candy, but Matti was perched on the edge of the sofa looking worried, while Henrik was slumped in the armchair with a blank expression on his face.

'What's the matter? Has something happened?' Linus asked.

Matti spread his hands wide. 'I don't know—Henrik had some kind of breakdown.'

'It's nothing,' Henrik said in a thick voice.

'Come on, talk to me. We have to be on the same side here.'

Henrik waved a hand in the air, pointing vaguely in the direction of various items in the Den. 'It's just…It's such a long time since I've been here.'

'And?'

'Things were so good for a few years. It was the only good time in my life. Sitting here messing around. It all came back to me. These days everything's shit.'

Henrik was on the verge of tears. Linus went over, squeezed his shoulder and said: 'Go and sit on the sofa. Then you'll see.'

Henrik did as he said. The pecking order must be established at every point. Linus was in charge, so he took the armchair. Subordinates on the sofa, hands resting on their knees. Matti shuffled sideways to make room for Henrik, but avoided touching him, as if he were afraid that Henrik's general wetness might spill over onto him. He glanced at Linus to show that he'd understood the demonstration of power.

Linus opened up the backpack, fished out the package and slammed it down on the tiny coffee table. Matti folded his arms and looked at it, then at Linus. He pushed out his lower lip. 'And you want me to believe this is what you say it is?'

The gun chafed against Linus's lower back when he leaned back, pointed to the coke and said: 'Snorting that is like the most mind-blowing orgasm. Only better.'

Matti laughed. 'Do you know what Julia did the other day?'

This was *not* the time or the place to talk about Matti's hot girl-friend. Linus rapped on the table with his knuckles; Henrik gave a start and looked up.

'I don't give a fuck what Julia did. You two need to understand what we've got here. People go crazy when they've tried it; they'd sell their own mother just to get hold of one more line. I've been dealing it for a while now, and they go. Absolutely. Fucking. Crazy. This…' Linus placed a hand on the package and patted it. 'Is a kilo of pure. Fucking. *Power*.'

His words had some effect. Matti was looking at the coke with greater respect, while Henrik's shoulders slumped even more. Then

263

Matti thought of something. 'You say you've been dealing this for a while. First I've heard of it. I haven't seen any money from it.'

Linus hated to sound defensive, but he didn't have much choice. 'Because I haven't made any money.'

'What, so you've been pushing top-class coke as a hobby? Because it's fun?'

Linus gave a theatrical sigh and tilted his head on one side. 'Matti. Sometimes you have to prove your worth. Before you're allowed to play.'

'And that applies to me and Henrik too?'

'No, you're in, so stop being so fucking suspicious. This is *me* you're talking to. Don't you trust me?'

Matti pursed his lips, gazed at the package and nodded slowly. In the silence Henrik took the opportunity to drag his voice from the depths of the sofa. 'I can't do this. I'm sorry, but it's impossible. I'm eighteen. I can't do it.'

Matti finally seemed to have chosen the right side. He patted Henrik's knee and said: 'Pull yourself together. This is what we've been talking about ever since we used to sit here *messing around*, as you put it. When we'd join the big time.'

'That's just it,' Henrik replied. 'That's what I'm saying. It's gone. And it makes me sad. Very sad.'

'What have you got on your arm?' Linus asked him.

'What?'

'Show me what you've got on your arm.'

'Oh, *that*.' Henrik stroked the arm where the tattoo was. 'Stupid idea. It looks ridiculous.'

Linus and Matti exchanged a glance, and this time when Matti patted Henrik's knee, there was rather more force behind the gesture. 'Show me. I want to see it.'

'Why? Do you think I've had it removed?'

'I don't think anything. Show me.'

Henrik shook his head, looking from one bear-brother to the other with an expression that said *are you serious*? When he saw nothing but animosity in their eyes, he shrugged and began to unbutton his shirt.

Linus was happy with the situation. Matti had snapped up his method of pressurising Henrik, made it his own and moved it on. That was a mark of true leadership. Only a hint was needed, then the subordinates did the job. Linus's demand to see the tattoo had been no more than a passing thought, but now a plan was taking shape. He got up and locked the door.

When he turned around Henrik had taken off his shirt and pushed up the sleeve of his T-shirt, revealing the blue uneven triangle. 'Happy now?'

Linus pointed to the tattoo. 'What does it mean to you?'

'It means that there was a time when we were really close. When it seemed as if anything was possible. So I'll always keep it, if that's what you're wondering.'

'No, that's not what I'm wondering. I'm wondering if you remember what it *means*.'

'Exactly,' Matti echoed. 'What does it mean?'

'Jesus, you two are hard work,' Henrik said, rolling down his sleeve. 'It was a stupid thing we did when we were kids. We did a lot of stupid things when we were kids.'

'That's not how I remember it,' Linus said. 'Is that how you remember it, Matti?'

Matti shook his head. 'No. I remember we swore we'd stick together. We swore that we had one another's backs. That we'd share everything. That it was the three of us against the world.'

'Mmm. And you think that was a stupid thing, Henrik?'

Henrik's eyes shone with unshed tears as he picked up his shirt. 'I just mean…'

'I couldn't give a shit what you mean,' Linus snapped. 'I hear what you're saying. And leave the shirt off.'

Henrik stopped with his right arm halfway into the sleeve. Frowning, he watched Linus cross the room and open the drawer where they kept things that might be useful. Right now a box cutter would be useful. Linus picked up the slender metal case and clicked out the blade with his thumb.

'If that's how you feel...' he went on.

Henrik snorted. 'For fuck's sake, Linus. This isn't cool.' His voice was steady, just a little subdued because he was holding back the tears, but Linus noticed his eyes darting towards the locked door. Linus went and stood beside him, then pointed to his upper arm with the blade.

'When you get married, Henrik, you put on a ring. If you decide to split up, you take off the ring. It sounds to me as if you want to split from us. Which means that has to go.'

Matti inhaled sharply and nodded. 'Absolutely.'

'I'm glad you feel that way,' Linus said, handing him the knife. 'Because you're the one who's going to do it.'

Matti took the knife and moistened his lips with his tongue. Henrik dropped his shirt and began to get to his feet. 'I'm not playing this game anymore. You...'

Linus pulled the gun and held it a few centimetres from Henrik's face. 'Sit down.'

Henrik slumped back down, and an angel passed slowly through the room. Henrik and Matti stared at the gun, the barrel of which was pointing straight at Henrik's right eye. Linus nodded at Henrik's upper arm. Matti seemed to have some difficulty swallowing before he spoke. 'Where did you get that? Is it...real?'

'Of course it is. Now do it. Slice it off.'

Matti stared at the knife in his hand as if it had acquired a new weight and sharpness, as if it had suddenly changed from a toy into something real. Something with a purpose. Henrik could no longer hold back the tears; they poured down his cheeks as he said: 'Come on, that's enough. This isn't cool. Stop now. I'm *eighteen*, for fuck's sake. I can't sell that stuff. I'd go down for life, my whole crappy life would be destroyed, don't you get that?'

Matti seemed to be paralysed, his eyes fixed on Henrik's upper arm, where the tattoo was hidden by his T-shirt. Linus took a deep breath and yelled: 'Do it!' Matti jumped and pushed up Henrik's sleeve. The blue triangle was visible once more, and even Linus felt a pang of melancholy when he remembered the afternoon long ago when he'd carved it into his friend's arm. It was all so far away. Right now, moving forward was the important thing.

Matti raised the blade, shook his head and lowered it again. 'I can't,' he said to Linus. 'You know that, right?'

Linus shifted his aim from Henrik to Matti. 'You can and you will. I'm ordering you to do it.'

With the barrel half a metre from his forehead, Matti glared at Linus. Something passed across his face, and he almost sounded cheerful. 'Shoot me if you want. I don't think you will, I don't think that's where we are. I could be wrong, and if I am, that's okay. But I'm not using this knife.'

Linus smiled. This was more or less what he'd expected. Matti was solid, a good guy to have in his crew. 'You're absolutely right. I'm not going to shoot you—it would be a terrible waste. But...'

Linus moved the gun again so that the barrel was resting on Henrik's knee. He pushed hard, creasing the dark brown designer chinos à la Täby that Henrik had started wearing. '...I can do this. We're definitely there, and I think you know that. So Henrik....' Linus looked straight at Henrik, who was sitting with his hands folded over his stomach, his teeth chattering. 'Now you get to choose. Your knee or the tattoo?'

'Th-th-the ta-ta-ta-tattoo, but for f-f-f-fuck's sake, Linus... Linus...'

'Don't bother, that won't work. You're a traitor and I couldn't give a shit about you. Do it, Matti, or I'll kneecap the fucker. I mean it and you know it.'

Matti looked Linus directly in the eye and saw that it was true. He took a deep breath, exhaled slowly and raised the knife once more. 'Sorry, Henrik.' He added quietly to himself: 'Jesus, this is horrible...'

'Okay!' Henrik yelled, raising both arms in the air. 'Okay, okay, okay!'

'Okay what?' Linus asked.

'Okay, I'm in!'

'What do you mean, you're in?'

'I'm in—I'll help to deal your fucking coke! I'll do it!'

Linus leaned forward and whispered: 'Maybe you could lower your voice a little.'

*

'What the fuck has happened to you?'

Matti's tone of voice was a mixture of admiration and scepticism, seasoned with a plea—*come back to us*. Linus hadn't told them about the field, and he had no intention of doing so. It would sound as if he'd completely lost his mind, and maybe he wasn't allowed to tell, so he simply replied: 'I've realised what matters, that's all.'

'Which means you get a gun?'

'Among other things. Okay, so…'

Linus went through the logistics. To begin with Henrik and Matti would receive twenty-five grams each—five four-gram and five one-gram bags. A hundred kronor commission, plus no more than a hundred on top for each gram. Five thousand profit each. He didn't care how they did it, but in five days he wanted to see twenty thousand on the table.

'Who's packaging the stuff?' Matti asked. 'Is it you?'

'No. It's the girl who finished third in *Idol* in 2014.'

'What the hell are you saying?'

'I'm saying it's none of your business.'

The corners of Matti's mouth twitched and his shoulders slumped, as if someone had punched him in the stomach. That was an unavoidable aspect of being the boss: you finished up alone. Linus could no longer share his concerns; he had to maintain a high profile with no cracks. It felt both sad and intoxicating.

Ever since Linus had told Henrik to lower his voice, he'd remained on the sofa with his hands tucked between his thighs, wearing the expression of someone who'd just been led away from a disaster wrapped in a foil blanket. Safe, but with everything in ruins behind him. Suddenly a change took place, as if he'd knocked back a Red Bull and it had just kicked in. He straightened up, rolled his shoulders and said: 'There's a party at college the day after tomorrow. I know a few people who smoke dope, and a few who probably snort coke.'

'You're going to be the king,' Linus said approvingly. 'Just make sure you warn them in advance so they've got cash.'

'They can pay using Swish on their smartphones too.'

'Won't that be registered? Traceable?'

'Yes, but we're not talking about huge amounts. It should be fine.'

'Okay, as long as you don't fuck it up.'

'I won't.'

A new flame had been lit in Henrik's eyes, just as Linus had hoped. During the lengthy period of apathy Linus had been afraid that his shock therapy had missed the mark, and that he would be dealing with a lump of jelly. But now Henrik had accepted that this was the way things had to be, and that was the key. More or less any situation was okay as long as you accepted it. No trying to wriggle out of it, no dreaming of something else, no regrets. Acceptance. Then it was just a matter of moving forward, one step at a time.

Linus was convinced that he'd done Henrik a favour. College in Täby? Who was he trying to fool? Linus knew it was possible for a kid with brains to fly away from Gårdsstugan on the wings of books, but Henrik wasn't that kid. Linus had made him see the reality, work with what he had, plus...

'There's one thing you two have to understand,' he said. 'You might think that I'm bossing you around, that I've changed. And you're right, I have. But there's a reason.' He paused to make sure he had their full attention. He had. Matti and Henrik were now sitting side by side on the sofa like the burning candles he'd expected from the start, hanging on his every word. He pointed to the package.

'This is once in a lifetime. This quality, this price, this supplier. We're in the middle of a gold rush, and it's happening *now*. If we make a good job of the distribution, we'll be able to chill later. We'll make so much money we'll be set for life. Apartments, cars, no problem. Staying in a luxury hotel by the beach, no problem. But this is happening *now*. You can't stand there and say: "I don't know, I daren't, I'm not sure." It's now we have this chance, and that's what you have to understand. I'm doing this for you. As well as myself.'

His pep talk worked. Matti and Henrik gazed into the future, seeing the pictures Linus had painted. Up until that point it was as if they'd been incapable of grasping the link between the package on the table and the joys Linus had just described. Now they could see it.

They spent a very pleasant half hour kicking around all the things that would be possible when you were as loaded as they were going to be. Linus allowed himself to soften, become one of the gang again, and it was like the old days and not like the old days at all. Even when he was babbling about how he was going to buy Bowser's car from Mario Kart, part of his mind was still up there in that black balloon, guiding him. The relaxed chat was also a strategy, a way of getting his crew to chill and think more about brotherhood and sticking together than shattered kneecaps.

When they got tired of their fantasies they sat in silence for a while, lost in their own thoughts, until Matti asked: 'How did they get hold of you?'

'Who?'

'You told us what Chivo did to you, but how did they get hold of you in the first place? Nobody can run as fast as you!'

'I was sold.'

'What, you mean someone...'

'Yes. Someone. His name is Tinnie.'

'Okay, so what are you going to do about it?'

'I'm glad you asked, because that's the next point on today's agenda. Henrik, you're coming with me.'

Henrik hadn't been following the conversation. His internal fantasy generator was working harder than anyone else's because there was so much emptiness in his life. He blinked at Linus. 'Sorry?'

'We're going to visit a cokehead. Who sold me out. That's not acceptable.'

One reason for Henrik's poor grades was his inability to see over-arching connections and draw the relevant conclusions. Which was why his next question was: 'What's not acceptable?'

Matti rolled his eyes. 'Didn't you hear? He sold out Linus. Do you think a brother can let himself be sold like some fucking whore?'

Linus didn't protest when Matti called him a brother. There was no reason to do so. Becoming a brother was merely a question of enough people *believing* you were a brother. Apparently Matti already belonged to that group.

Henrik wrung his thin hands. 'Wouldn't it be better if you took Matti with you?'

'Matti is as sweet as sugar in the sunshine, but he looks like a fucking gangster, and you don't. Which is why you're coming with me.'

Henrik tried another feeble protest, but he knew the race was run. He had no choice. They left the Den. Linus stood on tiptoe, reached up into the ventilation shaft and groped around until he found the wrench. Then they went to visit Tinnie.

*

After what had happened with Chivo, Tinnie ought to be a bundle of nerves contained in a bag of skin. He'd allowed himself to be used by someone who no longer existed, so when vengeance came knocking he would be alone, and no doubt highly suspicious. Linus would have to proceed with care if he was going to be successful.

Henrik rang the doorbell while Linus pressed himself against the wall halfway up the stairs to the next floor. There was a peephole in his own front door, so he knew exactly where the limit of the field of vision lay. The kilo of coke in his backpack was pressing between his shoulder blades, the gun was chafing in his waistband and the wrench was warm in his hand. He felt a tingling in his chest, and he was enjoying every second.

No one came, and Linus signalled to Henrik to ring the bell again in a series of short bursts. Eventually they heard someone creeping up to the door. Tinnie was looking through the peephole. Henrik did exactly as Linus had instructed him and performed a pantomime indicating that he had something important to tell Tinnie, but couldn't stand out on the landing shouting. 'CHI-VO' he mimed, exaggerating each syllable.

He dropped his arms, did his best to look harmless. The latch was turned and the door opened a couple of centimetres. Linus heard the rattle of the security chain as he'd expected. Tinnie whispered: 'What is it? Who are you?'

Henrik, the idiot, glanced up at Linus for guidance, and Linus had to hurl himself down the stairs to insert the thin end of the wrench into the narrow gap before Tinnie could slam the door. He put his whole weight behind it; it was no longer possible for Tinnie to close the door.

'Time for a little chat, Tinnie,' Linus said to the eye, wide with horror, that was just visible. He pressed the wrench against the wall, forcing the door as far as he could before the security chain stopped it.

Tinnie's breathing was rapid and shallow as he shook his head manically. 'I don't want a chat. It wasn't my fault, they forced me, they hit me…'

'I know, I know. And if you do as I say, nothing will happen.'

'I don't believe you.'

'What you believe doesn't matter. I can break that chain in a second, but then I'll be annoyed.'

Linus kept the mask in place even though what he'd just said was a lie. He needed something to put between the wrench and the door frame in order to apply pressure. All he could do was keep the door open, but Tinnie was hardly likely to be able to figure that out in his current state.

'What is it you want to chat about?'

'You sold me out, Tinnie. I want to discuss how you're going to pay, and it doesn't necessarily have to be with blood. If you open the door.'

He had underestimated Tinnie. The fucker moved his head closer to the door so that he could see the wrench, the frame and Linus's inability to carry out his threat. They looked each other in the eye. Dead heat. They could stand here until the end of time. Linus felt a hand moving across his back, then a flash of pain as the gun was yanked out of his waistband.

'Open the fucking door,' Henrik hissed, pushing the barrel into the gap so that it was pointing straight at Tinnie's O-shaped mouth. Linus was so shocked he almost let go of the wrench, but pulled himself together and took back control.

'I'll get you sooner or later,' he said calmly. 'And I'll be even more angry then. If you open the door right now, we can sort this out.'

A few seconds passed in silence. Tinnie had a great deal to think about. Linus and Henrik stood close together clutching their respective weapons, and it didn't feel in the least bit cool. Linus was starting to get seriously irritated. Fortunately Tinnie saw sense. With shaking hands he unhooked the chain and let them in.

Tinnie backed away until he was standing on the edge of the rug in the hallway. He looked terrible. Linus knew he worked as a bus driver, but in his current state he shouldn't be trusted with a kick sled, never mind a bus. The puffy, sallow cheeks were unshaven, and his sparse hairline was beaded with sweat. He was wearing a short-sleeved pale blue shirt that was wrongly buttoned up, revealing a hairy belly. He had dark sweat patches under his arms. In his right hand he was holding a large spanner, which he now raised.

'Seriously?' Linus said.

'What are you going to do?' Tinnie asked, his eyes shining with a desperation verging on insanity. Linus was about to say something reassuring when the gun appeared in his peripheral vision. 'Put that down or I'll shoot you, you fucker!' Henrik hissed, caught up in his own insanity. Linus felt a faint spray of saliva hit his cheek. He was standing between two lunatics, and there was no telling how this might end.

He took his left foot off the rug, put down his right foot as hard as he could, then immediately pulled back. Tinnie went down like a ton of bricks. He landed on his fat arse and dropped the spanner. Linus pointed the wrench at him, then turned to Henrik with his hand outstretched.

For a moment it looked as if Henrik was going to refuse to give up the gun, but then the film over his eyes dissolved. He blinked, passed the gun to Linus and said: 'I was just...'

'Ssh.' Linus turned back to Tinnie, who was staring at the gun. Linus showed it to him properly, then tucked it back in his waist-band with exaggeratedly slow movements. Tinnie focused his atten-tion on the wrench. With the same slowness, as if he were trying to calm a spooked horse, Linus placed it against the wall then spread his empty hands. He crouched down beside Tinnie, who stank of panic-sweat.

'The thing is, I need somewhere to live.'

Tinnie nodded frenetically; Linus didn't think he'd understood a word. If Linus had said there was a polar bear living in his fridge, he would have nodded equally enthusiastically. 'So I thought I'd move in here.'

Tinnie was still nodding. 'Absolutely, that's fine, no problem.'

'Good. But *you* won't be living here. You'll carry on paying the rent and the bills and so on, but you won't be living here.'

Tinnie's eyes darted from side to side, but the nodding continued. 'So...so where am I going to live?'

'That's not really my problem, is it? You've got five minutes to pack. Then I never want to see you again.'

It was beginning to sink in now, and Tinnie's eyes darted faster and faster as he searched for an escape route. Something to say, some-where to go, something that could make all this go away. His mouth opened and closed as he hyperventilated, and Linus discovered that he had bad breath on top of everything else.

274

Henrik walked past Linus and kicked Tinnie in the hip. His rolls of fat quivered and he let out a squeak. 'Move yourself, you fat fucker!' Henrik yelled. 'You heard what he said!'

Tinnie somehow got to his feet and stumbled into his bedroom. Linus signalled to Henrik to follow him into the living room.

*

Tinnie was about thirty, but his idea of interior design seemed to have stagnated in his teenage years. The walls in the living room were adorned with several badly framed fantasy posters featuring big-breasted women wielding swords as oversized as their clothing was minimal. A worn-down sofa, a large TV, and a DVD and Blu-ray shelf that covered half a wall. Gaps revealed where Tinnie had sold off box sets to finance his drug habit. There were dust bunnies all along the skirting boards, beer stains on the coffee table, crisps and popcorn scattered on the floor in front of the sofa. Henrik looked around and grimaced. 'What a dump.'

'Henrik.'

'Mmm?'

Linus waited until Henrik turned to face him, then slapped him so hard that his palm burned and the sinews in his shoulder screamed. It sounded like a whip crack. Henrik fell sideways towards the coffee table, but managed to save himself before he crashed to the floor. Tears filled his eyes and his cheek flamed bright red.

'Linus, what the…'

Linus positioned himself so that his face was right in front of Henrik's. 'Listen to me. Never, under any circumstances, take something from me unless I've specifically told you to do so. And particularly…'

Henrik straightened up, and there was a horrible sticky noise as he freed his hand from a patch of something unpleasant on the table. 'But he wouldn't have opened the door if I hadn't…'

Linus raised his hand and Henrik fell silent. 'And *particularly* not the gun. You do as I say, and you fucking calm down. Less of the initiative, okay?'

Henrik pushed out his lower lip like a sulky child and covered his cheek with his hand. He really didn't understand this new situation, and Linus had started wondering how and where to hit him again when Henrik said: 'Okay.'

'Okay what?'

'I get it. I have to do as you say.'

'And why is that?'

Linus's hand was hurting and he hoped Henrik wouldn't say *So you won't hit me*, because then he would have to do exactly that. Fortunately for both of them Henrik's reply was: 'Because you know best', which was the correct answer.

Linus relaxed and picked up the thread of the conversation. 'Well, it's not exactly the Grand Hotel,' he said as he inspected the film collection. It was dominated by fantasy and porn. Coupled with what he knew of Tinnie's coke consumption, Linus envisaged him as an idiot with a desperate need for escapism. Driving his bus like an automaton, longing to get home to his hovel where he could jerk off and dream of girls in metal corsets.

It was so depressing that Linus felt briefly guilty. Driving Tinnie out was like dumping a house cat in the snow and leaving it to get by as best it could. Then he thought about the hook, the electric shocks and the diaper. Any hint of a guilty conscience disappeared and was replaced by a desire to hurt Tinnie a little more. But he decided to leave it, as long as Tinnie didn't make waves.

Unlike Henrik, Tinnie seemed to understand perfectly: if he didn't cooperate, he was in deep shit. After five minutes he reappeared in the hallway with a bulging suitcase.

'Key,' Linus said. Tinnie pointed to a hook where a single key dangled from a Darth Vader key ring.

'How long will you be staying?' Tinnie enquired tentatively.

'As long as necessary. Spare key.'

'I haven't got one.'

'Yes you have.'

'No I haven't.'

Linus could hear Henrik moving impatiently behind him, but this time he kept his need to show initiative in check. This was standard nonsense, so Linus picked up the wrench, weighed it in his hand and said: 'Have you seen *Oldboy*?'

Tinnie nodded and his gaze was drawn to the teeth of the wrench, which could be used to remove his own. 'Good,' Linus said. 'If you're so stupid that you don't have a spare key, then you deserve to get your teeth fixed. Henrik, grab hold of him.'

Henrik took a step forward and Tinnie shook his head. 'Okay, okay.' He dug into his pocket and produced another key. This one was attached to a key ring with a girl in a bikini that disappeared when you tilted it.

'You're a sad bastard, you know,' Linus said, pointing to the door with the wrench. 'Get out of here before I give you a charming gap between your teeth.'

Tinnie gave Linus a pleading look and took a step closer. A gust of his bad breath made Linus want to back away, but he stood his ground. That's what a brother does. Tinnie lowered his voice, not wanting Henrik to hear.

'Linus...Have you got something for me? Just a little bit, before I go?'

That wasn't what Linus had been expecting. He stared at Tinnie, wondering what the idiot would say if he knew Linus was carrying a kilo while he was begging for half a gram.

'Tinnie.' Linus raised the wrench one more time. 'If you don't leave now, you won't have anything to snort coke with.'

Oddly enough, that was the first time Tinnie looked mutinous. He'd just lost his apartment and most of his possessions, but clearly that was nothing compared with losing a nose. The guy was a bona fide snorter. For a moment it looked as if he was going to kick off, but then he grabbed his jacket, picked up his suitcase and left without another word.

While Henrik checked out the film collection, Linus embarked on a tour of inspection. There was no table in the kitchen, and given the state of the coffee table, he assumed Tinnie had eaten in front of the TV. There weren't many utensils; no sign of a whisk or fish slice. He found the explanation when he opened the freezer, which was crammed with Gorby's pasties, cheap ready meals, ice cream, ice cream and more ice cream. There were two crumpled-up pizza boxes in the trash can under the sink. No wonder Tinnie had such a fat gut.

The bathroom wasn't quite as bad as he'd feared. A car freshener labelled *New Car* hung from the towel rail, its scent mixed with the acrid smell of Ajax. There was a *Star Wars* calendar on the door, and a row of plastic figures from *Lord of the Rings* were neatly arranged on the windowsill. Linus began to feel a heavy, creaking, painful ache in his chest.

The bedroom, finally. A shithole within a shithole. A thin red curtain at the window and a multicoloured rope light on the wall created the atmosphere of a particularly depressing night club. A pile of garishly jacketed fantasy books sat on the bedside table, while the bed itself sported a crocheted coverlet. The pain in Linus's chest increased when he saw the white teddy bear propped up against the pillow. It felt as if someone wouldn't stop telling a really sad story, and just kept on adding fresh details.

Linus opened the wardrobe door and found the explanation for Tinnie's name. The whole double closet was filled with empty beer cans, piled on top of one another with meticulous care. Several hundred, and as far as Linus could see, no two were the same. The inside of the door was virtually covered with a handwritten list, column after column giving the name of every beer, with a mark between zero and five next to each one. Those with a five had also been awarded a gold star.

Those little gold stars were the final straw. Linus's chest contracted, as if a pair of giant hands was wringing out his lungs like dishcloths. Everything went black before his eyes, and he had to lean on the wall to stop himself from sliding to the floor. *Sorrow and fucking sorrow and the black hell that's life and loneliness, try to find a meaning if you can.*

A bell as big as his body tolled through his bones, the noise inside his head was unbearable as the clapper met the dark metal, the vibrations made him start shaking as he broke out into a cold sweat. Panic. Sheer fucking panic.

What have I done?

You've done what you had to do.

Who am I?

You are nothing. Only the darkness exists.

Linus tried to take a deep breath and found that he could. Deeper and deeper until he was able to stand up straight. The tolling of the bell faded to a distant echo, he stopped shaking and the sweat dried on his back. He went over to the bed, grabbed the bear and chucked it in the wardrobe, then slammed the door.

*

Henrik had finished looking through Tinnie's film collection and was happily settled on the sofa with a can of Coca-Cola and a book of pictures from the making of *The Dark Knight*.

'What a crib,' he said.

Apparently he'd been so inspired by the encounter with Tinnie that he now thought he was a gangster.

'Don't even try,' Linus said. 'You sound ridiculous.'

Henrik finished off his drink, looking hurt. Linus couldn't have cared less. He'd had his moment of weakness, but now it was over. He still had things to do today, and he didn't have time for any crap.

'Let's go,' he said, heading into the hallway. When he opened the front door, he discovered that Henrik wasn't with him. He shook his head and went back into the living room, where Henrik was studying the dust bunnies on the floor. 'I said let's go. That means we go.'

Henrik looked up at him, his expression suggesting that he had something to say, but didn't know where to start. Linus sighed. 'Okay, spit it out. Now.'

'The thing is…I was wondering…Could I live here too?'

'Where?'

'Here. On the sofa.'

Linus thought for a moment, then pictured a scenario that appealed to him. 'Okay. But you'll have to be like a kind of Cinderella.'

Henrik's eyes narrowed. Hard to imagine anything less gangsta than a Disney princess. The hurt expression intensified, and he shook his head. 'Cinderella? I don't want to be fucking Cinderella.'

'Okay. Would you rather be my bitch? If you're going to live here you'll have to do the cleaning. The dishes. The laundry. The cooking.'

'I can't do that.'

'You can't do what?'

'The cooking.'

'Can you do the rest?'

'Absolutely.'

'Fine. I'm going home now. I'll be back in a few hours, and I want to see this place looking spotless. Okay?'

Henrik shrugged, his posture making it clear that it was anything but okay. However, he said: 'Okay.'

'Good. See you later.'

In a final attempt to retain some kind of dignity, Henrik grimaced and said: 'So where's the fucking vacuum cleaner then?'

'Henrik. If you look, I'm sure you'll find it. Along with the *fucking* mop and the *fucking* dusters.'

As Linus headed back to the front door he started whistling the mice's work song from *Cinderella*.

*

As soon as Linus turned the key he could hear running footsteps from inside the apartment, the flapping of his mother's slippers. When he opened the door Betty was standing in the hallway with her arms folded, her face bright red. She had dark shadows beneath her wide-open eyes, her pupils like lasers focused on him.

'Where have you been? Where have you been, Linus?'

'Out.'

Betty screwed up her eyes in pain, making the crow's feet at the corners of her eyes look more like paw prints. 'I know you've been out! But what have you been doing? Why haven't you been in touch? Have you any idea how worried your dad and I have been? How can you do this to us? Are you trying to hurt us?'

A lot of questions, none of which had a simple answer. Linus kicked off his shoes, kept his jacket on and went into the living room, where his father was sitting in his wheelchair with his distorted, inscrutable face. Betty was right behind him, still hissing, her face so close that he could feel her breath on the hairs at the back of his neck.

'We haven't been able to sleep, we haven't been able to eat, we thought you were lying dead somewhere. You always call, why didn't you call, I thought…I thought…'

His mother's voice dissolved into tears. Linus felt a pressure at his temples, everything seemed so thick, like wading through porridge instead of making the clear, cold decisions he was now capable of. He nodded to his father and continued out onto the balcony, where he rested his hands on the railing. Fortunately his mother didn't follow him.

Dusk was falling, and the neon advertising signs on the roofs around Norrtull acquired sharper contours as their lights braced against the darkness to proclaim their messages. Linus clutched the cold aluminium.

I have the stuff, I have the ability to move forward. It has begun.

Once again he became aware of the difference from when he'd stood here a few weeks earlier. How much the situation had changed, so much that he was someone else now. This Linus was heavier, darker. Better. He turned around.

His parents were looking at him from inside the living room.

Through the glass he saw them as figures in an aquarium, two tiresome examples of the human race exhibited for visitors to see. His father's downturned mouth, his mother's eyes, red with weeping. Just as before, he attempted to feel tenderness and partly succeeded; he felt sympathy.

The darkness that had taken up residence in his body was also within his father, even though he couldn't act on it. In his mother's case the darkness poured out in diffuse rivulets, a barbed-wire network of shadows digging into her guts. The same darkness as his, but with such a pathetic way of expressing itself. Hence the sympathy.

He went back into the living room and spread his hands wide. 'I'm sorry if I worried you. That wasn't my intention, and I'm really, really sorry.'

Betty had been about to say something, but her mouth snapped shut. She looked at her husband, who met her gaze with as much relief as he was capable of showing. Linus took a step closer. 'I know how hard things are for you both, and I know how hard you try. I haven't always been the son you deserve—please forgive me. I love you.'

It was easy to say and largely true, Linus discovered as the previously unspoken words left his mouth. They were no more than sounds his body produced to achieve a certain effect, but still true. More or less. He wasn't sure he loved his mother, but he had some kind of feeling for her; that would have to do.

It worked. Betty's hands flew to her mouth and tears filled her eyes. Her body swayed as if it had been struck by a sudden gust of wind, and her shoulders shook as she suppressed a sob. She mumbled: 'Sorry, I have to…' Then she disappeared into the bedroom and closed the door behind her.

If Linus had listened at the door, which he'd done a few times, he would have heard the sound of a bottle being opened, followed by the slimy glug of Baileys being poured into a glass. Then the gulping. His new insight allowed him to see that his mother was like him in this way too: powerful emotions, whether joy or sorrow, tended to become too much, too overwhelming, and so they had to be subdued. So Betty self-medicated, as they say. With Baileys.

'Iiinooo…'

A string of saliva dribbled from his father's mouth towards his shoulder. Linus took a napkin out of the box that always stood ready on the table and wiped his father's lips and cheek. Then he went over to the sideboard and picked up the photograph his father had wanted to look at the last time they'd been alone. He sat down on the sofa next to the wheelchair and placed the photo on his father's knee, angling it so that he could see.

His father in his jockey's silks, arms around his wife and son, bathed in sunlight. Linus remembered the feeling when he saw his father win a race, the knowledge that it was *his* dad on the horse that passed the post before all the others. Among the thousands of spectators, he was the only person who had a dad who'd just won. It made him feel special.

He looked at the photograph and felt nothing special. There they were, he and Mum and Dad about nine years ago. Things were one way then, and they were a different way now. Life changed, people changed. You just had to roll with the punches.

His father clearly felt otherwise. He was snivelling and sobbing, tears pouring from his eyes and snot from his nose. Linus cleaned him up again, stroking his head and whispering: 'There, there…' as if he were comforting a small child. His father could hardly do or say anything, and Linus was able to feel the tenderness towards him that he couldn't summon up for his mother. Linus hunkered down in front of him and rested his hands on his knees.

'We're going on a trip, Dad. Just you and me.'

His father made the small movement with his head that meant 'no', and slurred: 'C-C-Caaan't. C-C-C…'

Linus didn't wait for whatever was coming next. He took the jar out of his pocket and showed it to his dad, tilted it sideways so that the glutinous black substance moved.

'You can, Dad. I promise.'

Tommy

Tommy had spent the day packing two suitcases. Deciding how much to take to Anita's was a difficult balancing act. Too little, and it would seem as if he wasn't taking the project seriously, while hiring a van and taking the lot could be quite frightening for her. For him as well, to be honest. In the end he'd gone for a middle way: two large suitcases, like a traveller who's decided he's staying for a while.

Hagge padded around him, watching his activities with an enquiring expression and anxious body language, as if he were afraid that Tommy was going to go off and leave him. Tommy assured him that wasn't the case.

'You're coming too, boy. We're both going to live with Anita.'

Hagge's ears drooped at the mention of Anita's name. Tommy couldn't understand it, and it worried him. Hagge was good at reading people, and on the two occasions he'd been to Anita's apartment he'd reacted badly: nervous and wanting to leave. On the second occasion Tommy had had to drag him across the threshold into the hallway.

Of course it didn't necessarily mean that Hagge's radar had picked up any concealed malevolence in Anita. Maybe something about the apartment itself didn't appeal to him. The smell of candle wax and incense might bother his sensitive nose; the closed door to the mystery room might make him suspicious. Hagge's life as a puppy had left its mark on his character. When he arrived at a new place he always began with a thorough investigation of every area, presumably to exclude the possibility of danger. Being refused access to a room, even though he'd scratched at the door with his good front paw, could explain his nervousness.

Tommy had more or less finished packing when Betty rang at about four-thirty. He'd kept the phone in his trouser pocket all day in case he received a text, a picture or a call. He answered immediately.

'Hi Betty, how's it going?'

'He's home. He's come home.'

Tommy sank down in the armchair and let out a long breath. He'd been feeling as if he was wearing a shirt two sizes too small, constricting his chest. Now the buttons popped and he was able to breathe. 'Has he said anything about where he's been, what he's been doing?'

'He's said nothing.' Betty took a swig of something he was pretty sure was Baileys; he could almost smell it down the line. Betty's voice shook as she added: 'That's not quite true. He has said something, but not about where he's been.'

'Go on.'

There was a silence as Betty took another swig. 'Tommy, I'm scared.'

'Why? Because of what Linus said?'

'Yes. He said he loves us. That he's sorry for being a bad son. That he wants to apologise.'

Tommy laughed. 'Most mothers wouldn't be scared if their son said that.'

'Most mothers don't have Linus as their son.'

Tommy immediately regretted his dismissal of Betty's fears. She had a point. Declarations of affection weren't Linus's strong point, to put it mildly. Tommy adopted a more serious tone. 'What are you thinking?'

'I'm not thinking anything. But it feels as if…he's left us. That he's saying goodbye retrospectively. He doesn't think I understand, but I do. And I'm scared. Because I don't know where he is.'

More than once Tommy had been astonished by Betty's ability to see clearly in a crisis. In her everyday life she was often equipped with mental blinkers that made her closed off, prejudiced and pretty stupid, but when things heated up the blinkers came off and she had not just eyes to see but the words to describe what those eyes saw.

'Anything I can do?'

'Same old same old,' Betty said in a resigned tone of voice. 'Talk to him. See if you can find out what he's up to.'

'I will. But not today.'

When they'd ended the call, Tommy remained sitting in the armchair. Hagge curled up by his feet, happy that the upsetting upheaval had stopped.

He's left us.

Tommy knew exactly what Betty meant. In every relationship with another person there is an element of movement, a drawing closer or drifting apart. It's never possible to get so close that you achieve symbiosis, whereas it's perfectly possible to drift so far away that you become a stranger. Someone who has left. That's what Betty thought Linus had done.

X

The person behind the mask had the ability to change people's lives in a short time. As far as Tommy was aware, Linus had spent a number of hours in his company. What had happened? What had been said? Tommy would have given a great deal to know.

He sank deeper into the chair, into the labyrinth of facts, clues and possibilities. Hagge shuffled until his stomach was resting on Tommy's feet, grunting contentedly. After a few moments Tommy suddenly sat up straight. He waved his hands as if he were throwing open invisible curtains, and said: 'That's enough!'

The thought of falling back into his old ways was so attractive—sitting in his armchair and speculating until his stomach started rumbling and he could heat up a ready meal in the microwave. But he was on the move now, it was his turn to get close to someone. Ignoring Hagge's protests, he closed the suitcases and carried them downstairs, then put Hagge on the leash and hauled him along. Before Armchair-Tommy had time to protest, Tommy-on-the-Move had locked the door, fetched the car, put the cases in the boot and persuaded Hagge to jump in the front seat.

Tommy didn't believe in all that nonsense the magazines spouted about some celebrity who had embarked upon 'A new life'. We all have our own dull little life to take care of, and it's all about whether we stand still or keep moving. Tommy was moving now. Closer to Anita.

Since Anita was a total control freak, she usually referred to prostitution as her 'chosen career' rather than something she'd gradually slipped into. At one point in her thirties she had everything in order to the extent that she knew she'd made a carefully considered decision to continue with what she was doing, but before that it was all a bit vague.

Anita's father had left when she was three and her sister Ulrika was five, but Anita didn't really like talking about that, because it was such a cliché. Anita knew plenty of women who rented out their bodies, and two out of three had absent fathers. Anita didn't want to accept that she had been influenced by forces outside her control when she embarked on her career, that she was *one of them* and a victim to boot. Therefore she preferred to talk about growing up in a loving nuclear family in Katrineholm, where only the word Katrineholm was true.

The first time she hired herself out was in her second year at high school. She'd already had sex with a couple of guys, quick hookups when they'd all had too much to drink, no finesse. The situation was completely different for her sister, who was one of the prettiest girls in town. Ulrika was *wooed* by boys who were a couple of years older; they gave her presents and took her out in their smart new cars. Anita didn't think they dribbled in Ulrika's ear if she let them go all the way.

One evening she'd been to a hotel bar with two girlfriends. After an hour knocking back beers and shots, her friends stumbled onto the dance floor while Anita stayed at the table looking after their handbags. A man slid into the chair beside her. She gave him a quick sideways glance, decided that he looked okay for a guy over thirty, and demonstratively turned away.

'Hi,' the man said. 'I see you're on guard duty.'

Anita was drunk, but not drunk enough to numb the constant sorrow that gnawed at her heart, making her difficult and stiff. Without looking at the man she said: 'Forget it. You're too old.'

'I know, but let me just tell you: you're the prettiest girl in the room. The guys ought to be around you like wasps around a sugar lump instead of leaving you here on your own.'

Anita wasn't used to anyone talking to her like that, and she couldn't help smiling. 'So you're a wasp, are you?'

'More of a bee, I'd say. You can get some honey from me if you want.'

Anita turned and looked him up and down. Suit, fresh shave, good haircut, slim hands with nails that looked *manicured*. A businessman passing through, at a guess. She caught his eye briefly. 'It's kind of you to say such nice things, but…no chance. Try someone your own age.'

The man leaned closer, and she caught a whiff of expensive after-shave. 'But it's you I want. I'll give you fifteen hundred.'

'*What* did you say?'

'You heard what I said. And I promise I'm gentle, no weird stuff. You'll have a nice time.'

'Listen, I don't know what you think, but…'

'I don't think anything. I understand perfectly. This isn't what you normally do. But I'll be waiting for you. Outside. By the streetlight.'

The man nodded in the direction of the streetlight outside the station, and Anita couldn't help looking. When she turned back to tell the man he could forget it, he was on his feet. He gave her a warm smile before pushing his way through the crowd to the door.

When Anita's friends came back and asked who she'd been talking to, she told them it was some loser who'd dated her sister. When they swallowed her story, she glanced at the man, who actually was out there waiting, leaning on the lamp post. He wasn't unlike the guys who picked up Ulrika in their Audis and BMWs, just a few years older. Definitely not the image Anita had of a…punter.

During the next couple of hours she checked out the lamp post with increasing frequency. It was November, and the temperature had dropped below freezing. The man must be cold, standing there in an elegant but not particularly thick overcoat. She realised she was worried that he might give up and walk away.

Fifteen hundred was a lot of money. In the odd month when Anita's mother managed to make things work, she would give Anita three hundred in pocket money. Ulrika, who worked in a café, gave her a hundred occasionally, but that was it. Fifteen hundred was more cash than Anita had ever held in her hand. Plus...

She wondered, her body wondered what it would be like to go to bed with someone who knew what he was doing, who didn't behave as if he were hammering a nail into a plank, someone who was... gentle. Then again, he could be a complete perv who'd whip out the chains and the leather dildo as soon as he got her to himself. But she didn't think so. She knew she was going to go to him sooner or later, so it might as well be now, while her friends were gyrating to 'Living on a Prayer'.

She collected her cheap padded jacket from the cloakroom and tried out the words *teenage hooker* in her head as she crossed the car park. The man's face lit up when he saw her. Teenage hooker in a bulky jacket, crack whore spewing down a drain, her career path was neatly laid out. Anita was intensely aware of her body, her backside, her legs in her tight jeans as she approached the man and whispered: 'Where are you staying?'

'The hotel, I...'

'Room number?'

'203.'

'Go and wait there.'

She walked past without looking at him and continued into the station. If anyone had seen her from the bar they couldn't have guessed that an arrangement had been made. She hoped. She was pleased that she'd dealt with everything so quickly and professionally.

Like a real pro, in more ways than one.

She laughed. She was nervous. She felt hot between her shoulder blades, cold between her legs. She definitely wasn't looking forward to the man pushing his stiff cock inside her, but she did want him to caress her and say more nice things. He'd waited for her out in the cold, and he was prepared to pay a significant amount to gain access to her body. She felt valuable and worthless in equal measure; it was confusing, and she spent some time walking around and around on the marble floor of the station's entrance hall. She wasn't stupid. She knew that if she did this she was crossing a line, becoming a different person.

And?

On a scale of one to ten, how keen was she to remain the person she was? What did she have that she didn't want to lose? Nothing, apart from the cuddly rabbit her daddy had given her on her third birthday, a couple of months before he left. So. Fucking. Pathetic. At least someone was waiting for her in room 203, someone who appreciated her, even if he did see her as a transaction.

just be what you need to be

She repeated the words to herself, turning them over in her head like a mantra as she left the station and took a long detour towards the hotel. *Just be what you need to be.* There was something liberating in the simplicity of just being. She went into the hotel and waited until the girl on reception disappeared into a back room. Then she crept up the stairs.

just be

Let it happen. Let it be whatever it might be. At least she'd be able to afford a new jacket. Maybe a Moncler? Probably a bit expensive. She knocked on the door of room 203.

*

It was shortly after six when Tommy turned off the E18 heading for Bergshamra. He didn't want to admit it to himself, but he was anxious. His stomach felt like an aquarium filled with fantails, with someone swishing a net around. The fish, which were usually so languid, darted around tickling his insides with their feathery fins and tails as they tried to avoid capture.

He tried to console himself with the thought that it wasn't every day two people decided to combine their fortunes, or rather that it was something he'd never done before, so his anxiety was only natural. Sound logic, no help at all. Tommy parked outside something that looked like a bar, put Hagge on the leash and went inside.

'Okay to bring the dog in?' he asked the man sitting behind the counter messing around with his mobile. Judging by the frantic movement of his fingers, Tommy assumed it was a game. The man nodded without taking his eyes off the screen. 'A Famous Grouse when it's game over,' Tommy said, parking himself on a stool. Hagge settled down at his feet, gazing up at him with that expression that meant *do you realise you're treating me like a dog?* Tommy got his whisky, knocked it back and ordered another.

The barman poured it straight into his empty glass. With no real interest he asked: 'Tough day?'

Tommy was filled with a sudden urge to share his troubles with a stranger. He took a sip of his drink. 'Quite the opposite, to be honest. But happiness can be just as hard to handle if you're not used to it, wouldn't you say?'

Tommy could have sworn he heard Hagge sigh. The man looked up and his posture changed. Tommy knew exactly what that meant: he'd been recognised. Every word he spoke from now on would be stored in a special file marked 'things Tommy T said when he'd had a few drinks'. Plenty of those files had already been uploaded on Flashback. The chance of confiding in a stranger was gone, because he himself was no longer a stranger. He was *Tommy T*, for fuck's sake.

'What do you mean?' the barman asked, showing more interest this time.

Tommy shook his head and finished his second whisky. He paid, including a decent tip, and allowed Hagge to drag him out. Once they were back in the car, Tommy rested his head on the steering wheel. He'd hardly eaten anything all day, and the alcohol had made him feel slightly tipsy.

'Should have bought flowers,' he muttered. 'What do you think, Hagge? I should have bought flowers, shouldn't I?'

Hagge snorted. *Absolutely. That's your problem right there. No flowers.*

'So what is my problem?' Tommy asked. 'What is it I'm so fucking—I can say this to you, Hagge—so fucking scared of?'

He knew. Deep down in his fantail heart, he knew. He was scared of the *nakedness*. He'd dealt with the purely physical fear by abstaining from the activity with another human being that demanded nakedness, but the fear of the naked soul was something else.

He was more relaxed with Anita than with anyone else, and Tommy T rarely appeared in her apartment. And yet he knew that on some level he played a role when he was with her, that he kept up some kind of show that was hard to define, but that everyday life would slowly grind down. Anita would get to see the real Tommy, and the worst thing was that even he didn't know who that was. He might be a complete shit who'd send Anita screaming in the opposite direction.

Tommy-for-Anita was his last positive self-image, and if he lost it, then Armchair-Tommy would be all he had left, which was the same as nothing. He was scared of losing the tiny scrap of self-esteem that remained.

He raised his head and looked at Hagge, staring at him from the passenger seat. Tommy smiled. 'Sorry, boy. I think this is above your head. Or do you have a self-image too? Do you ever doubt who you really are?'

Hagge seemed to be considering the question, and Tommy was seriously worried that he was about to open his mouth and say: 'I feel like a Great Dane trapped in a mongrel's body, hence my recurring bouts of depression.' It had to be the whisky, creating crazy scenarios in Tommy's brain. He started the car and drove very slowly to Anita's.

*

He liked Bergshamra. It was as if one of the nicer suburbs to the west or south of Stockholm had grown feet and moved north, where it settled and remained an enclave of perfectly preserved 1950s style while new homes frantically popped up all around. There was a calmness beneath the tall pine trees among those asymmetric, three-storey apartment blocks.

Tommy parked outside Anita's block. He got out of the car, but Hagge was unwilling to go with him. He made himself feel heavy as Tommy tried to shuffle him off the seat.

'Come on, boy. This is where we're going to live. We can get through this together, can't we?'

Hagge's body language said *no* every bit as clearly as if he'd shaken his head. Tommy ignored his whining protests and gathered him up in his arms. With some difficulty he managed to get the main door open, then rang Anita's bell. Footsteps approached from inside. Tommy took a deep breath and plastered on a smile.

He could see right away that Anita had also knocked back a couple of whiskies to give herself courage, and in her eyes he saw the same fear that afflicted him. Hagge stopped struggling and slumped like a sack of potatoes instead. 'So,' Tommy said, heaving the dog into a more comfortable position. 'Here we are.'

'Yes,' Anita replied. 'Here you are.'

*

The man in room 203 wasn't *quite* as nice and gentle as he'd promised. Once he was inside her, the grunting and thrusting wasn't much different from what Anita had experienced in the past, but there had been a long time before that which had been okay. When he slowly undressed her and praised various parts of her body, which he then stroked and kissed. If Anita hadn't been so preoccupied with the line she'd crossed, she might have enjoyed it, might even have been turned on.

But that didn't happen. She wasn't really present in her body; she was watching from the outside with drunken astonishment. The lips moving over her thighs, the fingers caressing her hips. It was like observing someone becoming intimate with a statue, and the only

293

satisfaction was the abstract knowledge that the statue was her. That it was appreciated.

When he eventually laid her on her back, she was bone dry, and he had to use saliva for lubrication after he'd put on a condom. Then she lay there staring up at the ceiling while he did his thing. In-out, in-out, in-out. It didn't actually hurt and it wasn't actually unpleasant, just so *boring*. When he slowed down for a minute or so, she almost fell asleep. Then he picked up speed again, let out a whimper, and it was all over.

He asked if she'd enjoyed it, and she told him she'd enjoyed it very much. When he went to the bathroom she got dressed, then perched on the edge of the bed and waited. She felt just as empty and sad as before, no more and no less, but now the sadness was coloured with a few drops of fear, as if something dark and formless was approaching, and she couldn't work out what it was.

He emerged from the bathroom, picked up his wallet, removed three five-hundred kronor notes and offered them to her. She looked at the notes. At the man. He waved them in the air, urging her to take them; he was a man who kept his promises. She took the money between her thumb and index finger, got to her feet and tucked it into the front pocket of her jeans.

The formless took shape. She was a whore now. The word the boys at school sometimes used, the word that was written on the walls in the toilets. WHORE. Just something they said, but now it was part of her body. She had been paid for sex. She was a whore.

She left the room without looking at the man. The notes felt unnaturally large and bulky in her pocket. She couldn't shake off the word. The feet moving across the carpet were a whore's feet and when she reached the stairs she thought *look at that whore coming down the stairs.*

It had started snowing, small grainy flakes whirling around in the air and falling on her face.

the whore's face

She rubbed her eyes and inhaled the cold air. She had to stop this.

She'd been paid, well paid for something she'd done for free in the past. How long had it taken? Fifteen minutes? Six thousand an hour. She pushed her hands into the pockets of her jacket and set off for home.

The snowflakes grew bigger, covering her body and making her look like a ghost with a sheet thrown over it to make it visible. Her belly was aching slightly, but the lasting impression from the encounter in the hotel room wasn't what the man had done, but what he'd said. Now she had established a chilly, snowy distance between herself and the situation, she was able to appreciate it.

The way all his attention had been focused on her, his fingers playing over her body as he huskily whispered how wonderful she was. His tongue in her navel, his warm breath on her stomach, his kind words about her soft skin and glorious breasts. And she'd been *paid* for this.

Okay, so there was the in-out stuff as well, but that was like when the sports teacher told her to do twenty push-ups. It was just a matter of gritting her teeth and getting it done. Take the bad with the good. Anita looked into her heart and found that she wasn't particularly sad. So there.

*

She had crossed the line, crossed into a new country that she continued to explore, learning which types of men were receptive to which signals. Not all of them were willing or able to pay fifteen hundred, but she never went below a thousand. She acquired regular customers. Found out the hard way which types should be avoided, but she never suffered anything worse than a black eye and a split lip.

She'd realised one thing on that very first occasion: she hated the moment when the money was handed over. Even though she was renting out her body to strange men, it was only the financial transaction that made her feel empty or dirty. She tried telling them to put the money in her pocket, but the bad feeling simply shifted to the point

295

where she issued the instruction instead.

Her solution was unconventional, but it worked. She printed a little note stating that when it was all over, she would go to the bathroom and they were to place the money in her bag. She gave them this piece of paper to read as soon as it was established that they would be doing business.

She got her kicks from the appreciative words that sometimes flowed over her, the warm praise for her body, but as time went by the effect diminished, and the sadness returned as soon as the in-out stuff started.

There was gossip, and gossip became certainty, and by the middle of her third year at high school it was common knowledge that Anita was the biggest whore in Katrineholm. The boys started asking her how much she charged for a blow job. At about the same time one of her regular clients said he'd like to take her to Stockholm and rent a small apartment for her; in return she would entertain him once a week. She accepted.

After a year he tired of her. She was evicted, and the worst period in her life began. She had no qualifications and no particular talents apart from being on the receiving end of in-out, so she carried on along the path that would lead her to darker lands.

The kind of freelance activity she'd opted for in Katrineholm wasn't tolerated in Stockholm, and she ended up in the hands of a pimp who quickly got her started on cocaine. He didn't even need to push her over to heroin, because she became so heavily dependent on the coke, which initially seemed like the solution to all her problems. The emptiness and sadness were washed away in sparkling silver waves of euphoria and she felt happy, possibly for the first time ever.

Little by little, the solution became the problem. She could no longer live without the relief the powder gave her, and she agreed to do things she'd once decided she would *never* do. Soon she was doing them on a regular basis, enduring situations bordering on torture just for that hour, half hour, quarter hour of snow-white relief.

She lost all control, all sense of direction, allowed sleazy guys to do whatever they wanted just so that she would have somewhere to live, she drank, injected, snorted or smoked whatever she could get hold of. She didn't bother about her clothes, her hair, her nails, her life. It would soon be over anyway. The final darkness hung over her like a fire blanket, and she could feel it coming closer. Before long it would sweep her away, thank goodness.

*

It happened on July 12 2000. It was just after two in the afternoon when Anita walked down Odengatan and turned onto Sveavägen. She couldn't remember where she'd spent the previous night, and had no idea where she was going to spend the next one. She hadn't showered for a few days. She was wearing dirty jeans and a Bamse the Bear T-shirt. On her feet she had a pair of flip-flops that were much too big, and kept slipping off. The dregs of various substances were floating around her body, nauseating her. She needed a decent fix to scare away the ghosts of all the fixes she'd already had.

Some disconnect in her brain meant that the sun's heat was making her shiver with cold. As she passed McDonald's she grabbed half a burger that someone had left on one of the outside tables. She stuffed it into her mouth, ignoring the sparrows' protests. A little girl stared at her T-shirt as if she couldn't work out what Bamse was doing *there*. Anita smiled at her, and the child's face crumpled as if she was about to cry. Anita staggered into the Observatorielunden park and flopped down on a bench, the shivering and nausea tearing at her skin and guts. She just wanted to lie down and die.

She put her head in her hands, stared down at her feet and realised that she'd lost one of her flip-flops. She couldn't even bring herself to turn and look for it. She sobbed, but no tears came.

'God,' she whispered. 'God help me.'

In the distance, or deep inside her head, she heard a bell toll, just once. Then someone picked her up. Her immediate thought was that it must be a cop who didn't want her polluting a public place on this glorious summer's day, so she waved her hands around and hissed: 'Fuck off and leave me alone.'

There was no one there, but still she was being lifted. She could physically feel her body being straightened on the bench, and inside her something was also being lifted, just like in *Psycho* when the car is brought up from the swamp. She was lighter. Her whole self was lighter. She raised her head and felt rather than saw a light brighter than the sun; the sky was white. And there was a presence there, she thought she could make out a pair of wings, white on white, extending across the whole arc of heaven. They slowly moved, drawing her upward. In her head she heard a voice: 'It will be fine. Everything will be fine now.'

Afterwards she would be surprised that she hadn't for a moment thought she was dying, but simply allowed herself to be lifted, secure in the knowledge that she was being helped, that her prayer had been heard.

She didn't know how long it went on for, but at some point she found she was on her feet, and that the presence had gone, along with the shivering and the nausea. She stood motionless, contemplating the chestnut leaves quivering in a faint breeze, listening to the hum of the traffic behind her on Sveavägen.

In that instant she decided to take her vision seriously; this was her last chance. She took the subway to the Maria Poli clinic and booked herself in. She spent several weeks in hell, cursing the god who had given her back the will to live, but she didn't give up. All the way through the cramps and the vomiting she held onto the image of the white wings, the voice and the power that had lifted her. There was someone or something out there following her struggle, even though it never showed itself again.

*

When she came out she began to rebuild her life from nothing. She changed the SIM card in her phone and deleted all her contacts except for Goran, who was one of the few decent clients she'd had in the past few years. He was also good with computers. She'd been given a temporary apartment to help her transition, and she made sure she kept it spotlessly clean. She never left dirty dishes lying around, she showered and changed her underwear every day, and she went to aerobics. Step by step she achieved a normal and tightly controlled existence, but this time she was the one in control. She never forgot those who had helped her, and prayed at least once a day, sending thanks to a faceless god whose silence she interpreted as approval.

When she got the chance to rent the apartment in Bergshamra she began to build up the business again, but this time on her own terms. She'd considered an ordinary job; she'd even applied for a few, but with her lack of education and experience, she was offered mainly cleaning work. She spent a week or so cleaning a school, but it was mind-numbingly boring and badly paid. There was one thing she was good at—she'd been told often enough—so why not do that, if she could manage it without the nasty side effects?

In return for payment in kind, Goran helped her to set up a website with limited access and links to portals where punters could be found. Anita was thirty-four years old and looked good; the work-outs had tightened her skin, and self-discipline had put a sparkle in her eyes. She had some pictures taken by a semi-professional photographer, and had soon established a new clientele—of her own choosing this time.

No more shuffling from one seedy room to another, where even seedier men were waiting with their friends and their 'toys'. Her clients now mostly lived in nice houses and paid for a cab; she didn't really like them visiting her at home, because she didn't want problems with the neighbours. She still thought the actual in-out was as boring as cleaning, but it was significantly better paid. She would have liked to do a crossword while it was going on, but instead she put on the required show. Cries of ecstasy, pleas for more, no, no, no—all according to taste.

She had learnt one hard-won lesson during her years at the bottom:

never let them in. Physically that was exactly what she had to do, so it was all the more important not to let them penetrate her real self. She didn't want to hear about their problems, she didn't want to share her own. She never told them a single true word about herself, never gave them anything they could pick at and pull until her tightly woven self-image began to unravel. She had a number of entirely fictitious stories that she told about herself, and they had to make do with that. Plus the in-out, of course.

Until Tommy came along. As is so often the case when it comes to love, she couldn't say for sure what it was about him that touched her, made her open up against all the odds. She trusted him. She felt like a whole person in his company. She'd told him about her childhood; about what had happened in room 203 and many other rooms. He listened and neither condemned nor pitied her, plus he wasn't remotely interested in the in-out. They could happily spoon in bed, and Anita never had to deal with a throbbing bulge against her bottom.

There was only one important event in her life that she'd kept from him: the vision in Observatorielunden. It was a driving force as far as she was concerned, and she didn't want it probed or diminished by being reduced to a story. Plus it would be like a magician being ignominiously forced into revealing the secret behind his trick: *Look, this is how it works, here's the mechanism behind the illusion, Anita, it's just smoke, mirrors and a pair of white wings.*

If it was an angel that had saved her, then it must have been a demon that made her suggest they should move in together. There was nothing intrinsically odd about the desire for closeness, for a relatively normal relationship, but once the decision was made, Anita began to have her doubts.

She had methodically reassembled herself from the wreckage that had washed up in Observatorielunden and could present herself as a settled and lucid individual. However, she didn't believe in the reliability of this construct. She'd never had a long-term relationship, and didn't know what mental challenges it might involve. Tommy could easily crush her without meaning to, the way a child grasps a frog and accidentally squeezes it to death. She loved Tommy. She was afraid of him.

And then there was that damned dog, with its false leg and its gloomy expression; it seemed to have the ability to see right through her. Anita knew it was irrational, but she was convinced that Hagge knew exactly who she was, and she hated it. Hated being caught out. Hated that dog.

This was Anita's state of mind when she opened the door, slightly tipsy even though it was the afternoon, and let Tommy and Hagge into her life.

*

'So,' Tommy said. He put Hagge down and rubbed his palms together as Hagge crawled over to the front door and lay down, his nose almost touching the wood.

'So,' Anita responded, and Tommy hugged her in a way that felt formal rather than affectionate.

'My cases are in the car—and Hagge's basket. Where can we put it?' Anita looked slightly panic-stricken, and her eyes darted around her neat and tidy apartment. 'He won't be happy until he's got his basket,' Tommy clarified. 'He has to have a place to be.'

Only then did he realise how absurd this whole idea was. Hagge's basket was one thing, but what about Tommy himself? *Where was he going to be?* What did people do when they lived together in a small space? How did they move around each other, how did they find room?

Tommy had always liked Anita's home, but now he experienced a mild sensation of claustrophobia, as if the walls were closing in on him, making it hard to breathe. His reptilian brain or some other weird brain was shouting *Run! Run! Run!*, while a more civilised brain sublimated the impulse into the irresistible urge to move his feet up and down on the spot.

301

'Would you like a coffee?' Anita asked. 'Or a whisky? I know it's early, but…'

'Both sound good. I just need to…'

Tommy gave in to the reptilian brain. His tail was swishing as he opened the front door. Hagge shot out like an arrow, his prosthetic clattering on the concrete steps. When they reached the street Hagge ran straight to the car and looked meaningfully at it. *Home now? Yes?*

Tommy could easily have got in and driven straight home, never to return. He longed for his armchair, and it was this longing that made him think again. He lifted out the basket, wrangled Hagge into it, then carried the whole package back indoors. Hagge whimpered as if he were being transported to the vet's for the final injection, but didn't dare jump out of the basket, which Tommy was holding as high as he could. He placed it in the middle of the floor in the hallway and said: 'We'll find a better place shortly.'

He turned to go back for the cases, and both Hagge and Anita gave him a look that said *don't leave me alone with him / her*, but Tommy hardened his heart. He brought the cases in and moved the car to a legal parking space. He blanked his thoughts and simply concentrated on putting one foot in front of the other until he was sitting at Anita's kitchen with a cup of coffee and a glass of whisky, as promised. Meanwhile Anita had put out a bowl of water for Hagge, who was lying in his basket staring at it as if it were laced with arsenic.

'*Skål*,' Tommy said. 'Here's to combining our fortunes.'

'*Skål*,' Anita said, managing a little smile at long last.

They drank in silence, and a tiny fragment of peace crept into the uncomfortable silence between them. Things were getting back to normal. They could talk about Hitchcock films or something they'd seen, read, thought. Tommy was about to say something about the whisky when he caught sight of his cases, staring at him like passive-aggressive bulls.

'Where shall I put my clothes and so on?'

'I haven't thought about it.'

'You haven't thought about it?'

302

'No.'

'So what have you thought about?'

'Sorry?'

'You haven't thought about where Hagge's basket can go, you haven't thought about where I can put my things, so what *have* you thought about in terms of all this?'

'I haven't thought about anything much.'

'Because you didn't want to think about it? Or because you don't want me to move in?'

'I didn't say that.'

'No, but it's beginning to feel that way.'

'There's no need to get angry.'

'So how should I feel? Happy?'

They drank again, hunkered down in their respective trenches, and silence fell like poison gas. This wasn't what he'd been hoping for. He'd imagined a homecoming and he'd ended up in the middle of a war. He got enough of that in his everyday life.

'I want some kind of shared existence,' Anita said. 'I want you to be here all the time. But from a purely practical point of view, I haven't been able to…'

'Do you know what I think? I think you subconsciously see me as some kind of dog. You expect me to be around, but not make any human demands.'

'That's not a nice thing to say.'

'Not much of an argument, Anita, but okay, I'll take it back. If you want me as a dog, then you should at least have sorted out a place for my basket.'

Anita sighed, stood up and went into the hallway. When she grabbed the handles of Hagge's basket he leapt out and gazed at Tommy in horror. *Look what she's doing! She's crazy!* Anita carried the basket into the living room and placed it on the glass coffee table. She took out Hagge's blanket and spread it over one of the white leather armchairs. Hagge remained in the doorway, following her every movement.

Anita patted the blanket. 'Come on, Hagge. This is your armchair. This is your place now.'

Hagge glanced at Tommy, asking for permission. He was never allowed on the chairs in Tommy's apartment. Tommy shrugged and Hagge edged slowly towards Anita. Eventually he jumped up, turned around three times, then settled down with a contented sigh, his head resting on his paws. Anita scratched him behind the ears and he didn't protest.

'Do you know what I think?' Anita said. 'It might not be much of an argument, but you're not a dog at all. You're a fucking cat. You want to come and go as you wish, and you expect food and affection whenever you deign to grace us with your presence.'

Hagge was clearly waiting to see how Tommy was going to respond. No doubt he thoroughly approved of 'fucking cat'.

'That's not true. You're the one who's set these conditions for our...'

'Have I, Tommy? I think you've forgotten how things were at the beginning of our relationship, or whatever you want to call it. How many times I called you to ask if we could meet up, but Mr Cat was always too busy rooting around in some trash can. So in the end I let Mr Cat decide when we should get together, but he's conveniently forgotten about that now, because it suits him.'

Tommy looked at Hagge, who was still lying there letting himself be scratched, and he felt somehow betrayed. His main ally had crossed the minefield and gone over to the enemy. He searched his memory and recalled a couple of conversations about meeting up, but instead of sounding the retreat, he went on the attack.

'Your clients—have you told them you're quitting?' Anita's eyes darted from side to side, which answered the question. Tommy intensified his campaign. 'Okay, so how's that going to work? Is Mr Dog or Mr Cat, or whatever the hell I am supposed to be, going to sit on the end of the bed cheering you along, or do I go out? Sit at the kitchen table? What do I do?'

Anita scowled at Tommy, while Hagge shuffled around a quarter turn so that he couldn't see either of them. With ice in her voice, Anita said: 'Obviously I have no intention of continuing. I just haven't informed my clients yet.'

'Right. And where do you expect me to do my work? We know where you do yours.'

'I didn't think you'd sink that low, Tommy.'

'There's a lot you don't know about me.'

'I'm beginning to realise that.'

Anita had automatically continued to scratch Hagge, but now he moved his head and shook himself. He didn't want to be a counter in this game anymore. Anita sat down on the sofa while Tommy paced back and forth. Once again he felt the walls closing in on him and he longed for his cat life, his dog life, any life but this one.

'I guess this wasn't a good idea,' he said.

'No, I guess it wasn't.'

'It's going to be hard to fix this.'

'I don't think it can be fixed. It's broken beyond repair.'

'Yes.'

All the strength left Tommy's body and he sank down at the other end of the sofa. They could discuss the matter calmly now, but it was too late. The damage was done. It was impossible to bridge the half-metre gap between them on the sofa, and they both knew it. All that remained were diplomatic negotiations to bring the war to an end before they went their separate ways.

Fuck. Fuck fuck fuck.

Surely everyone knows it's not possibly simply to combine one's fortunes with another person? Collateral damage is inevitable. Tommy rested his head on the back of the seat, closed his eyes and examined his soul. It was cold and empty, nothing more than a shell. This had been his last chance, and he'd blown it.

He heard a gentle clicking, followed by the squeak of leather, a movement. Something warm and soft covered his right thigh, and he opened his eyes. Hagge had joined them and was lying at full stretch so that his chin was on Anita's lap and his back legs on Tommy's.

Tommy didn't dare look at Anita, but just as he reached out to stroke Hagge's back, she did the same thing, and their fingertips touched while Hagge's warmth found its way up through their palms, along their arms and into their hearts. Tommy moved his hand closer until it was resting on Anita's, then caught her eye and said: 'Sorry.'

Anita nodded. 'Me too.'

'We're like two kids.'

Anita continued to stroke Hagge. 'Just as well there's one adult here.'

They sat quietly until Hagge judged that his work was done, and returned to his armchair. Tommy shuffled closer to Anita and put his arm around her. 'Shall we start again?'

'Good idea.'

'Where shall we start?'

Anita didn't speak for a moment. Then she said: 'I was lying before. When I said I hadn't thought. I have thought.' She looked up at Tommy with a shyness he'd never seen before, then asked: 'Would you like to see my room?'

*

They held hands as they got up from the sofa. Hagge followed them with his gaze, but stayed on his armchair. In the hallway Anita reached up to a shelf and took down a sugar bowl with angels on it. There was a key in the bowl.

'So it was locked,' Tommy said. 'I did wonder.'

'You never…?'

'No.'

'Of course you didn't.'

Anita put the key in the lock and turned it. 'You mustn't laugh. You mustn't…There's a word. When someone has something holy and someone else spoils it.'

'Desecrate.'

'That's it. You mustn't desecrate it. Regardless of what you think.'

'I promise.'

'You promise?'

'I promise.'

Anita took a deep breath, pushed down the handle, opened the door and let Tommy into what he perceived as an eclectic shrine. The blinds were closed, but the light from the hallway shone in. The walls were covered in pictures of angels as they appear in different religions, from Islam's enormous winged beings to Judaism's creatures of light and Christianity's bookmark angels, watching over children crossing a raging river via a bridge. There were texts in Hebrew, Arabic and languages Tommy didn't recognise, phrases in Latin, Swedish and English.

On plinths, pedestals and shelves were three-dimensional representations of the same things: large and small statues and sculptures of winged beings with or without haloes, with large or small wings, and with expressions ranging from beatific kindness to stern vigilance.

Scattered among the angels were countless candlesticks and tealight holders, plus a couple of incense burners. The room was impregnated with a pleasant mixture of sandalwood and musk. In the middle of the floor lay a yoga mat, the focus of the angels' attention.

Tommy looked around slowly, checking out each item, and eventually said: 'Wow.'

'Not what you were expecting.'

'I don't know what I was expecting. You're clearly a believer, if you don't mind my saying so.'

'I don't know what I believe, but I know what I know,' Anita said. 'How are your knees? Can you sit on the floor?'

'I guess so. Whether I can get up again is another matter.'

Tommy lowered himself onto the yoga mat, using his hands to help him settle down cross-legged. Anita lit some candles, then gracefully sank to her knees in front of him. Tommy ran his hand over the mat and asked: 'Do you meditate?'

'I'm not sure. I think I pray in a way that's like meditation.'

'To the angels?'

Anita didn't reply, but looked at the biggest angel picture while her lips moved in a way that Tommy knew meant she was in the process of making a decision. She turned her head a fraction, patted her thighs and said: 'I'm going to tell you something. Something I've never told anyone else.'

'Why not?'

'Because…' Anita closed her eyes. If it hadn't been for the frown, Tommy might have thought she was praying. 'Because I believe that those who survive in this profession are those who manage to keep something to themselves. Something that's non-negotiable. Otherwise you just become…' A grimace that made her look ten years older passed across Anita's face. 'I've never told you how far down I was. And what happened.'

Briefly Anita ran through the years and events that had preceded her vision in Observatorielunden. She talked about the state she was in, the lost flip-flop, and finally the angel that had made her reassess her life. Tommy listened without interrupting. When she'd finished, he said: 'And this room is a…way of saying thank you?'

'Maybe it is, but more than that it's a way of not forgetting. It's so easy to let an experience like that become nothing more than a story, but I try to keep it alive.'

'And how's that going?'

Anita glanced at Tommy, saw that the question was sincerely meant, and replied: 'Pretty well. Not always, but I can often find my way back. See it. Feel it. Carry it with me.'

'Good.'

'Do you believe me? Do you believe this really happened?'

'What I do or don't believe is irrelevant. As far as these things go, I have only one motto: to each his own. Nothing like that has ever happened to me, but that doesn't mean it didn't happen to you. Will that do?'

'That'll do.' Anita nodded slowly, then looked slowly around the room with an air of melancholy. 'So this is what I thought. I'm going to move some of my angels to one corner of the bedroom, with the yoga mat in front of them. Then this will be your room. You can have a desk in here, a bed if you feel you want to sleep alone sometimes. Hagge's basket, maybe.'

'He seems to prefer the armchair.'

'But you get the idea.'

'Yes. Thank you. Why didn't you mention this before?'

'I wasn't sure.'

'But now you are?'

'Yes. When Hagge settled.'

Tommy glanced around the room with fresh eyes now it was going to be his. It would definitely work. A desk by the window and maybe, maybe a small armchair. He'd think about the bed later. He couldn't help asking one more question: 'So the idea is that I'll be replacing your angels?'

'Don't joke about that,' Anita said. 'It's far too close to the truth.'

*

On the way to the living room Tommy passed his suitcases. They gazed at him trustingly, gentle as lambs. When he and Anita sat down on the sofa, Hagge raised his head briefly, seemed happy with what he saw, and went back to sleep in his new nest. Tommy leaned back, finally able to take in the apartment that was to be his home.

In contrast to Anita's shrine, the rest of the place was fairly sparsely furnished. The living room walls were cream, adorned by only two paintings. Above the sofa there was a large Lars Lerin watercolour from Lofoten that Anita had bought ten years earlier; it was now worth four times as much as she'd paid. On the opposite wall next to the television was a framed original poster for the film *Notorious!*, the outline of a key surrounding Ingrid Bergman and Cary Grant as they gazed into each other's eyes. A fairly simple crystal chandelier. A beige rug, the drinks cupboard over in the corner, the sofa and armchairs, the coffee table. That was it. Tommy nodded to himself, and Anita asked what he was thinking about.

'I'm thinking this is lovely. And wondering why my place isn't as nice.'

'This is your place now.'

'Yes. Thank you.'

Tommy tucked his hands between his thighs, wondering what to say. Anita didn't say anything either, so they sat in silence, listening to Hagge's gentle snoring.

'So how do we do this?' Anita asked eventually.

'Do what?'

'Sort out our shared existence. Life. Everyday life. What do we do with all the hours?'

'I don't know,' Tommy replied. 'I don't have any experience, and I guess you don't either. It makes me feel a bit panicky, to be honest.'

'Maybe the secret is not to let ourselves panic. Just to let it be whatever it is. If we're bored, we're bored.'

Tommy nodded and stroked the back of Anita's hand. What she'd said was sensible, and yet that sense of being suffocated came creeping up on him. Not as powerful as before, but padding along. Over the past few years he'd got used to being bored, but he found the idea of being bored with another person slightly disturbing.

'Do you remember Albin, the psychologist?' he asked her. 'Have you had any contact with him.'

'Not for a couple of years. Why?'

'I once did him a favour.'

'And now you want him to repay that favour. Tell me.'

Tommy was still determined not to drag Anita into all this business with X, but the mere fact that he had moved into her apartment was enough to make her a target, if anyone was watching. It was most unfortunate that she lived on the ground floor. He got up and went over to the glass door, which at least had a sturdy lock. But the window…It had become fashionable among criminals to throw hand grenades into the homes of anyone they had a problem with. Anita must have sensed what he was thinking, because she said: 'Knock on the glass.'

Tommy cautiously rapped on the door with the knuckle of his right index finger. There was hardly a sound, because the surface was like stone.

'Bulletproof glass,' Anita informed him. 'Three centimetres thick.'

'And the window?'

'All the windows.'

On one occasion when Tommy had asked about the seven-lever lock on the front door, Anita had said she'd 'improved the security' of her apartment, but without going into detail. She needed to protect herself; there were people from her old life who thought she owed them.

'Expensive life insurance,' Tommy said.

'Home insurance too.' Anita pointed to the watercolour, depicting fishing boats beneath an unearthly midnight sun. 'That can be seen from the window, and it's worth half a million. So start talking.'

Tommy sank back down on the sofa and folded his hands over his belly. It was only fair that Anita should be aware of what she was getting into, so he told her what he'd learnt about X from Ernesto. His activities in the laundry, the attempted murder, the years in Colombia, the recently imported cocaine. Then he told her about Linus's abduction, Chivo's suicide and Linus's return.

'Have you spoken to him?' Anita asked.

'No. And I don't suppose he wants to talk to me.'

'I thought you were close.'

'We were. But lately...' Tommy's heart contracted. Ever since that day on the balcony when Linus asked about the 'really pure' cocaine, Tommy had suspected that he was heading into territory from which few returned, and what had Tommy done to stop him?

He knew perfectly well that the only effective solution would have been to lock Linus up and prevent him from setting foot outside. Linus was on a steep downhill path, and all he could do was keep hurtling along. That was how it worked, but Tommy couldn't help feeling he'd somehow let his nephew down. He massaged his chest with the palm of his hand.

'It's not your fault,' Anita reassured him.

'Maybe not, but that's how it feels.'

'Why do you want to see Albin?'

His heart was beginning to feel more normal. There was something he could do after all. Possibly.

'Albin worked at Huddinge when X was there. Before the laundry. He might have something to tell me, something that will enable me to…get to X. And eventually shut down his business.'

'For Linus's sake?'

'Partly. Obviously this makes me a risky person to know, and I'm living in your apartment. So if you want me to move out, you only have to say.'

'No. But now I understand why you were so interested in the window.'

*

Anita had Albin's number in her phone, and since he answered on the second ring with 'Anita!', he clearly had hers. She'd told Tommy that he'd made a few advances, but she'd rejected him. Tommy wasn't entirely comfortable with asking her to make the call, but he didn't want Albin to know he was the interested party. People of Albin's calibre had a tendency to forget promises they'd once made.

'Hi Albin. Listen, I've got someone who needs to talk to you…Yes, you could say it's urgent…No, not on the phone…Can you? That's great, you're really sweet. What? No, I'm not sure…Okay, see you later.'

She ended the call. 'He'll be here in an hour.'

'Well done. What was it you weren't sure of?'

'How much money is involved. Is any money involved?'

'Not one single öre.'

'Good.'

The feeling of suffocation had been blown away by the fresh

breeze of the hunt. Now the fox was being lured into the trap. Anita's eyes were sparkling when she said: 'Maybe we should start a private detective agency. You and me, Bogart and Bacall...'

'Anita, I have to say this one more time...'

'I know, I know. This is serious, but surely we can have a joke?'

'I hate to be a bore, but do you remember the guy who was found with his throat slit and his tongue pulled through the hole? He'd been tortured for something like forty hours. That's what we're dealing with now.'

The sparkle disappeared as a shadow passed across Anita's face, and Tommy quickly added: 'I'm not saying that's going to happen to you, that's absolutely not what I think, but...'

'Tommy, shut the fuck up.' The blackness in Anita's eyes was terrifying. 'You don't know the half of what I've been through. I haven't told you the worst of it. But I'm alive. And if we're going to live together, we need to set certain ground rules. Rule one: Anita can joke however much she wants about whatever the fuck she likes. Do you need to write that down? No? What's your rule number one?'

'That I want to be with you.'

Anita rolled her eyes. 'Don't even try.'

*

Albin arrived five minutes early. Tommy sat in the kitchen listening as he exchanged greetings with Anita. Even though he couldn't make out any words, there was something slippery about Albin's tone. There was a loud click as Anita turned the seven-lever lock, and the trap slammed shut.

The sound of Albin's voice moved closer. 'Okay, so what have you got for Uncle Albin today? Is it a...'

The question died away as Albin entered the kitchen and saw Tommy. For a second he looked blank and disorientated, a second later he half-turned to make his escape, and in the third second he pasted on a pale smile.

'Look, it's Uncle Tommy—who has a few little questions for you,' Tommy said.

'Good to see you, Tommy. It's been a while.' Albin held out his hand.

'Ten years.' Tommy shook the hand, which was just as thin and dry as he remembered. 'Did you read the book?'

'What book?'

'You know what book.'

Albin pretended to search his memory. Tommy was convinced that he'd grabbed the book on trafficking on the day it came out, just to check that he didn't appear under his own name or as a recognisable figure, which he didn't. Tommy had kept his promise, otherwise they wouldn't have been standing here now.

The past ten years had been kinder to Albin than they had to Tommy. Albin had the kind of appearance that dried out and stiffened rather than developing lines and shadows. It was as if he were undergoing a slow mummification. He must be getting on for sixty, but his skin was smooth, if somewhat parchment-like. He clicked his fingers and said: 'Oh, that one! Yes, yes. It was good.'

Anita came into the kitchen and told them to sit down, because people standing up while they talked made her nervous, unless she was at a party. Tommy and Albin sat down opposite each other with Anita at the head of the table, presiding over the meeting. She was the first to speak.

'Tommy's wondering about something, and both he and I would be very pleased if you could help us out here.'

'Go on.'

'It's a person you've come across in the course of your work.'

'I'm bound by a duty of confidentiality, as you know.' Albin leaned forward and peered into the living room. 'This person who needs help—where have you hidden her?'

'He's sitting right there.' Anita pointed to Tommy. 'And I've just explained the situation.'

Only now did the penny drop. Albin shook his head and began

314

to get to his feet. Tommy had been so taken aback by the way Anita had taken command that he hadn't made much of a contribution, but now he rapped on the table with his knuckles and said: 'Sit down. I did you a favour, and now you're going to do me a favour in return. That's how it works.'

'I have a duty of confidentiality. *That's* how it works.'

'Please, Albin...' Anita began, but Albin interrupted her. 'No chance. Now, if there's nothing else...'

'I know you're a bastard,' Anita said. 'And so does Tommy. In fact, what we know about you between us would be more than enough for a book—what do you think, Tommy?'

'I'm not sure about that, but certainly a few decent articles,' Tommy said thoughtfully. 'Sex, criminality and psychology. Actually, it doesn't get much better. *The psychologist turned punter.*' Tommy pointed to the empty chair. 'Sit down. Let me make this perfectly clear. If you don't cooperate, I'll finish you—very easily and with great pleasure.'

For a moment it looked as if Albin was considering an alternative escape route, presumably by using some kind of threat. The people he knew, what they were capable of—but then he looked at Tommy and Anita's expressionless faces and sank back down on his chair. His lips were clamped together so tightly they'd practically disappeared. Anita patted his hand. 'It's nothing dangerous, Albin. There won't be any comeback.'

Some of the tension in his jawline relaxed. Tommy was astonished. Instinctively he and Anita had fallen into a good cop / bad cop routine that seemed to work perfectly. Albin was wearing a martyred expression, but at least he seemed more amenable to being asked a few questions. Tommy took out his e-cigarette, and Albin glanced anxiously at the black metal case as if it contained a truth serum that was about to be injected into his arm. Tommy took a puff, pointed the mouthpiece at Albin and said: 'I want to know about a person who was admitted to Huddinge in the mid-eighties, and you were working there then.'

'I still work there.'

'Mmm. In around 2000 this person was given a job in the laundry at Gårdsstugan, as part of the preparation for his discharge. Does that ring any bells?'

Albin shrugged. 'We've got dozens of placements like that. It's sixteen years ago—how am I supposed to remember?'

'I think you'll remember this person if you ever came into contact with him.' Tommy drew an X on his face with his index finger. 'He has a scar like this.'

Albin's eyes widened, and before he could come up with an evasive answer, Tommy went on: 'Albin. I don't care if you say you don't know, you don't remember or you don't want to tell me. If I don't find out what I need to know, then I will finish you—figuratively speaking.'

'Tommy,' Anita intervened. 'If he really doesn't know anything…'

'Doesn't matter. I'll write the articles anyway. I'm sick and tired of this.'

'Wait,' Albin said quickly. 'I was there when he came in. Eighty-six. I'd only just started. He was in the young people's unit so I didn't have any direct contact with him, but there was plenty of talk.'

Tommy would have liked to make an ironic comment on the duty of confidentiality, but refrained. 'Came in, you said. Where from?'

'As far as I'm aware, they found him in the Brunkeberg Tunnel.'

Tommy's heart skipped a beat. He and Anita exchanged a glance before Anita asked: 'In the tunnel itself?'

'Kind of…There's some kind of ventilation system. A cooling room. It was just after the assassination of Olof Palme, when the police were searching for the gun. They found him in there and brought him in. He was in a very bad way.'

'What was his name?'

Albin gave a scornful smile. 'He had nothing on him—no ID. When he started to speak a little he often said "Sigge", but he seemed to be speaking *to* someone rather than about himself.'

'Who was he speaking to?'

'I wasn't there. It's just what I heard at the time.'

Albin ended the sentence on a downward inflection. He was about to stop. Anita reached for his hand, looked him in the eye as if there were only the two of them in the room and said: 'I'm so pleased you remember. This is really valuable. Do you recall anything else?'

Her performance was so convincing, her voice so sensual and warm that Tommy actually felt jealous. She never spoke to him like that. He knew why, of course: because she didn't need to. But still.

It had the intended effect on Albin. He brightened up and said: 'There was something else.' He glanced conspiratorially at Anita and lowered his voice. 'He was known as Walls.'

'Walls?' Anita repeated, not letting Tommy into the bubble she'd created around herself and Albin.

'Mmm. Right from the start they said *the kid who walks through walls*, but that was too long so he became Walls.' Tommy remained silent, not daring to break the trust Anita had established with her touch and her voice. Albin left a sufficiently dramatic pause, then continued: 'He could be locked in a room, and when the staff came along to do something, he wasn't there. He might be in a different room, which was also locked.'

'How did that happen?'

'That wasn't part of the story, but I know some people were really shaken up, as if something supernatural was going on. I guess he had keys—but then again it also happened when he was restrained, after he'd had some kind of episode. But of course it's only gossip.'

Albin was on a roll now, and the story carried him along. 'And another thing. There have never been as many suicides in the young people's unit as there were during the period when he was there—mainly those who'd upset him. It's not easy to take your own life in a secure unit; anything that could be used is locked away. But if you're determined…You can cut your carotid artery with a plastic knife, for example, although it takes a fair amount of sawing. This went on for a year or so, and then there was no one left who upset him anymore.'

Albin made a slicing gesture with his hand—*all gone*—which also indicated that he'd reached the end of his narrative. Tommy felt he could venture a question. 'Have you read any of my recent articles?'

Albin's face expressed sheer contempt. 'I don't read the *tabloids*.'

Anita gave Tommy a warning glance and he retreated, his brain boiling with things he would have liked to say to the stuck-up pervert who was holding his girlfriend's hand.

My girlfriend?

Tommy was fully occupied considering the connotations of this concept as Anita tried to wheedle a little more out of Albin. 'What happened later? When he grew up? When he was discharged?'

'He wasn't in my department then either, but I think he got better. Started talking. After a few years he was given a certain amount of freedom but he had no family, nowhere to go, so he kind of stayed around. Until he finished up working at the laundry, according to you.'

'Nothing else?'

'No, that's it. So now Uncle Tommy will have to decide whether that's enough to persuade him against taking revenge on someone who's never done him any harm.'

'I'm still thinking about that,' Tommy said.

Anita let go of Albin's hand, which seemed to trigger another memory. He clicked his fingers and said: 'That's it—Peter Himmelstrand! Apparently he hung out with Peter Himmelstrand a lot towards the end.'

Tommy felt dizzy for a second, and all he could come up with was: 'Peter Himmelstrand?'

'Yes—the journalist. The songwriter. *Somebody Up There…*'

'I know who Peter Himmelstrand is. What do you mean *hung out with*? How come?'

'Well, he was in there too, in the main hospital. COPD. Because of the smoking. And apparently Walls was there pretty often towards the end, like I said. I think Himmelstrand died in 1999, and Walls must have been discharged soon after.'

Albin grinned and nodded to himself, as if he'd just recalled an amusing detail.

'What is it?' Anita asked. 'Have you thought of something else?'

'Yes. Huddinge's a big hospital, right. Things happen. Over the years it's built up its own mythology, like in that Danish TV series *The Kingdom*, and Peter Himmelstrand is a part of that mythology.'

'In what way?'

'Well, the COPD—chronic obstructive pulmonary disease. He was hooked up to a whole lot of tubes and so on; he could hardly move because of the risk of his lungs collapsing completely. And rumour has it this was all hushed up afterwards, but apparently he didn't *die* in 1999.'

'So what did he do?'

'He disappeared. When they came in to check on him, all the tubes and cannulas were just lying there on the bed, but there was no trace of the man himself. It was as if he'd vanished into thin air.'

3. Beyond

The City and the Powder

It doesn't go unnoticed when a tonne of ninety per cent pure cocaine enters the bloodstream of a city. The fine powder seemed to be spread on the wind, and by the beginning of November it had arrived in every large suburb from Upplands Väsby in the north to Jordbro in the south. Stockholm was gripped by a minor outbreak of madness, and the police had their hands full.

First there were all those who overdosed. Cocaine isn't as unpredictable as heroin, but because the product was so pure, one person after another took a good big noseful as if it were the usual weaker mixture, then suffered palpitations followed by a collapse. Many were found with a blissful smile on their lips.

Then there were those who didn't overdose, but of course the drug had a much more powerful effect than anything they'd ever experienced, and they simply went bananas. Got in the car and drove off a quayside in the belief they were steering a submarine. Went crazy in a club because the dance floor had been invaded by aliens from outer space. Jumped out of a window to try out the wings they'd sprouted. And so on. Instances of people doing deranged things went through the roof, and there were countless individuals who had to be taken in because they were wandering around in a daze, completely unreachable. They came to be known as Teletubbies.

These phenomena alone would have been enough to bring the police to their knees, but that wasn't the worst of it. Secondary criminality rose sharply as well. Those who took the coke quickly became dependent and wanted more. When they ran out of money, they were prepared to do just about anything. The number of muggings, car thefts, robberies and break-ins soared, and so did the incidence of rape, because in some cases the powder seemed to settle in the testicles. The police barely had time to log all the reports, let alone investigate them. Extra overtime was approved, but they still had to ignore most of the break-ins.

There was one cooling breeze blowing in hell, if you chose to look at it that way. Since the wave of suicides ended, there had been very little gang-related violence. With so much top-quality cocaine swirling around, there should have been trouble between rival factions wanting a share of the snowstorm, but that didn't happen. After the initial burst of suicides and disappearances, things settled down on that front. Whoever was running the business was doing so with a firm hand.

In spite of staff shortages, the police had been forced to set up a special task force focused on the cocaine and its distribution network. 'The Powder Team' had managed to pick up a number of small-time dealers with their half- and one-gram bags, but they'd had no success in getting further up the chain.

Through witness statements from various parts of the city they had established that different groups were operating in each area. They always wore realistic masks representing people—some famous, some not—but the information about physique and skin colour changed from place to place. There was only one constant: a tall person with a slight limp, who had crooked fingers and often wore gloves. The police referred to this individual as X, because that was what he was called in the press.

Ah yes, the press. An experienced crime reporter called Tommy Torstensson had provided a number of suggestions that the Powder Team had gone over before he was allowed to publish. They knew quite a lot about X's background in Colombia, his activities in and around Gårdsstugan, and how the cocaine had been brought to Sweden. However, they didn't know where it had been brought ashore, and Tommy T claimed he had no idea either. Therefore they maintained low-intensity surveillance at Kapellskär and kept their options open.

The dream was to get to X, and on one occasion it looked as if they might succeed. An informant had told them that their elusive target was due at an address in Sundbyberg on a particular evening. Plainclothes surveillance officers were stationed nearby, and in an apartment with a good view of the relevant area. A SWAT team waited in an armoured vehicle one minute away. Imagine the tension when a tall, limping figure approached; the burst of frantic radio communication as he made his way down the cellar steps and disappeared through a door.

The building was surrounded and the SWAT team went crashing in, fully equipped with bulletproof vests, helmets and automatic weapons. Behind the door were two corridors running perpendicular to each other, lined with twenty or so storerooms. No other access point from the outside, apart from the door they'd just come through. They went over every inch of the place with a fine-tooth comb, but there was no sign of their quarry. The whole thing seemed so impossible that the SWAT team leader ordered his men to remove their helmets in order to check that X hadn't tried a particular move found in certain action movies. But no, all of them were wearing their familiar faces, none of which were removable. It was inexplicable.

One consolation was that they found a kilo of the crystal coke in a storeroom not registered to anyone. The seizure made the operation worthwhile, but it was still no more than a fart into the universe. How the hell had the man managed to disappear? X began to take on ever more mystical proportions, even within the police. The informant who'd given them the tip-off was found hanged two days later in the same storeroom. No indication of external force.

In the middle of November there were signs that the coke supply was finally dwindling. A tonne of powder had been absorbed by Stockholm's nasal membranes and had spread madness through its blood, but the overdoses, the acts of insanity and the desperate grasping for money dropped to a more manageable level.

Everyone knew what to expect, what was the top priority apart from tracking down and arresting X. If he was to retain control of his suburban empire, he had to be able to keep his business going. Therefore, one or more new deliveries should be on the way. This time the police were determined to stop those deliveries reaching the streets. They would strangle the sickness at birth to prevent the city from developing a fever once more.

Tommy

The Todos Santos boxing club was housed on a corner in one of Rissne's symmetrically arranged apartment blocks. Over the past thirty years it had been a convenience store, a key cutter and shoe repair service, a video store, another convenience store specialising in halal food, a computer repair shop, and finally Tomás's boxing club. The windows were barred, and the only adornment was a glittery sticker with the words *Confiamos en Dios*: we place our trust in God.

Tommy opened the heavy metal door and walked into a miasma of sweat, liniment, banter and hormones. The sound of blows, groans and fast-moving feet could be heard from the ring, where a young, skinny guy of Asian appearance was dancing around an older opponent, possibly of Middle Eastern origin. Tomás was leaning on one of the corner posts, watching closely.

The Asian guy's feet were moving as if he had springs beneath his soles; he bounced backward, forward, to the left, to the right, landing well-aimed blows on the other man's head guard or abdomen. The Middle Eastern guy tried the odd left or right hook, which the younger man effortlessly avoided. It was like watching a fight between a hummingbird and a walrus.

The Asian feinted left, ducked and went in for a killer punch with his right. A second later he was lying on his back, shaking his head. Tomás clapped his hands twice. 'Okay. Lennart…' The young man looked at him unhappily, and Tommy raised his eyebrows. *Lennart?* Hard to imagine a less suitable name for this supple, energetic boy. Rolf, maybe.

Tomás pointed to the tip of his nose. 'Remember. There's a string. Running from here. To Mahmoud's chin. Don't drop it. Don't lose focus. Good energy, good movement, but you need to…' Tomás slammed his fist into the palm of his hand, '…put more *weight* behind it.'

Lennart got to his feet, shook his head again, then said: 'He's… It's…like fighting with a sandbag.'

'Mmm. And Mahmoud? There's something called *parrying*.'

'No parry.'

Lennart's Swedish was perfect, but Mahmoud had a noticeable accent. Tomás sighed. 'What do you mean, no parry? You have to…'

Lennart interrupted. 'He means there's nothing to parry. That my punches are so loose he doesn't need to bother.'

Mahmoud grinned. 'Exactly. Little paws. Piff, piff.'

'At least I can talk properly.'

'Then maybe you can talk me into a knockout. Good luck.'

'Hey!' Tomás said. 'You know this isn't a match. Wrong weight class. You're just sparring. Learning the technique. And Mahmoud: if you meet Alfonso or Sebbe and you don't keep your guard up, you'll be the one lying flat on your back.'

Tomás jerked his head in the direction of the canvas, then spotted Tommy and raised a hand in greeting. 'Tommy! Don't just stand there like something the cat dragged in!'

'I'm watching with interest,' Tommy said as he approached the ring.

'Boys, this is Tommy. Tommy T. Sweden's top heavyweight journalist.' Both Mahmoud and Lennart smiled, and Tomás modified his assertion. 'He's the best in the business, and he's going to write about us. About you.' He looked Tommy up and down and nodded. 'I definitely got that wrong—you seem to be in fine form. Fit as a fiddle.'

'Not exactly,' Tommy informed him. 'I had a stomach bug for ten days. Couldn't eat. Lost about five kilos.'

'Every cloud,' Tomás said wryly.

*

After Tommy had finished his last article on X, in which he chose not to mention Semtex-Janne, as the only proof he had was the picture X had sent, he went down with a particularly vicious strain of the winter vomiting virus.

Anita told him he'd been overworking, that there had been too much stress in a short period. That might have been true, but the sickness and diarrhoea were a reality, and he felt like a bad person, lying there in Anita's bed letting her take care of him. He'd only just arrived, and now she was having to look after him, but he couldn't do anything about it.

He lay there with a bucket beside the bed and watched Anita as she set up a mini version of her shrine in the corner of the room. Once she'd removed all the angels from the other room and had a new bed delivered, Tommy moved in there so that she could sleep undisturbed while he shuttled back and forth to the bathroom.

It was Anita who took Hagge out, and during Tommy's illness the two of them formed a close bond. As if Hagge wanted to apologise for his previous aloofness, he became more doglike and affectionate towards Anita than he'd ever been with Tommy. He started rolling over on his back so that she could rub his tummy, something that had always been beneath his dignity.

When Tommy had recovered sufficiently to tackle the promised piece about Tomás's boxing club—Ove had promised him a full page, because the articles on X had been so well received—Hagge refused to go with him. He preferred to stay at home, canoodling with Anita.

*

Tommy chatted for a while with Lennart and Mahmoud and took some pictures with his Ixus—a few of each of them alone, then a couple with their boxing gloves on, arms around each other's shoulders. They were so different—the perfect image of human brotherhood. Maybe he wouldn't need to bring in a professional photographer.

The two of them continued sparring while Tommy and Tomás withdrew to the combined staffroom, office and storeroom, which had a pleasant smell of fresh coffee from the percolator on the counter, and well-worn leather from the pairs of boxing gloves hanging on the wall next to a poster of Ali and Foreman's Rumble in the Jungle.

Tomás poured two cups of coffee before sinking down on a squeaky chair behind a desk littered with papers. Tommy sat down on something that appeared to be both a stool and a stepladder. He could feel his upper thigh bone against the hard surface; maybe he'd lost all five kilos from his backside.

'So how's the club going these days?' he asked, blowing on his coffee. Even the steam coming off it smelled black.

'Not great. Some of the guys who used to come have given up; I think some are dealing and some are snorting the cocaine we looked into. But the wind is changing.'

'In what way? I've been out of the loop for a while.' Tommy sipped his coffee, which was red-hot and bitter. Some pure Guatemalan bean, at a guess. His stomach protested with a burning shudder, and he put down the cup.

'It's coming to an end,' Tomás said. 'Good or bad, depends how you look at it. There'll be trouble if no new product comes along, maybe even war. On the other hand it'll be nice not to have to deal with all the locos who think they're Rambo just because they've powdered their noses, so to speak.'

'Are you sure about this? Are you sure it's coming to an end?'

'I know,' Tomás said. 'As sure as *Amen* in church.'

*

Linus's number had stopped working; presumably he'd changed his phone or his SIM card or both. Betty had no idea where he was. She'd bumped into him once and had hardly recognised him—he'd shaved his head. He'd been pleasant and impersonal towards her, said he'd sorted out a place to live and she mustn't worry about him. Everything was fine.

Betty had bombarded him with questions about how he'd 'sorted out a place to live' when he hadn't been on a waiting list and didn't have any money, and Linus had refused to discuss the matter. He'd asked her to tell his dad that they would do 'that thing' one day when he had time, then he'd walked away.

Tommy was in the convalescent phase of his illness when Betty called him. She asked if he knew anything about Linus or 'that thing'. Tommy couldn't help her, but found the news about both Linus's accommodation and his new hairstyle worrying. Betty also told him that Linus was no longer going to college. Everything suggested that Linus was heavily involved in dealing the coke, which according to Tomás was coming to an end.

Good or bad, depends how you look at it.

Tommy understood what Tomás meant, but from his own perspective it was, paradoxically, mostly bad. Being responsible for the distribution of a product that then ran out was dangerous to say the least. It would leave an empty space, and *as sure as Amen in church*, someone would come along and fill it.

*

'He won't let that happen,' Tommy said.

'Who? Equis?'

'Mmm. He'll bring in another delivery.'

'I thought the police were watching every possible channel?'

'Maybe so, but…'

Tommy took another sip of coffee by mistake. The look on his face made Tomás smile and say something about *la fuerza guatemalteca*. Tommy got up to ease the pain in his backside, rinsed out his cup and placed it on the draining board. Then he leaned against the counter. 'Call me crazy if you like, Tomás, but I'm seriously beginning to wonder if there's something…supernatural about this Equis.'

Tomás's expression was grave. 'Why?'

Tommy explained what he'd found out from Albin, about *the kid who walks through walls*, and Peter Himmelstrand's disappearance.

He told Tomás the impossible tale of how the police had failed to catch him. In Tommy's absence the story had been given to Mehdi, and Tommy had read his article with a bitterness that didn't improve the state of his gastric juices at all.

'So what are you saying, Tommy? That he's capable of, what's the word, *teleportación*?'

'I know it sounds completely ridiculous, but...'

Tomás wagged his index finger as if he were correcting a trainee who had made an error. 'What's ridiculous, my friend, is not following your nose. Like the knife you use for shaving...'

Tommy sighed. 'Occam's razor. This sounds like a pseudo-intellectual crime thriller, Tomás. Occam's razor always comes up sooner or later. And Schrödinger's cat.'

'I don't know anything about a cat. But if everything is pointing to a simple explanation, then you'd have to be as blind as a bat not to look in that direction.'

'Would you call it the simplest explanation? The idea that we're dealing with someone who can *teleport*?'

'Listen to me,' Tomás said, embarking on a tale of *brujeria* from his home village. A woman had developed the ability to acquire other people's possessions with or without the help of magic, and she had been placed under house arrest. The villagers had guarded her hut 24/7, but somehow she had managed to get out and continue her thieving ways. In the end one of the men had become so angry that he beat her to death with a spade.

'End of story,' Tommy said.

'No. She was buried, but after a few days things started disappearing again, and guess what?'

'They opened up her grave and she wasn't there.'

'Have I told you this before?'

'No, but this isn't quite the same...'

Tomás spread his arms wide. 'Why not? Because my story is about superstitious peasants in Guatemala?'

'That's not what I said.'

'No, but that's what you meant. Just remember this, Tommy: a blind hen finds no corn.'

Tomás looked so angry that Tommy didn't dare point out that in fact a blind hen does still find corn, according to the saying. Plus he was right, of course. When the natural explanations didn't make sense, then you had to look at the unnatural. This wasn't the first time in Tommy's professional life that he'd come across this kind of phenomenon.

Towards the end of 1982 he was sharing an apartment with an old school friend on Islandstorget. He heard the call over the police radio, and was the first journalist on the scene in Blackeberg. The incident became known as the Bath House Massacre, thanks to Tommy. Bloodstains on the ceiling, as if the deed had actually been carried out by someone who could fly. A vampire, according to some.

A perfectly sane woman who drove a stake into the breast of a truck driver she didn't even know, because she'd been given the task of slaying this vampire.

'Somebody Up There Must Like Me' breaking into the messages on the police radio as soon as something happened in or around the Brunkeberg Tunnel. And now this business with X, who seemed able to move around regardless of what might be in his way.

'I'm sorry,' Tommy said. 'I started it. Sorry.'

Tomás grunted to indicate that the apology had been accepted. Tommy asked him about the history of the boxing club and its role in the local community, making careful notes. Finally he took a couple of pictures of Tomás with the boxing-glove wall as a background. Before he left, he asked: 'You're absolutely sure this coke is running out?'

'I'd put my last potato on it, Tommy.'

'Shit—I thought I was done with this. I'd better go and see Janne.'

'Want me to come?'

'No—he'll probably be more inclined to talk if I'm on my own.'

'More inclined to finish you too, maybe. Don't mention Zlatan.'

'No. And at least you know I've gone there. If anything happens.'

Tomás nodded and held out his right hand. 'I wish you luck, brother.' Tommy shook his hand and said: *'Confiamos en Dios.'*

Linus

'Do you understand?' Linus hissed, turning the gold snake's-head ring in towards his palm before slapping Wille across the side of the head again. It tore his cheek, his head flew to the side and he yelled: 'Oww!' as tears sprang to his eyes.

Linus grabbed his chin with one hand and put the index finger of his other hand to his mouth. 'Shhh. The neighbours. Shut the fuck up or I'll fetch a hammer instead.'

Wille swallowed, nodded and sat up straight on the kitchen chair Linus had placed in the middle of the living room. Linus ran a hand over his shaved head as if he were thinking of launching another attack. He grinned, and when Wille relaxed a little, he delivered a second vicious blow. This time Wille took it in silence.

Henrik had spent the whole time sitting on the sofa gazing out of the window, as if he were unaccountably fascinated by the snow-covered pine branches that could be seen through the grubby pane of glass. Now he brought his hands down on his knees and said: 'Anyway, I think I'll go and...'

'You're going nowhere,' Linus informed him.

'But what about dinner?' Henrik protested lamely.

'I've had enough of your fucking Bolognese sauce. Stay where you are.'

Linus turned back to Wille. With his hands clutching the edges of the chair and his lower lip trembling, he looked younger than his fifteen years.

'Let's try this one more time. Who else is scamming?'

'Nobody, you have to believe me...'

'Henrik, fetch the hammer.' Henrik muttered that Linus had told him to stay where he was. He didn't move. Linus clicked his fingers. 'Now! And the pliers.'

Henrik looked deeply unhappy as he dragged himself to his feet and headed for the kitchen and the toolbox. Linus fingered the heavy gold chain around his neck and gazed down at Wille, who had begun to move his head from side to side while whimpering quietly like a dog.

'Please, Linus, please,' he sobbed. 'I'll never do it again, and I swear I don't *know*.'

Linus allowed his fingers to trace the links of the chain as if it were a rosary for counting curses, not prayers. He loved that chain. He'd bought it two weeks earlier when he'd had his head shaved, and apart from the weight it gave him, which was considerably more than its physical weight, it felt good to walk around openly wearing something so valuable, knowing that nobody would dare try to take it.

Without a word Henrik handed him the hammer and the pliers, then returned to the sofa and his contemplation of the swaying branches. He probably thought Linus wasn't going to do what the tools suggested, and he was probably right. Probably. There was always room for improvisation.

What Wille thought was clear from his chattering teeth and the tears pouring down his face. However, Linus had to give him credit for being tough enough not to start yelling for help so that the neighbours would hear.

'Give me your hand.'

'Li-li-linus...'

'Your hand.'

Wille was about to hold out his left hand, but changed his mind and held out the right instead. Linus laughed. 'Use your left hand for jerking off, do you?'

'Wr-wr-writing.'

Some other time, like a month ago, Linus might have been moved by the fact that the boy wanted to save his writing hand. Not anymore. The darkness was everything, he was nothing. Wille was merely one of billions of fluctuations in the darkness, his fingers as unimportant as the legs on a daddy-long-legs in a dream.

He grabbed Wille's wrist and picked up the pliers, opened them up and positioned them over Wille's index finger. Wille mumbled something unintelligible. Linus tilted his head to one side: 'What?'

'Fuck, please, please Linus, the little finger. Please. The little finger.'

'What do you say, Henrik?'

Henrik shrugged. He didn't want to play this game. He was a conscientious bitch who cooked macaroni with meatballs or his fucking Bolognese sauce, did the washing up and the cleaning. Amazingly he'd also managed to find a few punters at his college and elsewhere, and was selling almost as well as Matti, even though unlike Matti and Linus, he was still keeping up with his academic work. He might lack both toughness and a sense of fun, but he certainly had discipline.

'Come on, Henrik. Shall we do a Petyr Baelish?'

'I couldn't give a fuck. Do a Varys if you want.'

Henrik had no interest in going out in the evenings, didn't even go to Primavera to party when the place became a nightclub at the weekends. Linus and Matti would hold court along with Alex and his two closest allies from Chivo's old crew, who had decided to accept the new leadership. Henrik stayed at home and studied.

The only thing Linus and Henrik shared in terms of entertainment was *Game of Thrones*—Tinnie had the complete box set on Blu-ray, of course. Wille also seemed to be familiar with the series and Varys the eunuch, because he started shaking so much that the chair began to move across the floor, and he opened his mouth to scream. Linus placed his free hand over the boy's mouth. 'Calm down. We're not going to go that far. Yet. Henrik's the only crazy motherfucker around here.'

Wille let out the air he'd inhaled, his lips puttering against the palm of Linus's hand. Linus shook it in disgust.

'Last chance,' he said, increasing the pressure on Wille's finger until the skin almost broke. 'Who?'

Suddenly it was as if a wind had passed over Wille—a wind called resignation. He shoulders slumped, he stopped shaking. He licked up a drop of blood that had trickled from the wound in his cheek to the corner of his mouth, looked up at Linus with a sorrowful expression, and said: 'I don't know. If there is anyone, then I don't know who it is.'

It had come to Linus's attention that Wille was involved in a scam—adding a few hundred to the agreed price per gram, thus earning twice as much as he should, twice as much as everyone else. Linus had three groups of boys aged between thirteen and fifteen who sold for him, just as he had done for Alex, and Wille was the leader of one of these groups.

Everything that Linus's subordinates did was Linus's responsibility at the end of the day. He was the one who was answerable to X, and if X found out that the product wasn't being handled in accordance with his instructions, then Linus would carry the can.

Through the jaws of the pliers his fingers and the palm of his hand were in direct contact with the bone in Wille's index finger, as tangible as if he were squeezing it in his hand, and he felt a powerful impulse to turn Wille's hand into a fist. The crunch. The scream. The thought of the scream brought him to his senses. He opened the pliers and placed them on the table. Wille let out a gasp and began to babble his thanks, until Linus stopped him with a gesture.

'Okay. At least you didn't mess with the product.'

'I would nev...'

'Shut up. Listen. If you messed with the product it would be your cock or mine, and guess which one I'd have chosen? But you've scammed me, and that costs a finger. But I didn't take your finger. Any idea why?'

'Because you're really nice, and honestly Linus I...'

'No. Wrong answer. Partly because you're a good salesman, and I don't want you to become, what's the word, disillusioned. I think you'll be an even better salesman after this, right?'

'Absolutely, thank you...'

'And partly because you're going to give me all that extra money you've scammed, right?'

A glimmer of uncertainty passed through Wille's eyes. Maybe

the money was already gone, exchanged for the designer jeans he was wearing and the Nike sneakers drumming nervously on the floor. Among other things. Linus only had to glance at the pliers. 'Absolutely, Linus. No problem. When do you want it?'

'In an hour would be good.' Wille's eyes darted all over the room, and a muscle in his cheek began to twitch. 'But tomorrow will be fine.'

Linus could see the cogs in Wille's brain beginning to turn. According to his calculations, Wille needed to produce around twenty thousand, and he didn't seem like the type who'd opened a bank account. Unlike Linus himself.

'The thing is...' Wille leaned forward and lowered his voice, excluding Henrik. Linus appreciated the acknowledgment that he was the boss, but at the same time he couldn't let this little runt diss someone who, however much of a sad fucker he might be, was part of Linus's inner circle. He drew back and said loudly: 'Yes, Wille?'

Wille glanced at Henrik as if he thought he might actually be a crazy motherfucker. In his normal voice he said: 'The product. I've run out, and people are waiting.'

Clearly Wille had spent his ill-gotten gains, and now needed to embark on a frantic sales drive so that he could pass on the profit to Linus. 'It's on the way,' Linus said, keeping his expression impassive.

'Is it? Because without a fresh supp...'

'Not my problem. You've scammed me, I want my money. Do you expect me to discuss my business with you? Do you want to *know*?'

'No, no. I don't want to know anything. I'll sort it.'

'Good. In that case we're done here.'

*

'Is that true?' Henrik asked when Wille had staggered out of the apartment. 'Is there more coming? I've almost run out too. I've had to sell half a gram to customers who wanted two.'

Without bothering to reply, Linus went into the kitchen and took a beer out of the refrigerator. He sat down at the kitchen table, which

337

he'd found in a dumpster, and opened the evening paper Henrik had brought home from college. He noticed an article by that guy Mehdi—Tommy had mentioned him. *Is the cocaine barn empty?*

Linus had read Tommy's articles with interest; he couldn't understand how his uncle had found out so much, or why he was still alive. Large parts of X's operation had been revealed in those articles, and maybe that was why there hadn't been a new delivery. Fucking Tommy, in that case. When Linus transferred his contacts list to his new phone, he'd deleted his uncle.

He hadn't seen X since that one time, and Tommy's articles told him why. This was a huge operation extending throughout Stockholm, and Linus was just one of many brothers pushing X's matchless product.

Today's piece by Mehdi was all about how this product seemed to be running out, which fitted Linus's own experience. But the fact that it was *in the paper* was a disaster. As soon as the sniffers and snorters realised that their tap was about to be turned off, they'd start looking for a new source, and the brothers who sold crap would realise there was a gap in the market and come galloping along like cows let out in the fields after a long winter. Minus the joy. Mehdi's article had probably sped up that process by several days. New stock was needed, and it was needed right now.

Linus's only contact with X had been a few brief messages via Snapchat. Where to pick up supplies, instructions for selling. The latest had arrived a week ago. Linus couldn't get in touch with X, and in any case it would have been pointless. If Mehdi was right, then every brother in every suburb was in exactly the same difficulties as Linus.

'Have you read this?' he called out to Henrik in the living room.

'About the coke? Yes,' Henrik shouted back.

Linus's cheeks flushed red with anger. He raced into the living room and hissed: 'For fuck's sake! Why don't you put a notice on the fucking door? Fucking idiot!'

'You asked, I answered.'

Linus caught sight of the hammer, which was still on the table, and the desire to beat Henrik to death came over him. His hands opened and closed as he breathed hard through his nose.

'Calm down,' Henrik said as he shuffled backward on the sofa. 'Calm down.'

Linus was anything but calm. His brain was crackling and sparking. The last few weeks might have been the best in his life. For the first time he was living in a way that chimed with his illness or diagnosis or just his fucking *character*. Rapid action, tension and sudden explosions of violence or partying. Plus status. No time for restlessness or self-loathing. He was on top, and yet he slept well at night.

Now there was a danger that it could all disappear, and right this minute Henrik, sitting there on the sofa, was the epitome of everything that was wrong. The hammer shimmered on the table like a *Resident Evil* treasure item. Here I am, take me, use me. Linus had to mentally grab himself by the hair, force himself to take one step back, and three to the side, and pick up two ten-kilo weights from the corner of the room. He pumped them twenty times until the worst of his rage had flowed out into his muscles. Between panting breaths he said: 'Why. Did you. Ask. About the. Coke. If you've. Read. The article?'

Henrik shrugged. 'I thought you might have more information. That you've got a special contact. That's the impression you gave.'

Linus gritted his teeth and carried on pumping. *That's the impression you gave.* Well yes, maybe he had slightly exaggerated his link to X. What would happen if that link disappeared, if X was out of the picture? Bad things. Very bad things. Over the last three weeks he'd worked with the weights at least three times a day, building up the muscles in his arms, but that wouldn't help much if the real muscle moved in and no one had his back.

He pumped until the sweat was pouring down his body and his arms felt like jelly. He couldn't cope with this crap anymore, he needed to talk to someone who understood. He hadn't seen Kassandra since he'd collected a batch of weighed-out packages a week ago, hadn't experienced her clear-sighted cynicism.

He put the weights back in the corner. 'I'm going out for a while.'

'When will you be home? Shall I make dinner?'

'We're not fucking married, Henrik.'

*

The temperature had risen to just above freezing, and the snow that had arrived a few days earlier lay heavy on the trees but had turned to slush on the ground. Linus hadn't got around to buying winter boots, and as he splashed along his flat-soled Adidas leaked at the toes.

Seeing a cop sitting in an unmarked Volvo outside the tanning salon didn't make him feel any better. Who did he think he was fooling? The idiot was wearing a leather jacket that yelled *cop* just as loudly as if he'd been sitting in a patrol car with its blue lights flashing. Linus was going to have to trudge through the slush past the carpet-beating rack in order to avoid being seen.

This guy had been sniffing around Gårdsstugan for two weeks. Crawling around in his white Volvo, talking to people, checking out storerooms and empty shops, but fortunately he hadn't managed to find the Den. Linus was pretty sure nobody in his crew would grass, but you could never tell what 'the public' might have seen, pensioners with nothing better to do than sit staring out of the window. The cop's presence was a source of anxiety, a disturbance, and maybe that was exactly what the fucker wanted to achieve.

Linus kicked the slush in front of him as he walked through the darkness; all the lights were broken. What was it with this fucking society? Linus was seventeen, almost eighteen, and he was running a complex operation that involved packing, storage and distribution with a turnover of millions, while the state couldn't even maintain the streetlights.

The thought that he was more competent than Swedish society cheered him up a little, and he felt even better when he saw himself.

Here he was in the dark, hands deep in his pockets, staring at the ground and thinking everything was crap. But was he scared, was he worried, was he on his guard? Not for one second. There was nothing to fear, because nobody dared touch him. He was at the top of the food chain.

He raised his head and stared into the bushes, looming up ahead of him like a blacker shadow in the shadows. *The darkness*. He no longer feared the darkness because he was a part of it, and the darkness was his essence. It was the same for everyone, but the difference was that Linus knew it, with every fibre of his body. So: nothing to fear.

He rounded the bushes in a somewhat better mood and emerged into the faint glow of the lights above the doors. He was out of sight of the cop, and continued towards Kassandra's apartment.

*

'It's so good to see you!'

Kassandra gave him a big hug and planted a wet kiss on his cheek. Linus wiped his face with the back of his hand and stared at her as she stood there in the hallway, smiling at him.

'What's going on? What's happened?'

'Nothing. It's just good to see you.'

'So you said.'

'Stop being so grumpy!'

Linus knew Kassandra was erratic, but he'd never seen her this cheerful. There was less kohl around her eyes, her hair no longer looked like a bird's nest, and over the past few weeks she'd dropped a few kilos. It was actually possible to see that there was a pretty girl sleeping behind the emo briar hedge.

She grabbed his cock and said: 'Take me now! Come on!' She rubbed his crotch and tried to pull him towards the bed, but Linus pushed her hand away. She might not be looking too bad, but he wasn't in the mood. He had a bad feeling about this. Kassandra adopted a theatrical pout.

Linus had handled so many bags of coke that he had a fingertip sense of the weight, and a few times recently he'd suspected that some of the two-gram bags were a fraction light, maybe by as little as one or two tenths of a gram. He hadn't been certain, and hadn't bothered getting himself a set of scales to check, but in light of this suspicion, he didn't like Kassandra's behaviour at all.

He grabbed her by the shoulders and looked into her eyes; the pupils were definitely dilated. 'Have you started snorting? Tell me the truth. Have you started skimming something off the top for your own use? If you have, tell me now!'

Kassandra twisted herself free. 'Are you crazy? Do you seriously think I'd steal from you? Is that what you think of me?'

'So what the fuck is going on then? What's happened to you? You're not usually like this.'

Kassandra looked offended. 'If you must know, they've changed my medication. Maybe it's just working, that's all.'

'What's it called?'

'Zoloft. Can't we talk about something else? If you don't want to fuck, then can you at least give me something to work with? Otherwise I'll just end up sitting here playing with myself.'

She was talking too fast and her fingers were drumming against her thigh, as if she were indeed about to start playing with herself.

'I haven't got anything.'

'What do you mean, you haven't got anything? There's hardly any left.'

'I haven't got anything.'

Linus went to the kitchen area, and Kassandra followed him. On the counter lay ten filled bags; Linus could see that each one contained two grams. Ought to contain two grams.

'That's all there is,' Kassandra informed him. 'Then it's all gone, finito, nada.'

'Mm-hm.' Linus picked up one of the bags and tossed it on the scales. The digital display showed 2.496. The bag itself weighed half a gram, and the absence of four-thousandths of a gram was nothing.

'What are you doing? Do you seriously think I'm sitting here skimming and snorting—is that what you think of me? If it is, you can fuck off!'

'I'll think whatever I like,' Linus said, picking up the jar with the cockroach in it. Nothing was moving, neither its legs nor its antennae. 'Is it dead?'

'No. It moves occasionally. During the night.'

Linus tilted the jar: maybe one of the antennae twitched, but it could simply be the jar's movement passing through a dead body. 'How long has it been now?'

'Five weeks. Five weeks since we started with this shit.'

Linus replaced the jar and pointed to the bags. 'Split those into ten one-gram and twenty half-grams. Put them in the usual place.'

'Yes boss. Then what? When those are gone?'

'Can I see your medication?'

'What?'

'Your medication. Zoloft. I'd like to see the prescription too. With the date on it.'

They stared at each other. This wasn't what Linus had been hoping for when he came to see Kassandra, but there was no going back. He couldn't have a packer who skimmed the goods. Pushing her like some social worker felt bad, but after all, it was for her sake too.

It wasn't true that Linus was at the top of the food chain. He might have no natural enemies at the moment, but in return he had an unnatural boss who could gobble up both him and Kassandra in a single bite if he had a reason to. Linus had to find out the truth before it was too late, and if he had to use violence, then he would.

Kassandra continued to stare at him with her arms folded, and Linus was about to start pinching, squeezing, punching until he elicited a confession when he heard from his phone the sound of a drop of water falling into an echo chamber. He quickly took it out of his pocket and clicked on the Snapchat icon.

It was a photograph of a map. A large, green expanse with a single building, which immediately drew his eye because there was

343

an X above it. At the bottom of the picture there was some childish handwriting: 'bromma golf clubhouse 1 hr mask.' Linus just had time to take another look at the building before the image disappeared.

Bromma. Fucking Bromma. How the hell do I get there? One hour, and I have to go and pick up my mask first.

'What was that?' Kassandra asked. 'You look stressed.'

'Nothing to do with you.'

'Is it a delivery?'

'You'd like that, wouldn't you?'

'Of course I would. That's what we do.'

'It's not a delivery.'

Linus glanced at Kassandra and thought he saw her face fall, but he couldn't be sure. He didn't have time for this crap right now. In spite of what he'd said, there could well be a delivery on the way. If nothing else, X was still around, so Linus was bound to find out something.

He hadn't even taken off his wet shoes. His feet squelched as he strode across the room, opened the front door and slammed it behind him, then ran down the stairs.

Tommy

It was dark in Janne's part of Värtahamnen. The buildings were in darkness, a light showing in only one window—Janne's office. Tommy parked next to the Ferrari, opened the passenger door and let Hagge out.

He'd gone back to Bergshamra to check with Anita if she wanted him to do any shopping for a late dinner, and to collect Hagge. He could have asked about dinner over the phone, but he liked the feeling of being able to go home and exchange a few words, maybe a hug, before he set off. His apartment in Traneberg provided accommodation, but Bergshamra was more like a home and, much to his surprise, he found he liked that. And of course he couldn't pick up Hagge over the phone; technology hadn't got that far yet.

He wanted to see Hagge's reaction, just as a diver uses an echo sounder to make sure there are no sharks around before he jumps in. Janne was unpredictable, and with no back-up it was safest to let Hagge sound out the depths before Tommy walked into his office. He had no idea how Janne felt about his articles—whether he was grateful that he'd been kept out of the story, or livid because they'd been published in the first place.

He put Hagge on the leash and the dog limped through the slush as if he were carrying the weight of the world's troubles on his back. Tommy went up the metal steps and knocked on the door.

Janne's voice came from inside: 'What the fuck!' Nothing else happened. Tommy knocked again, and was rewarded with another 'What the fuck!', this time with the addition of 'Fuck off!'

'Police! We've come to take your car! We want it!'

This time the 'What the fuck' was closer, and with a hint of appreciation in its tone. The door was unlocked and opened. Janne was silhouetted against the light from the office, and Tommy couldn't read his expression. Hagge's head drooped, and he drew back a fraction. He didn't like this person, but he didn't start to shake, growl or whimper, which was a good sign.

'What the fuck!' Janne said for the fourth time, and Tommy could smell the booze on his breath. He peered down at Hagge. 'Tommy. What the fuck's happened to your accountant?'

'He was no good. I got a new one.'

'Come on in, and bring your accountant. I think I might have...a bone or something for him.'

Before Tommy stepped inside he looked at Hagge again. The dog was no longer on the alert; he was gazing at Janne with an even gloomier expression than usual, as if he felt sorry for him.

The only light came from a small desk lamp, and it was hard to make out objects around the room. The wetsuits and dinghies seemed to have disappeared. Janne was leaning on the doorframe, watching him. He nodded. 'You worked it out perfectly, you old hack. How did you do it?'

'I got a photograph. Of you.'

The hint of a smile immediately vanished from Janne's face. 'Right. The photograph. It doesn't make any sense.'

'What doesn't?'

Janne seemed to be on the point of answering, but then he blinked drunkenly and said: 'So why the hell am I standing here? Why haven't I been arrested?'

'Because I didn't show it to anyone.'

Janne ran a hand over his face and shook his head, as if he were trying to sober up. 'No, I don't get it. Unless you're disturbingly fond of poor old Janne.'

'I can reassure you on that point. I'm not.'

'I didn't think so. Come in, for fuck's sake.'

*

Janne waved him towards one armchair, fetched an almost empty bottle of Seagram's from the desk and flopped down in the other chair.

He raised the bottle: 'Want a drink?'

'No thanks—I'm driving.'

'We're both driving. Seagram's not good enough for you? Do you prefer the stuff with a name that sounds as if you're clearing your throat?'

'No. Quite the reverse.'

Janne took a swig from the bottle, examined the label, then said: 'So I guess you're back in favour? The hard-hitting journalist from… where the hell did you say you were from?'

'Ängby.'

'Ängby.' Janne pulled a face as if someone had shoved a whole lemon in his mouth. '*Ängby*. And people talk to you, but you were the one who blew the whole thing wide open. I reckon you must be in line for some major journalism prize.'

'Did I?'

'Did you what?'

'Blow the whole thing wide open.'

'The…the key elements.'

'There's a lot I don't understand.'

'Mmm.' Janne took another swig, emptying the bottle. 'There's a lot I don't understand either.'

'Like what?'

Janne lowered the bottle and looked at Tommy. Something in his face and posture changed. Hagge, who'd been lying at Tommy's feet, stood up and let out a low growl. With surprising speed, given the state he was in, Janne slammed the bottle down on the table, shattering the glass and breaking off a corner of the table. Janne leapt up, clutching the jagged neck. He took a step towards Tommy and roared: 'Come fishing, have you? Just fucking try it!'

He waved the broken bottle in Tommy's face. Tommy jerked back and the sharp edges passed with a centimetre of his nose. Janne roared again, but this time it was just an inarticulate noise. Hagge had sunk his teeth into Janne's calf and was being swung from side to side with the movements of the leg. When Janne raised his weapon to slash at

Hagge, Tommy stood up and punched him hard in the chest. Janne staggered back, collapsed in the armchair and dropped the bottle.

His rage subsided as quickly as it had flared up. His head wobbled up and down as he contemplated Hagge, whose jaws were still locked around his calf. He sighed. 'Could you ask your accountant to let go, please?'

'Hagge, let go.'

Hagge obliged and backed away from Janne, never taking his eyes off him. Janne examined his leg; his jeans were torn and bloodstained. He contemplated the wound. 'Does your accountant have rabies?'

'Not as far as I know.'

'Fine.' Janne pointed to a cupboard behind Tommy. 'Can you fetch a fresh bottle?'

Tommy refrained from speculating about which of the occupants of the room was more likely to have rabies, and opened the metal door. Just like Anita, Janne had a drinks cupboard, and just like his furniture, it was crap. There must have been thirty bottles of Seagram's lined up on the shelves. Tommy took one, picked his way over the broken glass and handed it to Janne, who unscrewed the cap and took a swig.

'Oooh, that's better. Sorry I got a bit annoyed before.'

If Tommy hadn't had the presence of mind to pull his head back he would have been disfigured for life, but Janne had already forgotten that. He'd *got a bit annoyed*—nothing to worry about, in his opinion.

This was something that Tommy found both terrifying and attractive when it came to certain criminals: their immeasurable capacity for sublimation and suppression with regard to their own actions. Seconds after they'd done whatever it might be, it was all water under the bridge, what's done is done, time to move on. He was terrified by the total moral relativism and attracted by their carefree attitude.

Things that were done *to* them, on the other hand, were an entirely different matter. In those cases their memories were unhealthily good. A wrong word or an ill-considered shove could sit there like a ticking time bomb for years before suddenly blowing up in the face of the unfortunate who'd shown disrespect. No doubt Hagge would have had a death sentence hanging over him if he'd bitten Janne without provocation.

Janne ripped open the leg of his jeans and studied the double row of teeth marks, from which blood was still seeping. He waved the bottle. 'Is it only in cowboy films that...' He tipped whisky over the wound and yelled: 'Jesus Christ! Aaah! Fucking hell!'

When he straightened up he looked brighter than he had since he opened the door—almost energised. The impression lasted only a few seconds, then it was as if he remembered how things really stood. He sank back in the chair, sighed and took another swig.

'You think you know everything, Tommy. But you know nothing.'

'I'm not going to ask what it is I don't know.'

'Good. If you choose to play the game, then...'

Tommy thought he'd found a strategy for dealing with Janne's volatile temperament, so he continued along the same lines: 'I'm not going to ask what you mean.'

'No. I feel like telling you the whole lot, just to see your jaw drop.'

'I'm not going to ask you to do that.'

'No. We don't want Janne to end up like the guy in the Brunkeberg Tunnel, do we?'

'I'm not going to...'

'For fuck's sake, Tommy! You sound like a broken record.'

'I'm just trying to make sure you don't get annoyed again. I know it's hard to believe, but I'm quite happy with this face.'

'Jesus...Have a drink, why don't you.'

Janne passed over the bottle and Tommy took a cautious sip. It tasted much better than the whiskies Anita kept, the ones *with a name that sounds as if you're clearing your throat*, a phrase he had made a mental note of. He handed the bottle back and Janne shook his head. 'You drink like a woman. I thought all hacks were alcoholics.'

'Exactly. Listen, about this biography...'

'What fucking biography?'

'Your biography.'

'Oh, that.' Janne's eyes narrowed, and Tommy guessed he was remembering the reference to Zlatan. Hagge shifted uneasily at Tommy's feet, then Janne appeared to decide that it wasn't worth getting upset about. He waved a dismissive hand. 'No point.'

Tommy went for a variation on his earlier strategy. 'Do you mind if I ask why there's no point?'

'Jeanette. My daughter.'

'She was going to marry a doctor, right? From some aristo family?'

'Mmm. It all went wrong. Her family had me checked out. Told the son they'd disinherit him if he married Jeanette, and he didn't like that idea.' Janne nodded slowly to himself. 'I'll probably have to terminate every last one of them.'

This was said with no conviction whatsoever and Tommy didn't set any store by it. Hagge had gone back to staring at Janne with sympathy in his eyes.

'Is that why you're sad?' Tommy asked.

'Who said I'm sad?'

Tommy nodded in Hagge's direction. 'Him.'

Janne leaned forward and studied Hagge, whose expression remained unchanged. 'When did he say that?'

'He says it all the time.'

Janne tilted his head on one side as if he were listening for a whisper. When he didn't hear anything, he rubbed one eye. 'You're crazy, Tommy, you know that? Maybe that's why I put up with you.' He picked up his phone, an old Nokia with a diagonal crack across the screen. 'What's your number?' Tommy gave him his mobile number, and Janne laboriously entered it into his contacts list, his tongue sticking out of the corner of his mouth. Then he gave Tommy his number.

'Are you thinking of calling me?' Tommy asked.

'You never know.' Janne sank deeper into the armchair, his eyes fixed on the broken corner of the glass coffee table. A minute or so passed, and Tommy had started to think about leaving when Janne suddenly said: 'I'm not sad, Tommy. I'm completely destroyed. If only you knew. Now get out of here. Before I tell you something.'

*

As soon as Tommy got in the car he opened the glove compartment and took out a bar of chocolate. He unwrapped it, broke it into small pieces and placed it in front of Hagge, who was sitting in the passenger seat eying him with suspicion. Tommy stroked his head. 'You're a good dog. The best and bravest dog in the world.'

Hagge pressed his head against the palm of Tommy's hand, and even if he appreciated the praise, he didn't seem to fully understand it. When he'd eaten his usual quarter of the bar, he looked enquiringly at Tommy, who pointed to the remaining pieces. 'It's for you. All of it. You've earnt it, and more.'

Hagge gazed at the chocolate as if he couldn't believe his luck and didn't know where to start. He swallowed the smallest piece, then checked with Tommy one more time before finishing the lot.

Before I tell you something.

Janne had actually told him quite a lot, indirectly. *If you choose to play the game* was probably a reference to the fact that having started to do business with Equis, he now couldn't get out of it. *Completely destroyed.* The game that Janne had embarked upon had taken a turn that made him deeply unhappy. He'd been forced or was going to be forced to do something he didn't want to do. *Just to see your jaw drop.* Something above and beyond.

Janne had given away one concrete detail: the tortured police officer hanging in the Brunkeberg Tunnel did have a direct connection with Equis, who had himself been found in the tunnel's ventilation system in the mid-eighties. The interference on the police radio. *Somebody Up There Must Like Me.*

Tommy let Hagge finish his chocolate before he drove away from the docks. It didn't strike him until he'd negotiated the traffic around Slussen and was heading down towards the Old Town: *Shit,*

351

I'm doing it again. It was just before eight when he parked illegally on Luntmakargatan, on the steep hill leading down to Tunnelgatan. He pulled on the handbrake, got out of the car then remained where he was, staring at the door opposite: number fourteen.

What was it?

About thirty years ago he'd picked up on a story here, but it had gone to a more experienced reporter. Tommy closed his eyes and allowed the spiders of his memory to spin their web.

The Palme murder...video camera...bodies...blood...a couple... symbiosis.

His eyes flew open.

Jesus, that was *here*. A married couple who'd never drawn any attention to themselves had tried to become one single body. They'd pushed their way into each other's orifices and opened up new ones in order to get further in. When their bodies were found, in a state of advanced decomposition, they'd been stuffed full of strong painkillers in an attempt to complete the project.

If Tommy remembered correctly, several centimetres of loose videotape had been found up by the church. It was lying next to a heap of ashes, suggesting that a larger number of tapes had been incinerated. The intact tape showed a few seconds of the couple carrying out their physical symbiosis, and apparently it was enough to turn the stomach of even the most hardened observer.

Nothing to do with Tommy's current investigation, but didn't someone—or more than one person?—disappear at about the same time? People had a tendency to vanish when Equis was around, so maybe it was worth checking out.

He opened the door. Hagge jumped out of the car, landed in the slush and fell over. He got to his feet, shook himself and held up his prosthesis as if to say: *I'm actually a very graceful dog, but this makes me clumsy.* Tommy had to clamp his lips together to suppress a laugh. Hagge hated being laughed at. They made their way down the hill.

Behind the glass doors, the entrance to the tunnel shone with a greenish glow. Tommy looked up at the cast-iron plaque above.

KNUT LINDMARK
ENGINEER

What was the story again? Lindmark had also been responsible for the Katarina Elevator, which was a success, but the construction of the tunnel had been beset by problems and fatalities. Hadn't Lindmark taken his own life in the end? At least that was one suicide Equis couldn't be blamed for. Then again, what did Tommy know? In the end everything is connected, and maybe Knut Lindmark's death was somehow linked to the same phenomenon.

Tommy, lost in thought, didn't notice that Hagge had stopped moving until he felt a tug on the leash. Tommy took a couple more steps, dragging Hagge through the slush. The dog cowered and whimpered, making himself as small as possible as he stared at the entrance to the tunnel.

'What's the matter, boy? Don't you want to go in there?'

Hagge didn't need to answer to make his aversion clear. He pulled away, his prosthesis sliding on the slippery surface, his back legs kicking slush all over Tommy's trousers.

'Okay, okay. I get it.'

Tommy took Hagge back to the car where he settled on the passenger seat with his head on his paws, looking pleadingly at Tommy. 'It's all right, boy. I'll be back soon. Move the car if a cop comes along.' When Tommy closed the door, Hagge got to his feet and started barking. The sound followed him all the way down Luntmakargatan.

Tommy couldn't help being affected by the dog's behaviour. He trusted Hagge's instincts, and when he approached the tunnel this time he did so slowly, his whole body on the alert. He couldn't imagine what had made Hagge react like that, but there had to be something.

He pushed open the door and found that he couldn't see all the way along the tunnel, because it curved to the right a dozen or so metres up ahead. He stopped and listened. Nothing, apart from a faint clicking that he couldn't identify. He wished he could see all the way.

Pull yourself together, Tommy.

The tunnel was well lit by a series of lights along the sides, reflected in the shimmering green metal plates covering the lower half of the walls, while the ceiling had been left as it was—rough, dark stone. Tommy looked behind him and saw an old lady with a wheeled walker approaching at a snail's pace, which made him start moving. He wanted to be alone. He passed the curve and now he could see the full length of the tunnel, all the way to Birger Jarlsgatan. It was empty, and there was nowhere for anyone or anything to hide.

Except...

As he walked he glanced up and saw a ventilation grille in the ceiling. He remembered that the ex-cop's mutilated body had been found hanging from a grille near Tunnelgatan. It could well be the one he was looking at now. Behind it there was only darkness. An icy finger stroked the nape of his neck and continued down his spine, and he was convinced he was in the right spot. The man had hung from that very grille, with his tongue pulled out through the hole in his throat. Behind that grille, Equis had been discovered thirty years earlier. It couldn't be a coincidence.

The icy finger kept moving, like a faint but concentrated draught from the tunnel wall behind him. He turned and studied the metal plate. No cracks, no draught. But there was something...He placed his hand on the smooth, cold surface and closed his eyes. He could sense the massive, ancient rock behind civilisation's thin plate. He kept his eyes closed and lowered his head. Something was happening.

The darkness behind his eyelids began to glow green. At first he thought he'd unconsciously opened his eyes and was looking at the metal, but this was a different shade, with a different texture. A field. He wasn't there, but he was observing it like a pair of eyes suspended in mid-air. He was also able to use these eyes to look up at a bright blue sky with no sun.

Between the field and the sky, two figures were moving away from him: a small child and a big cat, coal black with a long, swinging tail. The animal's back and the child's head were at exactly the same height as they walked along side by side. Tommy couldn't work out what kind of cat it was. Its coat was too rough for a panther, and it was much too large to be a puma.

And the child? It was wearing tracksuit pants and a T-shirt. From behind, it was impossible to see whether it was a girl or a boy, but it was striding out with purpose and confidence, as if it owned the whole place. Suddenly the two figures stopped and looked at each other, then slowly turned around.

The child was a five- or six-year-old boy, with deep-set brown eyes and rounded cheeks. The animal beside him was, in spite of its black coat, a tiger. The size and shape of the head, the yellowish, bloodshot eyes. A tiger. The two of them stared straight at Tommy.

They can see me!

Tommy wasn't actually in the field, which seemed to stretch towards infinity. He was merely an observer without a body, in some incomprehensible way, but in the same incomprehensible way, the child and the tiger could see him. He didn't like it. Didn't like it at all. He made a huge mental effort and pulled away from the vision, took his hands off the wall. He was back in the tunnel.

He stood there panting, palms resting on his knees. He didn't know how long he'd been inside the vision. The boy...the gaze hadn't been that of a child. The eyes were clear, but as deep as bottomless forest tarns. *The kid who walks through walls.* Tommy crumbled the last of his scepticism towards the supernatural between his fingers like flakes of ash. He was convinced that he'd just seen Equis, or one aspect of him. And Equis had seen Tommy.

He became aware of a squeaking sound that was growing louder; he looked up and saw the lady with the wheeled walker approaching with agonising slowness. She was so old and frail that it was impossible to tell her age—eighty? Ninety? She looked as if she'd risen from her deathbed for one last outing. Tommy thought he recognised her. The woman stopped and peered at him with cloudy eyes, and a name popped into Tommy's head: *the Mora whore.*

She'd called to see Anita a few years ago, begging for money 'for old times' sake'. Later Anita had told him that she'd been known as the Mora whore during her working life, because she always carried a Mora knife for protection.

'I know who you are,' the woman rasped. He was used to that comment and was about to say something appropriate for Tommy T when she went on: 'You're Anita's bloke. Are you still Anita's bloke?'

'Yes, I am. Definitely.'

The woman smiled, pleased at having fished up a correct detail from her memory. 'What are you doing here?'

Tommy couldn't help glancing at the wall. The woman nodded. 'I see.'

'Do you know anything about…that?'

With unbearably slow movements the woman applied the brake to the walker, shuffled around it and sank down on the seat. She dug a packet of cigarettes and a lighter out of her coat pocket. She lit a cigarette with a trembling hand and took a shallow drag. What was it with dying people and smoking? Unlike Ernesto, at least she wasn't racked by a fit of coughing.

'Once upon a time,' she said, waving the cigarette towards the wall. 'A bloke asked me to feel. There. Fifty kronor.'

'Who was this bloke?'

'No idea. He was young. Close your eyes and put your hands here,' he said. 'So I did.'

'And?'

'What do you mean, and? You saw it for yourself, didn't you? I was shit scared. I didn't come down here for many years. And then…'

The woman shrugged and took another drag. A man appeared from the direction of Tunnelgatan. He was aged about thirty, wearing the obligatory thin quilted jacket and walking with a springy gait. He wrinkled his nose, stopped next to the woman and said: 'Excuse me—we don't smoke in here.'

'DON'T we? Well you can kiss my arse.'

'I'd rather not.'

She jerked her head at Tommy. 'What if he forces you?'

Tommy held up his hands to show that he had no such intentions. The man scratched his artistically overgrown beard, shook his head and muttered: 'Idiot', then carried on towards Birger Jarlsgatan.

'Is that the best you can come up with, you hairy fucker!' the woman croaked after him before turning back to Tommy. 'Where was I?'

'You saw the field. The tiger.'

'Exactly. Sigge.'

'What did you say?'

'Sigge.'

'Sigge who? Sigge Cedergren?' That was the only association that came to him, partly because Sigge Cedergren had been active in the area, and partly because he'd allegedly lost a revolver like the one used to assassinate Olof Palme just a few months before the incident. The woman stared at him as if he'd lost his mind. 'Why would you bring up that bastard?'

'Sorry. Go on.'

Sigge. Sigge. Tommy had heard that name in another context recently. Yes! That was what Equis had said when he was first admitted to Huddinge.

'I was scared,' the woman continued. 'For many years. But then— well, I suppose I got too old for that kind of nonsense. And it's a long way round. So I started using the tunnel again. Sometimes I hear or see something—I suppose I got tuned into the right frequency that first time.'

'And Sigge? Who's Sigge? Is the tiger Sigge?'

The woman tossed aside her cigarette without bothering to stub it out. 'Oh, that's just something it does when it wants to be seen.'

'It?'

The woman hauled herself to her feet and began to shuffle around the walker, using the handles for support. 'It, yes. Haven't you understood yet? There's something in the rock here. Something ancient.

That fucker Lundmark or whatever his name was set it in motion when he started digging.'

'And this something old is called Sigge?'

'Sounds like it. If you listen you'll hear it.'

The woman released the brake, pushed the walker over to Tommy and said: 'I don't suppose you can spare a hundred or so? For old times' sake?'

Tommy gave her two hundred-kronor notes, which was all he had in his wallet. She thanked him with a toothless grin and continued on her way. After a couple of metres she stopped. Presumably a one-eighty-degree turn was too much for her, so she called over her shoulder, her words echoing around the tunnel: 'Say hello to Anita from the Mora whore—she'll know who you mean!' Before she set off again she patted her coat pocket, letting him know that she still carried her signature weapon.

Tommy had no intention of listening or making any further contact with that field. He crushed the still-smoking cigarette butt beneath his foot and left the tunnel the same way he'd come in.

*

When Tommy had climbed into the driver's seat and closed the door, Hagge did something he hadn't done since he was a puppy. He shuffled onto Tommy's knee and licked his face. His breath still smelled of chocolate, and Tommy turned his head so that Hagge could only get at his cheek. 'It's all right,' he said. 'I'm still alive. Everything's fine.'

Hagge eventually decided he'd expressed enough affection and returned to the passenger seat. He settled down and looked at Tommy: *Okay, let's hear it.*

'You were right. There was something there. But I don't know what it was.'

Tommy couldn't make sense of what he'd seen, but as the woman had seen it too, he had to accept it as a kind of reality. An apparently endless green field, the grass cut short; a blue sky with no sun;

a child and a black tiger. The image reminded him of an illustration, somehow. If the two figures hadn't reacted to the fact that he was watching them, Tommy would have happily accepted that he was seeing something static. But they had reacted, and the woman hadn't seen the child, only the tiger.

Sigge. Just something it does when it wants to be seen.

If the story had been strange from the start, it had now taken a huge stride in the direction of myth and saga—and delirium. That didn't suit Tommy at all. He loved stories, but they had to be anchored in concrete facts and believable human behaviour. What he was experiencing now wasn't believable, it could hardly even be called...

'It's not fucking *realistic*!' he said, slapping himself across the side of the head and making Hagge whimper, as if he'd been struck instead.

Time to forget all this, stick to his area of expertise: facts and evidence. He didn't mind a bit of blood and guts, when reality was in that kind of mood. And there was still one loose thread dangling. He took out his phone and scrolled down to Don Juan Johansson.

There was no music in the background—even though it was after eight o'clock—and Henry's voice was weak.

'Tommy. How are things?'

'Okay. How about you? I thought you might be out on the town.'

'I've got some kind of vomiting bug. Not quite up to dancing at the moment, but I'm on the mend.'

'Good to hear. Listen, I've got something for you. You know Semtex-Janne? I'm pretty sure he's helping Equis with another delivery. A big one.'

'Doesn't he work from Värtahamnen?'

'Yes. I was there earlier.'

'But the last lot came into Kapellskär, didn't it?'

'A very small part of the shipment was in a box from a ferry that uses Kapellskär. That doesn't mean the whole lot was brought in that way.'

'Really?' Henry's tone was ironic, but Tommy knew he'd gone in hard on the Kapellskär lead. The only result was a fourfold increase in the seizure of cigarettes and spirits, which had led to Henry being given the temporary nickname Ration Book. His voice had soured a little when he added: 'You were the one who gave me the tip, if you recall.'

Henry had rewritten the story of the coke found in Hans-Åke's car to suit his own self-image. *Hans-Åke*, for Christ's sake. That felt like a lifetime ago. Tommy sighed and suddenly felt down; he couldn't be bothered to argue with Henry.

'And now I'm giving you another tip. It's your decision, but if I were you, I'd keep a close eye on Janne. He's done something, or he's going to do something. I'm not sure which.'

Tommy could hear Henry making notes, so presumably his tip wouldn't fall on stony ground. He enjoyed talking to Janne, but he belonged behind bars.

'Anything else before I run to the bathroom? It's pretty urgent, so make it quick.'

'Yes. Svante Forsberg. The ex-cop who was found hanging...'

'I know, I know. We checked it out. No links to Colombia, nothing. So you were wrong. Again.'

Tommy refrained from mentioning how much he'd brought to the investigation; this wasn't the time or the place. Instead he simply said: 'I want to know everything about him.'

'Didn't you hear what I...'

Now it was Tommy's turn to interrupt. 'I'm not talking about that. I want to know what he did beforehand. I want to know about his whole life. You said he was a nasty piece of work—okay, so when did that happen? What did he do?'

'You expect me to...' Henry didn't get any further; he whimpered in pain. Tommy knew what he was going through; it was hard, trying not to shit yourself. Henry let out a groan and cut to the chase. 'Why the fuck would I do that?'

'Because I told you about Janne. You know people at every level. You can easily find out.'

'For a tip that's probably worthless? Seriously, Tommy…'

'I know it might take a while, but…'

'Jesus Christ!'

The call ended. Tommy decided to leave Henry in peace to change his pants and possibly his sheets. He might be a real ladies' man when he was fit and well, but when he was sick he had no one to look after him. Unlike Tommy. He started the car, released the handbrake and drove home to Anita.

*

'Greetings from the Mora whore.'

'Goodness—is she still alive?'

'Just about. I met her in the Brunkeberg Tunnel today.'

'What were you doing there?'

Tommy told Anita everything, from Semtex-Janne and Hagge's heroic intervention to the tunnel, the field and the tiger, the Mora whore and the conversation with Henry.

They'd had a late dinner of rice and leftover chicken, which Anita had cheered up with saffron and cinnamon. When Tommy had finished his tale, there was one thing that particularly caught Anita's attention. She whistled quietly, and there was a thud from the living room as Hagge jumped down from his armchair and approached her. She stroked his head and said: 'Are you a good dog? Are you the best dog in the world, protecting my Tommy?'

She took the remaining piece of chicken out of the dish and offered it to Hagge. He'd never been allowed to beg at the table; unlike Anita he looked at Tommy to check it was okay. Tommy shrugged and Hagge gently took the chicken, ate it up then licked his nose.

'He doesn't usually have stuff like that.'

'He saved your life!'

'I know,' Tommy said. He knew exactly how pathetic it sounded when he added: 'I did give him a bar of chocolate.'

'And now I've given him a piece of chicken.'

'Okay, okay. As long as it doesn't become a habit.'

Living with Anita wasn't exactly conflict-free, and they'd clashed several times. She would come into his room because she needed something out of the wardrobe when he was writing, breaking his concentration. She would wake him in the middle of the night because she'd had a weird dream. She'd more or less taken over Hagge. Every time she did something that irritated or disturbed Tommy, he returned to his mantra *as long as it doesn't become a habit*, even though a number of these things had already done just that.

Anita was bothered by the fact that Tommy was such a restless sleeper, that he could be a know-all who didn't allow her to say her piece, that he grunted like an old man when he sat down, that instead of engaging in an argument he withdrew into himself and became difficult. Among other things.

During Tommy's illness these conflicts had been temporarily set aside, and many of them hadn't caused a problem since. They were slowly getting used to each other.

'This Svante Forsberg,' Anita said. 'Why is he so important?'

'There's a gap. The rest of the story makes sense, but there's something missing. Something I don't understand at all.'

'So you understand what you saw in the tunnel?'

'To be honest, I'd prefer not to think about that.'

*

But when Anita had gone to bed and Tommy had settled down at his desk to finish the article about Tomás's boxing club, the image came back to him. The field, the child, the tiger.

There's something in the rock here. Something ancient.

He'd never been in direct contact with anything that could be called supernatural. It was possible to find an explanation for what had happened in Blackeberg. There were ways the blood could have got on the ceiling, and the children who'd talked about someone flying were in shock and therefore unreliable. Plus on that occasion he'd been faced with a fait accompli; it was all over when he arrived. Now he was right in the middle of whatever it was. The field, the child, the tiger.

Sigge.

He might have been able to push his thoughts aside if it hadn't been for that look. When they turned around. *You don't belong here. You are seeing something you're not supposed to see.*

Gradually, however, Tommy managed to return to Lennart, Mahmoud and Tomás. As he'd hoped, the pictures he'd taken were perfectly fine and, given that the name of the club was *Todos Santos*, he thought he would headline the piece 'All Rissne's Angels', if Tomás didn't find it too cheesy.

He wasn't due to submit the article until the following day, and was intending to allow himself the luxury of a final revision when he'd slept on it. There wasn't usually time. He'd just saved the text when his phone pinged to tell him he had a message. In the current situation he was grateful not to hear a drop of water falling into an echo chamber. He opened the message, which came from an unfamiliar number:

Linus here. You saw him. He wants to see you. I gave him the address. Don't reply to this.

Tommy put down the phone and stared at his own reflection in the blank computer screen. *He wants to see you.* Suddenly he saw his face stiffen. There was someone in the room. Someone was behind him, even though he couldn't see whoever it was. Tommy pushed off from the desk and spun around half a turn.

There was no one there, but when he lowered his eyes he realised why the presence hadn't been visible in the reflection. Hagge was standing there looking up at him with that expression Tommy recognised all too well: *What did I tell you?*

Linus

Linus could have been at a really bad fancy-dress party. He was surrounded by about twenty people, none of whom was showing their real face. Half were wearing rubber masks representing famous people, from Freddy Krueger to Donald Trump, while the rest of the masks represented anybody, just not themselves. The only one Linus recognised was Alex, who had adopted his persona from the field and was in a Joker mask.

Linus had chosen something neutral, a black guy who looked tough. He might be a rapper—Linus wasn't sure. He certainly wasn't familiar with his work, if that was the case.

The only light came from a crescent moon, casting its pale glow over the clubhouse, the snow-covered ground and the silver-coloured caravan which had taken on a bluish tone. They were all facing the caravan, and no one said a word. He and Alex had nodded to each other, but that was the only communication Linus had had since he arrived five minutes before the agreed time.

He understood the point of the masks. If no one knew who anyone else was, then no one could betray the group, nor could there be any co-ordinated action if a few people were unhappy with the leadership. But there was also a risk. What if they'd been infiltrated by armed cops, ready to whip out their guns when the performance began?

Linus looked around, trying to imagine what kind of mask a cop would choose. The Devil over there on the far side? The old man flapping his arms to keep warm? At least he couldn't see a leather jacket like the one on the plainclothes cop in the Volvo.

Shortly after eight, the door of the caravan opened and everyone straightened up, just like the congregation when the priest steps into the pulpit. Linus had wondered what face X would be wearing, but he wasn't wearing a mask at all. Linus was grateful for the faint light, which spared him the inexplicable details of that face. What had X been through? The moonlight enabled him to see the deep X etched into the flesh, and that was enough to make him uncomfortable.

X stepped down and stood in silence for a moment, looking at his congregation as if he were counting heads, or waiting for a question, a challenge. When none came he raised his hands and made the usual gesture: 'Fall down.'

Linus wasn't sure whether he complied of his own free will, or whether something forced him. His legs bent, or he bent them, and he fell prostrate on the cold, wet snow. The dampness immediately penetrated his trousers, chilling his thighs as he lay there looking down at the dark blue slush. He heard the sound of other falling bodies, muffled splashes. Here they all were.

Slow footsteps as X approached. Linus was struck by a fresh thought: all those lying in the snow on the deserted golf course were about to be executed. The vulnerability of his position and those squelching footsteps evoked the image, and it made him shudder.

Another minute or so passed in silence. Linus had time to turn the thought over, consider it more carefully. He realised he didn't find it unpleasant. Or rather, it didn't matter. He'd always been terrified of death, but now he found that he didn't really care whether he lived or died, because basically it was the same thing. So why the anxiety, the fear?

It was probably the actual method—would it happen with a knife or a bullet to the back of the neck? Then again, neither would take very long. Linus relaxed as the dampness found its way through his jacket. Everything was fine. He wasn't even cold anymore, not really.

Maybe everyone around him had gone through the same thought process, and maybe that was what X had been waiting for, a kind of extra lesson before he spoke. The surprisingly high, childish voice came from directly above Linus, and he closed his eyes.

'I know you're having a hard time,' X said. 'I do know that. But soon everything will be fine. A delivery is on the way. A huge delivery. Everyone will get their share. Tomorrow.'

If it was as Linus had suspected, and all those around him had reconciled themselves with imminent death, then X's assertion gave them renewed hope. A collective exhalation of relief passed through the prostrate bodies, and somewhere to his right Linus heard a quiet *Yesss*.

'Everyone will receive a hundred kilos,' X went on, and the exhalation changed to a sharp intake of breath, a gasp. *A hundred kilos.* Linus couldn't imagine how he was going to shift that amount, but one thing was clear: if he succeeded, he was set for life. Two hundred in commission per gram would give him a profit of…Linus double-checked the sum he came up with. Twenty million. Unbelievable. But Jesus, a hundred kilos.

All the others must have been involved in similar calculations, and a sense of unease was clearly perceptible in the way they were breathing, the way they moved their bodies in the snow. It didn't get any bigger than this; it was going to be total fucking madness. In order to cool down overheated brains, X added: 'You'll get plenty of time. But it's arriving tomorrow. You will be given addresses. On notes I've written. Everyone will have a note. You need to be there at eight o'clock. In the evening. At the place that's written on the note.'

As before, Linus drifted away on the hypnotic sound of X's voice and his simple, childish statements. Footsteps moving away through the slush, a door opening and closing. When Linus looked up he saw a white glow coming from the fluorescent light in the window of the clubhouse. Everyone got to their feet, brushed down their clothes and looked at one another. Donald Trump, who was almost two metres tall, scratched the tattoo on his neck, gestured towards the clubhouse and said: 'Shall we…?'

When no one responded he took the initiative and walked over to the door. He stopped, his broad chest heaving as he took a deep breath before pushing down the handle. The others waited, their rubber faces ghostly in the cold light. Linus's eyes were drawn to the caravan, which was hooked up to a Toyota RAV. What the hell was it, and where had it come from? The shining chrome and the egg shape made it look like a spaceship. The field and the sky were inside it…

Linus made a decision. If everything went well now, he would take his father on that trip, as soon as possible.

After a minute or so Donald Trump emerged from the clubhouse. As if he were casting a vote for himself, he waved a piece of paper, then carefully folded it and placed it in his wallet. When he gave the thumbs-up sign he was even more like the real Trump: he'd sniffed out a good deal and come running. Without looking back, Trump set off across the golf course.

As if on a given command, the group lined up outside the clubhouse. They might all be brothers or gangsters, but the Swedish culture of queuing politely sat deep. Linus ended up somewhere in the middle, watching as the next person opened the door and went in. Once again it reminded him of a church service, the bit where people kneel down to get bread and wine—communion, that was it. This was like taking communion.

It took ten minutes for Linus to reach the front of the queue. No one else had waved their piece of paper since Trump, they'd simply headed off across the snow-covered grass without saying or doing anything. Even though there was no indication that anything bad had happened inside the clubhouse, Linus's mouth was dry when he opened the door.

He walked into some kind of reception area; it wasn't much warmer than outside. No doubt the golf toffs didn't waste much money on heating at this time of year. The walls were covered with diplomas and certificates and pictures of people in white clothes looking stupid.

X was sitting behind a desk like the receptionist in *Hotel Transylvania*. The comic association didn't help. It was painful to have to look at X's face in the clinical light; it was hard to believe it was the face of a living person, and yet another involuntary thought popped into Linus's head: *He's dead. That's why he can do the things he does.*

Dead or not, when X glanced up Linus forced himself to step forward. He tried to maintain a blasé front as the animated wound said: 'A hundred kilos. You can do it.'

The voice was so monotonous that it was impossible to tell whether this was a question or an assertion. Whatever. Linus replied: 'Absolutely.'

'You don't think it'll be difficult?'

When they first met, Linus had thought that X had very thin lips. As he moved them now, Linus could see that in fact they'd been cut away, and consisted only of scar tissue. He avoided running the tip of his tongue over his own lips, and said: 'Difficult, yes. Not impossible.'

'Good.'

The hand with the bent fingers appeared above the counter, holding a piece of paper in its claw-like grip. When Linus reached for it, X pulled back. 'One more thing.'

Linus had to fight to keep his voice steady. This didn't bode well. 'Oh yes?'

'You have an uncle.'

'I don't have any contact with him! I have nothing to do with all the crap he's written!'

X looked Linus directly in the eye, and with an enormous effort Linus managed to place his mind in the black balloon and stand firm.

'Did I ask you that?' X's voice rose slightly at the end of the sentence, as if he really was wondering.

'No.'

X shook his head. 'So why would you say that?'

'I don't know. Sorry.'

X lowered his eyes as if Linus's behaviour was a tricky human nut to crack. He would have frowned if he could, and Linus had no idea what was going to happen now. X seemed to have cracked the nut, or deemed it impossible to crack. He looked up again. 'Where is he?'

'I don't know. I don't have any contact with him.'

'You already said that. Where does he live?'

Surely anyone could find that out, so Linus said: 'Traneberg. Margretelunds…'

'No. He's not there. Where is he?'

368

Linus felt a mounting sense of panic. It began like a tingle in his fingertips and spread like a paralysis up his arms. His head was empty, the balloon was empty. X got to his feet and leaned across the desk. Fortunately Linus's legs were also paralysed, so he couldn't back away.

'He saw me. I want to see him. Where is he? Answer me.'

The paralysis had now reached Linus's throat and turned into a lump. At any moment Linus would burst into tears, and then he would be killed. A name flashed through the vacuum: *Anita*, and a second later it flew out of his mouth.

'Anita!' he almost yelled. 'The old whore! In Bergshamra! He's moved in with her!'

'The address. Of the old whore.'

Linus searched his memory, but drew a blank. Only then did he realise that he'd been so busy saving his own skin that he'd sold out Uncle Tommy. Bergshamra wasn't very big. Tracking down Anita wouldn't be a problem. Clearly X had reached the same conclusion. When Linus shook his head, he held out the piece of paper once more.

'Good. That's all.'

Linus took the paper and left the room.

*

He saw me. I want to see him.

Linus's clothes were soaked through. He didn't dare put the piece of paper in a pocket in case it became illegible, so he folded it over several times then held it between his palms as if he were praying. He weaved his way across the golf course, where a track had formed through the slush.

He didn't understand what X meant. How had Tommy seen him? More importantly, what did he mean when he said he wanted to see Tommy? Had Linus just signed his uncle's death warrant for a reward of twenty million? But what the fuck else could he have done? If he hadn't answered, then X would have killed him, or rather made him take his own life. The fact that he was reconciled with the idea of death didn't mean he *wanted* to die, just that he would accept it if it happened.

It had been him or Tommy, it was that simple. And yet he found it difficult to come to terms with what he'd done as he walked across the grass, lit only by the moon and stars. He was wet and frozen, totally absorbed in pointless self-recrimination, and it was several hundred metres before he realised he was still wearing the mask. He pulled it off and tucked the note inside it, then pushed it in his pocket and closed the zipper.

He wanted to travel now. Get away from all this. He broke into a run, heading for Åkeshov subway station.

*

During the journey back to Gårdsstugan by subway and bus, Linus managed to keep thought of his uncle at bay by concentrating on the *amount*. He remembered what Kassandra had said when he placed the kilo of coke on her kitchen table. *This is something else.* He wondered what she'd say about a hundred kilos.

Needless to say, he wouldn't be able to carry on dealing as he'd done before. This really was something else, at least from a purely logistical point of view. Kassandra could no longer be solely responsible for storage and packing; it just wasn't practical.

A hundred fucking kilos.

The more he thought about it, the less he was actually capable of thinking about it. A hundred kilos was unreal. The cops would cheer if they seized a kilo, throw a party if they picked up five or six. That was *a significant amount*. Linus was going to have a hundred kilos to sell.

Which meant that somewhere *two tonnes* was being brought into the country. Linus had read Tommy's articles, overcome with admiration for the super-advanced method of using the parasite. But surely, since Tommy had exposed the whole process, that route must now be closed? The cops must have submarines out there.

He took out the piece of paper and opened it up. It was a map with a cross above a rectangle next to Gårdsstugan's football pitch. Linus knew exactly which building it indicated: the Heil Hall. Once upon a time it had been a gym, until someone realised in the eighties that asbestos wasn't a good thing, and that the gym was full of the stuff. Removing the offending material would have been too expensive, so the authorities did what they always did at Gårdsstugan—closed it down and left it, hoping everyone would eventually forget about it.

At the beginning of the nineties an unexpectedly talented member of the BSS (Keep Sweden Swedish) had decorated one outside wall of the gym with an enormous swastika and an image of Adolf Hitler, happily raising his arm in the traditional Heil Hitler salute. The council had managed to find the money to remove *that*, but the name had stuck. The Heil Hall, tomorrow at eight.

*

It was twenty past nine when Linus let himself into his old home. He'd been back to the apartment, dropped off his mask and picked up the jar containing the black substance. He burned the map on the way from the subway station. Henrik had asked if Linus would like to watch *Game of Thrones*, and when Linus said he didn't have time, Henrik had looked terribly disappointed. This was getting too much like having a girlfriend, Linus thought. Not that he'd ever had a girlfriend, not in that way, but he assumed similar discussions took place. *Where are you going? You're never home!*

This was Betty's bingo night. There were others—at any moment a bonus night could be tossed into the routine—but Wednesdays were sacrosanct. The last game ended at about nine forty-five and it took Betty fifteen minutes to get home, so Linus had plenty of time, particularly if time behaved as he thought it had during his first visit to the field.

The television was switched off; his father was dozing in

Frankenstein mode in the shadows in the corner of the room. When he heard the sound of Linus's footsteps he raised his head and said: 'Wr-wr-ET-ET-d-d-d!'

When Linus was little, his father used to read Astrid Lindgren's *Emil in Lönneberga* aloud to him, and had placed extra emphasis on the phrase Emil's father so often used: 'Wretched kid!' It had become a private joke between them. It was a long time since his father had said or tried to say those words, and Linus had assumed he'd forgotten. It made him happy to know he hadn't.

'It wasn't me!' Linus responded, holding up his hands. 'Well—it was me, but I didn't mean to do it!'

His father grunted, pleased to know that Linus had both under-stood what he said and what he meant. Linus went and sat down on the sofa beside him, leaned over the armrest and said: 'Dad, we're going to do something together, you and me. That thing I told you about. But we have to do it before Mum gets home.'

Linus took out the jar and showed it to him. His dad's eyelids twitched. 'OOOPE?'

'No Dad, it's not dope, it's…It's impossible to explain without making it sound like dope, but it's something else altogether.'

His father groaned, his head moving from side to side, and Linus realised it really was impossible to explain.

'Can't you just trust me?'

His father snorted. His reference to Emil might have proved that he could rise above the crap Betty presumably trotted out on a regular basis, but that didn't mean he was prepared to trust Linus, sitting there gangsta-style with his gold chain and his shaved head. Linus tried a different tack.

He held up the jar. 'Okay. If I told you this was the best fucking drug ever, and I want us to take it—what would it matter? What, Dad? What would it matter? Have you got anything better to do?'

His father stopped moving, and Linus thought about all the times when he'd tormented Linus with his endless *kill me*. When it came to the crunch he wasn't even prepared to risk a bad trip. Contempt began to grow like a slimy embryo in his breast, then his father said: 'Nnnnnottt-uuu.'

Not you. Okay, so that was the problem. The embryo was still-born, sluiced away in a second. 'It's fine, Dad. I've done this before. It's not dangerous. And it's not dope.'

His father's head twitched and he uttered a stream of words that Linus interpreted as yes, Linus could give him whatever the fuck he liked, as long as Linus himself didn't take any of it.

'All right, we'll do it your way. I just want you to experience this.'

Linus went into the kitchen and fetched a teaspoon. He unscrewed the lid of the jar, then hesitated. What if it didn't work? The black substance might be perishable. Linus had had the jar for almost a month; its contents might have…died.

There was only one way to find out. He dipped the spoon into the glutinous substance and knew at once that his fears were unfounded. His fingertips tingled, the spoon became warm and he knew the contents of the jar were alive in the same way as he'd known that the bodies in the darkness were dead. It was alive, just like Kassandra's cockroach in its jar.

It moves occasionally. During the night.

Linus lifted the spoon to his father's mouth. His father's expression was sceptical, and Linus said: 'Am I going to have to pinch your nose? Trust me, for fuck's sake.'

His father opened his mouth. Linus pushed in the spoon and waited until he saw the Adam's apple move as the substance slid down. Then he dipped the spoon in the jar once more, scraped up what was left and swallowed it.

*

Close. So close now.

Once again the feeling of approaching something tremendous that was the portal to something indescribable. Swimming in the depths with your eyes closed, then opening your eyes and finding yourself

373

face to face with a blue whale. Being swallowed by the whale then hurled out into the universe and at the same time *close, so close.* Chaos or mystery only an arm's length away, but no arm to stretch out and touch it. Linus didn't know if he was falling or rising, what was up or down until he felt grass beneath his palms

pads

and opened his eyes.

The field stretched out before him, the blue sky rose above him. In the corner of his left eye he could see a dark body that was much bigger than his own. Linus turned his head, staggered back and sat down on his hind legs. What he saw was as astonishing as it was obvious. His father was a horse. A beautiful, gleaming black purebred Arabian.

The horse's coat rippled, it tossed its head and rolled its eyes, its legs as unsteady as those of a newborn foal. Linus stood up, walked around so that his father could see him and said: 'Dad? Dad? It's okay. This is how it's meant to be.'

The horse chewed the air as if an uncomfortable bit had been inserted in its mouth. Its tongue whisked around and it uttered a series of tentative sounds. It lowered its head to Linus's level, nostrils flaring as it inhaled. 'Linus?'

Linus wanted to laugh out loud with delight, but his current body didn't allow that expression of feeling. What emerged was a purr from deep in his belly, and a couple of cheerful swishes with his tail. 'Yes,' he said. 'It's me. This is me.'

'I...' His father gazed around, but apparently it was neither his surroundings nor his metamorphosis that surprised him the most. 'I can talk again.'

'Yes Dad. You're a horse and you can talk.'

His father looked down at his forelegs with their powerful muscles, turned his head and rubbed his muzzle over his broad flank, shook his mane, then flicked his tail a few times before turning his attention back to Linus.

'This is a hallucination, right? Because of...that.' He remembered and drew back his lips, exposing his teeth, and snorted. 'You promised you wouldn't…'

'Maybe I'm just a part of your hallucination.'

His father lowered his head, ears twitching. He blinked. Linus was glad he was such a strong, magnificent horse. It wouldn't have been as cool if he'd been a scabby donkey. Linus realised that his father could ponder until his hooves rotted, but he would never know for sure whether all this was his own experience, or whether the two of them were involved.

'It doesn't matter, Dad. We're both here now. You can walk, you can run, you can talk. Just enjoy it.'

His father tilted his head to one side and stared at his son. 'You're a cheetah.'

'Yes. And you're a horse. That's the way it is.'

'Is this for real?'

'Yes. We're in another place, and this is what we really look like.'

'What was in that jar? Where did you get it?'

His father lowered his head still further and stared at Linus. Now it was Linus's turn to bare his teeth, a growl rising from his throat. Without unsheathing his claws, he swiped his father across the muzzle.

'Seriously, Dad—just fucking leave it! You're not stuck in that wheelchair anymore—you're a horse in a field, okay?'

His father's head jerked back in pain and surprise. Then he gazed around, eyes wide, nostrils quivering. At last his tone of voice was what Linus had been hoping for when he asked breathlessly: 'What… What is this place?'

'That's a reasonable question, and I haven't a fucking clue. But I know that our time here is limited. In a while we'll be back in our normal crappy lives.'

His father looked around again, and Linus could see the blue sky reflected in his big black eyes. Suddenly he reared up on his hind legs, whinnying and moving his front legs through the air. When he landed on the grass with a heavy thud, he leapt forward, then he began to run. Linus stood and watched him pick up speed; he could feel the vibration of his father's hooves through his sensitive pads. He gave his father a fifty-metre start, then took off after him in an explosion of power.

He caught up in seconds, then they ran side by side. The ground flew by beneath their paws and hooves. His father ran even faster, his mane streaming in the wind, but Linus had no problem matching him—he was a fucking cheetah!

His father glanced at him, shook his great head and made a sound that was somewhere between a human cry of joy and a whinny before he engaged top gear, and for the first time Linus had to make an effort to keep up. His strength lay in sprinting over short distances. His father's legs were moving so fast they were no more than a blur, his hooves thundering across the grass, *ta-da-damm*, *ta-da-damm*, *ta-da-damm*. The smell of burnt flesh drifted into Linus's nostrils. On his left he saw something that looked like three people, walking along a line a few metres apart. Their skin was charred as if they'd been barbecued; it was hard to believe they were alive, let alone moving.

His father didn't seem to have noticed them. Linus shot past him and veered to the right. This place had secrets. Maybe one day he would learn about them, but not now. He continued on the same trajectory until he was on the same line as the figures, but heading away from them.

Once again he and his father were running side by side. This was what Linus had dreamed of since he received the jar containing the black substance—maybe even before that. Maybe he'd dreamed of this ever since his father's accident, but been unable to formulate the dream until it was within reach. But now they were here. Now they were running. *Close. So close.* They kept going at a steady pace until the old white caravan appeared on the horizon. His father ran straight towards it.

'No!' Linus shouted. 'Not that way!'

'Why not? I can see people.'

There were indeed two men in their fifties standing outside the caravan; they looked like farmers. They shaded their eyes with their hands against the harsh, sunless light from the sky as they looked at Linus and his father.

That's Lennart and Olof. They're nice. I go and visit them sometimes.

Linus didn't have the chance to see any more, because exactly what he had feared happened. The black tiger appeared, blocking their way to the caravan. Head down, all its attention on Linus and his father.

'No Dad!' Linus yelled again. 'No!'

His father was so preoccupied with his own strength and ability to move that he didn't hear. Linus leapt up and sideways, claws out, and swiped at his father's side, making him cry out in pain and slow down to a stop.

'What are you doing?' he shouted. Blood trickled from four deep scratches in his left flank. Linus didn't take his eyes off the tiger. It was only about ten metres away, walking towards them. The power emanating from it was neither human nor animal.

'Back away,' Linus hissed. 'For fuck's sake Dad, back away.'

At last his father picked up on the level of the danger that was approaching. He looked at the tiger then turned sideways and galloped off perpendicular to the line they'd been following. Linus was right behind him. He glanced over his shoulder; the tiger had sat down and was licking its lips as if to say: *Next time, little cheetah. Next time.*

Sweat poured down his father's flanks, mingling with the blood. 'What was that?' he panted.

'No idea, but nothing good.'

They carried on running, but Linus was so preoccupied by the tiger that he could no longer enjoy the experience. He knew it could move across the field at will and turn up anywhere. He was so busy looking behind and to the sides that he didn't see the line of darkness on the horizon until it had already begun to take on the appearance of a wall.

It was moving so fast that in a very short time it covered a considerable part of the sky, extending as far as Linus could see to the right and left. At the same time, something else began to happen: a tingling in his muscles and bones not unlike the sensation he'd had when he pushed the spoon into the black substance. It was as if carbon dioxide was slowly seeping into his body, dissolving the solid outline. He understood.

We're on our way back.

'Can you feel it?' he asked his father.

'I can feel it,' he replied, jerking his head at the black wall. 'What's that?'

'The darkness. You can't find your way out. You have to stay in there.'

As Linus spoke his father increased his speed, and Linus realised what he'd said. The wall of darkness loomed over them, covering the sky as the carbon dioxide surged through Linus's blood.

'No, Dad! It's just darkness, it's nothing!'

'Thank you,' his father said without turning his head. 'Thank you for bringing me here.'

Linus summoned every scrap of strength in his hind legs and made a huge leap upward and forward, landing on his father's back and digging his claws in to stay put. His father's muscles worked beneath his paws like a tangle of angry snakes as sweat spattered Linus's face. The darkness was flying towards him. His father made a huge effort to shake him off, and Linus slid across his slippery coat.

'Dad, Dad!' Linus shrieked. Then the darkness smothered everything. He fell off the horse's back, landed on the grass five metres from the edge of the darkness and saw his father's black body swallowed up by the deeper blackness as the carbon dioxide became whirling, stabbing ice crystals.

It was so agonising that Linus threw his head back and howled in pain, despair and confusion while the world around him disintegrated. He became one with the whirling ice, he was washed away in a river of ice. His body was battered and broken, his limbs stretched and transformed. He was crushed. He screamed.

*

He was shaking and twitching just like when he'd been given the electric shocks, joints and sinews aching just like when he'd been suspended from the hook. The difference was that the sensation was fading, and he could feel the external pain of something tearing at his face and hands.

He was in a thicket of bushes, thorns scratching his skin as he shook. He wrapped his arms around his body and managed to wriggle free.

The bushes were a few metres from a shoreline, ice floes and half-frozen sea water bobbing up and down. He had no idea where he was. He gazed out across the water and he thought how lucky he was not to have landed there. Although the darkness had been where the sea was now. In the other place.

Dad!

Strips of light from houses on the opposite shore were reflected in the blackness. Nothing was moving, apart from that slow, rhythmical bobbing up and down. If his father had landed there, Linus ought to be able to see some sign.

Of course, you idiot.

In this world his father was disabled. If he'd landed in the water he would have sunk like a stone. But surely bubbles would rise to the surface from his…Linus folded his arms over his belly and bent double. He didn't like that image at all, his father sinking into the cold, black water as his final breaths left him in the form of air bubbles and…

Shit, shit, shit. What was I thinking?

He knew exactly what his intention had been. The black substance allowed the person who took it to zone out, to disappear, but afterwards you would return to the place where you took it, as long as you didn't enter the darkness.

Only now did he realise how stupid he'd been. They lived on the thirteenth floor, for fuck's sake. He and his father could have reached the other place thirty metres up in the air. Not even a cheetah could survive a fall like that; he would have lost all his nine lives when he hit the ground. That hadn't happened. Maybe the field took no account of height differences, because there were no height differences in the other place. But still. So fucking stupid.

His only excuse was that he hadn't thought it was a physical transportation. That explained X's ability to get himself out of tricky situations. Linus cupped his hands around his mouth and shouted: 'Dad!' He listened for a sound, an answer. Nothing. He walked along the shoreline and shouted again.

A jetty ran out into the water on his left, and suddenly he knew where he was: Brunnsviken. To the south he could just see the upper floors of Gårdsstugan above the treetops. The field wasn't endless, but he couldn't work out its geography. He checked the time on his phone. He been gone from this world for six minutes. He had no idea how long he'd been in the other, but longer. Much longer.

'Dad! Where are you?'

The only sound was the drip, drip, drip of melting snow falling from the trees. If his father had been nearby, he would have heard him. Linus consoled himself with the thought that he didn't understand how the field worked. His father had raced into the darkness. Maybe that meant he would return to the point from which he'd started?

That was the last possibility if this was to end well. If Linus had had any faith whatsoever he would have been sending prayers up to God as he ran through the slush. But he didn't believe in God, so the only thing in his head was a directionless *Please, please, please…*

*

It was just before ten when he reached the front door that he still thought of as his. He wiped the sole of his left shoe on his right trouser leg and vice versa; he didn't want to leave any traces of his presence in the apartment. He was clutching his bunch of keys so tightly that it had left an impression on his palm. He found the right key and opened the door.

'Dad? Dad?'

The apartment was silent. At least Betty wasn't home yet. Linus crossed the hall and stopped dead in the living-room doorway. The wheelchair was empty. He sank to the floor and wrapped his arms around his head.

Fuck. Fuck fuck fuck.

He felt he ought to search the apartment, but he knew it was pointless *He's in the darkness.* His father was in the darkness now. Linus took a few deep breaths.

Now I have no one.

In spite of his father's pitiful state and the fact that Linus had spent most of his time avoiding him, there had been *something.* That last look Darth Vader gives Luke Skywalker. A spark of warmth. Now it was gone. Now it was in the darkness.

Linus straightened up and went into the kitchen. Betty still had an address book; Linus found Tommy's number and entered it into his phone. Linus still had one person left. And he'd sold out that person a couple of hours earlier.

Fuck fuck fuck.

He looked at the wheelchair one more time, just in case his father had materialised while Linus was in the kitchen. He hadn't; there was only the impression of his body on the worn cushions and the shabby neck support. Before leaving the apartment Linus waved to the empty chair. 'Bye Dad.'

As he closed the front door behind him he realised that the elevator was on its way up. He crept down the stairs, but it stopped a couple of floors below. It would be a while before Betty got home and discovered…Linus shook his head. He couldn't imagine what his mother would think.

Once outside he headed for the carpet-beating rack and sank down, his back resting against the post Rabbit Boy had been tied to. Before he had time to change his mind he took out his phone and sent a text to Tommy: *Linus here. You saw him. He wants to see you. I gave him your address. Don't reply to this.*

He had a stack of unanswered messages from snorters and sniffers wanting their next fix. He looked up at the night sky and his heart felt a little lighter. There was one thing he hadn't considered, because he'd panicked. His father had chosen to do what he did. Linus had tried to stop him, but his father had raced into the darkness of his own free will. Maybe that was…a good thing?

Ever since the accident his father had wanted nothing more than to die, to put an end to being trapped in his useless body. And now he was free. He had chosen to be a horse inside the darkness rather than a human being made of darkness. And that was perfectly understandable.

Linus laughed out loud. The more he thought about it, the less guilty he felt. He'd done his father an amazing favour, and they'd had one last trip together. At last he could think about the experience they'd shared. The laugh died away, became a smile that lingered on his lips.

Good luck, Dad. Canter on. Stay away from the exit, because then you'll become human again.

What about Tommy? The smile disappeared. He hadn't done Tommy any favours, whatever spin he tried to put on it, but surely X would have been capable of finding out where Tommy was living without Linus's help? And after those articles he'd written, Tommy must be aware that some people wouldn't be too happy.

And hello—if X hadn't asked Linus for Tommy's address, then Linus wouldn't have known that X wanted to *see* him, whatever that meant, and he wouldn't have been able to send Tommy a message to warn him. So in the end that was good too.

Everything was good. It was just a question of how you looked at it. As a brother he couldn't afford to brood on things. What was done was done, and if it was possible to look on the bright side, then so much the better. Linus no longer had any problem seeing this evening's events in that way. Like a brother.

He scrolled through the messages from his increasingly desperate customers. Then he sent Matti a message: *Den in ten.*

Enough. Time to sort a few things out.

Matti had had the sense to give up the bear-paw greeting since they became brothers—yes, Matti could be regarded as a brother too, because he was shifting a considerable amount of product and had the right attitude—but the problem was that no other greeting had replaced it. When they met in the corridor outside the Den, they had no easy way of affirming their solidarity. They exchanged a brief nod.

Unlike Linus's, Matti's appearance hadn't changed since he became a brother. He still had that long brown hair that made him look a bit like an Italian lover boy, but was probably down to his Roma heritage. He'd already been pumping iron; maybe he'd improved on his six-pack a little since he'd started to make some serious money. There wasn't much he could do about his lack of height.

The only thing he'd bought himself was a bracelet studded with real rubies; it was so bling it was almost gay, but Matti insisted that it turned Julia on, and no small-time dealer would dare suggest that a brother might be gay.

Matti ran a hand through his hair, his bracelet sparkling in the light. 'Okay?'

'Okay. You?'

'The thing is…'

'I know. But it's under control.'

A crack opened up in Matti's laid-back attitude and light seeped in. 'No shit?'

'No shit,' Linus said. 'I wanted to talk to you about that.'

'What about Henrik?'

'Henrik makes a good bitch, but I can't trust him.'

Matti's eyes narrowed. 'Really?'

'He's okay, but he'd crap himself. We're talking about a hundred kilos.'

The crack widened until the façade collapsed. Matti's jaw dropped and his pupils darted around like pinballs. '*A hundred?*'

'A hundred.'

Matti raised his hands and pressed his palms on either side of his head as he inhaled, then slowly exhaled. His brown eyes met Linus's. 'You're serious.'

'Absolutely serious. A hundred kilos. Eight o'clock tomorrow evening.'

'But how the fuck are we supposed to…I mean…It's…' Matti was now waving his hands in the air—not behaving like a brother at all—as he paced back and forth.

'It'll be tricky, but we have to sort it. Build up an organisation. A structure.'

'But that's…A hundred kilos…I…*Where?*'

'I'll text you half an hour before. Seven-thirty.'

Matti stopped pacing. He took a step closer to Linus, anger flaring in his eyes. 'Why? Do you think I'd…?'

'I don't think anything. But that's how we roll.'

Matti resumed his pacing, breathing hard through flared nostrils. He reminded Linus of an angry bull. It wasn't so much that he didn't trust Matti; it was a matter of making it clear who was in charge. And did Linus really trust him? Yes: ninety-nine per cent. But that one per cent was enough to make it necessary to exert his authority, angry bull or no angry bull.

'Enough,' Linus said. 'You're in. The two of us are doing this together.'

'I don't like that. I don't like the fact that Henrik's in the dark.'

The image of his father disappearing into the black wall flashed through Linus's mind and he lost patience. 'Matti. My decisions aren't based on what you like or don't like, but on what's right. And by the way, that bracelet is so fucking gay.'

Matti stopped. He didn't even glance at the bracelet. His expression was cold and calm now. 'Okay Linus, I get it.'

'You get what?'

'I get it. You'll text me half an hour beforehand.'

Linus wasn't happy about the sudden calm that had come over Matti. It reminded him of the still moment after the safety catch has been slipped off and everyone is waiting for the bang. Hoping to restore the safety catch, he said: 'Do you realise how much money we're talking about here? What we're going to be able to do? Everything we've dreamed of—but for real this time.'

Linus's deliberate and repeated use of *we* melted away most of the ice in Matti's eyes, and he nodded. 'I get that too.'

'So now we just have to hold firm. It'll be a few days before we can start dealing, and I'm guessing some of your customers are pretty desperate?'

'You think?'

Linus went into the den and fetched the wooden chair that he'd put there for this very purpose. He placed it under the hot water pipe, where he'd cut a hole in the insulation. He climbed onto the chair, groped around and found to his relief that Kassandra had done her job. Ten one-gram and twenty half-gram bags. Keeping his back to Matti, he weighed one of the one-gram bags in his hand. Seemed okay.

He stepped down and gave Matti half the bags. 'Take a strategic approach. Start with the most...'

'I get it,' Matti said.

'You're on it today, aren't you? And you can hint that there's fresh stuff on the way so they don't go off to someone who's dealing crap in the meantime.'

'No problem.'

Matti was giving the correct answers, but something felt off. Linus knew that being the boss was a solo job and demanded a certain distance, but now it was as if the distance had grown too great. He didn't quite know where he was with Matti and, given the task ahead, that wasn't okay.

'It'll be a challenge,' Linus said, gazing at Matti with warmth and affection. 'But together we can do it. We've coped with everything so far—we can cope with this too.' He swallowed his pride and held out his right hand, palm down, fingers bent inward. 'Paws?'

Matti looked at Linus, at his hand. Then he gave a smile that was possibly ironic, possibly genuine, held out his own hand and squeezed. 'Paws.'

*

Linus felt okay by the time he left the basement. He didn't need Matti to love him or even like him, but he did need to know that he was loyal. The product they were due to receive, the situation they were facing didn't just mean they were venturing into deep water, it meant they would be walking around with an entire fucking swimming pool suspended overhead. It ought to be impossible, which was exactly why it made Linus's spirits rise. Nothing excited him more than being told he couldn't do something, that it was out of the question. As long as it didn't involve reading he'd always found a way, and he would do it this time too.

It was after eleven, but he still felt wide awake. It would take half the night to reassure all the customers who had nothing to snort. He squeezed the bags in his pocket. He was looking forward to making one last round of deliveries. After tomorrow evening everything would be organised differently; someone else would be taking care of direct sales. He went through his messages to see who appeared to be the most desperate. He made a list, sent a few texts and received instant replies.

He left the building and checked to make sure that the cop in the Volvo had gone home to bed. He glanced up at the window of his apartment; the light was on and it looked perfectly normal, although of course it couldn't be. He didn't want to know. It was no longer his problem.

Tommy

'He's gone, Tommy! He's gone!'

Tommy hadn't managed to leave his desk when his phone rang and he heard Betty's hysterical voice on the other end of the line. He massaged his temples. 'Who's gone? Linus? But he's already…'

'No, Göran! Göran's gone, Tommy!'

Tommy looked at Hagge, who was still sitting on the floor by his chair wearing that same expression: *What did I tell you?*

'Göran? Surely he can't have…'

Betty interrupted him with a sound that could have meant anything. Eventually she managed to explain: 'I was at bingo. When I got home. Göran was gone.'

'You mean somebody's driven off with…'

'No, Tommy! His chair's still here!'

'What?'

'His wheelchair's still here. It's just…the straps, the cushions, the impression of…He's *gone*, Tommy! He…'

The words continued to pour out of Betty as if she was trying to fill the emptiness, break the silence in the apartment. Tommy took the phone away from his ear for a moment. This sounded horribly familiar.

All the tubes and cannulas were just lying there on the bed, but there was no trace of the man himself.

Peter Himmelstrand's disappearance from Huddinge in 1999. He too had been virtually incapable of independent movement, and X, Equis, Walls had been around at the time.

You saw him. He wants to see you.

What could Linus's father possibly have to do with any of this? Was it a punishment? A warning? That seemed very unlikely.

'Could someone have carried him away?' Tommy asked.

'I don't know! I don't know anything! He's gone, Tommy!'

'Okay, I'll be there as soon as I can.'

Anita slept in a very determined way, as if sleep was something she had to hold on to even when Tommy wasn't lying beside her, tossing and turning. Some people look peaceful and angelic when they're asleep, but in Anita's case it was as if her inner demons seized the opportunity to take control of her face, and there was something almost evil about her.

Tommy fixed his gaze on the curve of her hip beneath the thin cover and gently shook her shoulder. 'Anita. Sweetheart. Something's happened.'

Anita released her grip on sleep and immediately sat up, her eyes wild and staring. 'What? What's happened?'

That was why Tommy's restlessness had been such a problem for her. When she was alone she could sleep through the night, but a part of her was always alert. As soon as a noise or a movement penetrated her consciousness, she was wide awake in seconds. On this particular occasion, that was an advantage.

'Göran. Linus's father. He's disappeared.'

'I thought he was paralysed?'

'That's the problem. We need to get over there.'

'We? What use will I be?'

'I daren't leave you here alone. Something else has happened too. I'll explain on the way.'

During the drive to Gårdsstugan Tommy told Anita about the message he'd had from Linus, and that her apartment couldn't be regarded as safe.

'But I've got bulletproof glass. And high-security locks,' Anita objected.

'I don't think any of that will stop him.'

'What do you mean?'

'I think he uses that field to…transport himself. I think he can disappear somewhere in this world, cross the field and reappear somewhere else.'

'That sounds completely crazy.'

'I know. But I'm convinced that was what I happened to see. In the tunnel. And he didn't like it. So now…'

Tommy made a gesture encompassing the E18, the streetlights, the university they were driving past, the Circle K gas station up ahead. This was his area now, like an outlaw without a safe place to rest his head.

'Do you really believe all this?' Anita asked.

'I'm not sure what I believe, but I do know I can't write an article about any of it.'

They fell silent, and the only sound in the car was Hagge's discontented grunting from the back seat. He didn't like being driven off in the middle of the night, and he didn't like being ousted from the passenger seat, even if it was by Anita.

'Okay,' Anita said as they left Roslagstull.

'Okay what?'

'I can't say I believe it's all true, but I'm prepared to act as if it were. For your sake.'

'Thank you.'

*

Anita's fears that she wouldn't be of any use proved unfounded. As soon as they entered the apartment she focused all her attention on Betty, who in her despair let go of all her misgivings about Tommy's choice of life partner.

This wasn't the first time Anita had dealt with devastated women, and she consoled Betty with soft words and a gentle touch as they sat side by side at the kitchen table.

Tommy went into the living room. The wheelchair was empty, of course, but he had to see it with his own eyes. The balcony door was slightly ajar. Tommy opened it, walked across the plastic grass, which rustled beneath his feet, and leaned over the railing. Same thing—he knew, but he had to see for himself. The draught from the door told Betty what he was doing.

'For goodness sake!' she shouted from the kitchen. 'Do you think I didn't check?' Her voice broke and thickened as she turned back to Anita. 'I knew, but I still had to…'

'Same here,' Tommy said to himself.

Regardless of what he knew about X's capabilities, he had to exclude the natural explanations—the possibility that someone had got into the apartment, carried Göran onto the balcony and thrown him over the railing. But there was no broken body down there on the ground.

Göran, where are you?

Tommy decided to ignore Linus's instructions. He took out his phone and replied to his text message: *Your father's disappeared. Do you know anything? Answer now.* When no response had arrived after thirty seconds, he sent another message. And another. Thanks to Anita, Betty's sobbing had gone from hysteria to sorrow.

Fucking kid.

The next time Tommy saw Linus, the gloves would be off. This had gone way, way too far, and even if Linus didn't care how much he hurt those who loved him, Tommy did. He needed to shake some sense into the little fucker. Tommy realised he was furious.

His phone pinged and some of his anger drained away. At least the little fucker had bothered to reply. But the message wasn't from Linus, it was from Semtex-Janne: *The code to the safe is 23-13-9-12-45.* That was all.

What the hell was going on tonight? No doubt the code to Janne's safe was hard currency for anyone who wanted to find out about his business, so why had he sent it to a hack from Ängby? Because there was something he wanted to get out there, something he wanted to pass on.

Tommy stood there on the plastic grass for a moment, then went into the kitchen. Betty was slumped on a chair while Anita gently stroked her back in slow circles. Hagge had settled down at Betty's feet. Tommy couldn't leave them alone to drive over to Värtahamnen. Janne would have to wait until tomorrow.

His phone pinged again. Betty looked up, her eyes red and swollen with weeping. 'Is that...?'

Tommy shook his head. Another message from Janne. This one was even shorter: *So long.*

He rubbed his eyes and looked at the little trinity at the kitchen table. 'Will you be okay for a while? I have to go.'

*

It was almost half past midnight when Tommy arrived at the docks. Janne's car was still in the same place, and the buildings were still in darkness, apart from the light showing in Janne's office. In spite of the circumstances, he couldn't suppress a yawn. He was no longer the man for all-night stake-outs, the pursuit of a story 24/7, but that *So long* was too alarming to ignore.

He was starting to wish he'd brought Hagge. Both his company and his intuition made Tommy feel safer, and today Hagge had also proved that Tommy could rely on him when things got sticky. However, that was also why Tommy had left him with Betty and Anita; there was only so much you could ask of a ten-year-old dog with a prosthetic leg. Plus he'd seemed a bit out of sorts. Maybe a whole chocolate bar had been too much for him. Hagge deserved a rest.

Unlike Tommy. He had absolutely no desire to get out of the car. Today had been filled with impressions to process even before Betty called—and now this. It wasn't just lack of sleep; he didn't have the energy to deal with anything else.

He leaned back and closed his eyes, trying to clear the rubbish from his hard drive, but therein lay the problem: he didn't know what was rubbish and what wasn't. He had so much information, and some of it made sense, but he found the general lack of cohesion or overarching narrative very wearing. Everything was so much easier to deal with when it was a neatly packaged story, preferably nicely written up and published.

What finally made him open the car door was the possibility that Janne's safe might contain one of the links he needed. Something that would bring this story together and leave him in peace.

*

The door wasn't locked. Tommy went inside and looked around with the help of the LED light on his car key. He found a length of copper piping, which he picked up and weighed in his hand. It was simultaneously reassuring and pointless. He was useless when it came to a fight.

'Janne? Hello? Janne?'

The office door was ajar. Tommy edged closer across the dusty concrete floor. Stupid. Shouting then creeping, but he kept going until he was able to push the door open with the pipe. He stopped dead, sighed and dropped the pipe, its metallic clang echoing through the building.

Janne was sitting in one of the white armchairs. One of the armchairs that *used to be* white. Both armrests were soaked with blood, the front of Janne's T-shirt was covered in blood, the walls, desk and floor were spattered with blood pumped out by a main artery. Janne's head was drooping, and Tommy could see the beginnings of a bald patch towards the back.

His left hand was resting on his thigh, the stiff fingers clutching a box cutter. His right hand was on the armrest, holding his phone. Everything was sticky with the blood that filled the room with the smell of rusty nails hammered into raw meat. Janne had sat down in the armchair, sent his *So long* text to Tommy, then cut his own throat.

I'm completely destroyed. If only you knew.

There were two alternatives. Either Janne really had been so disgusted by what he'd done with or for X that he hadn't been able to bear it, and had decided to check out. Or he was yet another in the long line of suicides that X created around himself as he moved through life.

In spite of Janne's hard image, Tommy was inclined to the former explanation. Janne really had been at a pretty low ebb, and maybe he'd tried to carry out one last act of penance. Maybe the safe contained information that could finish X. When Janne sent the code he was as good as dead, and chose to die by his own hand.

We don't want Janne to end up like the guy in the Brunkeberg Tunnel, do we?

No, he'd eliminated that risk. There was nothing in the room to suggest that Janne had been subjected to violence or duress by another person. Then again, that applied to all suicides. But Janne hadn't been tortured; he'd simply bled to death, all alone.

Taking care not to step in the blood, Tommy made his way over to the safe under the desk. When he reached out to enter the code, he felt a sudden surge of paranoia. His eyes scanned the desk, which was strewn with blood-spattered papers. He spotted a roll of tape, tore off a piece and wound it around his right index finger.

He was sabotaging an investigation and contaminating a crime scene. Sooner or later the police would turn up, and they wouldn't be happy if they found out that an old hack had been poking around. He took a couple of photographs of Janne and the room, then crouched down.

He keyed in the code, justifying his actions with the thought that Janne had chosen to send the numbers to him. He was merely fulfilling a dead man's last wish. He might be on the wrong side of the law, but he was on the right side of…whatever. Tommy knew he shouldn't be doing this, but he also knew he had no choice.

There was a click and the heavy door opened. The safe contained two folders, plus four one-kilo bars of gold—totally Janne's style. On top of the folders lay a piece of paper with writing on it. A farewell note?

Tommy looked at Janne. From this angle he could see the deep, dark red gash in his throat where Janne had begun the cut; he shuddered. He didn't think he'd be capable of doing that, whatever the circumstances. He picked up the piece of paper, which turned out to be two pieces of paper; he didn't bother about fingerprints, because he had no intention of putting the papers back in the safe.

It wasn't a farewell note. Janne hadn't even written it. The pen appeared to have been wielded by someone who'd only just learnt to write, or was clutching the pen in a clenched fist. Thin, sprawling letters that combined to form a list.

Tommy glanced down the pages and the world began to spin; he almost had to lean on the desk for support. His suspicions had been correct. Janne had wanted to drive a stick, or rather a log, into the wheels of X's operation before he bowed out. Tommy was holding a list of twenty addresses in Stockholm where *one hundred kilos* of cocaine would be delivered at eight o'clock the following evening.

He glanced at his watch. *This* evening. In just over nineteen hours. He couldn't breathe. This was huge. He'd spent forty years grubbing around without getting anywhere near information of this magnitude before the police got their hands on it. Should he put the papers back after all? He thought about fingerprints, then spun around and looked at Janne.

What the hell have you dragged me into?

He couldn't discount the possibility that Janne had had another reason for sending the code to Tommy rather than the cops. He wanted to have the last laugh—to put Tommy in exactly this situation, to make the hack from Ängby's *jaw drop*, and even if Janne wasn't there to see it, at least he was in the same room. Tommy waved the papers at the dead body and whispered: 'What am I supposed to do with this? What do you expect me to do with it?'

Tommy stopped waving as a plan began to form in his head. Obviously he had to hand over the list to the police, but the question was *how* he should do it.

He folded the papers and tucked them into his inside pocket, closed the safe and double-checked mentally that he hadn't touched anything else in the room. He remembered the copper pipe and kicked it into a corner. He looked at Janne one last time, sitting there in his armchair with the whisky bottle in front of him on the table.

'So long,' Tommy said. 'And thank you.'

*

'What the fuck, Tommy? It's half past one in the morning.'

'I thought that was when your evening began, Henry.'

'Not when I've been ill. This had better be good.'

'It is. How are you feeling?'

'Better. Not that you care.'

'I do, actually. It would be useful if you were on your feet tomorrow.'

Tommy had stopped in a lay by outside Norrtull. Since leaving Värtahamnen he had gone over the plan, what he could say to Henry without putting himself in danger. He was counting on the fact that Henry was always keen to advance his career, but it was still a risk.

'What are you talking about?' Henry sounded a little more awake now.

'I've got some information for you, and it's pure gold—like medal-from-the-king gold. But the question is: do you have something for me?'

'About what?'

'Svante Forsberg.'

There was a brief silence, then Tommy heard the rustle of sheets as Henry swung his legs over the side of the bed. Henry cleared his throat and adopted an authoritative tone: 'If you withhold information which…'

'I have no intention of withholding information; I'm prepared to pass it on to the police. I'm merely wondering *which* police officer I'm going to speak to. Maybe I should call 112?'

'Okay, okay.' Henry made a sound that was somewhere between a laugh and a cough. 'Don't be like that. I have actually asked around a little; I even met up with a guy earlier this evening. Yesterday evening.

Fuck's sake, Tommy.'

'What guy?'

Henry ignored the question, and Tommy could see him holding up his index finger like the former prime minister Göran Persson as he said: 'Let me be perfectly clear, Tommy. You can't write about this. The guy I spoke to had only heard rumours, but what he told me... There are some bad people out there, really bad people, and unfortunately *Svante*'—Henry uttered the name as if he were spitting a fly out of his mouth—'just happened to be a cop. If you wrote about him it would blacken the name of every police officer.'

'You don't need to worry. I'm not going to write anything.'

'Why not?'

Tommy smiled and played along. 'Because you're telling me not to, Henry, and to be honest this is all beginning to sound like something nobody would believe.'

Henry sighed. His voice was weak as he said: 'This much I can say. Svante Forsberg died in the worst way imaginable. If there was any justice, he would have died several times over.'

'But what the hell had he...'

Henry's momentary humanity disappeared and he interrupted Tommy as brusquely as he could manage, given his current state. 'We're not sitting here making small talk, Tommy. You're not my friend. What have you got for me?'

Through the fabric of his jacket, Tommy stroked the papers in his pocket. 'I can't tell you over the phone, but like I said: If there was a Nobel prize for police work, it would go to what you'll be able to achieve with this.'

Henry was breathing heavily, and Tommy wasn't sure if it was down to tiredness or the fact that he was picturing himself at the Nobel prize ceremony. Eventually he simply said: 'When and where?'

'The Railway Restaurant at the Eastern Station. Eight o'clock in the morning.'

'Nine would be better.'

'You should be saying 'Seven would be better'. If we meet at eight you'll have twelve hours to get your troops together.'

'Troops? What troops?'

'Anyone you can get hold of. I'll say it one more time: This is *big*.'

'Okay, seven then.'

'Eight is fine. We're getting old, Henry. We need our sleep.'

'Speak for yourself.'

When Tommy had ended the call he sat there for a while without starting the car. He gazed towards Gårdsstugan where lights were showing in only a few windows, mostly with a bluish flicker. People were sleeping or staring at their screens, unaware of the enormous events taking place in the darkness around them. Tommy wished he could be one of them. He'd been one of them, he could become one of them again, God willing. And the Devil. The blond Devil.

*

When he got back to Betty and Göran's apartment, Anita was standing in the hallway. She put her finger to her lips and whispered: 'Ssh. I think she's fallen asleep.'

'Just like that?'

Anita raised an eyebrow. 'There's no shortage of pills here, if you know what I mean. Let's go into the kitchen.'

Tommy closed the door and they sat down side by side at the table. He didn't need to ask if Göran had been found; Anita would have told him. He took her hands in his and said: 'I need to ask you a big favour. Two big favours, actually. Could you stay here with Betty?'

Anita frowned. 'And where will you be?'

'He wants to get hold of me. He's going to get hold of me. And when that happens, I don't want to be in the same place as you. Or Hagge, for that matter.' Tommy was about to continue but stopped himself and shook his head. 'Or Betty, of course.'

'Same question—where will you be?'

'Traneberg.'

Now it was Anita's turn to shake her head. 'But he must know that address, it would be really easy to…'

Tommy held up a hand to silence her. He hated the gesture, but he didn't want to be in the same apartment as her for any longer than absolutely necessary. 'Sooner or later he's going to catch up with me, wherever I am. So I might as well be in Traneberg. And I will not allow you to be anywhere near. It doesn't matter what you say. I *will not allow* it.'

Anita looked at him for a long time. Her eyes expressed so many different feelings that the result was the same as when all the colours are mixed. Black. She nodded and said mechanically: 'And the other favour?'

Tommy took out the pieces of paper, opened them up and placed them on the table. 'I'd like you to photograph these with your phone.'

'What are they?'

'It doesn't matter. Take a picture.'

Anita did as he asked, and once Tommy had checked that the addresses were legible if he zoomed in, he added Henry's number to her contact list and showed it to her. 'If anything happens to me…'

'Tommy, please.'

'No. That's just the way things have to be. There's nothing I can do about it. *If* anything happens to me, if you haven't heard from me by nine o'clock in the morning, then you send the photo to this number. Okay?'

Anita peered at the pieces of paper and Tommy hurriedly picked them up, but it was too late. Her voice filled with disbelief, she said: 'Two *tonnes*?'

'I don't want you to know anything about this. I wrote about a tonne before, what's the difference?'

Tommy realised that retrieving the papers was pointless when Anita simply found the photo on her phone and zoomed in. 'The difference is that I saw the date and the time. You're going to try and stop it, rather than writing about it afterwards. That's a hell of a difference.'

'Exactly. Which is why I have to go now.'

*

After a few more frank exchanges, followed by resignation then tenderness, they embraced in the hallway. Hagge appeared and looked up at them pleadingly. Even if he didn't know exactly what was going on, he picked up on the general atmosphere of sorrowful parting, and began to whine.

'Be a good boy,' Tommy said, scratching him under the chin. 'You're going to stay with Anita for a while. I'll be back soon. You're the best dog in the world.'

For a moment Hagge looked as if he was going to fling his paws around Tommy's legs and shout 'Don't go, don't go!', but instead he lowered his head and ambled back into the living room, where he'd found temporary accommodation in the empty wheelchair.

'Take care of Betty,' Tommy said, and kissed Anita.

'Take care of yourself. I love you.'

Anita's words remained in Tommy's overheated brain like a zinc paste bandage on a burn as he got in the car and set off for Traneberg. Those three words. Said in the right way, they could mean so much. He might be driving to his death, but he was doing so as someone who was loved. It made a huge difference. He didn't want Anita to be hurt, but it felt good to know that someone would miss him if he disappeared.

Then there was Hagge. His eyes prickled as he crossed Traneberg Bridge. Despite the value of Anita's human love, it was the image of Hagge that caused a tear to run down his cheek. Hagge waiting by the door, waiting for Tommy to come back, unable to understand why he hadn't returned, why he'd abandoned his dog. Tommy dashed away the tears and slammed his hand down on the wheel. He would make sure he survived this. For Hagge's sake.

*

He hadn't been in the apartment for a few weeks, and it had acquired that desolate smell of settled dust, the absence of human odours. He closed the door behind him, stood there in the darkness and said: 'Hello?' When there was no response he switched on the light.

A drift of post and junk mail lay on the floor, but unpaid bills were the least of his worries right now. He stepped over the pile and went around switching on the lamps in every room. There was no one there. He texted Anita to tell her he'd arrived safely, then sent what must have been the twentieth message to Linus.

It was almost three o'clock in the morning and he should have been exhausted, but he'd gone past that stage. He felt numb, but not sleepy. He placed the pieces of paper on the kitchen table, took a photograph with his own phone and attached it to a message to Henry. He saved it ready to send quickly if necessary.

Tommy was well aware that Linus could be involved in the receipt of the package, and that by handing over the list to Henry he might be consigning his nephew to jail. However, Linus had used up the last scrap of Tommy's goodwill, plus he was better off in prison than under X's black wings.

With his phone in his hand, Tommy sank down in the armchair. In a few hours he would meet Henry and bust the biggest delivery of cocaine in Swedish history. He couldn't help feeling a little aggrieved that his own role would have to remain a secret. He would never be safe if he owned up. People were going to lose a great deal of money all the way along the chain from the Colombian jungles to the suburbs of Stockholm, and when those kind of people got burnt, they turned nasty.

Shit!

There was a sinking feeling in his chest, as if a bottomless pit had opened up behind his ribs. *Janne's message!* If X or anyone else checked Janne's phone, they would see the text message with the code that Janne had sent. To Tommy.

He got to his feet and scrabbled in the drawer of his desk until he found the pay-as-you-go card he'd kept for occasions such as this.

With sweaty fingers he changed the SIM card in his phone and called 112 just like any other law-abiding citizen and asked to be put through to the police. When a woman answered he said: 'Oh, hello. There's a dead body in the one of the storage depots in Värtahamnen. The one with the light on.'

He ended the call before she could ask how he knew this, or who he was. In his experience the police usually followed up that kind of call pretty quickly, and he just hoped they would be first on the scene. Apart from him. He switched back to his usual SIM card and started pacing the room; he was too agitated to sit down.

X had already made it known that he wanted to *see him*, so it was a question of preventing other people from reading Janne's message. Ordinary, human criminals. Had he stopped regarding X as human? What was X, in that case? Tommy thought about the child he'd seen in the field, the sprawling, awkward handwriting on the pieces of paper in his pocket. Maybe Henry would be able to fill in the gaps, if Tommy lived long enough to speak to him.

Towards four o'clock he sat down on the bed. He set an alarm to be on the safe side, then lay down and stared at the wall. If X came to him, how would it happen? What would he do?

At some stage Tommy's eyes closed. When the alarm woke him three hours later, he found to his surprise that he had eyes to see with and a hand to turn off the alarm.

A new day had begun, and Tommy T was still in the game. He texted Anita to let her know that everything was okay, got to his feet and began the complex procedure of making himself a cup of coffee.

Linus

It had been a good night. By the time Linus arrived home at four in the morning, all the Ziploc bags had been exchanged for cash.

After arranging appointments with his customers Linus had switched off his phone, because he couldn't stand the constant pinging from Tommy's messages. His conscience was clear when it came to his father, but explaining the situation to Betty and Tommy could be a little tricky.

So we took this black stuff, okay, and then Dad became a horse and I became a cheetah. It was fucking fantastic until Dad ran straight into a wall made of darkness. But that kind of thing happens, right?

If it ever came to a confrontation, Linus would simply deny everything. He had no fucking idea where his dad had gone. Maybe he'd regained his mobility and headed off to the Canary Islands? To be fair, that was a more reasonable explanation than the truth.

Anyway, he couldn't cope with the pinging in his pocket; apart from Tommy, he didn't have enough coke to supply all his customers, so even though it was unprofessional, he turned his phone off so that he could have this one last night as a small-time dealer, like a kind of paid holiday.

He had a skeleton key and could come and go as he wished between the apartment blocks, but whenever possible he used the basement passageways that linked them, or in certain cases the roofs; each block had four access points. By combining these different routes he hardly needed to show himself outside. This made him feel like a shadow—a superhero, or at least a highly skilled brother, slipping unseen through the night.

He was met with joy wherever he went, and even if the snorters and sniffers weren't too happy when they realised he had only a small amount to offer at the moment, they soon cheered up again when he hinted that something big was coming, and if they had the resources they would be able to snort and sniff away to their heart's content.

When they asked for details, like *when*, Linus treated them with the casual disdain his new position allowed. He told them they would have to be patient, and if they decided to source crap from some other dealer in the meantime, then it was thank you and goodnight to the crystal coke as far as they were concerned.

He also took the opportunity to start recruiting. Seven or eight of his clients had their wits about them in spite of their habit, and three of these had already asked to buy larger amounts for friends and friends of friends.

Linus had long conversations with all three; they could become a major part of the operation, as long as they stuck to the terms and conditions. They would receive a certain percentage on what they sold, no independent pricing, and maybe they'd already heard what Linus thought of those who scammed him?

They assured him they had, even though Linus had only given a few people—like Wille—a hard time. He hadn't yet carried out a severe punishment, like the removal of small or large body parts. He wasn't looking forward to it, but at some point he would probably have to do it, just to make sure he had the respect he deserved. Maybe he'd go for the methods he'd experienced directly—electric shocks and the hook. Effective, and not much to show the cops, if anyone was that way inclined.

Finally Linus made it clear to his future subordinates that he would be keeping a close eye on them. If they started snorting so much themselves that they fucked up the business, what would happen with the crystal coke as far as they were concerned?

'Thank you and goodnight,' they all repeated obediently.

Linus couldn't remember where he'd heard the phrase, but he felt it had the magical quality of being so dumb that it was cool.

Needless to say he couldn't keep tabs on everyone who snorted his coke, but like Varys in *Game of Thrones* he had his little birds in the form of the younger boys and a few girls who dealt for him, plus their friends. If anything happened, he would find out about it sooner or later. In addition, X seemed to know exactly what was going on around Gårdsstugan, and had his own network of informants in the suburbs he controlled. What might look like criminal chaos was in fact as tightly coordinated as if the Stasi had been running it.

*

When Linus unlocked his front door at four in the morning, he was both tired and happy. It had been a productive night. A hundred kilos was still a crazy amount, but he'd begun the task of making the impossible possible. He was a brother to be reckoned with.

He kicked off his shoes in the hallway then stood in the living-room doorway for a moment, looking at Henrik on the sofa. The light from the streetlight fell on him as he lay beneath a thin blanket, curled up like a child. Only the thumb in the mouth was missing. For a second Linus felt a stab of tenderness, which was instantly replaced by his usual irritation at Henrik's pathetic feebleness. Things were going to have to change. Soon.

He went into the bedroom and emptied the money from his pockets onto the bed, draped his jacket over a chair, then gazed at the lovely notes strewn all over the crocheted coverlet.

A contact of Alex's had helped him set up an account with a bank registered in St Lucia, and via a series of transactions Linus's money ended up there, impossible to trace. Linus had understood maybe ten per cent of what the guy told him, but Alex had guaranteed that he was sound.

Linus yawned. When the new business got under way he'd be able to buy an apartment, and in that apartment there would be no pathetic wanker sleeping on the sofa. He hadn't dreamed of what he would have instead, except that it would be as white as snow and coke.

A wave of exhaustion came over him, a burst sandbag falling down through his head, weighing down his neck and scattering grains of sand beneath his eyelids. He yawned again, almost dislocating his jaw. He contemplated the blanket of notes, gave a foolish smile and thought *oh, what the fuck*. He lay down on top of it and closed his eyes.

The last thing Linus normally did when he went to bed was to check his phone, but this time he fell asleep in two seconds and forgot all about it. He didn't even remember to switch it on.

Tommy

Tommy parked in the usual place, the car park to the north of the Eastern Station. Something must have gone wrong with the planning for general misery here, because there were always spaces. It was ten to eight when he went over to the machine and bought a ticket for one hour. When Henry saw the list he wouldn't be in the mood to sit around chatting.

The temperature was above freezing and most of the slush had melted away, with only the odd exhaust-fume-grey clump still lingering under the trees along Valhallavägen where the morning rush hour was in full flow. Tommy wandered towards the square, where people who looked as weary as him were getting on and off buses. When he ended up in the middle of a stream of commuters emerging from the subway, he automatically placed a hand over his inside pocket, where the papers lay.

Up in the restaurant he found Henry in the corner furthest away from the bar. He had his back to the room, and was staring down into a large cup of coffee. All he needed was a fedora and a trench coat. As Tommy drew closer he could see that the stomach bug had really taken its toll. Henry's skin was sallow and his cheeks sunken. Even his transplanted fringe had suffered, hanging lank and lifeless over his forehead.

'Hi,' Tommy said, sitting down opposite him. 'Bad night?'

'Idiots keep on calling,' Henry replied without looking at Tommy. 'Then I have to call other idiots.'

'What kind of idiots?'

'Idiots who know something about what the first idiot wants to know.'

'Henry, I'm touched. Have you been up all night making phone calls just because I…But I thought you'd already spoken to a guy?'

'I had. But I don't really trust him, so I wanted to follow up with a couple of idiots.'

Tommy didn't understand. Henry wasn't in the habit of making any more effort than absolutely necessary, but he'd clearly been calling people—and presumably waking them up in the middle of the night—to double-check on the story Tommy was after.

'That's not like you,' he said.

Henry grimaced, picked up his coffee cup and looked at it with distaste before putting it down again. There was another hint of uncharacteristic humanity in his voice when he said: 'I wanted to know too. I've never heard anything like it. Not in real life.'

'And?'

'And. What have you got for me?'

Tommy patted his breast pocket. 'I want you to tell me first. When I've given you what's in here, you're going to be…stressed.'

At last Henry looked at Tommy. His blue eyes seemed faded, and there were dark circles beneath them. He gestured to indicate that he was too tired to care. 'I'll say it again: all this is hearsay and second-hand information. And you absolutely cannot write about it.'

'You have my word.'

'Your word has lost something of its golden lustre since that stunt you pulled at the gym.'

'Oh, you know about that.'

'Everybody knows about that. But then you did contribute to the investigation, so I suppose that evens things out a bit.'

It was the first time Tommy had heard Henry state directly that the knowledge about X's methods that Tommy had passed on to the police had been useful.

'Svante Forsberg,' Henry went on. 'To say he was a bastard is the understatement of the decade. He was pure evil, and the icing on the cake is that he was some kind of Satanist.'

'Like…a devil worshipper?'

'He had some idea about *the darkness*. That darkness isn't only the absence of light, but that there's an *absolute* darkness, which is also a god. That it was possible to reach this darkness, to gain control over

407

it, and then…something would happen.'

'What?'

'The stories I've heard didn't include that information, but apparently he managed to persuade a couple of colleagues into the same kind of thinking, and it's colleagues of these colleagues that I've spoken to.'

'This sounds crazy rather than horrific. And I know there are plenty of cops who regard evil as an absolute. Which they have to combat, of course.'

'Are you done?' Henry asked, resting his chin on his hand. 'Your insight into police psychology is astonishing, and I could sit here all day listening to you, but maybe it's better if I tell you what I found out?'

'Sorry. Go on.'

'He had a caravan. Silver-coloured—one of those small ones known as an "Egg". And in that caravan he had…a child. A little boy.' Henry sighed, ran a hand through his hair and, as if his facelift had suddenly collapsed, he looked his age. Older.

'What he did to that boy…As I understand it, he did everything you can imagine, short of killing him. He raped him, beat him, cut him and burned him. Broke his fingers and his leg, knocked out his teeth, stuck needles in his ears. And this went on for *years*. Inside that caravan. Now maybe you can see why I said it was a shame he only died once?'

Tommy had planned to order a cheese sandwich for breakfast, but when the waitress came over he settled for a cup of coffee. He wasn't even sure he could get that down. Unless he was completely wrong, this was the story of X's childhood. But there was one question. The eternal key question.

'Why?' Tommy asked. 'Why did he do all that?'

'To get to the darkness. I don't know where he'd found the boy, but apparently he thought he was a special child who had the darkness within him. It was just a matter of forcing it out. With systematic torture.' Henry rubbed his eyes and repeated: 'For years.'

'And did he succeed?'

Henry looked at Tommy in disgust, as if he'd made an inappropriate joke. Then he made the too-tired-to-care gesture once more and said: 'He kept moving the caravan around. And sometimes…things happened close to where it was.'

'What kind of things?'

'There was some mention of a field, but that was just according to the first guy. The idiots hadn't heard about it.'

Tommy's coffee arrived and he looked down at its black, shining surface as if it were an opening into the darkness, then into the field he'd seen in the Brunkeberg Tunnel. He couldn't say that he *understood*, but some of the connections had become clearer through Henry's narrative.

Given what X was capable of, maybe Svante Forsberg had been right. Maybe he really had found a child with extraordinary abilities. Or was it possible to create darkness from nothing, if you were determined enough? The boy might have been a perfectly ordinary boy until Svante broke him down to X, and the darkness leaked out. Tommy could see it in his mind's eye: the egg-shaped caravan, the child being carted around and beaten, destroyed over the years. A caravan filled with darkness.

'And now,' Henry said, pushing away his coffee cup in which he'd completely lost interest. 'Now I'm the one who's listening.'

'First of all: This X you're looking for and the boy you've just told me about is one and the same person. I'm almost certain.'

'Unlikely. When he was about twelve Svante got rid of him. I don't know how or where, but he's dead.'

'In fact it's very likely that he somehow ended up in the Brunkeberg Tunnel. He was found there and taken to the child psychiatric unit at Huddinge. He grew up there and was gradually reintegrated into the community, then set up his business in and around Gårdsstugan.'

'Sounds pretty unbelievable to me,' Henry said.

'And do you think what you've told me is any more believable?

The difference is that I do believe what you said, because I know what I know. I could go on, but I think you're more interested in these.' Tommy took out the pieces of paper, unfolded them and placed them on the table in front of Henry. 'I'm glad to see the back of them, to be honest.'

Henry read through the list of addresses, then said: 'So you claim this is exactly what it looks like?'

'Yes. A list of addresses to which one hundred kilos of cocaine will be delivered at eight o'clock this evening.'

'It looks as if it's been written by a child.'

'That's *his* handwriting. On some level I think he's...got stuck in his childhood.'

'Seriously?'

'Remember what happened to him when he was growing up.'

Henry began to bite his nails. Tommy realised that he was caught between belief and disbelief. Of course he wanted to believe that this information was for real, but at the same time he was afraid of the consequences if he cried wolf and it turned out to be a kitten. Or nothing at all.

'You could at least have a SWAT team on standby,' Tommy suggested. 'Keep an eye on those addresses, see if anything seems to be happening, then bring in the cavalry at the right moment.'

Henry sighed. 'I'll say it again, Tommy. Your insight into police work is so comprehensive that I can't understand why you're not national police commissioner already. The question is: where the hell did you get this?' Henry tapped the papers with his index finger.

Tommy had his answer ready: 'I have the right to protect my source.'

'You have the right to protect your source. Aha. So someone *gave* you this, of their own free will.'

'Something like that.'

'I have interesting news for you,' Henry said. 'You suggested we should put Janne in Värtahamnen under surveillance.'

A lump of the dirty slush he'd seen out on the street formed in

Tommy's belly, and he looked uninterestedly around the restaurant to hide the chill spreading through his veins. *Shit. Somebody saw me.*

No doubt Henry knew exactly what was going on in his head. He savoured the moment, then went on: 'We didn't do it. As I might have mentioned, I'm not too keen on allowing you to tell us how to do our job.'

Tommy was off the hook temporarily, but the problem of Janne's text message remained. The fact that Tommy had been given the code to the safe didn't *prove* he'd been there, even if Henry clearly realised that he had.

'A call came through this morning. An anonymous tip-off about a death in Värtahamnen. A patrol car went out there and bingo, Janne was sitting in his armchair with his throat cut.'

'I'm sorry to hear that.'

'I'm sure you are.'

He's just playing with me, Tommy thought as he went through his movements in Janne's office. If Henry knew that Janne had sent the code to Tommy, he wouldn't give up until he'd found proof that Tommy had been there.

'So now I'm asking you: are these lists and Janne's suicide in any way related?'

'Not as far as I know.'

Henry looked him in the eye, but he knew that Tommy was far too experienced to let himself be stared down. He gave up and turned his attention back to the addresses, his fingers moving unconsciously as if he were calculating something in his head. Presumably they hadn't yet checked Janne's phone.

'You can think what you like,' Tommy said. 'But I can pretty much guarantee that those lists are the real deal, and it would be a big mistake not to act on that premise.'

Henry nodded. He seemed to have accepted that the wolf was indeed nearby, and that the consequences would be even more serious if he didn't take the appropriate steps. He brought both palms down on the table.

'Okay. As you so rightly predicted, I have things to do. Maybe you'd like to come along and run the surveillance operation?'

'A little gratitude will suffice. Nothing else on Svante Forsberg?'

'No, that's the lot.' Henry got to his feet, looking significantly better than when Tommy had arrived. The care—almost tenderness—with which he folded up the lists and tucked them in his pockets showed that he thought they were valuable. He tapped his temple and said: 'Actually, there was one more thing—a really creepy detail. When the fucker was torturing the boy in the caravan he always had music on, and do you know what it was? Do you remember that journalist from *Expressen*, the guy who...'

'Peter Himmelstrand.'

'Exactly—how did you know that? The fucker only played songs by him, and he was particularly fond of the one Jan Sparring sang.'

'Somebody Up There Must Like Me.'

'That's the one. Imagine putting that song on repeat while you torture a kid. Disgusting.'

'Absolutely,' Tommy said.

Linus

There was a rustling sound as Linus turned over and opened his eyes. Ingmar Bergman was staring back at him from a two-hundred kronor note. The sheet covering the window glowed pale pink, suggesting that the sun was as high as it was going to climb in November. He must have slept for hours.

Fuck. Fuck.

As he reached for his jacket and his phone, he remembered that it had been switched off since the previous evening. That was fuck number one. Fuck number two was that his phone wasn't in his pocket.

He scrambled to his feet, sweeping several notes onto the floor. He patted his jacket all over, hoping the phone was in another pocket. It wasn't. His head began to spin, and panic rose in his chest like mercury in a thermometer. Losing his phone was like losing his *life*. All the contacts, all the messages…Coded, admittedly, but very useful to the cops if they got their hands on it.

He looked under the bed, behind the bed, under the pillow. He shook the crocheted coverlet, scattering notes in all directions. The fucking phone was gone. He didn't know how, but it was gone. He felt sick, almost to the point of throwing up.

He remembered arriving home, looking at Henrik, then coming straight to his room. His phone couldn't be anywhere else in the apartment, but still he flung open the bedroom door and peered at the floor in the hallway. Out of the corner of his eye he saw Henrik sitting on the sofa.

'Good morning,' Henrik said.

'Shut the fuck up. I've lost my phone.'

'No, you haven't.'

'Yes I have, you idiot!'

'Your phone is here.'

Linus glared at Henrik, who had his hands on his lap like a young lady waiting to be asked to dance. On the table in front of him lay Linus's phone. Enormous relief mixed with confusion made Linus stagger slightly as he went into the living room.

'Sit down.'

'I haven't got time,' Linus said, reaching for the phone. 'I need to check...'

'I said: Sit down.' Something in Henrik's tone made Linus look up. In his right hand Henrik was holding the gun he'd picked up once before, and this time it was pointing at Linus.

'Seriously, Henrik, you're way out of line. Was it you who took the phone? Out of my pocket?'

'Yes.' Henrik waved the barrel of the gun in the direction of the armchair. 'Sit down.'

Linus weighed Henrik up. He had that cold, muted madness in his eyes that was probably a legacy of his upbringing; it rarely appeared behind the feeble face he wore in everyday life. It was like looking at a mad dog on a chain that was about to snap. Linus raised his hands and sank down in the armchair.

'This isn't good, Henrik. This isn't good at all. Do you remember what I said about...'

'I remember *everything* you've said,' Henrik hissed, a fine spray of saliva landing on the table. 'Every. Fucking. Word. But now *I* want to talk, and this seems to be the only way.'

'Talk away. But you're skating on very thin ice—I hope you realise that.'

'Thin ice? You have no idea.' Henrik put the barrel of the gun to his own temple. A blood vessel burst in one eye; was he really going to pull the trigger? Linus gritted his teeth. Henrik glowered at him with real hatred before he lowered the gun. 'Actually, there's only one thing I want to say. You've turned into a real shit, Linus.'

'Okay, you've said it. Can I check my phone now?'

Henrik shook his head. 'Allow me to clarify my point. You're a shit because you treat other people, especially me, like shit. You talk about respect, but you have zero respect for anyone else. You think you're the King because your pockets are full of little plastic bags—have you any idea how pathetic that is?'

'That's not what you said when…'

'Shut up. I'm talking now. You strut around with your dumbbells and your shaved head and you think you're a real gangster, but in fact you're just arrogant. I don't know if you're familiar with that word, but it kind of means you only care about yourself. We're *friends*, Linus. We grew up together, we had each other's backs, but now? Now it's all you, you, you and you're *lonely.*'

'You're lonely too, Henrik.'

'Yes, but the difference is that I'm smart enough to realise it and feel sad about it. I've tried, Linus. I really have tried. I've sat here like a lonely old woman, *crying* because the person who used to be my best friend is so fucking *horrible*. But it's over now. I hope you die, Linus. I won't be at your funeral.'

The last comment hit home. Somehow Linus had regarded the balance of power in his relationship with Henrik as entirely natural in the current situation; he'd never considered how Henrik might feel. They had indeed been best friends for a long time. With the gun pointing at him, he saw things in a different light. Apologising was out of the question, so instead he said: 'This is what's happening, Henrik. A huge delivery is coming in tonight. You can help. We're talking millions here. Matti's already on board. The bear-brothers ride again, okay?'

Henrik got to his feet, keeping the gun trained on Linus. 'You don't listen. You really don't listen. It's broken. You've broken it. It can't be fixed. I want nothing more to do with you or your business, Linus. I don't care about the money. I did it mostly for your sake. And because you threatened me, of course. That's how it began. And now it's over. I'm done, Linus, and let me say this one more time: I hope you die.'

Linus remained in the chair as Henrik backed out of the room, unlocked the front door and said: 'I'm leaving the gun on the hall stand. I'm assuming you won't dare shoot me on the stairs.'

The door opened and closed. Footsteps descended the stairs and faded away. Linus didn't move.

*

Linus was still sitting with his hands on the armrests, glaring at the dumbbells in the corner. Since the business got seriously under way, no one had dared to give an alternative view of his behaviour. He had encountered only appreciation, respect or fear. It was depressing to see himself in the way that Henrik had described him. Admittedly it was only one opinion, one way of looking at things, but it was the opinion of his childhood friend, which was why Linus was still sitting in the armchair.

It was only when the image of Michael Corleone came into his mind that he managed to move. Michael Corleone, sitting in the armchair after he's given the order to murder his brother Fredo. The empty gaze, something hardening inside him. The loneliness. Sad— tragic—but necessary. Linus was no Corleone, but the issue was the same. You didn't get to the top by being nice, and you couldn't make an omelette if you just stood there stroking the egg. Unfortunate but true.

He picked up his phone and switched it on. What should he do about Henrik? He'd threatened Linus with his own gun, he'd walked out. That was unacceptable. If you were in you were in, and punishment must follow if…

Linus's train of thought was interrupted when he saw that he had countless unread messages, and not all of them were from Tommy. He opened the top one and read it, then leapt to his feet, rushed out of the door and ran down the stairs.

*

'Kassandra? Kassandra?' Linus hissed through the letterbox. 'Answer the door for fuck's sake—I know you're in there.'

He'd tried texting and calling on the way over. He'd rung the bell and banged on the door before resorting to the only remaining chance of communicating with her. He pushed the flap open as far as possible; he could see parts of Kassandra's gloomy apartment, but no doubt she was hiding in a corner somewhere.

'You're in real fucking trouble,' Linus continued, hoping no one else would be able to hear his irate hissing. 'We're *both* in trouble. If he finds out, we're dead—so talk to me for fuck's sake!'

The messages on Linus's phone had come from the customers he'd supplied overnight. They'd all said basically the same thing: *What kind of crap is this supposed to be, it's nothing like the crystal coke we had before.*

Kassandra had been messing around.

Just as he'd suspected and tried to prove when he was interrupted by the message from X, Kassandra had started snorting the coke herself. At first she'd done it by skimming off tiny amounts from lots of bags, but when only a few bags remained she'd cut the coke with caffeine powder or fuck knows what.

Linus banged his head against the top of the letterbox. He'd *known*. Kassandra was never as cheerful and carefree as she'd been the last time he saw her, not without powerful chemical assistance. *Zoloft*, she said, and Linus had chosen to believe her because that was the easy option. He'd dropped his guard, and now they were both fucked.

Matti had taken half of Kassandra's adulterated coke, and not surprisingly several of the messages were from Matti, who'd had the same reaction from his customers. It was out there—everyone knew that Linus and Matti were supplying crap.

It was just after two in the afternoon—six hours until the delivery arrived. Still no response from Kassandra. Linus let go of the flap and sank down by the door, wrapping his arms around his head. Which was empty. He had no idea what to do.

He remained there for a couple of minutes. There wasn't a sound from inside the apartment, but down below the elevator began to move. Linus leapt to his feet. Fucked or not, he couldn't let anyone see him in this state, and when there was no way out, at least he had one thing left.

He went home to fetch his running shoes.

*

Fifteen minutes later Linus was up on the roof. Dusk was creeping in, and part of the courtyard below was already in shadow. Linus looked to the west and saw the sun glowing behind the tops of the pine trees and on the Heil Hall's rusting metal roof. He glanced at his phone. Five hours and thirty-five minutes until the delivery. He'd turned it into a superstitious countdown. If he made it that far, everything would be fine.

He tucked the phone into the breast pocket of his hoodie and began to run. Lap after lap, but the lump in his stomach refused to shrink. The sky grew darker, the few remaining streetlights came on and he kept on running. After around thirty laps, or ten kilometres, his body felt a little lighter.

He stopped on the side overlooking the square and stepped up onto the wall. People were criss-crossing the area, with or without bags in their hands. Seen from this distance their efforts seemed so meaningless.

And what about him?

You're a shit, Linus…pathetic…I hope you die.

There was one solution. Now that the cacophony of voices inside his head had faded away, everything became much clearer, much simpler. He edged forward a few centimetres so that his toes were just over the edge, and his stomach turned over. What was it Kassandra had said? *I'm just giving the universe the opportunity to take my life.*

Jesus, how he hated her. And loved her. He was completely entangled with her. He moved his feet another centimetre, spread his arms wide and for a moment everything felt absolutely fine. Then a buzzing came from his breast pocket, and he heard the sound of a drop of water falling into an echo chamber.

That drop almost became another kind of drop. Linus gave a start and only just saved himself from plunging to the ground. He waved his arms around, and the minimal friction against the air enabled him to regain his balance and step down from the wall. He took out his phone and opened Snapchat.

The message was a picture of Kassandra; it looked as if it had come from an old school yearbook during her worst emo period. She was glaring scornfully into the camera, her eyes thick with kohl. The text, in that sprawling handwriting, read: *her or you two hours*. The picture disappeared.

The information had reached X. Within two hours either Kassandra or Linus must be dead, as a punishment for cutting the coke. As Linus lowered the phone, he felt a counterintuitive sense of peace.

*

'Kassandra, he knows. I got a message. In two hours either you or I must be dead. Otherwise I'm guessing he'll kill us both. Should we save him the trouble, or the pleasure? We're not going to get out of this. And we had a plan. The promise we made. I'm in.'

Linus closed the letterbox and shuffled to one side so that he could sit with his back against the wall, legs spread in front of him. His hands lay between his thighs, his knuckles resting on the concrete. He didn't understand why, but he was almost happy. Or at least significantly calmer than he'd been since he woke up.

He heard a faint rustling from inside the apartment, like a mouse finding its way through insulation fibre. The rustling became tiptoeing steps, then the lock turned. Kassandra looked out and saw Linus sitting on the floor. Her eyes were bloodshot and her mascara had run.

'I'm sorry,' she whispered. 'I'm so sorry, I…'

'It's okay.' Linus got to his feet. Kassandra shivered and said: 'Are you going to kill me now?'

'Didn't you hear what I said? We're done. Both of us. We made a promise.'

'Is that what you want?'

'I wouldn't go that far, but it's just the way things have to be. It's time.'

'I'm so sorry.'

'Don't be.'

Kassandra sighed and gazed around the stairwell as if she wanted to check for one last time whether the world was worth having, then an expression of restful calm came over her face. She gestured towards Linus's running gear and said: 'So is that what you're going to wear?'

Linus shrugged. 'I guess this is me.'

Kassandra looked down at her faded sweatshirt with Marilyn Monroe's face on it. 'I'd like to get changed.'

'Okay.' Linus glanced at his phone. One hour and thirty-five minutes left. 'Just don't take too long.'

*

It took Kassandra twenty minutes to plaster her face with make-up and change into several layers of tulle skirts with pockets that made her look like a cross between a gypsy woman and a fairytale princess. She'd applied enough product to her fringe to make it stand up straight and sprayed it pink. She stood in front of Linus and spread her hands wide. 'How do I look?'

'Fucking horrendous. There was a brief improvement for a while, but now…you're definitely back.'

Kassandra didn't take offence; she merely nodded. 'I just thought—if that's you, then this is me.'

'Jesus. Shall we go?'

As they were about to leave the apartment, Kassandra stopped. 'Hang on—I need to write a note.'

'What kind of note?'

'You know—this is no one's fault, I did it because I wanted to and so on. Haven't you written anything?'

'I didn't get around to it, and to be honest I can't be bothered. You carry on—I'll go up and wait for you.'

*

It was several degrees colder now. There were no clouds in the sky, and the stars were sparkling indifferently, as they had done for millions of years before man clambered down from the trees and started babbling. Everything was so vast and eternal, one single human being so small and insignificant.

But still. It was a fine evening. Linus's breath froze as he went over to the corner between the courtyard and the square. Arms folded, he looked down at the place where he grew up. He was still totally calm; he must have passed some critical tipping point.

He saw the sandpit where he and Henrik and Matti had played with plastic soldiers, built fortresses of sand which they then bombarded with stones. The bike shed where he and Kassandra used to sit and whisper until Linus got twitchy and had to go for a run. The bench where Alex had spotted him with his medication. All the broken streetlights. A real shithole, but the only place he could call home.

He looked across at the apartment where he'd grown up, and saw a woman who wasn't his mother pass the kitchen window. Had Betty already moved out? Fast work if she had, but it didn't make any difference to Linus. Those days were gone, like so many other things.

It was less than an hour to the deadline, and he'd begun to think that Kassandra had got cold feet when she finally emerged through the metal door, closed it behind her and came towards him. She had draped a thin cardigan over her shoulders—why? She glanced down, then up at the stars, which were reflected in her dark eyes as if she was in some Disney movie. Linus stroked her cheek. 'Are you scared?'

421

Kassandra pulled her cardigan more tightly around her and shivered. 'A bit. A lot. How about you?'

'Same.'

'It's so fucking high.'

'That's kind of the point.'

Linus took her hand, and side by side they stepped up onto the wall. Kassandra swayed when she looked down at the square, forty metres below. There were more people around now, doing their shopping after work. There were no shops directly beneath them since the video store closed. No streetlight either. Only darkness.

'Shit,' Kassandra said, squeezing Linus's hand and shuffling her feet until her toes reached the edge. 'Shit, shit, shit.'

Linus raised his chin. 'Don't look down.'

Kassandra did as he said. The grip on his hand loosened, but her palm was wet with sweat and she was breathing hard, like someone concentrating on a particularly difficult task.

'I'll count to three,' Linus said. 'Okay?'

'Okay.' Kassandra turned to face him. Her eyes were open wide, her mouth distorted in an ugly grimace as she said: 'I love you.'

'I love you too. Let's do this. One...'

Kassandra closed her eyes and held her breath. Her hand began to shake and slip in Linus's grasp.

'Two.'

A low whimper began in Kassandra's throat and her teeth started chattering. She already sounded like an unhappy ghost, and Linus shuddered as he shouted: 'Three!'

Neither of them moved. Kassandra's teeth were still chattering, her eyes were filled with tears and snot dribbled from her nose as she whispered: 'I can't do it, Linus. I can't do it.'

'No.' Linus pulled his hand free and gave her a push. 'No, you can't.'

Kassandra went over the edge. She caught Linus's eye and opened her mouth to say something, but it was too late. Arms flailing, skirts billowing around her, she disappeared into the darkness with a drawn-out scream.

Linus jumped backward off the wall. A second after his feet touched the concrete he heard a thud from the square, that was all. It was over. He'd finally crossed the line.

What have you done, Michael?

Only what needed to be done.

*

He couldn't stay on the roof. It wouldn't be long before the cops arrived to check out the place Kassandra had fallen from. Linus looked around. All the snow had melted away, and there was no sign that two pairs of feet had been here. Plus of course Kassandra had written that note; he would check it out when he was clearing any trace of their operation from her apartment.

He moved away from the edge and headed for the door, but after only ten metres he stopped and turned around. He felt a powerful urge to run, run as fast as he could and leap after Kassandra.

Should have done it.

He hadn't been sure of what he was going to do until the very last second. When Kassandra couldn't do it. If she'd simply allowed herself to fall, there was a real chance Linus would have done the same. The plan had been to let Kassandra take the punishment for cutting the coke, but when they stood there hand in hand, Linus had felt differently. It was only when she lost her nerve that he finally made up his mind.

What's done is done.

He had a delivery arriving in three hours, and before that he had to sort out Kassandra's apartment. He turned again and walked towards the door. He didn't feel good, in fact he felt fucking terrible. Tentacles of darkness reached out to him from the abyss behind him, trying to drag him over the edge and down to Kassandra.

All the evenings and nights they'd sat up here on their sun loungers laughing at crap. That would never happen again, thanks to him. He felt as if he was struggling in a headwind, and the will to live in his breast was a flickering flame, about to go out. The only thing that stopped him giving in to the impulse to run, then fly, was that he thought of a different way to obey it.

He *would* go down to Kassandra, but he would take the stairs. Go and see her. He owed her that much.

*

When Linus rounded the corner of the square he could see about thirty people gathered in a wide, loose circle around the spot where Kassandra should have landed. They were talking quietly, glancing over their shoulders from time to time. Presumably someone had called an ambulance.

Linus looked up at the roof. It was possible to make out the lower part of the façade by the light of the unbroken streetlights further away, but the roof itself was indistinguishable from the night sky. At most someone might have seen his and Kassandra's silhouettes up there, but it seemed unlikely. There was no danger that someone in the circle would turn around, catch sight of him and point the finger.

He moved closer. The air grew thicker, as if it contained almost no oxygen. His head began to spin, and he found it difficult to breathe. There was an opening in the circle right in front of him, and as he reached it white light flooded the centre as someone took a photograph with their phone.

The image of Kassandra's body was seared onto his retina in a ghostly light that sent waves of fear pulsing down into his chest. She looked so *thin*. He just had time to see the pool she was lying in, bodily fluids that had been forced out of her when she landed on the concrete. The back of her head was missing. Her eyes were wide open, as if she'd continued to stare up at Linus as she fell.

You did this.

The people around Linus were talking, but he heard their voices only as a meaningless hum. He was standing in a tunnel that contained him, and Kassandra's body, nothing else. In the darkness it was just a pile of clothes dumped on top of extremities sticking out at odd angles.

You need to look. You need to see.

Linus stepped forward and broke the circle. With numb fingers he took out his phone and switched on the torch. The hum took on a tone of complaint, protest as he shone the beam directly on Kassandra.

The pink fringe was smeared over her forehead, which was mercifully undamaged. Her mouth was open; a filling gleamed in the white light. Linus allowed his gaze to travel down her body. He gave a start and almost dropped the phone when he saw her heart beat.

Impossible.

Impossible or not, the fabric moved over her flattened left breast. Linus closed his eyes tightly. When he opened them again he saw a black segmented body crawling out of a pocket, and he heard the faint clink of broken glass.

When Kassandra went back to the apartment to write her note, she must have decided to bring the jar containing the cockroach with her. The fall had smashed the jar, and the eternal survivor was free once more. Its antenna felt at the air as it made its way over Kassandra's shoulder and down onto the concrete. It didn't even appear to be injured.

With unexpected speed for something that had been without food for such a long time, the cockroach headed straight for Linus. He let out a gasp, switched off the torch and backed away. Total paranoia, surely—but he suddenly got the idea that it was Kassandra's soul that had left her body and was now hell-bent on revenge.

He turned and walked to the middle of the square, sat down on a bench and failed to resist the impulse to switch on his torch again and check that the insect hadn't followed him. It hadn't. He bent down and buried his head in his hands. However hard he tried, he was no Michael Corleone, sitting stone-faced in his armchair and simply absorbing the weight of what he'd done. Linus was a teenager on a broken bench in a run-down Stockholm suburb, and he couldn't take any more.

You do not exist. Only the darkness exists.

Yes, he knew that. He had it within him, but it was no longer carrying him as it had done recently. Kassandra's death had made the darkness change colour; it was now sickly green and treacherous yellow. He'd murdered the only person who understood him, who could look at him and tell him who he was.

I can't do it, Linus. I can't do it.

He saw her face before him, the last time she'd looked at him. His own words, his final farewell, then the push. He couldn't bear it. He'd thought he could, but now it turned out that he couldn't. It would have to be the barrel of the gun to his temple or in his mouth, then thank you and goodnight.

A hundred kilos. Twenty million.

Linus sat up, hands resting on his knees, and took several deep breaths. He had a job to do, a task that had been allocated to him. But how was he going to manage that when he was incapable of moving his body, when he saw Kassandra's death as the heaviest lead weight around his neck? His shoulders slumped again.

Like this...

He thought about the darkness, about the interchangeability of everything, billions and billions of fluctuations within the blackness, as black as a cockroach.

Like this.

The cockroach had been trapped in its jar and Kassandra had intended to keep it there until it died, just to see how long it took. If Kassandra hadn't plummeted from the roof, the insect would have faded away, dried up in its isolation. Cockroaches didn't live forever, even if it seemed that way. So. Kassandra had lost her life, but the cockroach had been saved. On the cosmic, overarching plane, one life had been exchanged for another. It was a non-event.

Linus realised that from one point of view his logic was sick and perverted, but from another it was perfectly correct. The point of view of the darkness. He felt neither enlivened nor in the least bit cheerful, but it was enough to get him on his feet, to tackle what had to be done.

As he was leaving the square he met the ambulance that had come to collect Kassandra. He glanced back as people moved aside to let it through. In the headlamps he saw the heap of clothes that had been the person closest to him in the world. He raised a hand in farewell.

I love you. That bit was true.

Tommy

Tommy spent the day working on the puzzle. Henry's account had given him a corner piece that he could build on. The Egg. The silver-coloured caravan and the strange things that happened when it was around.

First there was the incident on the campsite near Trosa. When Svante Forsberg was abducted, he'd been staying at Saludden campsite in just such a caravan. He'd taken his darkness with him, and when he left it, his kidnapper had grabbed him.

Tommy read several articles about the other incident a month earlier, when four caravans had inexplicably disappeared from the same site. In one of the photographs showing the spot where the caravans had been, it was possible to make out a silver-coloured caravan in the background. Was that how X had found out where Svante was?

Tommy clicked between articles using different search terms, and discovered that some of those who'd vanished had returned. A married couple who owned an ICA store, along with their young son. They didn't want to talk about what they'd experienced, but mentioned that they'd somehow been transported to a different place. They refused to go into detail about this place, but Tommy guessed that it had been a field.

He stretched in his office chair. His eyes were burning from a lack of sleep and staring at the screen. He got up and stood for a while with his hands in his pockets, checking to see if anything was happening out on the street. It wasn't.

One of the addresses on the handwritten list was a canoe club on Tommy's side of Traneberg Bridge. As far as he was aware, it had closed down a couple of years ago, but the clubhouse was still standing. He passed it occasionally on his walks with Hagge.

He was completely washed up as a journalist, given that he had no intention of exploiting his knowledge of a major police operation that was due to take place virtually in his backyard, but for one thing he didn't want to expose himself, and for another he just didn't have the energy. He'd considered calling Mehdi and tipping him off; he might have done so if it hadn't been for that one phrase: *with legend Tommy T in tow.* He might still tip him off, but not until it was too late.

He called Anita, who told him that Betty was more or less okay, wandering around in a haze of Baileys and pills. Anita had taken Hagge out, but he hadn't wanted to stay long because he didn't like the area. How long was this nonsense going to go on?

'What nonsense?' Tommy asked.

'How long are we supposed to live like this?'

'Just until...'

'You've got twenty-four hours,' Anita said firmly. 'At this time tomorrow I'm moving back to my apartment, and as far as I'm concerned, X, Y and Z can come calling. I couldn't give a fuck.'

They discussed the matter for a while, but in the end it was decided that Anita would do exactly what she wanted. As usual. When Tommy asked her to give Betty his love, she replied frostily that she would. When he also asked her to give Hagge a big wet kiss on the nose, they were able to end the conversation in a reasonably civilised manner.

Tommy sat back down at his desk and looked up articles on police radio, interference, and 'Somebody Up There Must Like Me'. He didn't have much success. The unlikely song had been played continuously while the child was being tortured, and had then been transferred to the Brunkeberg Tunnel, where it was sent out as interference, even after the child had been removed. Had the song remained buried in the rock, with...Sigge?

He tried the disappearances on Luntmakargatan instead. The incident had happened over thirty years ago, and it wasn't easy to find anything. If he searched for '1986' and 'Luntmakargatan', most results referred to the assassination of Olof Palme. However, it seemed that three or possibly four people had gone missing. Bloodstains from several individuals had been found in the laundry room.

Tommy went into the bathroom and splashed his face with cold water. The fact that things got more complicated the more you knew never ceased to fascinate him. It was after six o'clock now, and he had one more thing to do today. He returned to the computer and spent an hour going over his article on Tomás's boxing club, then called the man himself. After some small talk, Tommy said: 'I've finished the article. It's good, but I just wanted to check that you're okay with the title.'

'Shoot.'

Tommy cleared his throat. 'All Rissne's Angels'.

'Angels? Let me tell you, Tommy, those guys are no angels.'

'No, but I just thought, *Todos Santos*, All Saints…'

'I'm not completely stupid, Tommy. I get it. It's cheesier than Julio Iglesias, but it's fine by me. How are things?'

'Complicated. Very complicated.'

'Anything I can do?'

'Not really, Tomás, but thanks for asking. The article will be out tomorrow.'

'The boys will be as proud as a rooster on a dung heap.'

'Glad to hear it.'

Tommy ended the call, sent the article and shut down the computer. He went and sat in his armchair. The beam of car headlights from Margretelundsvägen passed over the ceiling, slowly at first, then with increasing speed. The day had been filled with impressions, circling one another in his head in a chaotic whirl. The caravan, the tunnel, the field, Tomás's boxing guys. Henry's haggard face and Hagge's gloomy expression.

The images flowed together and merged. The caravan was travelling through the tunnel, Hagge was sniffing around in the field, the boxers were beating up Henry in Janne's office. At some point Tommy realised he was asleep, and his conscious thought process ceased.

*

He was woken by a sound, the rustle of fabric as something thin and sticky landed on his face. Still half-asleep he attempted to wipe it away, and a substance that felt like a spider's web attached itself to his fingers. He opened his eyes.

In the darkness of the room he was able to make out the shape of someone sitting on the Josef Frank stool in front of him. Tommy had been prepared for this moment; he wasn't even afraid. He simply thought: *so it's time.*

He sat up straight as a truck drove past. The light crossed the ceiling, illuminating the face of the person opposite him. Tommy hadn't been prepared for *that*, and couldn't help grimacing. He'd never seen such damage, at least not on a living human being. What stood out most sharply in that moment of indirect light was the deep X carved into the flesh.

'So that's what you look like,' Tommy said. He knew this was X's real face, not a mask.

'Yes,' X replied in a high, childish voice. 'This is what I look like.'

*

Tommy didn't know how long he'd slept, what time it was. X sat with his elbows resting on his knees and gazed at him for a while. Then he bounced his bottom up and down and said: 'This chair isn't very nice.'

'It's a stool.'

'This stool isn't very nice.'

'Would you like me to fetch you a chair?'

'No. I'm not staying long.'

Tommy wished for the hundredth time that Hagge was here. The contrast between X's appearance—a war veteran in a torture chamber—and his pleasant, confiding tone made it impossible to read his mood or intentions. On the other hand, it was from precisely this encounter that he'd wanted to protect both Hagge and Anita.

I'm not staying long.

At least he wasn't planning to do a Svante Forsberg on Tommy.

Maybe he was just going to *talk* until Tommy fetched his Japanese kitchen knife and got into the bath with the water running. He surprised himself by asking a question that was hardly a priority under the circumstances: 'What's your name?'

'I don't know. Is it important?'

'No. It's just good to know the name of the person you're talking to.'

'I might have had a name. But it disappeared.'

'In the caravan?'

'Yes.'

And with that they had reached the dark heart of this story. There was no trace of regret in X's tone, and Tommy didn't think he was after pity, so he came straight out with it: 'What happened? In the caravan?'

'They were horrible. Really horrible. It hurt. For a long time. So I made the other place. So that I'd have somewhere to be. Sometimes.'

'You *made* it? But how?'

'I don't know. I had nothing to do. It hurt. So I thought. A lot. Until it became real.'

X got to his feet, and Tommy involuntarily recoiled. X didn't even glance at him; instead he went over to the window and looked out. His profile stood out against the light from the street, and there was a monster standing in Tommy's living room. A monster and a little boy.

'They thought you were dead,' Tommy said, without specifying who *they* were.

'I was almost dead. I don't know. Maybe I was dead. Then Sigge came. He was nice. I was allowed to stay with him.'

'In the Brunkeberg Tunnel?'

'Yes. Sigge was there then. He took care of me. And I gave him some of what I had. I didn't have much. The field. The songs. He liked those.'

'This Sigge—who is he?'

X turned to Tommy, his face mercifully in shadow. 'That's all people can say.'

'What do you mean?'

'His name. It's really difficult to say. For people. I can. But I practised a lot. It's a very long name and it means lots of things.'

X took an old-fashioned Nokia phone out of his pocket and looked at the screen. 'I'll have to go soon.'

Tommy stared at the Nokia and a chain of ideas began to form—until X took a step towards him. *It's going to happen now*, Tommy thought. *Somehow it's going to happen now*. With the aim of readying himself for the actual moment, he asked: 'Why have you come?'

'Because I wanted to see you. You saw me. Everything I did.'

'You mean I've been your witness?'

'I don't understand.'

'You wanted to have someone who saw and understood what you did, then told your story.'

X tilted his head on one side and looked up at the ceiling, the whites of his eyes glinting like a pair of torches in a ruin. 'Maybe partly. But only partly. I wanted you to see. And write. They were horrible.'

'Who were?'

When X checked his phone again, Tommy could see the numbers behind the diagonal crack across the screen: 19:55. X slipped the phone into his pocket and said: 'I have to go. Close your eyes.'

'Are you going to kill me?'

'No. Why would I do that? You're not horrible. I don't know if you're nice. But you're not horrible. Close your eyes.'

'Wait. Just one more thing. Peter Himmelstrand. What happened to him?'

'I was going to make him dead. Because he wrote the songs. But he was nice. So I let him come with me instead.'

'What do you mean…'

X made a sweeping gesture with a claw-like hand that Tommy recognised from the photos. 'Close your eyes!'

Compelled by an internal force that Tommy knew was coming from himself, his eyelids closed. He heard a rustling sound, or a brief burst of static, like interference on a radio. Somehow he managed to open his eyes and saw a network of fine threads falling towards the stool where X had been sitting. They drifted over Tommy's head and body, entangling him in a black gossamer web.

Linus

Linus checked the time on his phone: 19:55. Neither he nor Matti had decent winter jackets, just hoodies that weren't much use against the wind that swept in and bounced off the graffiti-strewn walls of the Heil Hall. They pushed their hands deep in their pockets and jumped up and down on the spot.

Earlier that evening Linus had cleaned up Kassandra's apartment. Among other things, he'd found a bag containing fifteen grams of coke that she'd skimmed off. Fifteen out of twenty. It was hardly surprising that their customers had reacted badly. Linus had told Matti that Kassandra had been responsible for the packaging, and that she'd been so terrified by what she'd done that she'd taken her own life. He relayed the contents of her farewell note—she was doing this of her own free will, the world was shit, et cetera et cetera.

Matti didn't seem particularly bothered, which Linus found irritating to say the least. Matti had also unwittingly sold the adulterated coke, and Linus had taken it upon himself to clear up the mess in the worst possible way. Matti's indifferent expression when he heard about Kassandra made Linus want to rearrange the features of his bear-brother.

At least he'd arrived five minutes after Linus sent him a two-word message: *Heil Hall.* Everyone in Gårdsstugan knew the place; it was still adorned with a number of Nazi tags, which had been added after the main attraction had been removed.

The door to the storeroom was unlocked, and together they'd cleared a space among the crap. They'd decided to store the coke temporarily in a mouldy vaulting box, leaning drunkenly against the wall in one corner like a half-dead pony. Then they would distribute it to the new packaging centres.

Linus checked the time again. 19:57.

'Nervous?' Matti asked.

'No—I'm just like you. I couldn't give a shit about anything.'

'What the fuck are you talking about? I'm here, aren't I?'

'Yes, but you're not really here. This is like the biggest thing ever, and you just…I don't know.'

'Maybe I've had enough of your style.'

They didn't get any further before they were interrupted by the sound of a car engine. Two cones of light were approaching from Paradisvägen, casting huge shadows of Linus and Matti on the wall of the Heil Hall. Linus felt for his newly purchased shoulder holster; he'd practised drawing his gun and removing the safety catch in one smooth movement. In case it proved necessary for some reason.

You didn't need to have seen many films or TV series to know that the moment when the goods changed hands was critical. It was a question of trust. Linus had no idea who was driving the van marked *Flora's Flowers*. The trust level was zero. Hence the gun.

The vehicle came to a halt three metres away from Linus, and a guy in his thirties who looked like any other van driver stuck his head out of the side window. 'Delivery,' he said. 'What's your name?'

'Linus. You can back up to this door here.'

The guy nodded and began to turn the van. He didn't look dangerous at all. As long as he didn't have a gang of armed brothers in the back, everything should be fine.

And why would he have?'

No reason. Just general paranoia regarding anything that could go wrong. Linus looked at Matti, who had brightened up since the delivery arrived bang on time.

'Here we go,' Linus said.

'Yes. Here we go.'

As the van was reversing, Linus's phone pinged. He took it out and saw that the message was from his uncle: *RUN LINUS RUN*

The driver stopped a couple of metres from the storeroom and jumped out. Linus put the phone back in his pocket. Had Tommy somehow found out what he was up to? If so, Linus would have to deal with that problem later, because the driver was now unlocking the back doors of the van. Linus had his right hand ready for action, just in case, but there was nothing to see apart from two large blocks wrapped in plastic. The driver pointed to them and said: 'They're fucking heavy—you'll have to give me a hand.'

Linus's phone pinged again, but he ignored it. Together he and Matti managed to help the driver lift out the two fifty-kilo packages and place them on the ground between the van and the hall.

'Okay,' the driver said, brushing his hands together. 'I guess that's...' He broke off, staring open-mouthed towards Gårdsstugan.

Linus spun around to see a catastrophic scenario he hadn't even thought of unfolding before him. A SWAT team of seven or eight officers was approaching in a semi-circle, dressed in black, automatic firearms at the ready. A voice called out: 'Show your hands and get down on the ground!'

He spun around again and saw at least fifteen cops coming from the other direction, cutting off any possible escape route.

RUN LINUS RUN

Uncle Tommy had known. Why had he sent the message when it was already too late? The frustration exploded inside Linus's head. He slipped his hand inside his jacket and grabbed the gun.

Tommy

Tommy sat still in the armchair as the gossamer web dissolved like candy floss melting in hell. There was an image in his mind that he couldn't shake off. *The Nokia. The diagonal crack across the screen.*

X couldn't possibly have used that phone to communicate via Snapchat; it was impossible to take a photograph with such an old device.

Tommy picked up his own phone and opened the archive of pictures he'd taken in Janne's office. Found a clear photo of Janne's body. Zoomed in on the phone in Janne's hand. It was an old Nokia, same model, and it had a crack across the screen—but from top to bottom rather than diagonally.

Tommy closed his eyes and thought back to when Janne had entered his number in his phone. He'd found it funny that Janne was so low-tech in that area. Tommy was absolutely certain: the crack on the screen had been diagonal. And that was the phone X had been holding in his hand just now.

The message giving the code to the safe hadn't come from Janne, but from X. Tommy pressed his wrists against his eyes. *I wanted you to see. And write. They were horrible.*

They?

They?

It was 19:58. Tommy's fingers slipped and slid as he found Don Juan Johansson's number and called him. He shook the phone as if to make it work faster. When Henry answered, Tommy could hear that he was outdoors, and very tense.

'Bad timing,' he said.

'One thing. You said that Svante Forsberg managed to talk a couple of colleagues into thinking along the same lines as him. Were these colleagues also involved in torturing the child?'

'Yes, I told you that. Listen, I have to…'

'You did *not* tell me that! You have to abort the operation—right now!'

'No chance. I've got over three hundred officers in twenty locations, and…Something's happening here!'

'Henry, listen to…'

The line was dead. Tommy tried calling again, but there was no answer. His hands were shaking so much he could hardly hold the phone as he found Linus's number and wrote *RUN LINUS RUN*. He sent the message and immediately began to write another.

Sweat was dripping from his forehead onto the screen, sweat was trickling down his sides from his armpits. He knew he was too late.

Linus

'You fucking traitor!'

Something had been wrong with Matti all evening—since the previous evening, in fact, when he'd said, 'I get it'.

Maybe I've had enough of your style.

Linus would never have believed that Matti was so hacked off that he would go to the cops. That hadn't been on the cards at all, but Matti had clearly been dealing cards of his own and had chosen a completely different game. He was no longer a brother or even a person, just a worthless little shit. Linus drew his gun and shot him in the stomach.

The second Linus fired, it felt as if someone had hit his legs with a sledgehammer—first the right, then the left. The sound of his own shot had drowned out the muted reports of two G36 assault rifles that had been fired almost at the same time. One bullet entered the calf muscles of his right leg, while the other hit his left thigh bone, sending a shockwave through his skeleton and causing him to collapse on top of one of the packages.

The phone fell out of his pocket, then he dropped the gun. It landed on the phone and cracked the screen.

Unlucky. Seriously unlucky.

He looked up and saw the delivery guy lying on the ground with his hands on his head. Matti lay beside him wriggling like a worm, pulling horrible faces and pressing his hands to his belly as if he were trying to keep his intestines in place. *Serves him right.*

The echo of the shots died away, and in the silence Linus could hear the cops' boots coming closer and closer. He pressed his cheek to the package, which was surprisingly hard. He raised his head a fraction. Beneath the plastic, right in front of his eyes, he saw a mobile phone wrapped up with the goods. There was a wire running from it.

Unlucky. Seriously fucking unlucky.

Linus glanced at his own phone. Through the spider's web pattern on the cracked screen he could just read Uncle Tommy's last message: *NOT COKE BOMB RUN*. Right. He'd worked that out now, but there wasn't much running left in his legs.

The cops were only a couple of metres away now. The only sound was the crunch of their boots and Matti's dying groans. Soon it would be a lot less quiet. It was just a shame that Staffan and Margot weren't part of the circle surrounding him. Oh well, maybe they were doing the same thing somewhere else. This was *big*. The biggest. Which was some consolation at least.

Linus looked up at the cops who were nearest, guns pointed at the ground.

'Come closer,' he said. 'Come and see what I've got for you.'

He felt a vibration pass through the package, saw a rectangle of light beneath him as the phone came on. Everything went white. Then black.

Tommy

Even though the canoe club was a kilometre away, the shock wave shook Tommy's apartment block, rattling the windows. Tommy ran out onto the balcony and saw a pillar of black smoke rising behind the trees beyond Traneberg Bridge. He grabbed hold of the railing and sank down onto the cracked concrete floor. He scrabbled at the corrugated metal sheet surrounding the balcony, the green paint flaking beneath his fingers.

Over three hundred officers in twenty locations.

Three cops had tortured the child, and he had taken his revenge a hundredfold on the whole police service. That had been his aim all along; the coke had merely been a ruse to attract attention. And Tommy had given him attention. Too much attention.

I wanted you to see. And write. They were horrible.

It was hardly surprising that Janne had regretted his actions. A tonne of coke was one thing, contributing to a carefully planned massacre was something else. But he was Semtex-Janne, and part of his legal business involved importing explosives. He was the man who could organise it without anyone raising an eyebrow, and it was he and Tommy who'd made everything possible.

Tommy was on all fours, panting. He was so devastated that he couldn't even shed a tear. X had led him along a neatly laid-out track, and Tommy had eagerly raced from one checkpoint to the next with his tongue hanging out. For four articles and a little rehabilitation.

He could see the destruction in his mind's eye. Fifteen or more officers gathered around a hundred kilos of plastic explosive when it was detonated. There would be nothing left but lumps of flesh, scraps of uniform, fragments of guns whirling through the air. No doubt also a number of dealers, plus innocent bystanders who just happened to be in the area. Children. Linus.

Tommy had never considered taking his own life, and he wasn't considering it now either, but this was unbearable. A future where he would always be the man who'd paved the way for the worst mass murder in modern Swedish history. No.

Still on all fours he crawled indoors, then sat for a while in the grip of a mild insanity as he stroked the Josef Frank stool and thought about the child who had been treated so badly. The fear. The pain. The darkness that grew, billowed out and filled the caravan.

It hurt. For a long time.

The sound of a drop of water falling into an echo chamber came from Tommy's phone. He shuffled over to the table and picked it up. He couldn't be anywhere else but on the floor right now. He didn't know when he'd be able to get up. He touched the Snapchat icon.

The photograph showed a note in that same handwriting, the letters as crooked and splayed as the fingers that had printed them. The note said: *thanks for your help goodbye.*

The image disappeared and Tommy looked up at the window. He could hear sirens in the distance. The whole of Stockholm must be in a state of chaos and shock.

Goodbye.

Only a small percentage of Sweden's police officers had died today. Those who remained would put everything into finding the person who had murdered their colleagues. If this was the worst mass murder, then it would also be the most extensive and thorough murder hunt in Swedish history. It would be impossible for X to hide anywhere.

Except for one place.

Epilogue

Peter Himmelstrand's 'Somebody Up There Must Like Me' was playing on the radio.

'Liberal academic to employ. Seven letters. Starts with P, ends with E and in between...'

'Let me see.' Lennart pulled the crossword across the table, his tongue protruding from the corner of his mouth as his forefinger tapped the letters Olof had already filled in. 'Ha!' he said, bringing the palm of his hand down on the table with such force that Benny the beagle, who was dozing on the sofa, raised his head.

'Profuse,' Lennart said triumphantly. 'Prof is an academic, use is another word for employ, and the whole thing means...'

'I get it,' Olof said. 'Thank you very much.'

'No need to sulk.'

'I'm not sulking, I just think I should have been able to work it out for myself.'

'We help each other. You help me sometimes.'

'Not as often.'

Silence fell around the table. Benny slid off the sofa and went outside. Whenever Lennart or Olof happened to mention something to do with time, there was a weird atmosphere. The word 'often' was associated with time.

They didn't know how long they'd been in the field. The dates on the puzzle magazines indicated that it was three years, but it felt like much less. Weeks. The boy who brought the magazines along with food and drink every few days told them not to think about it. He said he was the one who decided how time passed, quickly or slowly.

But it was impossible not to think about it. The idea that three years had passed in the world beyond the field, the world that had been theirs before they decided to come to Trosa on a camping holiday.

How were the cows, for example? Had their respective offspring, Ante and Gunilla, taken over the running of the farms? Had their shared worries about their missing fathers brought them together? Had they got married? Had children? Hard not to think about it.

The two men sat with their callused hands resting on the table and gazed out over their vegetable patch. At their request the boy had brought seeds and seed potatoes that grew unnaturally quickly, and Lennart and Olof had already harvested one crop. Beyond their plot there was nothing but the endless field, the endless sky. Everything that had frightened them in the past, the burnt figures, the white figures and the acid rain, had disappeared since the black tiger started watching over them. All they had was the vegetable plot, the grass, the sky, the puzzle magazines and each other.

Lennart gently stroked Olof's cheek. 'We'll survive, my Olof. We will survive, won't we?'

'We will.' Olof placed a hand over his. 'Of course we will. It's just that things get a little monotonous sometimes.' He glanced over at the sofa. 'Where did Benny go?'

Lennart couldn't help smiling. 'He doesn't have much choice, does he?'

*

Benny jumped down from the caravan and peered underneath it. Cat was lying in her usual place next to one of the wheels, looking back at him. Benny shook his head and sniffed the air. There it was. The scent that had made him leave the comfort of the sofa. Grandchild.

When Grandchild came he sometimes wanted to play with Benny. Benny obliged for a little while, because he felt he ought to. Grandchild brought food and treats for him and Cat. But there was something odd about Grandchild. He didn't smell like Grandchild, he smelled like Big and the smell of Big was mixed with the smell of those who had burnt and those who were White. He smelled like this place, but Human.

Grandchild also walked with the big Cat. The black one. Benny didn't like it at all. It was completely different from ordinary Cat, Benny's Cat. Big Cat refused to let Benny go where he wanted. Once when Benny got too close it had bared its teeth. Benny had turned tail and hidden under the caravan.

Grandchild was coming closer. Benny could see him, so he went and lay down next to Cat. She made the noise that sounded like a growl, but meant that Cat was happy. It calmed Benny down. He shuffled closer and tried to make the same noise. He could almost do it. He'd been practising.

*

'Hi.'

The boy was carrying two bags of food that seemed unreasonably heavy for his small frame, so Olof relieved him of his burden and placed the bags on the kitchen counter. The boy looked around and asked: 'What are you doing?'

'Not much,' Lennart replied. 'Crosswords. Making up stories. Eating. Exercising.'

'Will you tell me a story?'

'Another time, maybe.'

The boy sat down on the sofa and tucked his hands underneath his thighs. 'There won't be another time,' he said.

'What do you mean?'

'I'm going to live here now. I've done what I wanted to do.'

Lennart looked at Olof, who spread his hands wide. They both found the boy disturbing, because he spoke like a child, but with the authority of an adult. He was also closely connected with the field that held them captive, and ruled it as he wished. The idea that he had created it, as he claimed, was perhaps a little far-fetched, but not impossible. The assertion that he was intending to live with them was alarming, or was he saying…

'If you're going to live here, does that mean we can leave?'

'No. I don't want you to leave.'

Olof came over and placed his big hand on the child's shoulder. 'But how long do you intend for us to stay here?'

'I don't know,' the boy said, frowning before he laid his cheek on the back of Olof's hand and broke into a smile. 'But you're nice. I want to stay with you for a long time. Maybe forever.'